THE DRESSAGE
CHRONICLES

THE DRESSAGE CHRONICLES

KAREN MCGOLDRICK

BOOK II: a MATTER of FEEL

Deeds Publishing | Atlanta

Published by Deeds Publishing
Marietta, GA
www.deedspublishing.com
Printed in the United States of America
Cover design by Mark Babcock
Library of Congress Cataloging-in-Publications Data is available upon request.
ISBN 978-1-937565-xx-x
Books are available in quantity for promotional or premium use. For
information, write Deeds Publishing, PO Box 682212, Marietta, GA 30068 or
info@deedspublishing.com.
First Edition, 2013
10 9 8 7 6 5 4 3 2 1

Acknowledgment

I am daily living my own Dressage Chronicles, and although I am not Lizzy exactly, she exists vividly inside my head as does every other character imagined in my story, because I know her well, as I do the Margots and the Franks and Francescas and the Debs and Ryders who populate our world. I am glad to say I do not know any Patricks!

The horses, too, are amalgams of horses I have known and ridden and am still riding today.

The characters of Kiddo and Petey, were "won" at a silent auction to benefit The Georgia Dressage and Combined Training Association at their annual banquet. I hope that owners Caryn Caverly and Kimberly Murray will be happy with their horses' depictions and that they will forgive me for any liberties I may have taken!

Part of the fun of writing these books is the "research" that I do. It gives me an extra reason to do what I already want to do: go to horse shows and ride in clinics and continue to train daily.

Thanks go to my friend and training buddy Anne Pagel. Anne happily read early versions of the novel and was always encouraging and sparking new ideas in my head. She inspires me daily by her own riding and training of her gorgeous young horse, and her German accent helps me imagine that I could be riding in Warendorf.

For this book I drew on my childhood experiences as a member of a vaulting team. I lacked the gymnastic ability to go very far, but at least I do know what it feels like to jump up, and stand, on the back of a moving horse, even though today I use a mounting block!

Part of my research was learning about Liberty work. I had the pleasure of working in a clinic with the amazing and talented Sylvia Zerbini whom I first saw perform with the horse circus, Cavalia.

I also self-studied equine behavior and aggression. I think I learned the most reading the works of Linda Tellington-Jones, although I have never met her. I would still love to attend one of her clinics. My new horse, Gia, was terribly insecure when I got her, and as "mare-ish" as they come. She has already taught me much, and she is an ongoing experiment.

I am lucky to live in an equestrian-rich area in Milton, Georgia. I currently work (when possible) with talented trainer/instructor, Roel Theunissen. With Roel's help I took my mare Wasabi up through the levels and beyond my expectations.

My sometime-student and longtime friend Elisa Wallace is an exceptional eventing talent, and she also won the regional Extreme Mustang Makeover with her Mustang, "Fledge." Elisa, and local young-horse dressage trainer Ashley Marascalco of High Valley Hanoverians, are two local young women who have incredibly bright futures. Watching them develop has been exciting and inspiring, and I am lucky to have front row seats to watch.

Although I draw energy from watching our local talent bloom, it is not the bright young things that have impacted me the most. Some of the most important members of our dressage community have now stepped out of the limelight, but are the richest source of wisdom and just keep getting wiser. I am proud to count Jessica Ransehousen as one of my teachers and friends. Whenever I find myself in her presence (which is not as often as I'd like these days), I always know she is the smartest person in the room. Jessica is always first and foremost for the horse, absolutely what I consider "classical," and with the highest ethical standards; a worthy role model for us all.

My thanks also to Annetta Coleman, owner of High Valley Hanoverians who allowed me to come watch her imprint and turn out for his first outing her newborn colt, whom I then had the honor to christen. I expect great things from High Valley Hanoverians' "High Voltage." He is stunning.

As before, I depended on writing coach, Christina Ranallo, to help me shape and pare and cut the mess of scenes and dialogue I presented her, into something readable!

I am grateful again to Deeds Publishing for launching me on my career as a published author. They now know more about dressage than they ever could have imagined!

I am also thankful to Selene Scarsi for the amazing front cover photo. Selene is a true Renaissance girl (she is a published author/professor/scholar of Renaissance literature!). But she is also a dressage rider whom I met while training in Germany. On top of that, she is an incredible photographer; her photos and articles have appeared in such magazines as Sankt Georg. Selene's photographs also grace my Riders Training Journal.

The filly on the spine of the book is "Superbarbie," bred by Cathrin Schlemper of GermanPremiumFoals.com. I fell in love with Superbarbie (San Amour x Donnerhall) on Facebook. She is the most beautiful foal I have ever seen.

The back-cover photo, "Peek-a-Boo" is by Alicia Frese Klenk of Frese Frame Photography. Alicia has the eye of an artist, as is evidenced in this charming shot.

My greatest thanks go to the love of my life and partner of over 33 years, husband Lawrence. He combed through my long manuscript word for word to be sure my commas were in the right spots and I hadn't confused my tenses. Not only has he edited everything I have ever published, he has been a non-horsey horse husband supreme. He has stayed up long cold nights with colics, helped me get cast horses up and made the terrifying trip in the dead of night to the vet school. He too felt the grief when we lost our beautiful Wasabi.

One of the aspects of dressage is that you never know it all. Each horse is a new challenge that demands your intellectual engagement in a long-term commitment. Your partner outweighs you by a lot, is a flight animal, and hasn't read a single book on how it is all supposed to work. Yet, step-by-step, and day-by-day, you forge a partnership, and amazing things begin to happen.

Writing and publishing turns out to be a similar process, and so a natural fit.

I hope you will enjoy this installment of *The Dressage Chronicles.*

Karen McGoldrick

DEDICATION

I dedicate this book to my father, Harry V. Jaffa.

Daddy is an author many times over. He would be classified as an expert in political philosophy, but that hardly touches his areas of expertise. They include Abraham Lincoln, Winston Churchill, Aristotle and Thomas Aquinas, Shakespeare, The Declaration of Independence, and the U.S. Constitution. But he can practically recite the Jeeves and Wooster books by P.G. Wodehouse too. As children of two reader-parents, my brothers and I learned by example to love books and reading. In all three cases, it took.

Daddy told us children that we could be anything or do anything we wanted; but whatever it was, to be good at it. I have tried to do just that.

I was horse-crazy from an early age, and Daddy knew nothing about horses, nor could we afford much on a Professor's salary.

Yet, after it was clear I was not going to be interested in any activities that did not include horses, he asked his publisher for a book advance; the only advance he ever took; and I got my first horse.

Thank you, Daddy.

Contents

CHAPTER 1

Teeth. Hooves. Cat Hair In My Tea.

WILD CHILD HAD HIS HEAD DEEP in the grass, the picture of contentment. I stood at the gate bracing myself for battle. I had the lead shank with the chain on it, ready to bring him in, tack him up, and hand him over to Margot.

I held a big fat carrot in my other hand as a small bribe that I hoped would persuade him to leave the sweet spring grass.

Wild Child's chestnut coat glowed like a polished copper penny. Anyone walking by would have marveled at his beauty. He was lean and hard as a rock, with muscles stretching his skin tight. He was world class. It was a privilege that Margot wanted me to be his exclusive groom; to be her groom.

But I hated him.

The feeling was mutual.

I rattled the chain on the gate and called his name.

"Wiiiild Child, c'mon boy!"

Yeah right. He didn't even pick up his head, only swiveling one ear my way. I was going to have to make the first move.

I tried to put on a nonchalant air, but I hated going into his paddock. This was his territory. I hung the gate's chain around the post, but I didn't latch it. I wanted to be able to get out quick.

As I got nearer, Wild Child picked up his head to give me a nose-toss with his ears pinned back. Then he charged at me, just a couple steps, before he stuffed his nose back down into the grass. After a few big tearing bites, his head came back up, his ears went back, and he lowered his head again, but not to graze. He was arching it like a bow; coiling like a snake. He was ready to strike.

It was all I needed to decide to retreat.

I quickly turned back toward the gate, looking over my shoulder as I went. He could just rot out here for all I cared.

I grabbed the gate and jumped back outside.

At first he just trotted, striking out with his front legs, but he soon accelerated into a sprinting gallop, open mouth and lips pulled back to show his ugly teeth. He thrust his neck over the gate, knocking into it with his chest and rattling the chain. He looked like he was going to come over the top of it to kill me. But it was my opportunity to snag the sucker.

"Asshole, you love this game don't you."

I simultaneously stuffed the carrot in his mouth and snapped the shank on the nearest ring of his halter.

"Well I don't. I don't love it at all Shark-face."

With shaky hands I ran the chain around and around his mouth, and then pulled the leather part of the lead line through the halter, sort of tying his mouth shut. It was unconventional for sure, a kind of crazy-looking chain muzzle I had improvised.

But it didn't really make him any nicer to lead. He either pulled and tried to go ahead of me or hung back and pinned his ears. Pulling was preferable. Then I could jerk on the lead line and make him back up. But if he lagged behind me, I expected him to lower his head and pull his lips back, ready to strike out with a front hoof or possibly even rear and lift me right off the ground.

Hateful creature. He made me want to beat the crap out of him, except he had about 1300 pounds on me and four steel-clad hooves. But even if I got some kind of perverse pleasure from doing that, I knew he would come back and kill me later when I wasn't paying enough attention. I needed to be smarter than fight a battle I was doomed to lose. I just needed to be smarter than a horse. That shouldn't be so hard.

I put him in the cross-ties, took off the chain shank, and began grooming him. Every time I had to cross in front of him or get near his head, he snapped his teeth, barging toward me in the cross-ties. I had gotten accustomed to walking wide around him to avoid that head and mouth. To brush his face I ran the chain around his mouth again. I knew enough to know this was all wrong, that my approach could never make this better, and that I was playing with a loaded weapon.

Ryder came in leading a sweaty Papa. As soon as I heard the clip-clop of Papa's hooves, I unwrapped the chain from around Wild Child's nose. The last thing I wanted was advice from our newest addition, a hot-shot teenager. I tried to put on a cheery voice.

"How was your ride?'

"Fantastic."

"That's great."

Yeah. The more fantastic Ryder's lessons were, the sorrier my riding seemed to be getting.

Margot appeared, and Wild Child clearly stood up taller in the cross-ties. In fact, we all stood up taller when Margot appeared. She had been a dressage superstar for decades. She was always elegant, the picture of sophistication. Petite, blonde, and stylish. And the woman could ride. She was the reason I was here; to be her working student.

I offered Wild Child his bridle; a moment that always made me break into a sweat because once when I was putting the bits into his mouth he had bitten me on the thigh. Today he grabbed the bits impatiently, and as soon as they were in, he lifted his chin, sliding them into position. Margot ignored him as he champed on the bits. But he never took his eyes off her.

When I handed him over to Margot, I felt like a limp dishrag. It was such a relief to be free of him. Margot walked him to the mounting block, and he followed her. I noticed he did not try to bite her.

He looked submissive following her, but I knew otherwise. He was a challenge even for Margot. The two were a new combination as the Cavellis had just purchased him in Florida during the winter show season, and Margot was still trying to figure him out.

As soon as they walked out the door, I said, "I hate that horse."

Shit, I had said it out loud. Ryder heard me.

She turned from hosing off Papa and scowled at me, shaking her head.

"Wild Child getting the best of you again?"

"Nothing I can't handle. He's just an ass, that's all."

"Don't get in over your head, Lizzy."

I looked back at Ryder, but could not think of a single snappy comeback. I murmured something inane, like, "thanks for your concern." She was looking down her nose at me once again.

I wished she still wore that nose ring she arrived in because I would have loved to give it a yank; little prig. Francesca had forbidden her to wear it, so I was out of luck. But of course, Ryder was right to caution me. I was in over my head with Wild Child, and I knew it.

Once Margot finished her two horses, it was my turn to ride. Margot had trained Winsome for me in Florida, but I was back on my own horse again. Margot had been trying unsuccessfully to teach us walk pirouettes. I was praying that Margot would pick another topic today.

Fat chance. After my usual warm-up, Margot called me over.

"Lizzy, I know a walk pirouette looks easy, because it's done at the walk, but it's not easy. You have to feel what's going on underneath you. You have to stay in perfect balance through the turn, and you have to get control of the shoulders. At the same time you must keep the hind legs stepping forward and under the horse. It's a highly technical movement. But once you really ride these well, you will understand so much about the elements for canter pirouettes, and canter half-passes too for that matter."

Margot's words ran over me without sinking in. I knew the definition from the rule book. And I knew the purpose and benefit of the exercise. But words and actions were worlds apart.

"Margot, I did canter pirouettes on Rave."

Our eyes met. It seemed that no one was talking anymore about losing Rave. But for me it was still a fresh wound. And looking at Margot I could see it was the same for her. Finally Margot nodded and answered softly.

"I miss him too, darling."

"He still had so much to teach me. I was going to ride the Prix St. Georges. Now it will be years and years."

Margot sighed and pressed her lips together before speaking."

"And I still look for him every morning when I arrive; that will never change, even though I know better."

She turned away and walked to her chair on the deck.

And then she went back into teaching mode.

I had been blind and selfish. Rave's worth was more than what he still could have done for me. She was hurting more than I was. I just needed to suck it up and apply myself.

"Lizzy, let's get back to work. This is important. What I want you to do is ride quarter turns on a square. Be able to start and stop the steps and ride out of them. Riding out of them is the most important part. You must always be able to go forward. Avoid at all costs any backward or stuck feeling."

I began to ride Winsome on the square pattern. March, march, march, shoulder-fore position, outside leg and rein, keep inside flexion, and bend. One step, two steps and walk forward back on the square.

"Lizzy, that was a turn on the middle. You let the outside hind step out. Did you feel it?'

"No," I answered honestly.

"Well, pay attention next time to the outside hind leg."

March, march, march, turn one step, and two steps, and walk forward. I focused like a laser beam on the outside hind leg.

"OK, that was better, but now the inside hind leg stepped sideways like leg yield. The inside hind can step a tiny bit forward, but never to the side. It's the pivot point that the rest of the horse turns around. And Lizzy, you're leaning to the right. The horse is turning left. You must turn with her, not against her."

On and on I rode that stupid square. My entire freakin' lesson was at the walk. I sat too much to the right, and I pulled too much on the inside rein. I tried to watch too long in the mirror and was looking the wrong direction. Then I committed the sin of "sticking" on the inside hind. One time Margot shrieked because Winsome stopped and backed up a step, a cardinal sin. It wasn't Winsome's fault. Winsome did whatever I told her to do. It was just that I never did tell her to do the right thing.

I didn't remember any of this torture when I was riding Rave. I remembered riding Rave alongside wonderful FEI horses and riders in our quadrille, and doing flying changes, extended trots, and even piaffe and passage. But the memory was really faint and growing fainter by the day.

I WAS trying. I wanted points for trying. But the harder I tried, the more I tied myself into knots. I just wanted to hear Margot say, "Yes! Great job, Lizzy."

Clearly that wasn't going to happen. Not this day.

"OK, Lizzy, that's enough for today. Stretch your girl out, and get all the kinks out so you both go back to the barn loose and relaxed. While I'm off in Texas, I want you to come in here and practice your square. Next week, I know you will have it mastered. Just be sure to keep the right attitude. Don't get frustrated; stay focused. An inner calmness is how you discover subtleties. Patience my dear; patience and perseverance are the keys to mastery."

I stretched Winsome out in a forward working trot and then walked her outside, making a lap around the outside of one of the paddocks. I reached down and stroked a section of her mane, the bit right in front of her withers, and felt my eyes get hot.

"I'm sorry, sweetie. I'm so sorry. You're my good girl. You did fine. It's not you, it's me. Forgive me. And keep forgiving me. I don't know what I'm doing, and I'm afraid I'm doomed to repeat this muck-mess all weekend long."

Winsome was swinging along, ears pricked, taking in the scenery; and not a bit of tension in her body. She wasn't worried. She didn't care whether she had performed a correct walk pirouette. She didn't care if she wasn't meeting some standard written down in the rule book. Heck, she didn't know what a rule book was. It occurred to me then that as long as I kept the right attitude, just like Margot said, I wouldn't be hurting the horse.

KAREN MCGOLDRICK | 21

Patience. Patience and perseverance. They were two qualities I needed to learn.

I looked down the hill to see Ryder standing outside the barn, talking on her cell phone, but looking up at me. She seemed to have been watching, and suddenly my vow of patience and perseverance went out the window. I wasn't patient. I was angry; angry at myself for not being better than Ryder Anderson, and angry that Ryder knew it without a single doubt.

Then I noticed Margot come out of the barn, and Ryder turned to follow her back in, but not before I saw Margot look our way.

I was putting Winsome back in her stall when Margot found me.

"I've planned your afternoons for you, Lizzy."

I slid Winsome's door closed and hung up her halter neatly. "How's that."

"I've told Deb you're going to help her with the youngsters up at the mare barn. This summer you'll be starting the three-year-olds with Deb and Ryder too, but Deb could sure use some help now. And I have a feeling you two will get on famously. Deb's an incredible horsewoman. Anyway, I just called her, so head on up; she'll be waiting for you."

Margot smiled broadly before waving goodbye.

I climbed up the hill on tired legs to the mare barn and found Deb, the Cavellis' resident young-horse specialist, leaning on the pasture fence. Deb was a part of the farm that didn't move to Florida during the show season, so I hadn't met her until we came north. I'd only exchanged a few words with her up until now. She was short and slight, with small rimless glasses and a long blonde braid that hung over her shoulder. Even though she was a lot older than me, there was something young and pixie-like about her.

"Hi, Lizzy, come meet the yearlings; my little wildlings."

Deb pointed across the pasture to three shaggy soon-to-be yearlings gathered under a tree. One looked butt-high and mutton-withered with a saggy belly. One had a chewed-off tail. Even the one that looked half-way attractive, with four white socks and a blaze, was still no beauty.

But I felt impatient and was shifting from foot to foot. It was chilly that afternoon. The sky had turned steel grey, and the wind was picking up. It was definitely going to rain.

Deb flicked her long braid over her shoulder and put two fingers in her mouth, blasting out one of those ear-piercing whistles I could never figure out how to do. Then she straightened her glasses. I was not sure how old Deb was, maybe late thirties, although I was terrible at guessing ages. No fancy breeches here. She wore ratty old jeans, and I doubted she had ever worn make-up; but she was pretty without it.

The shaggy youngsters immediately picked up their heads from the grass. The black one even stopped chewing, letting the long grass hang from his mouth.

Deb said, "He's studying his options. He's the leader, and he won't come at first. He likes to play it cool, but once he commits they'll all come."

All it took was a gust of wind and a smattering of raindrops. Then, sure enough, first the black and then the two bays began moving our way. They began at a walk, broke to trot, and finished in a galloping race to the gate, the black one letting fly a high-placed kick and a loud fart.

I looked over at Deb and she was grinning. Her smile was broad with pretty teeth and two dimples which gave her a mischievous look.

"Help me get these guys in. But watch yourself. They are rebels. Not one of them can be trusted. Our little gang leader there is quite the punk. You know Hotstuff right? That's his half-brother. At least he's way better-looking than Hotstuff ever was."

That piqued my interest.

"Oh. Does that mean one of them is a sibling of Bounce?"

"Yeah. The bay with the little star and the chewed-off tail. He looks just like his big brother."

I sighed. He was the homeliest thing I'd ever seen.

"That's Bounce's brother?"

"Yeah. Half-brother. Don't look so disappointed. He's growing, Lizzy. He'll be beautiful one day."

"I rode Bounce in Florida. He was my project. He had the most wonderful round shape and lovely eye. And the other one? Is it a sibling of Romp?"

"Different fathers. But yes, all out of the same mares as your crop that went to Florida. The mares have been easy breeders, so we have three more coming soon. Francesca's been really lucky. Seems like her luck never runs out."

"Except for Rave."

"Well, yeah. I'm sorry about Rave. I hate that he didn't get to come home. He deserved a retirement in my green fields up here with the youngsters. I watched him make Margot who she is today."

Then she turned to me, "I understand you got to show the old boy."

Deb handed me a lead rope, turning away from me before I could ask questions. She talked over her shoulder while unlatching the gate.

"Maybe you should take the rebel boy, and I'll take the other two. It's not so easy leading two at once, but it's how they usually come in."

"Does that bad-boy have a name?"

"Yeah. Hi-Jinks. Don't blame me," she smiled, "Margot names them."

Deb snapped the lead rope onto Hi-Jinks' halter and handed him off to me without a single instruction. How hard could it be to lead the little "punk" into the barn?

Then she snapped up the other two, finagled them so she had one on each side of her, and gave me a nod.

"Get that gate open wide for me, Lizzy."

The rain picked up as I gave the gate a push. And before I could give a tug on the rope, we were off.

Hi-Jinks may have been a baby, but he was turbo-charged, and I was trotting to keep up with him.

Then he stopped, bowed himself up, rolled his neck down, and shook the rain out of his ears.

"Hey!" I tried to pull his head back up.

The rain got heavier. I was already hopelessly chilled and now soaked through. I could hear Deb yell at me to keep moving.

I gave the rope a few more tugs, and he flung his head up in the air. Within a few steps, he was doing little launches off the ground, and I was bounding alongside him, flying my weird hair-covered kite. He finally stood up on his hind legs, still bouncing his way toward the barn.

I tugged on the rope, "Hey, get down here!"

He came back down to earth, and somehow I hustled his little black butt into a stall, but not before he stepped on my foot with one of his little hooves. Even little yearling hooves without shoes hurt. I unclipped the lead and then slid the door shut. Deb seemed not to notice my limp.

"Lizzy, take one of these guys from me, please."

One of Deb's babies had somehow decided to turn around and was walking backward down the barn aisle. I grabbed that one, and Deb pointed to a stall.

This was the woman who was going to teach me all about training babies? All I could think of was how incredibly dangerous horses were; even little ones.

"Come on in and dry off, and I'll get you a cup of tea. You look like a drowned rat."

"Thanks, Deb. I feel like a drowned rat, too."

"Let's just forget about doing anything with these guys today. There's always tomorrow, and you can't teach anything to an excited horse. Sometimes it's just better to let horses be horses."

Deb led me down the barn aisle to what looked like a tack room door, but it opened instead to her laundry room in her cottage. Ingenious. On bad winter days, she could care for the horses without having to step outside. A laundry basket sat on top of her washer, full to the top with folded towels and a tabby cat. Another cat darted out of the room like a flash. I only caught sight of the end of a tail. It was red like a fox, with a white tip.

"Ah, those are my clean towels." Deb growled, "Midget, out of the basket!"

The tabby made no move, and Deb lifted it out. It opened its green eyes and gave a little squeaky protest as Deb placed it on top of the washer. But as soon as she lifted out two towels, the cat crawled right back in the basket and curled up again, giving us a disgusted look.

"Damn cats. When I moved in, I had no cats. Zero. But somehow the word got out, and they started showing up. I'm not sure how they know. Maybe they beat on little kitty tom-toms, or a leave a mark that means "sucker lives here." Of course then I put out kitty chow, and now look at me. I've got seven prowling around the house and garden. Seven, maybe more, I'm not really sure. Some I can't even touch."

I looked down at the hairy towel I had just been handed.

"I'm really more of a dog person myself."

Deb turned to look at me, flipping that long, blonde ponytail over her shoulder and examining me through her tiny rimless glasses. Oops. Clearly I'd said something wrong.

The glasses got another little push up her nose. I thought she really ought to get them tightened. Then she said, "Francesca hates cats. Just hates them, and the Jacks run them right out of the main barn. I guess the cats stay up here so they can still live on the farm without ever having to see her; just like me."

I folded my towel inside out so the cat hair would at least be on the inside and then squeezed my wet ponytail in the folds and rubbed down my face and arms.

So Deb, like most of us, felt no fondness for Francesca. But for Deb it was clearly more personal.

I followed Deb into her kitchen. It was warm, with two loaves of homemade-looking bread sitting on the counter.

Deb busied herself with putting on the tea kettle. It was nice that she had invited me in, but clearly she hadn't been expecting company. The place was in shambles. She removed a stack of papers and magazines from a chair just so I could sit down. I tried not to stare at the piles of dirty plates and mugs stacked on the kitchen counter and instead did my best at polite conversation.

"So, Deb, it seems you and Margot go way back."

"Yeah. She and Walter kind of raised me."

That surprised me. Looking at Deb I couldn't see Margot's influence at all. Margot was so polished and stylish, with hair and makeup never out of place. Emma always looked like Margot's "mini-me," always camera-ready. But not Deb; with those glasses that wouldn't stay put, and ratty jeans. I responded as politely as possible, "I didn't know that, Deb. And you've been with Margot all these years?"

Deb set a box of sugar cubes on the table and a quart of milk. She rummaged around in a drawer and handed me a long-handled teaspoon.

"Oh you know, on and off. After Walter died—you know who Walter was right—Margot's husband? Anyway, we moved here; the whole Francesca thing really got going; and ultimately I had a parting of the ways with Francesca."

I stirred my tea distractedly, pulled out my spoon, and noticed a cat hair swirling on the surface. I plucked it out quietly and looked back at Deb, who clearly had not noticed.

I nodded encouragingly. "Francesca is difficult."

"I suppose Emma told you the whole story."

"Emma didn't tell me anything really. Not about Margot, or Francesca, or Frank, or…"

Deb interrupted, "But I'm back now."

I was thinking I had heard nothing about Deb. Nothing. Until we arrived in New Jersey, I didn't know she existed.

Deb sat down at the table with her cup of tea. She dropped at least four sugar cubes into her mug and sighed.

"I'm here because of Margot. But."

Deb smiled, and there was a long pause. Her focus had drawn inward, like she was watching an internal movie, an old favorite. She said, "I wouldn't trade that wonderful, awful time away from her for anything."

I was hoping to hear more. But Deb then turned the conversation to me. She seemed really interested and encouraging, and kind. So I spent the afternoon telling Deb all about my jump from an office job and a steady boyfriend, with my horse on the side as a hobby, to this:

All horses, all the time.

I had thrown that old life away for this opportunity. I had gambled everything to train with Margot, to be a dressage rider. Not just a dressage rider; I wanted to be a great dressage rider. I understood by now that there was no turning back for me. But what was in my future?

I hoped it was more than teeth and hooves, and cat hair in my tea.

CHAPTER 2

Ears Up, Eyes Wide

THE BARN WITHOUT MARGOT IN IT felt different; less comfortable. I was glad for Emma that Margot would be helping with Emma's new stallion this weekend in Texas. But I missed Margot, and I missed Emma, too. Margot had orchestrated Emma's new job in Texas and the ride on a Grand Prix stallion. It was a point of pride to Margot that Emma would be successful with her new horse; after all, Emma had worked for Margot for eight years and was her star protégé. I wished I could have gone with Margot to visit Emma and see the new stallion. Being alone with Ryder and Francesca and the monster-horse Wild Child made me edgy.

There was no strict schedule to follow. To be sure that Ryder and I weren't idle, Francesca had assigned barn-wide "beauty parlor." So that was how our morning had begun. I had just finished with Wild Child, and Ryder was working on Francesca's horse, Lovey.

I looked up when I heard the dogs' nails tap-tap on the herringbone brick aisle. Francesca, the owner of 'all we could survey,' would be right behind. The dogs were always her advance guard. She came into view, walked a few paces toward us, and stopped, putting a hand up to smooth her hair which was pulled back into a bun. Francesca was dressed in beautiful chestnut-colored breeches that I was sure were her own design. However, they were way too pristine to have ever been ridden in.

Francesca looked over at me, and her red lips turned down at the corners.

"Lizzy, is Wild Child groomed?"

"Yes."

"Good."

Then she turned to Ryder.

"Ryder, come to my office. We have something to discuss."

What the heck? Was Ryder going to ride Wild Child? Or was Ryder in trouble? No matter what Francesca did or said around here, it had the effect of making me slightly queasy.

Francesca gave a directional nod toward her office and then turned her back.

Her dogs followed her. Snapper stopped to pee against a stall front, mouth open, tongue lolling, and he looked right at me, sharing the joke. Chopper, the rough-coated one, quickly gave a squirt right on top, and then they hurried on their stubby, crooked, little Jack Russell legs to catch up.

I looked over at Ryder, who had been busy pulling Lovey's thick black mane. She didn't look the least bit concerned.

"What do you think is going on?"

Ryder simply shrugged, hopped off her stool, and turned to me, clearly unfazed.

"Even up his mane for me, Lizzy. I'm almost done, but I need to trim-clip him before I put him away."

"Sure. I'll pray for you, OK?"

Ryder gave me a smirk and shook her head.

I started stressing on Ryder's behalf. Maybe she was going to get a dressing down. Maybe she was even losing the ride on Papa. Oh, I was ashamed at how my mind was working. Was I jinxing her? I would feel bad if she got fired. I would.

On the other hand, maybe she was going to get a ride on Wild Child behind Margot's back. No. That couldn't be, could it?

I leaned my broom against the wall of the grooming stall where I had been sweeping up mane from Wild Child, and I climbed up on the mounting block next to Lovey. Unlike Wild Child who tried to eat me, and my horse Winsome who had to have her mane razored she hated it so much, good old Lovey stood like a rock for mane-pulling. In fact his top lip poked forward, and his eyes half closed. He was such a sweet boy. I never saw Francesca give him the affection that he so clearly enjoyed. I tidied up the bottom edge of his pulled mane, making it uniform.

When I was finished with his mane, I got him a nice fat carrot. While he chewed I put my arm around his head and rested my ear against his cheek, which he let me do without worry. He was Saint Lovey. I closed my eyes and listened to the crunching sound as he made fast work on the carrot.

"Lizzy, you are such a freak."

I opened my eyes and gave Lovey a pat and an extra-long hug around his neck. He had centered me; Ryder could call me a freak. I no longer cared if she'd been reamed by Francesca. I turned back to Ryder, thinking, hey, let the chips fall. I took a light tone.

"Francesca let you live another day. So, what terrible sin did you commit?"

Ryder shook her head in disbelief along with a little horse-like snort of disgust.

"Mom's been talking to Francesca. She told her about my modeling, and now Francesca wants me to do some print ads for her breeches."

"Modeling?"

"Yeah. Crazy right? I hate it. It's incredibly boring. Mom had this idea when I was little that I was going to be a model and an actress, and for years I got dragged around to photo shoots. I finally went on strike. I'm kind of pissed that she sent Francesca some shots. So Francesca asked and I said I'd do it, but only 'cause I'm riding Papa. If it wasn't for that fact, there'd be no way."

A model? I was stunned. Ryder didn't look anything like how I imagined a model would look. OK, she was skinny, but I was skinny. She was tall...I was tall-ish.

Of course when I first met Ryder, she had a pierced nose, multiple piercings in her ears, and pink-streaked hair. She was just punk-ugly. Maybe that was intentional to keep her out of modeling jobs. Francesca had insisted her hair become a normal brown, and she was allowed only one earring in each ear. Still, I wouldn't have called her pretty. I summoned up my politest tone.

"Wow, that's great, Ryder. Clearly your Mom is very proud of you."

"She needs to butt out."

"I think it's sweet that she wanted Francesca to know about all of your talents."

"The only talent Francesca needs to know about is that I can ride her horse and that I can win the individual gold medal at Championships."

My politeness evaporated. Her attitude once again put my teeth on edge. It was hard to keep that light tone now.

"Aren't you getting ahead of yourself? You haven't even shown yet. You have to qualify for your spot on a team from Region One. And even if you do make a team, you shouldn't expect to win a medal, certainly not the individual gold medal on your first try."

Ryder turned away from me and plugged in the small clippers. She unhooked Lovey's throat latch on his halter and flicked the switch. The little clippers began to hum. Lovey stretched his neck out making it easier for Ryder to clip the hairs under his jaw. Ryder kept her eyes on her job while answering.

"What you don't get, Lizzy, is that I have Papa; and I have Margot; and the other kids don't. If Margot has confidence in me, that's all I need."

I sighed.

Maybe she was just terribly naive. She was only eighteen. I knew I shouldn't try and squash her dreams, but I knew it wasn't going to be that easy for her. I guessed she could find that out herself.

Ryder put Lovey away, and I was contemplating going for Hotstuff when the Jacks reappeared, leading Francesca and a tall slender man our way. Even though the guy was wearing jeans, I could tell that he was a rider. I'd always noticed that good riders move and even stand a certain way. I was not sure what it is, but they seem to own any space they occupy, and this guy was no exception. He was listening to Francesca, but he was looking with a discerning eye at the horses in the stalls as he passed; as if he were shopping. I knew in my heart he was looking for Wild Child, and I was surprised at my own reaction. I was concerned because Margot was not in the barn.

Francesca was nodding toward me.

"Lizzy, go ahead and bring Wild Child out for us."

My fingers curled into fists, and my feet felt like traitors as I did what I was told.

I went to the tack room and grabbed a big fat carrot, a pocketful of sugar cubes, a whip, my deerskin gloves, and of course, a chain shank. If I could have put on armor, I would have. But even as I braced for battle with Wild Child, I hoped he was not for sale. I hated him, but I did not want him sold out from under Margot.

As I passed Ryder, I knew without looking she would be sneering at my weaponry.

I drew a fortifying breath. This was my job, and Francesca was the big boss.

Francesca and her guest and the dogs followed me. I knew Francesca would be scrutinizing my every move. I didn't dare show hesitation or timidity in front of these two, and I didn't want to come on too strong either and incite Wild Child's aggression. I had to play it cool.

I could hear the two of them chatting behind me. Francesca said, "I had no idea you were bidding against us for this guy."

My heart began thudding in my chest.

"We were a day late and a dollar short I'm afraid. I can't lie, I was terribly disappointed. I know I could do great things with that horse."

Surprisingly, I had no problem putting the halter on Wild Child. He came to the front of the stall and hung his head out into the aisle.

He never did that for me before.

He was on high alert, his ears pricked, nostrils wide. He was staring transfixed at our guest. I cut my eyes briefly toward Francesca, and I could see both of them were entranced by Wild Child. My hands were trembling. I hoped no one noticed.

I ran the chain over his nose and had to back him up to open the sliding door. He refused the offered carrot and did not pin his ears or try to bite.

I pulled Wild Child out in the aisle and shook the chain shank at him to get him to stop and stand. He made himself extra tall, and his widened eyes showed white around the edges.

The guest reached his hand out to touch Wild Child on the neck but never made contact. Wild Child scampered to the side, arching and twisting his neck and blowing suspiciously at the man's hand.

The man dropped his hand and crossed his arms, his eyes still appraising.

I quietly moved toward Wild Child, and he let me. He didn't even pin his ears when I laid my hand on his neck, but I could see the tension around his mouth, the edges of his lips pulled back almost in a smile, and I could hear his front teeth weirdly tapping, as he nervously pulled his tongue far back inside his mouth. I'd never seen Wild Child act like this.

Francesca put a protective arm on her guest, drawing him back toward her.

"He's not a friendly sort of horse."

I almost laughed out loud. What an understatement.

But the guy seemed unconcerned. He put one hand on top of Francesca's and smiled at her in reassurance, and she almost giggled. I realized that Francesca was lapping this up. He was good-looking. He had a rugged look from too much time in the sun and was sandy-haired with lots of smile wrinkles.

He was patting her hand and still smiling.

"I know his type. He just needs a firm hand. I'm actually surprised that Margot agreed to ride him. I know she doesn't like stallions."

Wild Child moved into my hand ever so slightly.

"Nonsense," said Francesca, "Her best horse was a stallion."

"Yes. Of course I know that. Magnus was before my time of course. It's just the stories I've heard."

I tentatively began scratching Wild Child's withers. He did not indicate that he was enjoying my touch, but he didn't seem to dislike it either, so I kept lightly scratching. His ears stayed fixed on the guest.

Francesca continued, "Magnus was before I knew her, too. But remember, I trained with Walter before I trained with Margot. And he always spoke of Magnus in glowing terms. He said Magnus was a "once-in-a-lifetime-horse.""

The guest nodded in agreement before answering, "I've always heard that Walter was the one who rode and trained Magnus, that he was a man's ride and gave Margot a devil of a time. I bet this guy is the same."

Before I could think, I had butted into their conversation, "Oh, Margot's got this guy's number. She worked his rear off on their very first ride. You should have seen it. He even had white foam on his eyelids!"

Francesca shot me a dirty look.

But the guy smiled and looked me right in the eyes. I noticed his were pale blue. He held my gaze just a beat too long and then turned back to Francesca. I knew she had not liked my intrusion.

"Ah, Francesca you know how much I like the difficult horses; they suit me more than they do you ladies. You know what they say about "madness and genius;" it's a fine line, one that I tend to share with my favorite horses."

Francesca smiled thinly.

"Oh, Patrick, we're all a bit mad in this horse world if you ask me."

So our guest's name was Patrick. Then it dawned on me, I knew who this was but would only have recognized him in a top hat and tailcoat from the magazines.

Patrick looked down into Francesca's face and smiled as if she had said something profound.

"So if you guys need me to help with the stallion, just call. Heck, you could practically whistle and I'd hear you; Claire's place is so near."

"That's kind of you to offer, Patrick."

Wild Child and I watched as they turned and walked away.

When they were gone, Wild Child deflated, but after I put him in his stall and pulled off the halter, he chased me right out of his stall with pinned ears.

I hung everything back up, feeling exhausted and relieved. Wild Child was not for sale. I guessed Francesca had been rubbing it in that she had Wild Child and Patrick didn't. That would be like her. But still, I hadn't liked the way that guy had looked at Wild Child, or at me for that matter.

Ryder was fuming.

"Francesca should have introduced me to him. He's the Chef d'equipe for the Young Riders. I should have just gone up to him. Maybe I could still catch him."

"Ryder let him go. He was a total jerk. That guy even had the nerve to dis Margot to Francesca; in front of me, too."

"Lizzy, he's a renowned trainer."

"I don't care who he is. I don't have to like him. Wild Child didn't like him either."

Ryder was shaking her head again.

"Lizzy, you can't know that. What you're doing is called anthropomorphizing."

I looked over at Ryder. Her arms were crossed, and I could tell she was feeling superior.

"You can call it what you want. I know what I know. I could see it in his ears and his eyes. Horses don't lie."

CHAPTER 3

A Cup Of Kindess

I GRABBED MY MOM'S LATEST CARE package. It was a large tin full of her great Tollhouse cookies, big chocolate chunks and walnuts, my favorite. I was headed to Deb's to share my bounty. Deb had been nice to me. I thought it would be friendly to share my package with her. I trudged uphill along the drive while watching two furry colts in a pasture push each other around a bit before putting their heads back down to graze.

DEB'S LITTLE SHACK OF A COTTAGE hugged the side of the mare barn. Around the stoop and door was a garden unlike the organized beds set out by Francesca's gardeners. Here were disorganized bunches of daffodils and crocus, with leathery tulip leaves breaking the surface here and there. Large clay planters were sitting against the wall, full of soil and ready for something to be planted. A long-haired tortoiseshell cat was sprawled on the concrete slab stoop, soaking up heat. The cat glared at me with its gold-flecked eyes and darted away as soon as I knocked on the door.

No answer.

Her little car was there, so I strolled through the empty barn. I thought about how the farm felt more like two farms, and how Deb seemed to own the mare barn and fields more than Francesca or Frank did. This was clearly her territory. I had never seen Francesca up there.

But I also noticed that Deb never came to watch her mentor and friend Margot ride down at the other barn. That was Francesca's territory.

I had been told that Deb didn't ride anymore. Actually, Deb had said so herself. That's what Margot said, too. But yesterday her jeans had the tell-tale crescent of dirt on her behind. I kept quiet, but it was a dead giveaway that she wasn't telling the whole truth.

Her old dressage mare was heavy in foal, not exactly riding fit. Of course it wasn't her mare anymore. She had sold the big black mare, "Regina," to Francesca and Frank some years ago. But she was riding someone. I imagined that by announcing she did not ride anymore, she had gotten herself off the hook of starting the baby horses. At a certain age, most riders handed that job off. Someone else got to be cannon fodder. I guessed this year it would be Ryder and me.

I walked to the end of the barn aisle and gazed out to the back field.

Then I saw her.

Deb was indeed riding the heavily pregnant Regina bareback in a halter and lead rope. In fact the lead rope hung loose around Regina's neck. Deb carried a dressage whip. Regina was piaffing. And even without a bridle, her neck was raised and arched. Even the heavily pregnant Regina was beautiful. She must have been brilliant as a young horse. She trotted almost in place, her tail bouncing in rhythm, then step-by-step the piaffe gathered. Slowly the mare raised one front foot. She found her balance and lifted the other, her knees level with each other. I knew it was a Levade only because I had seen photos of the famous Lippizan stallions of Vienna performing it. I had never seen one live.

Then they stopped, and Deb gave her a pat. To my surprise they started up again, picking up the trot, doing a few steps of medium trot, and then transitioning back to passage. Deb patted the now-puffing black mare. They stopped again and just stood there for the longest time, seeming to take in the scenery.

At first I was frozen to the spot. I had never seen anything like it. I felt a longing for that to be me and my Winsome, and a pain in my chest because we were so far from what I had just witnessed.

I came unstuck and instinctively backed up behind the barn door. I felt like an intruder, a spy, but at the same time, just couldn't make myself yell out to her and make my presence known. There was something intensely private about the moment. I backed away and then turned to hurry back down the barn aisle.

The next thing I knew, I was heading for the floor.

"Oooof!"

"Yeeoww!!"

A flash of electrified tabby cat disappeared into a stall.

I landed right on my elbows. Ouch. The tin went flying, clattering loudly against the concrete. The lid popped off, and wax paper and precious Tollhouse cookies scattered.

So much for sneaking away unobserved.

First I examined my elbows. They hurt, more from the impact than from losing a little skin. I got on my hands and knees, and I started crawling around gathering the cookies, but of course they were mostly broken. What a waste. For some reason I felt overwhelmed, and I sat back on my haunches and started to cry. Not "sniff-sniff" either, but "boo-hoo."

Maybe skinning my elbows like a kid on a playground, and then crawling around on my hands and knees, was cause for emotional regression. Maybe it was just the sight of wasted Tollhouse cookies.

I felt a light touch of a hand on my shoulder.

"Lizzy? Are you OK?"

I stopped picking up cookies. She was looking down at me through her little rimless glasses, her long braid hanging forward over her shoulder, whip and lead rope in her hand.

"I'm sorry, Deb. I'm being silly."

Then I was embarrassed. I pulled myself together.

"It's just I brought my Mom's care package to share with you; cookies. And I tripped over a cat and look; I've ruined them."

"Nonsense. These are all perfectly good."

Deb put down the whip and lead rope and started picking up cookies. She blew off one broken piece of cookie, and then it went right into her mouth. She closed her eyes for a moment while she chewed, opened them back up, and smiled at me.

"Delicious. It's sweet of you to share. C'mon in. I'll put the tea kettle on. Tea and cookies are the best."

She put her hand out and helped pull me up off the ground, and I followed her in to the house.

Piles of magazines were pushed to the edge of the kitchen table and the tin of cookies placed in the middle.

Deb knew how to make me feel at ease. She simply asked me to tell her about my mare. I had many questions I could have asked her, and wanted to ask, but she had shorted the circuitry. When the tea kettle began to whistle, I had hardly drawn a breath, and Deb was smiling slyly at me.

"Lizzy, things can't be so bad if you own a horse like that. I have a special fondness for mares myself. Once they bond with you, I find the bond is intense. Then they'll leap through rings of fire for you. It's something you can't buy and you can't fake."

When we finished our tea, I cleared our mugs and took them to the sink. I found a brush and soap and washed them and put them in the drain rack. Then I looked at the stacks of dirty dishes on the counter.

"Deb, can I wash these too?"

Deb grimaced, "I know I'm a lousy housekeeper, Lizzy, but you don't need to do that."

"I want to do something for you. You've been nice to me."

"Suit yourself."

"You don't mind?"

"Knock yourself out."

So I washed, and Deb picked up a wrinkled dishtowel. I watched as she shook crumbs off of it and onto the floor. But it looked fairly clean. After I had handed her a few dishes, I asked, "Deb, do you know this guy Patrick that has a farm near here?"

Deb made a small grunt.

"Sure, he works for Claire Winston. I could tell you some stories about that one. Better horse training through 'chemistry,' if you know what I mean."

"Geez, I knew I didn't like him. He's famous though. I always see his picture in the magazines on amazing-looking horses. Why do you think Francesca would have him looking at Wild Child?"

Deb stopped drying and turned to look me full in the face. Her mouth hung open for a moment. Then she picked up another dish and slowly began to turn it inside the wadded-up towel. She answered me out of the side of her mouth, "Because she's a damned fool."

CHAPTER 4
Modes Of Flight

I COULDN'T WAIT TO GET ON Winsome. I wanted the bond that I had seen between Regina and Deb. I tacked her up with images of Regina playing in my mind like a movie.

Winsome and I headed out the front gates for an afternoon ride. Even though the April air still had a chill in it, it smelled of spring. It was a green smell, the smell of new bright grass, with wet earth underneath. Every step Winsome took crushed the tender shoots and filled the air. People would not smell this in the suburbs yet. Not until the army of lawn mowers emerged from garages to cut lawns.

Winsome kept her ears pointed forward, watchful for chipmunks and deer, ever alert for a need to twirl and scoot, almost looking for a reason to work off the extra energy I felt bubbling underneath the saddle.

I turned her up a long grade and let her have her head. A bounding trot became a rolling canter and then accelerated into a gallop. I could feel her bunch herself and then explode, her hind feet pushing and pumping together. I leaned low and forward and gave her outstretched neck a pat, the sleeve of my windbreaker fluttering like a flag. By the time we crested the hill, she was done.

She stopped and stood, panting and surveying the fields and farms below us. Her veins stood up, clearly visible on her recently clipped liver-chestnut coat. She pulled in a deep breath, exhaled loudly, and gave a strong, all-over shake that made me yelp and grab the front of the saddle to steady myself.

I checked my watch. Crap. I guessed I was having too much fun. I would be late. Ryder would be on time, and I would look bad. Ryder and I were to help unload the two new arrivals and get them settled. It was some old friend of Francesca's. It was hard to imagine Francesca had any friends, old or otherwise.

It seemed like a long walk back to the stable. My nose was running, and I wiped it on the back of my gloves. Winsome was still blowing hard, and I needed to walk to cool her down. I assured myself she would still make good time with her big walk. I was sure the judges would give it a 9 or 10 if we could get it in competition. She could really cover ground when she was heading back. I checked my watch about a dozen more times. How had so much time passed?

We came out of the field, through an open wooden gate sagging on its hinges, onto a dirt road, and passed barns and schooling rings. This really was a horseman's paradise. Because there was still foxhunting in the area, there was plenty of land we were allowed to ride over. We just had to stay to the edge of any planted field.

We rounded a bend in the road, and up ahead appeared the farm, Equus Paradiso North. It was unlike the Florida farm in almost every way. It was old and rustic. I thought it might have been historic. The barn's foundation was fieldstone; the top half was timbered and painted a faded red. The stalls, compared to the Florida barn, were not as roomy, the aisle not as wide, and the ceilings not as high. The windows on the stalls were small and barred, so the horses could not hang their heads outside. But I liked it. It was a snug barn, meant to shelter the horses and riders from the cold.

Although the barn was smaller, the acreage was more expansive than the Florida farm. This farm had acres of green fields. It had two arenas, an outside one and a fully enclosed indoor.

Each arena had a full short-side of mirrors and a viewing stand with chairs. The landscaping was not as formal as the Florida barn, and most of the plantings were mature. The outdoor arena was surrounded by old hedges that ran the entire perimeter. They were set just outside the timbers that framed the arena. Thick and glossy-leafed, the hedges formed a natural sort of kickboard.

Winsome clip-clopped up the driveway, and we sidled up to the keypad outside the iron entry gate. The farm might have been old, but the gates weren't. They were clearly new. The bronze plaque "Equus Paradiso" was set in one of the stone posts, just like the Florida farm. The ironwork was intricate, with the farm logo of olive branches framing a horse in pirouette.

Winsome found the keypad entry and electric gate highly suspicious. Usually she got over things like this pretty quickly. Last time I got off her to punch the numbers and got my foot stepped on for my troubles. This time I decided I was safer staying on board.

The keypad was mounted on a post and set at a height that was just a little bit too low to reach comfortably from the back of the horse. I had to lean over to push in the code, grabbing a piece of mane for security. I braced myself for what I knew was coming. Each number I pushed on the keypad made a little beep, and each beep would make Winsome startle sideways away from the keypad.

"Good girl, c'mon, just a bit closer."

Steeling myself, it was time to give it a go, so I gave it a poke. "Beep."

Winsome's hoofs clattered against the pad of concrete as she scampered sideways.

"C'mon sweetie, over, over, over, Winsome, over. Yes."

I leaned over and stabbed again at the keypad.

"Beep."

She once again bounced away from the post.

Then I was growling at her, "Winsome, get your ass back over there."

I turned a small circle and grabbed mane again, pushing at the pad as we did a "fly-by."

"Beep."

She jumped sideways once again and then added a few steps backward so she could turn and snort at the keypad. I looked over my shoulder to see that this time she had put more than one hoof print in the bed of pansies.

"Winsome, honestly, now I'm gonna' have to come out here later and cover your tracks. C'mon, get back over there. It won't kill you."

Winsome sashayed herself back over to the keypad, and I steeled myself for the last beep. I knew it was going to be the mother of all beeps. Once you hit the fourth number correctly, you had hit the jackpot. You were allowed in.

"Beeeeeep!"

It was followed by a pleasant female computer voice, a voice that had slept through the commotion.

"Access granted."

How kind, I thought. If Francesca had seen her pansies, she wouldn't have sounded so nice, or necessarily granted me access.

I was just getting myself upright in the saddle when the gates began their inward swing. This time Winsome surprised me by throwing her head down and spinning hard to the right. I heard myself make a roaring sound mid-flight. I hit surprisingly-soft ground with a thud, sitting up in time to see a flash of chestnut, my mare, running away.

Winsome had tucked her tail, scooted, and run from the offending gates, and from me, the one she was supposed to be bonded to. She had cantered off in the other direction along the fence line, churning up the pansy beds as she went. There would be no covering up those tracks.

Winsome began to slow down, sensing that she was missing something. Me. She slowed to a trot, turned back around, stopped, arched her neck, and snorted like a fire-breathing dragon. It was the danger call, the one that would raise every soul in the barn, horse and human.

I reached into my jacket pocket and found a peppermint. All I had to do was crinkle the plastic, and then she carefully tip-toed back to me and gave me a hard nudge as I unwrapped her treat. Nervously she took her peppermint, and I led her through the gates to safety. Or maybe not.

There was the firing squad, lined up and ready to take aim. I guessed I deserved it.

There stood Ryder, leaning on a broom and standing next to Francesca and the two Jacks, Chopper and Snapper. Francesca had her arms crossed. She never looked friendly, even on her cheeriest day, but now she looked livid.

"Lizzy, can't you and that mare leave my flowers alone?"

I felt like I couldn't swallow or speak for a moment. My face felt hot. Francesca was not ever going to let me forget Winsome trampling her bed of Begonias in Florida. I finally sputtered.

"I'm sorry, Francesca. I'll pay for new pansies. I'll plant them myself."

"Of course you'll pay, but I'm not letting you near my flower beds, at least not if I can help it. Why are you so late anyway? Cara should have already arrived. Oh my God, what a mess you are. You're filthy."

I looked down at myself. My left leg was black with good potting soil and bits of mulch; a petal of a yellow pansy was crushed against my zippered pocket. I guessed the pansies had been recently watered.

Ryder walked up to me and handed me the broom.

"I'll take care of the mare. Go change clothes. I can clean her up, and after you change you can finish sweeping the tack room."

Ryder just couldn't open her mouth without sounding condescending. I was the one who should be giving her orders. And how about showing concern for my well-being? I had just fallen off a horse. Did anyone care?

I looked down at the dogs, and they were smiling as usual. Their little stump-tails did mechanical-looking slow wags, mouths hung open, and tongues lolled. They liked nothing better than a good skirmish.

I tried to sound polite, but it came out strained.

"Ryder, I can take care of my own horse, but thank you. Why don't you go finish the tack room?"

Francesca flashed an annoyed look at Ryder, but then turned back to me, giving me the same look.

"Not another peep, Lizzy. Go change."

Ryder took Winsome's reins, and I found myself holding the broom. As I started to walk away, Winsome tried to follow, but

I stopped and looked at her. She seemed to understand, and she stopped too. She turned her head and touched Ryder on her shoulder. I did not like leaving her with Ryder, but I did as I was told.

As I passed Francesca, I handed her the broom. It gave me some small satisfaction. I thought she could fly away on it.

CHAPTER 5

Tough Broads And Tiaras

I CAME DOWN FROM CHANGING TO find a trailer pulling up to the front of the barn. A short round woman jumped out of the truck and gave Francesca a big hug. No air kisses, but a real old-fashioned bear hug.

The woman's voice was nasal and most definitely New Jersey.

"Oh let me have a good long look at you! My God, how come you look so young, Franny? You don't even have wrinkles."

Francesca looked startled by the hug, but she was smiling.

"Cara, it's been too long."

Then Francesca looked over Cara's shoulder at us.

"What are you two staring at? Help Cara get her two horses off the trailer and unpack her things. Take care now, girls."

"Franny, they don't know my horses. I'll get the boys off myself."

"No, Cara. You just tell them what to do. Supervise if you need to."

"Now I'm feeling spoiled already."

Cara turned to gaze at us, and then shrugged.

"OK. Take the one on the left off first. That's the young one, that's Petey. He's a bit of a handful, pulls like a freight train; sorry I forgot my chain lead rope. Stand Petey nearby while you take off Kiddo. He's my old man. He's the one you girls will be fighting over. It breaks my heart to leave him."

So we carefully unloaded the two. Kiddo had once been a plain dark brown, but now had a face flecked with grey. I guessed by his size and muscling that he was probably a Quarter Horse.

Petey was a true black, tall and powerfully built, with a graceful arching neck set on high. His face was more "noble" than pretty. He clearly was a warmblood.

Cara was right; I was happy to be leading the quiet Kiddo into the barn. Ryder was following me leading Petey, and I could hear her scolding him and jerking on his lead rope. I looked over my shoulder to check on her and was surprised, not by Ryder and Petey, but by Francesca.

She and Cara were walking arm-in-arm, heads bent toward one another. The sight was unnatural.

Francesca caught my eye, just for a second.

"Lizzy. Ryder. Get Cara's trailer clean as a whistle and unpack her horses. Then you can go park her trailer. She's leaving it here until she gets back from Florida."

"Sure thing, Francesca," I responded.

Francesca and Cara ducked into the lounge. Cara was saying with conviction, "Frank Cavelli is a Prince among men..."

Ryder and I put the horses into stalls and headed out to the trailer with a muck cart.

I turned to Ryder, "So, why do you think we're taking in these two?"

"Don't you know? Cara's Mother isn't doing well down in Florida. Francesca offered to take care of the horses."

"How do you know? Did Margot tell you, 'cause she didn't mention it to me?"

"Francesca told me about it."

"Francesca talks to you?"

"Apparently."

"Anything else you can share?"

Ryder shrugged.

"All boring stuff, like how they grew up together on the same street. Y'know, that kind of stuff."

I took a big breath in through my nose and furrowed my brow in disbelief. Francesca was confiding in this teenager, really? Maybe Ryder had just been the warm body who happened to be present when Francesca started traveling down memory lane. That must be it.

So Francesca actually had a friend. I figured that meant she must have a heart and soul, even if I had never seen any evidence of it. Maybe she once had them, but like Voldemort had shredded her soul into itty-bitty pieces by her relentless acts of bitchiness. I guessed there still must be a little shred left to do this nice thing for Cara.

Ryder and I had just finished when Francesca and Cara came out of the lounge. They were laughing, even Francesca, and Cara was wiping tears from her eyes.

"Franny, I'll never forget that day. Whew."

Cara collected herself and sighed, "Well, I guess I'll take the guided tour, and then head out. Let me tell you girls about my boys first."

Ryder and I stood at attention while Francesca drifted back to her office.

"Now Kiddo here, he's not really a horse. Well, I guess he's a horse, but he thinks he's human. He's so smart, he'll keep you on your toes. Plus, he's sort of the Ghandi of the horse world; believes in total non-violence and teaches it to any horse or human he comes into contact with. He's also a good counselor. Any problems you need sorting out; just go into his stall. He's a good listener, rarely interrupts."

I looked into his stall. I could see nothing exceptional. He was contentedly munching our good hay.

Cara turned to me and put her hand on my wrist, giving it a squeeze. Then she said something that surprised me.

"I've heard such nice things about you, Lizzy. I want you to ride him for me. I think you and Kiddo will become the best of friends."

I nodded back at her.

"I know he doesn't look special, but you'll find out on your own that he is. Just know that whatever he tells you, he's right."

"Now Petey here, he's a talent that needs a talent, but he's a tough one. I'm in the process of turning him around. Francesca and I thought Ryder would enjoy the challenge."

Ryder responded, "Yup."

Ryder almost leaned forward in quiet eagerness.

"Just the kind of horse I enjoy working with."

"Well, I've heard a lot about you too, Ryder. In fact, I almost left Petey in the field, but after talking to Francesca, I brought him along just for you."

Cara followed us as Ryder and I rolled a wheelbarrow loaded down with a bag of feed and a bunch of supplements into the feed room. She was chatting non-stop in a nasal voice, barely catching her breath.

"You girls don't know how lucky you are. I sure wish I could turn back the clock and have your jobs, this life."

Ryder and I couldn't stop ourselves; we made eyes, and Cara saw.

"Aw, c'mon now. It can't be that bad. I know Franny can be a pain-in-the-ass. But Franny has waited all her life for this. I hope you girls make nice."

I tried to respond, nodding my head. Who was she kidding? Nice? Polite, yeah. Nice would probably get your head snapped off. But Cara was on a roll.

"In our day we just did as we were told. Her mother was quite the dragon-lady. Franny was gonna' dance, and Franny was gonna' be Miss America whether she wanted it or not. I think she bought Franny a tiara and white gloves at age three and entered her in every pageant she could find. Man they had some battles, right in front of me."

I giggled a little nervously. If you asked me, Francesca walked around the place every day as if she still had on a tiara.

"Today you girls can be whatever you want. We had few choices. Maybe you could be a nurse or a teacher, but only if you couldn't catch a man. Glamour girls became the wives of rich men or gangsters, truth be told. It was a different time. Her Momma and Papa were second generation who had made money in liquor, but money won't get you into high society."

Cara's voice was extra nasally now, and her hands were gesturing.

"Her folks wanted only the best for her. Franny was their only child and a girl, too. In our neighborhood, that was something to be pitied."

Cara paused. So I chimed in, because this WAS interesting stuff.

"So Francesca didn't get to ride?"

"No, no, we both rode. Our private school had a stable and a good European instructor. But the ballet-master finally put a stop to it for Francesca. He said it was ruining her body for dancing."

Cara shook her head, clearly reminiscing.

"We had a hell of a good time on our crazy Thoroughbreds. It was the most freedom we were allowed. But it came to an end for both of us, eventually. But did you know, she did make the cut into the Miss America pageant. Did you know that?"

Ryder had a sneaky little smile. Maybe it was more like a smirk. I piped up before she could.

"Frank told me. He said she danced beautifully."

"She made it to the top fifteen girls. Her Mama wept like a baby when Franny got eliminated. I was there, Atlantic City. But she got Frank. He was the better prize anyway. But still, it was another time."

Cara shrugged her shoulders.

"You went from being a daughter to being a wife, and then a mother. Did you know they started out with only a little neighborhood grocery store? It belonged to Frank's parents."

Ryder and I shook our heads.

"Franny worked her ass off building that business. She deserves this as much as anybody I know. I sometimes think about how good we'd both ride if we'd been allowed to keep it up all those years. Franny and I are two tough broads."

I chimed in again. "I believe you."

"Well, both of us are getting old now. I wish she could at least sit on that fancy new stallion of hers, but she says he's almost too much for Margot even, and Margot won't even put Franny on him on the longe line. What a damn shame. He's the best-looking horse I've ever seen. I guess we old broads need to be grateful we can still put a leg over any horse."

Ryder put the grain away and set the tubs of supplements on the shelves. She wiped her hands on her breeches, "So we'll switch the horses over to our feed, y'know, over the next week. And I guess both the horses get the supplements?"

"Oh, yeah. Sorry. I guess I'm rambling."

I shot Ryder a dirty look. Why would she want Cara to stop? Clearly Cara was someone Francesca actually talked to. I wanted to know more. I tried to re-start her.

"I love hearing about Francesca from you. I like to think of her all dressed up in a gown and being in a pageant, and you two riding your Thoroughbreds. Did she jump, too?

"Like a kangaroo. We weren't always pretty, but we stayed in the tack."

Cara grinned.

"You know, after Frank watched the Olympics, well, the only discipline where he didn't see anyone fall off was dressage. Isn't that a hoot! So dressage it was gonna be."

Cara slapped her thigh.

"I still jump a little. I probably shouldn't. Not Petey though. He's destined for dressage. But Kiddo, he and I did the Ammie Hunters together. Carted my butt around like a champ and found every distance. I just grabbed mane and pointed. But if you want to jump him Lizzy, keep the jumps low. He's old. He will still fly over them like he thinks he's a Grand Prix horse, so be sure and grab a little mane if you do."

"Oh, I doubt I'll do any jumping, Cara, but thanks. We do have wonderful hacking trails around here. I love to ride out."

"Yeah. This is the part of New Jersey where we never would have been welcome in the old days. But now, we own it."

Cara grinned.

"I'll bet Francesca's Mama is smiling down from heaven. Take good care of my boys. I guess I gotta go."

And then Cara surprised us both with big bear hugs. Ryder received hers rather stiffly. I was happy to get mine.

CHAPTER 6

A Good Turn

MARGOT WALKED IN HOLDING HER LARGE cup of coffee. I felt happy and relieved to have her back. Margot was my movie star. I didn't think she had any idea how I worshipped her. Even the horses stood up taller and strained forward against the cross-ties as soon as they heard her voice. She always greeted Alfonso and the other guys and asked about their families, so I had to wait for her to work her way down to Ryder and me, as we groomed Wild Child and Hotstuff.

And then of course, Francesca came out of the office and caught up with her. Chopper and Snapper jumped up for their pats on their heads with her free hand. They wiggled their butts and licked her hand until Francesca called them off. Francesca seemed to have urgent business to discuss, and although Margot nodded her head with interest, I knew it was the horses, her horses, that she really wanted to see. I assumed Francesca was telling Margot about Patrick's visit. It put me at ease to know Margot knew about it. Francesca would be sure to tell her so that she wouldn't hear it first from Ryder or me.

Margot was dressed immaculately, as usual, and ready to ride. Her hair was plastered into its little blonde bun, her light brown cotton shirt crisp with starch. Her breeches today surely were tailored for her by Francesca's "High Horse Couture." They were peach with brown fleur-de-lis stitching around the pockets, and she had on highly polished brown boots to match. However, the inner sides of Margot's boots were worn thin and held no polish. She had worn them thin from countless hours in the saddle.

I wanted her attention too, and I was eager to ask about Emma. I wanted to hear all about Texas, all about the new stallion Emma was training. I hated to admit to myself how much I missed Emma. Ryder was no replacement. Emma had her quirks for sure, but, geez, at least she would talk to me. Margot's voice was genuinely cheery. If she knew about Patrick's visit, it hadn't bothered her. I guessed Margot was secure enough in herself that Patrick posed no threat to her.

"Hello, girls! How are these two boys?"

I piped up first because I knew Ryder would only mumble something anyway.

"They miss you. They get depressed when you're gone. I swear."

Margot was smiling as she lifted an eyebrow. "I doubt Wild Child missed me."

I wanted to say that he did. I wanted to tell her how much I could tell he hated that hot-shot trainer Patrick, but not in front of Ryder who would only defend him.

Margot continued, "Wild Child was pretty surly last week. I think it's because it's spring. He knows it's breeding season, and he has to sit this one out. He has to live down here like a monk while there's a harem right up the hill."

Then Margot gave me a nod as she focused in on me. "How goes the walk pirouette exercise, Lizzy?"

Then it was my turn to mumble, "Ah. Yeah. Not so good."

"Well, we'll get right back on it then. And Ryder, how is Papa?"

"Stellar."

"Francesca has told me about our two new guys. It should be fun for you girls to have projects. Lizzy, I'm putting you on Kiddo, OK?"

"OK."

"Ryder, looks like you'll be riding Petey."

"Sure."

"OK then. I'll get on Wild Child in about ten minutes."

I piped up, "Uh, Margot?"

"Yes?"

"How is Emma doing?"

Margot smiled and shook her head.

"I almost forgot, thanks for asking, Lizzy. She's doing just fine."

Margot had an impish grin. I wanted details.

"You have to tell me a little more than that."

"Well, she has shaken up that little corner of Texas. I can tell you that much. I don't think they've seen the likes of Emma around there before. The cowboys are falling over each other trying to get her attention, and she's turned her nose up at every one of them.

But she's got that stallion dancing. He is a good-moving horse and well-mannered too. I think it's going to work. I'm actually rather proud of myself for arranging it."

"Is she wearing her pink cowboy boots?"

Then Margot was smiling broadly. "Not yet. She has an image to maintain doesn't she? But I predict she'll soften up in time. Things just take time, Lizzy."

After the initial buzz of Margot's return, it was time to get back into the rhythm of the work. Avoiding Wild Child's teeth was enough to distract me from the dread I felt about my lesson for at least a while. But by the time it was my turn for my lesson, my stomach was churning. I still got nervous over a lesson with Margot.

And I figured I had good reason. I was still terrible. And poor Winsome was confused too. Then Ryder walked in on Papa, and I got even more tense.

Margot must have felt my agony and taken pity on me.

"Lizzy, darling, go on and jump down, and I'll give it a go."

I jumped off, and Margot stepped right into my stirrups. They were a little short, but she didn't stop to change them. She gave my mare a small kick and then a mighty one. "Whump!"

Winsome gave a little jump forward.

"Pay attention, Lizzy. Winsome is not enough in front of the driving aids; in fact she's gone to sleep. Now I want you to watch and tell me when the mare is set up for the turn. When do I have her in shoulder-fore and ready to turn?"

March, march, march. Off they went. I could see Margot shorten Winsome's steps, and I saw her then position Winsome's poll to the inside.

"Now. She's ready."

Then it was one-two steps of turn and straight on the line. Winsome stuck in the first one, so "whump" came the leg, and this time Margot added the stick.

Winsome shook her ears in protest but upped the energy.

I could see the look of concentration on Margot's face. She had drawn her attention away from me and totally onto my horse.

March, march, march. This time Winsome's ears focused completely on Margot. Then it was one-two steps to turn, and Winsome practically leapt forward out of it onto the line of the square.

Then Margot did the square technically perfect.

She came to a halt in front of me, keeping the reins short and keeping Winsome "on-duty."

"There, you see, it can be done. Now quick, get on and feel it. Once you feel it, you can reproduce it yourself."

I got on and gathered up the reins. Winsome felt electric, and I could feel her chewing nervously on the bit. But her ears were turned back to me, and she felt eager to move.

I moved off onto the line, using my eyes as Margot had taught me. March, march, march. Winsome felt like a little steam engine. I shortened the stride and waited, and then positioned her to the inside. I was ready; she was ready. She was up and light and easy to turn; one-two and forward. March, march, march, shorten, position, one-two and forward. March, march, march, shorten, position, one-two and forward; again, again, again. It was easy. Margot was now clapping for me and yelling, "Good, good, good." But I didn't share in her excitement. I felt like a fraud. I knew it would disappear if Margot even moved more than fifty feet away from me.

I shouldn't have, but I looked around the arena and spotted Ryder. She had been watching. And then I looked back at Margot. She shook her head at me and pursed her lips before speaking softly.

"Darling, you did that beautifully. Be happy for now, and don't worry about what others think."

I nodded dutifully while Margot tilted her head slightly, studying me, trying to read me. But how could she? I couldn't read myself.

"We'll talk more later."

And I was dismissed with a puzzled feeling about 'later.'

***

FRANK, FRANCESCA, AND MARGOT SAT AT the wrought iron table on the patio in front of the barn enjoying a glass of wine. It was another perfect spring afternoon; the air was cool, but the sun was warm. They were having their own private pow-wow, leaning in toward the center of the table where Francesca had laid out papers of some kind. And I was spying on them from my apartment window above.

Frank had shown up that afternoon with a wicker basket, simply waving as he passed me in the barn aisle.

It was clear to me from that small gesture that I was not invited to the picnic. So I had headed up the stairs. Ryder had gone into her bedroom and closed her door. I put a frozen dinner in the microwave and then walked over to look out again at the threesome down at the little table. Margot was leaning back, and Francesca was tapping the table with one finger, obviously making an important point.

The microwave started beeping. But I was glued to the window. They laughed, and Frank upended the bottle, filling the three glasses to the brim and then making a toast. I strained my ears, but of course I couldn't hear a thing. Their heads leaned in again, and the earnest discussions continued. The microwave repeated its beep-beep-beep, so I retrieved my soggy heat-'em-up eat-em-up and ate it right out of the cardboard container, watching while they nibbled on crackers and dip and drained their glasses.

The picnic on the patio came to an end, and I waited until the last car had pulled away before heading back down the stairs. The time had switched to daylight savings, so there was still plenty of light.

***

HARMONY WITH MY HORSE WAS WHY I started this journey. But harmony with my horse was something I had only when I was outside the arena. Inside the arena was just a mess. It wasn't dressage at all. It had become some kind of anti-dressage. There was obviously some critical piece of information that was missing. Something that Margot either wasn't giving me or I wasn't hearing.

I wanted to go and see Deb and ask her to share her secrets. Maybe she would tell me how she trained Regina so beautifully. When I saw her riding, it was awesome. No bridle and no saddle, and yet any judge would have been impressed at Regina's light-footed piaffe and passage and medium trot, even with her big pregnant belly. The harmony was a ten.

I found Deb sitting in a battered lawn chair outside her front door. It was the old-fashioned kind with the plastic woven strapping, and several straps hung down under a sagging seat. She had a bottle of beer in her hand and a cat in her lap. She was leaning back with her legs stretched out. She seemed happy to see me.

"Hey, Lizzy."

Deb raised her beer bottle.

"You like beer?"

"Thanks no, but you enjoy yours. I don't drink."

"Too bad 'cause you need to relax, Lizzy. I can see you're all in knots. I know what it's like down there, with Francesca walking up and down the barn aisle like some kind of proctor during final exams. You should have one drink, Lizzy. Just a little, y'know, dull the hard edges."

I looked a little more closely at Deb. So far she didn't seem to have any hard edges.

"Yeah. You're probably right, except that I don't like the taste, and I'm asleep before the bottle is empty."

"Well, more for me I guess. Hey, I'm sorry I can't offer you a chair. This is my only one, and it's about to break through anyway."

I looked around for a place to sit. I chose the small concrete stoop. Immediately a little tabby cat with four white paws crawled out of the flower bed and began rubbing back and forth under my arm, purring away. After a few strokes, he started bumping my hand with his head. Then he was in my lap, rubbing his chin against my chin.

"Aw, see, Lizzy. You should be honored. That scrawny little thing started out scared of his own shadow. Cats and horses have one thing in common. They have to come to you. If you move toward a skittish horse or cat, they will always move away. But they crave companionship nonetheless. If you're patient, they just can't help coming to you; and when they do, just treat them right. Be fair. In time you'll win their trust and their friendship."

I took my finger and rubbed the cat's chin. My own chin was already itching because I was a little allergic to cats. His eyes closed, and he began to drool. He then threw himself down on my lap, and his purring amped up a few decibels. As we sat there, each of us with a cat in her lap, other cats began to slink into view. One appeared in the tall grass of the pasture. I spotted one under a bush against the cottage. One sat next to a watering can. Most were tabby, blending into the surrounding environment like soldiers in cammo.

"So, Deb?"

"Lizzy."

"I saw you on Regina. You were amazing. No saddle. No bridle. Piaffe. Passage. Medium trot, and a Levade. I'd never even seen a Levade before."

Deb took a sip of her beer and then sighed.

"Of course you realize Regina isn't being ridden anymore. She belongs to Francesca now. You understand?"

"I didn't tell anyone," I stammered. "I wasn't...I just saw is all. I thought you two looked wonderful. And I want to ride like you."

Deb's voice softened to almost a whisper, "You sure you didn't say anything to anyone?"

"I'm sure."

"Good." She leaned back in her chair and closed her eyes.

I started again.

"Deb, I'm still struggling with those damn walk pirouettes. I feel like I'm still missing some gigantic piece of the puzzle. Like there's something Margot hasn't told me. It's like I'm being hazed before I'm allowed to join the advanced riders' sorority or something."

Deb was then smiling.

"Let me guess, you're learning Margot's dreaded square. We all had to do it"

"I try but it just isn't happening."

"There is no try, Lizzy, only do."

Not that bullshit, I thought. I wanted answers. I was suddenly irritated, and I sounded it. More than I meant to.

"Oh no, you're going all Yoda on me. I need information, Deb. Besides which, I think Yoda or somebody also said that 'when the student was ready the teacher will appear.' Well, you're the teacher. You've appeared. I saw you on Regina."

"The master teacher is always the horse. Margot taught you that one yet?"

"Please help me. C'mon. No one is here. No one will know."

"Now you're whining."

Deb started to move.

"You want to learn pirouettes? I'll have to see if the Doctor is in."

Deb was then standing and staring down at me and the cat. "C'mon then."

"Now?"

"Right now, and then I don't want to hear another word about it. OK?"

I felt a victorious thrill. The secret of pirouettes was about to be revealed.

"Yes. Yes. OK. I promise."

I tried to take the cat off my lap. It didn't really want to go, and I had to carefully pull its claws one by one from my breeches. Damn thing was like Velcro. I had to trot to catch up to Deb.

Regina had her head buried in a pile of timothy hay. The barn air was suffused with a rosy light as the sun was sinking.

Deb reached for the halter on the door and then slid it open, making a kissy noise.

"Miss R, we have a student for you here. This is Lizzy. She would like to order up some technical skill Stat."

Regina lifted her head, looked at Deb with alert ears, and greeted her with a low-toned nicker.

"Huh-huh-huh."

Looking at Regina standing there, it was hard to believe this was the same horse I saw Deb riding in the pasture, floating on air. She was coarse, with heavy bone and a shaggy mane. Her whiskers were long; brown hair stuck out of her ears; and hair hung from her pasterns. And then, much bigger than it looked while she was moving, there was her huge pregnant belly.

Deb had picked up her whip from somewhere. She had the mare's full attention. She gave Regina a sugar cube as she slipped on the halter. And then in a very serious tone she asked, "What do you think about teaching Lizzy walk pirouettes? Do you think she can learn them?"

Regina nodded her head up and down in the affirmative. It was a cute trick. I smiled.

Deb continued. "If she screws them up will you cover for her?"

Then Regina gave her head a vigorous shake no. She had me laughing.

"How many minutes can you spare, Regina? I know that's some good hay you've got there."

Regina started pawing and Deb was counting. "One, two, three, four, five, six, seven, eight, nine, ten." Regina miraculously stopped at ten.

I was shaking my head. "That's brilliant. You are an amazing trainer, Deb."

"Yeah, well, I'm pretty good with horses. I can't brag about training humans. "

Deb led Regina out to the paddock, clipped the lead rope to the ring on one side of Regina's halter, and tied it to the other side like a rein. Then she used the fence to wiggle up on Regina's back. After doing a few half-passes at walk, she began turning walk pirouettes.

Then she couldn't resist showing off. While still turning the pirouettes, she made a transition to piaffe and, still turning, made a transition into canter. Then back to walk, all still turning. Then she came to a halt.

"Ta-da!"

She gave Regina a tap on her shoulder, and of course, Regina bowed.

"OK, Lizzy, now climb up here so I can see just how terrible those walk pirouettes really are."

Deb sidled Regina up to the fence, and I clambered on, none too gracefully. Regina was taller than Winsome and twice as wide. Her neck was shorter and rose straight up in front of me, with those incredibly big hairy ears.

I felt like I was sitting on someone's Barca-lounger with lumpy stuffing. I looked behind and found a roomy back. This girl could have been an old-fashioned school bus. Instead of reins, I gathered up a thick cotton rope. This was weird, weird, weird. I gave a little kick, and surprisingly Regina grunted and jumped forward, and then began to piaffe.

"Whoa there, Lizzy. She's a sensitive girl. Use less leg, OK?"

"Wow. She is way more sensitive than she looks."

"So let's see a walk pirouette."

I proceeded to piaffe and then did turns on the middle. Regina picked up canter once and did haunches-in. Pretty much everything except walk pirouettes. I looked over at Deb, and she was sitting on the fence shaking her head.

"Man. You're screwed up every which way. You are so over-thinking this. Come on over here."

Regina gave a big sigh as I headed at a walk over to the fence.

"Scoot yourself forward a bit and grab some mane. I'm joining you."

I looked at Deb. What the heck was she up to?

"C'mon, get closer to the fence. I'm not one of my cats."

I leg-yielded Regina tight up against the fence, and Deb slid on right behind me. Then she took the rope reins away from me.

"OK. Pay close attention. This is what it's supposed to feel like."

Then we did a whole slew of walk pirouettes. Or Deb and Regina did them, while Regina's withers dug uncomfortably into my crotch. I grabbed a handful of mane and hung on.

"Feel how the shoulders always have to stay in front of that inside hind, just a smidge. You gotta' always feel that in every pirouette, every half-pass. Lose that and you are so screwed. That's what makes the bend. That's what makes the balance. That's how you load the bending joints of the hind leg. That's engagement, Lizzy. That's dressage."

I was a dolt. I couldn't lie. "I'm trying, Deb. It all happens so fast."

Not to mention how hard it was to concentrate through the discomfort.

"Well, feel this, Lizzy. We'll do it in piaffe."

And then they began to piaffe. And it was still a small feeling. It wasn't much to feel, but I could tell that the balance to stay back on the hind leg was delicate.

"Hang on, how about this?"

Regina lifted up into canter, like making a small rear. Wow. Yeah, my crotch was pretty much screaming, but this was definitely cool. Very, very, cool. And she was turning a pirouette.

After a few turns I knew. This was the ultimate. I wanted to be able to do these on Winsome. It wasn't just an exercise, it was a friggin' key. A little light bulb began to glow in my brain. That epiphany filled me with hope. I had never experienced anything like this. Maybe I hadn't produced this, even as I hadn't produced them yet with Winsome, but I knew somehow that in time, I was going to get this.

When we both slid off Regina it was dark. But I had never noticed that the sun had set.

I gave Regina a scratch on her withers and thanked Deb.

I walked back down the hill in the dark with an understanding of walk pirouettes that could not be written down in words. It was not "information" that Deb and Regina or Margot and Winsome had given me today.

It was a feeling.

CHAPTER 7

While You Were Sleeping

I HAD TOSSED AND TURNED ALL night re-imagining my ride on Regina but substituting Winsome for Regina. I knew I wanted to teach Winsome how to bow. I fantasized about doing a kick-ass dressage test on Winsome, and after it was done, leaving the arena, turning to the cheering fans, and having her bow. Of course I was here to learn from Margot, and Margot was the greatest. I would die to ride like Margot. But I had stumbled onto this amazing, crazy, horse trainer. Deb was unlike anyone I had ever met. And no one had told me how awesome she was.

There was no point in trying to sleep, so I got out of bed early and headed to the feed room to start the morning feeding. Ryder usually beat me out of bed, but I was awake before her today. As I rolled the cart down the aisle, I smiled to myself. I was getting an extra education that Ryder was not. I knew Ryder would have turned her nose up at Deb's unconventional methods, but she would have missed out on a genius. Being in the magazines is not what made you a horse trainer. But Ryder did not understand that yet.

I started rolling the loaded cart down the aisle. There weren't so many to take care of in this barn, but it was still a noisy affair. Horses whinnied and banged on their feeders. But when I got to the end of the aisle, to Kiddo's stall, it was empty.

I stared at the empty stall, having trouble believing my eyes.

I walked out into the parking lot. It was just my old red truck and Ryder's little white car. Then I walked back into the barn. Kiddo's door had been pushed all the way open, and he was most definitely gone.

My mouth went dry.

Someone had stolen Kiddo. No, that couldn't be. I marched out of the barn and headed to the paddocks. I couldn't see him anywhere. All of our paddocks were empty. Soon an old truck pulled into the driveway. Alfonso.

Thank God it wasn't Francesca or Margot. I had to find Kiddo.

I trotted up to his window, dancing around like I had to pee or something. He stayed calm as he parked and got out.

"Hola, Lizzy."

"Alfonso, Kiddo is gone! I just fed the horses and he's gone."

"No. He can go nowhere here."

"Francesca's going to kill me. Somehow this will be my fault."

One of the horses in the barn gave a loud whinny. I turned around to see that Deb was riding Kiddo bareback in a halter toward us. Alfonso patted me on the back.

"See, Lizzy. Miss Deb has him. Don't worry."

Deb rode up to us.

"You lose something?"

"Holy crap, Deb. His door was wide open. What the heck?"

"I found him scrounging around my barn aisle this morning. He cleaned out the bowls of kitty chow. Who knew horses would eat cat chow."

"How do you suppose he got out?"

"Better add an eye bolt with a double-end snap on it to his door latch. That should keep him in. In the meantime skip his grain this morning; grass and hay only. Who knows what other crap he ate last night."

Deb slid off and handed me the lead rope.

"Thanks."

"You're welcome. Bring me back the halter and rope later, OK?"

"Sure."

I could see Francesca's little sports car pull up to the farm gate, and of course the gates swung open automatically. Deb saw her too, and turned away to walk purposefully up the hill.

I hurried Kiddo back into his stall. He went right to his feed tub, checked it out, found it empty, and then looked right at me.

"No way. You heard Deb. You are getting nothing. You are a bad horse, Kiddo."

He looked not so much at me as into me, studying me, and then weirdly he slowly lowered his head. It was as close to "sorry" as I'd ever seen from a horse. But sorry didn't last too long. He came a little closer and gave me a shove. Gentle enough but begging. I rubbed his forehead.

"OK. I'm sure a few carrots won't hurt."

So I went into the fridge in the tack room, broke four carrots into small pieces, and went and put them in his feed tub. He had begun his training program; of me.

Chapter 8

Addicted To Heartbreak

HANDLING THE YOUNG HORSES WITH DEB meant never being in a hurry. Tea and bread and chit-chat preceded every session. And sometimes the sessions never happened at all. Learning from Deb was different in every way from learning from Margot. Deb was as informal as Margot was formal. I was learning to wait for Deb and be patient. I understood that epiphanies could not be scheduled, but I was here each afternoon and would be ready.

Deb placed a pot of tea right on the wood table. She went to grab the honey bottle from the counter, but it was stuck. I tried not to laugh as she tugged, finally freeing it.

"Milk?"

"Sure, thanks."

When she opened the bottle, she smelled it before placing it on the table. Then she plopped down on a chair next to me and poured a long stream of honey into her tea.

"So, how's it going with the walk pirouettes, Lizzy?"

"Oh they're better. Or at least I think they are since Margot has finally let me get out of the walk."

She squinted at me and then nodded.

"Yeah, you do look way more chilled. I'll bet your ears were burning this morning. Margot said some really nice things about your riding."

Now that was a surprise.

"…About me? After all that struggle over the pirouettes?"

"Lizzy, don't let yourself become one of these stressed-out uptight dressage divas. I mean we have the greatest job in the world. We get to play with horses and call it work. Feeling too much pressure will suck the pleasure right out of it, and the horses hate feeling that pressure too."

I watched Deb sip her tea and wondered again why in the world she wasn't riding. She was no dressage diva for sure. But she was a hell of a rider.

Then she brightened.

"I helped Margot with Wild Child again today. He is something else. Walter would have loved that horse. He always liked the horses with strong characters."

Deb had "helped" Margot? Again? I almost choked on my tea.

"You were down in the arena? I missed seeing you. You should have come in and said hello. I want you to see Winsome go."

Deb looked down at her hands, examining a callus on her palm and then looked back up.

"Margot needs eyes-on-the-ground just like anyone else. I'll come watch you ride someday soon too. I promise."

Deb sat up straighter and took a cleansing breath, "But as for the present, what should we do with our wild crew out there today? Pick an age group; yearlings, two-year-olds, or the coming three-year-olds?"

Deb was avoiding any further questions. And it meant today was a day we would work.

"I guess I should look at those three-year-olds, see what kind of trouble I'll be getting myself into this summer."

"OK, we'll start there."

Deb got out of her chair. It was time to move. The bread was delicious, and I had just slathered another piece with butter. I crammed what I could into my mouth as I stood up.

"Whoa there, Lizzy, there's more where that came from. You know, I can send you home with some."

We headed out to the paddocks, the ones furthest from the barn. There, standing under a big tree, were the coming three-year-olds.

I thought how they had been born on this farm, suckled side-by-side with their dams in these same green fields. They were weaned together and had grown up together. And now they would learn together how to be riding horses, just like the three we had down in Florida: Bounce, Romp, and Hotstuff.

And then they would be sold. I remembered Bounce's pitiful cries as the trailer carried him away from his friends on the day he was sold. Then Romp went to Texas with Emma to be sold. Only Hotstuff remained here at Equus Paradiso Farm.

Maybe I did have "Black Beauty Syndrome." But I knew for a fact that horses were capable of deep and lasting attachments. These thoughts flooded my mind just standing there looking at three young geldings snoozing under a tree.

They were three different shapes and sizes, but all with the look of teenagers; all angles and bones, with shaggy manes and tails. I thought I could have guessed who each of their siblings were, I knew their big brothers so well. But Deb was already filling me in.

"The really tall black guy, that's Regina's baby. He's a full brother to Hotstuff, but even better; more sensitive and lighter on his toes. Margot named him Habenero. But I just call him Pepper. He's special. I'll bet you Margot won't be able to let him go. You gotta' check out his blaze."

Deb unlatched the gate and handed me a halter. She put her fingers in her mouth and gave her ear-piercing whistle. All three heads whipped around. Pepper had what I'd call a broken blaze. It went about two-thirds of the way down his face but stopped about where the noseband would go. Then, after a few inches of black, it restarted with a small splash of white above his nostrils.

"Wow, cool blaze."

"You won't be able to see it with a noseband on, but I think it looks like an exclamation point. Now the chestnut…"

"Romp's brother," I butted in.

Deb nodded. "Half brother. Margot named him 'Quester.' His sire is very hot right now, although not too many of his 'get' are old enough to tell what kind of horses he's going to make. Lots of suspension in this guy though. Quester is out of Wink.

"And the plain little bay is also a rubber-band man. His name is "Boingo," and he's a full brother to your friend "Bounce" out of Glimmer."

Boingo. I could see he was Bounce's baby brother, and I practically teared up just looking at him.

"We've got a lot of work to do, Lizzy. By the time these boys head down to Florida next winter, they need to have earned their "Equine-Good-Citizen" badges, if you know what I mean."

"Equine-Good-Citizen? You made that up, right?" I noticed Deb was grinning.

"Yeah. But what I mean is we need to be sure amateurs can safely try them out, since Francesca has to sell horses to prove this is a legit business to the IRS. I try to amateur-proof them as much as possible. People don't appreciate how much time it takes to get the horses used to such basic things as picking up their feet, leading, loading, and clipping. They aren't born knowing these things. Someone like you or me has to teach them."

Deb and I brought the youngsters into the barn, Deb leading two, and me leading little Boingo. They came in a lot better than the weanlings or yearlings. And then Deb had me put Boingo in the cross-ties.

She put her two away and then came over to the cross-ties.

"I've handled this guy from his first breath. He knows me and trusts me, and he has no reason not to trust you too. He has never known anything but good handling. Just remember that in case you ever meet with resistance from him. He's an innocent child. Be patient, and be satisfied with very little. Remember my shy cat? They all come around in time, but if you go after anything too hard, you'll drive the horse further away from you and undo your good work."

I clipped him in and then spoke softly to him.

"Hi, Boingo."

I held the back of my hand up to his nose, the way I'd been taught as a child, since the back of your hand was supposedly less threatening. He looked a bit surprised and arched his neck, lightly touching my hand. Then I reached up and stroked his neck lightly. He wasn't as round and roly-poly as Bounce, but he had the same lovely large eye and the same bushy mane and thick heavy tail. I loved him instantly and at the same time felt a real pain in my chest.

I was mourning the fact that I was going to put my heart and soul into his training, only to watch him leave. I ran my hands over his body, trying to find the best scritchy-scratchy spots. Most horses love to have their withers scratched, and Boingo was no exception. Horses scratched each other's withers as a way of establishing friendships, so I was trying to do the same.

It worked.

I caught Deb's eye. She was looking at me and smiling her easy smile.

"Lizzy, you have a good touch."

Before long Boingo was poking out his top lip and rolling his eyes back in his head. This is why I would never have fingernails, and the nails I had usually had dirt under them. Deb was laughing, and I thought to myself that she was an easy laugher, something I found appealing about her. She unclipped his cross-ties so he could reach around and scratch my butt.

"Hey, Deb, keep an eye out and tell me if he tries to use his teeth."

"OK, but I can't promise to catch it in time."

Boingo and I stopped scratching each other at about the same time, and he sighed.

"Would you like him to be your project?"

"Oh, I'd love that, Deb."

"I think that would work. Me, I'm dying to sit on Pepper, and I can let Ryder take Quester. I know once Pepper is going well, Margot will want him for herself. I think he's destined for something big. But we'll see."

Deb showed me her grooming procedure. Boingo was a bit wobbly as I picked out his hind feet, but he let me touch his ears. He didn't like the fly spray, so Deb had me simply spray it on the ground and then on a rag instead of on the horse. Then I wiped it over him.

We rubbed his lips and gums with our fingers, ran soft cotton ropes around his girth area snugging it up and releasing it, and we stroked him all over with a long whip. All these things almost put him in a trance. The last thing we did was have me stand next to him on a mounting block and lean over his back and gently tug on his mane.

"You see, Lizzy. We're just playing. All this will make his first saddling, girthing, and bridling just another game."

"That was easy, Deb."

"Well, there's enough drama in life without intentionally creating more. Let's do the other two, and then I'm sending you home with some of that bread."

Later I followed Deb into the house and watched as she wrapped a short loaf in foil for me.

"Deb?"

"Yeah?"

"Do you ever get used to saying good-bye to them. I mean, as a professional I suppose you have to."

"You're worrying again. Hard stuff should only be lived once, Lizzy."

"So it's still hard?"

Deb handed me my loaf of bread and our eyes met. She paused for a moment before answering.

"Some good-byes are harder than others. Dressage horses work hard, and not every buyer can ride well. Not every story can have a happy ending, hard as we try to make it so. Good-byes can still be heartbreaking no matter how many times you do it."

"And yet this is what you do."

"Yeah. I'm addicted. I keep coming back for more. I'm looking forward to seeing those three under saddle. I've been looking forward to it from the first time they stood and nursed."

I had just met my little Boingo, and I was already thinking ahead to the day when I would ride him and then the day when I would say good-bye.

It was a bad sign. In my head I had already called him "my" Boingo.

And then I thought of the horses in the barn below. I cringed at the thought that I felt a jealous ownership toward every single one of them, even the big red nasty one.

I was doomed.

CHAPTER 9

Boys' Night Out

I SHOT BOLT UPRIGHT IN MY bed. Three AM glowed on my little clock radio.

I punched my pillow flat and flopped over on my stomach. There was absolutely no good reason to be awake, but I couldn't get back to sleep. A feeling of unease coursed through every cell of my being. I flipped and flopped until my nightshirt was twisted around my body. There was no use. I was wide awake.

So I sat up and straightened out my oversized T-shirt and listened. The barn was awake too. Horse bodies below me were moving in their stalls. I sensed it more than heard it. I should get up. I should investigate.

I got up and flipped on my light, pulled my barn jacket on over my nightshirt, and slipped my bare feet into my clogs. This was pretty ridiculous, but if a horse was colicking or cast, then I would feel terrible if I hadn't gone down to check.

As soon as I opened the door into the barn aisle, someone whinnied. I flipped on the lights. At first I thought everything was just fine. Winsome popped her head out the yoke opening on her stall door, blinking at the harshness of the suddenly well-lit barn.

"So sorry, sweetie."

She nodded her head up and down, and then gently tapped the door with her hoof.

"No, no. It's not time for breakfast. Go back to sleep."

Down the aisle other horses began to talk. Confused, I thought. I decided to walk down the barn and have a check on everyone.

When I got to Wild Child's stall, my blood went cold. His door was partially slid open. And he was gone.

I tried to call out at first; or scream really. But it was silent. Like one of those nightmares where you try to yell for help but you've lost your voice completely.

In fact I couldn't even swallow for a moment. My lips suddenly were stuck to my teeth. I staggered to the end of the barn aisle, feeling for sure that Wild Child was gone for good: stolen.

But when I got to Kiddo's stall, he was gone too.

Kiddo? I had put a double-end snap on his door.

But there was the double-end snap still hanging there. Or at least it was hanging on the part of the latch on the face board.

I walked on leaden legs outside and stared up the hill toward the mare barn. The moon was full. The air was soft and cool. And then I saw them, two beautiful silhouettes.

Kiddo and Wild Child; standing together. That horrible vicious stallion looked, well...happy.

Kiddo was giving Wild Child a vigorous grooming. Kiddo's teeth were raking over Wild Child's withers. And Wild Child was returning the favor.

My knees were like jelly. So I sat down on the wet grass.

Then Kiddo stopped grooming, and he turned to look my way. His ears were pricked with interest, as if to question why in the world I would be out at three AM. Then he turned away from Wild Child and put his head down to graze, and Wild Child did the same.

It occurred to me then, as some kind of epiphany, that the horses had a private life of their own that I had no part of. Try as hard as I might, I would never be included in it, and was not welcome in it.

I felt, of course, relieved that Wild Child had not been stolen, at least not by a human. He had been chosen by Kiddo; too weird. How in the world had Kiddo opened a double-end snap? And then of all the horses to choose to let out, he chose Wild Child.

The next problem to solve would be how to catch Wild Child and put him back in his stall. He had no halter on. And I had no fence to contain him.

I should go wake up Ryder; but not yet. I felt weak but relieved at the same time. I just couldn't seem to haul myself up off the grass. Instead I sat there watching the two of them with amazement until my butt was not only soaked but numb.

Without really formulating a plan, I finally hauled myself off the grass. On stiff knees I walked up the hillside. What was I thinking? I wanted Deb, not Ryder.

I banged a little too hard on her door, and I had to keep banging. She finally called through the closed door.

"Who the hell is it?"

"It's me, Lizzy."

The door flew open.

"For crying out loud, what's happened? Why are you up here at...?" Deb looked at her watch. It was one of those heavy diving-type watches.

"Three-thirty! It's three-thirty."

"Deb, I don't know what to do, and I didn't want to get Ryder. But Wild Child is out."

"How the hell?"

"Kiddo."

"What do you mean?"

"He can open a double-end snap. I don't know how he did it. Alfonso put it on right away just like you said. But he got out again, and this time it looks like he let Wild Child out too."

Deb smiled that big wide smile which brought out her dimples. When she smiled, everything softened about her. In the moonlight, with her hair loose and without her glasses, she looked younger.

"Well, I'll be damned. I've had a lot of smart horses, but none who could open a double ended snap; and for sure not one that would be so bold as to let out another horse, the farm stallion to boot. This I've got to see. Hold on, let me get my sweater and some shoes, and I have to find my glasses too."

Deb and I made an odd-looking pair as we walked back down the hill. Deb had put on a pair of lace-up paddock boots and had pulled on a cable-knit cardigan over her short flannel nightgown. Her bare legs were so pale, they practically glowed in the dark. Mine must have looked the same. We each carried a halter and lead rope, swiped from the broodmares, and pockets full of peppermints.

As soon as we saw them, we spontaneously stopped. They were beautiful. Wild Child was always beautiful, but in the moonlight he was breathtaking in a new way, almost cinematic. He lifted his head and huffed at us. Kiddo looked up and then put his head right back down, seemingly unconcerned.

Deb touched my shoulder and half-whispered. "Wild Child is loving his freedom, and he won't want to give it up. I can tell that if we move toward him now, he'll only run. Let's not let that happen. We need to be smarter than that. We need him to make the decision himself."

"How the heck are we going to do that?"

"You stay here. I'll be right back."

So I sat once again on the wet cold grass. And I waited. As each minute ticked by, I got more and more nervous. What if the stallion started running and hurt himself? That stallion was worth a lot of money. I didn't know how much, but I knew it was a lot. And here he was, gallivanting around the farm loose. One crazy twist of a tendon or ligament, and it would be over before it started. I could somehow be blamed. But it wasn't my fault. Deb was here with me. The catching him part would be our shared responsibility.

Wild Child suddenly picked his head up out of the grass. This time he whinnied. It was a whinny I remembered from the clinic we had taken him to in Florida where he had been smitten by a beautiful big black mare. It was a low and deep whinny. I looked behind me to see Deb riding down the hill on another black mare, Regina. As Deb got closer, I could see her smiling.

She pulled Regina up next to me. "How about this? Regina as bait."

"Brilliant. I guess Wild Child has a thing for big black mares. But everything about him is aggressive and unpredictable. Please be careful. You know he scares the shit out of me daily, don't you?"

"Oh, Lizzy, chill. I think this is kinda' fun. But you have to do your part or the whole thing falls apart. It could go south fast. Always can with horses. So here's how I hope it will work. I've closed the barn door at the far end and opened it at the near end. Once he follows us in, shut the door."

"OK, I can do that. But what about Kiddo? What should I do about him?"

"Don't worry about Kiddo. I get the feeling that boy can take care of himself. But no more talking; start for the barn 'cause he comes."

He was moving, neck arched and tail up like a flag. He was impressive as all get out. Deb spun Regina around and headed for the barn. Regina couldn't possibly outrun Wild Child with her big pregnant belly. I started after them as fast as I could. But there was no way I could outrun those two. I saw Regina and Deb make it into the lit-up barn. My legs were screaming, and I fell off my clogs a couple times as I hit clumps of grass. But Deb was brilliant; there he went, right into our trap. I made it to the door in time to see Deb and Regina duck into a stall. Deb reached up as Regina entered the stall, and she grabbed onto the boards overhead, neatly sliding off of Regina's butt, dropping to the ground, and sliding shut the stall door. At least Regina was safe from Wild Child. I was shaking as I slid the first door shut. It was heavier than it looked. Wild Child heard it slide. He spun around and snorted at me.

"The gig is up, asshole."

I heaved on the second door, but it was sticking. I got it mostly shut but for about a two -foot gap. He was making a break for it, and he twirled and sprinted toward me. He had way too much steam going. I had a horrific thought that he was going to slam right into me. Wild Child was going to take me down with him on his last break for freedom.

I had to get the damn door shut all the way, preferably with me on the outside. But no way, there was no time to jump out of the thin gap like I did in his paddock. I was trapped. I heaved and heaved and I got another foot or so closed. Wild Child saw his opportunity was gone, and he tried to stop. Sparks flew as steel shoes slid on concrete.

He stopped mere inches from me. Veins stood up; ears pinned back; and nostrils flared with his mouth open the way it was every damn day at the paddock gait. I threw my arms over my head. At least I would preserve my face from being savaged by his teeth. But nothing happened.

I lowered my arms and opened my eyes to see that he was just standing there puffing. I reached up and put my hand on his face.

But then he turned away to look back at the barn full of horses. Every horse in the whole barn, from pregnant mares to yearlings, whinnied. He walked back over to Regina's stall and pressed his nostrils against the bars. Regina had gone to the back of her stall and wanted nothing to do with him.

Deb threw a rope around his neck and wiggled the halter on him while he focused on Regina.

"Good job, Lizzy. That was something wasn't it?"

"Deb, I thought I was a goner."

"Naw. You were great. Sorry those doors are so damn heavy. I think they're kind of warped or something. They don't slide smoothly in their tracks anymore."

Deb put a chain over Wild Child's nose, and he followed us pretty calmly back down the hill. I thought he was just plain spent and had a belly full of grass, or he would never be that polite about going back to his barn. We didn't see any sign of Kiddo on our walk, and I was getting anxious. Even though the farm was completely fenced in, that horse was just plain quirky.

But as soon as we walked into their barn, Deb and I cracked up laughing. Kiddo had put himself back into his stall.

Deb and I looked over Wild Child and couldn't see a scratch.

"So Deb, what do you think we should do?"

"Well, first off, we have to find a snap that Kiddo can't open."

"Yeah. But what I meant is, should we say anything?"

"About what?"

Deb was grinning her big wonderful smile.

CHAPTER 10

At Liberty

DEB INVITED ME TO GO OUT with her to an all-horse circus. Deb knew the head trainer; evidently very well. So this was where Deb had learned Liberty and trick training. Deb was letting me in, bit by bit. I was excited.

Deb had been able to score us front row seats at the Sunday matinee performance. This was an annual stop for the circus on their tour, their most popular venue. She was bringing me as her treat, but it had to be our secret. She didn't want Ryder to feel left out, but she also said something about Francesca having a tantrum if she knew. So, "mum" was the word. I didn't press for more…yet. I had been "chosen" by Deb. That was good enough for now.

Deb said that these horses and trainers, unlike some other shows she'd seen, were beautifully trained and that the horses were sound and happy. There would be many different breeds appropriate for the different acts. We would be seeing vaulting, trick riders, aerialists, and her friend's liberty act, now performed by his son. There was also to be a clown act and miniature horses. All the horses would be either stallions or geldings. Not a mare among them. It evidently kept the horses from going to war with each other.

The lights went down, and new-agey flute music started softly and grew louder. Everyone finished getting settled, and mothers hushed their children. Suddenly drums began, and from stage left a white Andalusian stallion came galloping onto the stage, his mane and tail longer and fuller than anything I'd ever seen and sparkling silver in the spotlight. He made a lap at speed, so close that I could feel the vibration of the floor. Then he stopped suddenly, threw himself down on the ground, and rolled.

Just then another white horse galloped in, then another, and then another. The first horse jumped up in the air bucking with joy. The joy infected each horse as they were released into the arena. There were finally six of them, all white or silver or grey and all with fantastically long manes and tails. The light played off the silver coats with muscles flexing and relaxing while the music gave each buck or leap additional drama.

I realized the music could not have been canned. The choreography was being designed by the horses themselves, and the musicians had to follow the horses' lead. They rolled, bucked, and cavorted freely around the stage.

One especially magnificent horse wandered up to the front and looked into the audience, his eyes dark and large. He examined us thoughtfully it seemed. And then he circled his head, flipping his long forelock out of his face, as if to examine us better. But another horse would not let him stay long, running up behind him and giving him a nip. He turned and rejoined the game. I fought back a lump in my throat as I realized there were no humans here. This was pure horse.

I knew my emotions were being manipulated, but I couldn't help myself. I rummaged around in my purse, searching for a Kleenex, but then I felt a tap on my shoulder. Deb handed me one of those miniature packs of tissue.

Next, without any fanfare, a young man walked into the mix. He was dressed in black with a silver vest. He walked with such presence that all the horses immediately stopped what they were doing. They turned together like the needle of a compass seeking true north, and then as a group they went to him. The beautiful horse that had come to look at the audience touched the young man lightly on the shoulder. I had a weird feeling that I too wanted to rise from my seat and go to him.

He stroked each horse, lingering a little with the magnificent one who was now my favorite. After each horse had been greeted, he raised his arms. When he did, the horses spun away from him to line themselves up, shuffling to get the order right, like dancers in a chorus line.

He then conducted the dance. The horses circled, turned, and wove intricate patterns. At one point he jumped up on one horse's back, as light as a cat. He walked from one horse's back to another's. Later he had them all lie down, and he even rolled one over on its back and crawled through its legs. At the finish, when they lined up facing the audience, they bowed. He then went horse to horse, stroking their necks and kissing each one on the muzzle. Once each had gotten a kiss (and some kind of treat he pulled from inside his vest), they spun away and ran off the stage.

I wasn't the only one who stood to applaud. I was sure I wasn't the only female heart aflutter in the audience either.

Deb gave my arm a light punch.

"C'mon, let's slip backstage."

My heart gave a lurch.

"Are you kidding me?"

"These are my friends."

"Oh, Deb, I want to run away and join the circus!"

Deb smiled so big she showed off her dimples.

"I know how you feel. I actually did that once, but that's a story for another day, Lizzy."

My ears pricked. I wanted to hear about that, but as soon as the show was over, Deb was moving and I had to follow.

As we filed out, Deb peeled away in a hard right turn, lifted the corner of a tent flap, and motioned me to follow.

Some people were staring, and I felt a little nervous following her.

"Won't we get into trouble? I don't think we're supposed to be back here, Deb."

"We'll be OK. Just shut up and follow me. Once we're in the stabling area, I'm sure I'll see someone I know. But, yeah, if some ticket puncher catches us, we're toast."

So I felt like soldier sneaking my way through the enemy camp. And it really was a camp. Tents connected to other tents. We passed stacks of hay and a dozen or so wheelbarrows and muck forks and brooms. Then a room full of some kind of generators humming away. Deb seemed to know where to go. We entered a tent that was really just a round riding arena.

Deb stopped for a moment. "Training arena; we're almost there."

The next tent was it, a normal stable really, row upon row of temporary stalls. What a hassle I thought to have to take your buildings and stalls with you. What an amazing amount of work. It started to make our horse shows look simple.

People were moving around, putting up tack. Grooms were standing in stalls braiding up those gorgeous long silver manes and tails to keep them clean and tangle-free. I understood why they were doing it. Once a tail was braided up, the horse couldn't step on it when they lay down or got up, and they couldn't break any hairs. That's how the tails grew so long. We had kept Ace's tail braided in Florida to keep it silver-white instead of manure-stained green.

Of course not every horse had a real tail at all. I saw one of the grey horses having a false tail removed. Once it was out, I watched them hang it up on a hook and saw the groom comb it out and braid it up just like the real thing. One thing that did strike me as I peered into stalls was that away from the music and the lights, these horses looked like ordinary horses. Some of course were more beautiful than others, but they no longer appeared mythical. And no horse was as beautiful as Wild Child. Not even any of these.

It was a hive of activity in that tent, and no one seemed to notice us. There was a certain electricity in the air. Sunday matinee was the last performance before their day off. Monday and Tuesday the show would be "dark." Grooms were chatting and laughing, and I figured they were ready to get the barn ship-shape and to go out or crash. Who could be bothered with us? We wandered around awhile, but then Deb saw someone she knew.

"Pali!"

A short muscular man with curly silver hair stood at some distance with his back to us talking to a group of performers still in their costumes. It was clearly a meeting. Deb should have seen that and kept quiet. He was clearly annoyed when he turned to face us.

When he turned, I saw an older heavier version of the young man in the arena. He was weathered but had the same eyes, the same mouth, and the same erect bearing.

"What?" He barked out.

The two of them stood without speaking. I was getting a little uncomfortable. Deb wasn't smiling and neither was he. OK, I immediately got it. Deb's face was flushed. The air almost crackled between them. The tent was quiet. But then he walked over and gave her a hug; a long one. I stood to the side feeling very, very uncomfortable.

When they broke apart, Deb turned toward me. She looked so happy. Radiant. Really she was very pretty.

"Pali, this is Lizzy. She's Margot's newest protégée. I had to bring Lizzy to see what you do. She needs to see other kinds of riding masters, y'know, for a complete education."

"How do you do, Lizzy?"

He reached out for my hand, looked into my eyes, and then took my hand in both of his hands, holding it for just a moment before releasing it. He then looked over his shoulder at the milling group of performers who were restless and had picked back up their chit-chat but clearly felt they had not been released to leave.

"Excuse me for a moment. Deb, don't leave. Please. We'll go to dinner."

We waited while Pali finished his meeting. Deb had gotten quiet, but was shifting around, fidgeting.

"You OK, Deb."

"Do I look OK?"

"Of course you do. You look great."

"Pali always has this effect on me when I first see him. I'll just take a minute to settle. He is a master horseman, and Marco, his son, is probably going to be an even better one."

She was thoughtful for a moment.

"Marco is...softer."

Then she sighed, and continued talking while still watching Pali talk to his group.

"If the opportunity comes for you to learn from him, you take it. You understand? This is an opportunity you shouldn't miss. For me it was first Walter and then Pali, and of course Margot."

She turned to look at me.

"Did I tell you who Walter was?"

"He was Margot's husband."

"Yeah. Anyway, I've been privileged to know some of the best. Walter was a genius with a horse. Walter never liked to show, but God could he train a horse."

I had never seen Deb nervous like this. I just nodded.

Deb was nodding.

"Walter and Pali are a lot alike. When Walter got on a horse it was transformed right in front of your eyes. He had tranquilizers in his fingertips if you know what I mean. He gave them confidence. He was confident. He wasn't always as patient with people though as he was with his horses."

Deb pressed her lips together.

"I'm sorry that you're too late to know Walter."

The circle of performers broke up, and Pali came over, this time with his son.

Deb quickly whispered.

"But you're not too late to know Pali and Marco."

"Deb, you and your friend here will come with us to dinner. We have our favorite place expecting us. But first, of course, we must see to the horses. You'll wait?"

Thankfully Deb answered for us because I was sure I couldn't have answered.

"Of course. Oh, and Marco, this is Lizzy. Lizzy is a very good rider too and will be helping me with the young horses this year."

Marco very politely asked, "Oh, so you are a horse trainer too?"

When I tried to speak I found I had to stop and clear my throat first.

"I'm a working student. I'm trying to learn. But, I have a lot to learn."

He smiled, "But isn't that true of all of us?"

And I just nodded, and then found myself staring at his mouth, the shape of his chin, his big brown eyes with heavy lashes, his wonderful heavy black curls, and then back at his big brown eyes. This was the guy from the liberty act, as I knew it would be, but now I was up close, and it felt almost too close for comfort.

I finally found my voice and it came out in a croak.

"Yes, the more I learn, the less I realize I know."

His brows lifted, and his smile back seemed genuine and warm.

CHAPTER 11

In The Company Of Kings

I HAD TOLD PALI ABOUT WILD Child and about how difficult it was for me to handle him.

He leaned in and locked eyes with me, smelling a bit of wine. But his voice was low and melodic with an accent from I didn't know where.

Deb rested her chin in her hand and silently gazed at Pali through half-closed eyes. Pali was talking to me but constantly checking out Deb. Marco leaned back in his chair turning the stem of his wine glass, seemingly assessing all three of us.

Pali asked me a question I knew he didn't expect me to answer.

"Do you consider how the horse is made? What is the natural state of a horse?"

His eyebrows went up.

"You must work within their natures, Lizzy. Look at our stallions. Why do you think they are so beautiful? You must understand that a stallion brimming with health, young and strong, is naturally arrogant. But he has a right to be. He is full of power. He has grace without our tutoring. He has by the gift of nature everything he needs to fill us with awe. There is nothing that we can teach him that he doesn't already know how to do."

I nodded in agreement. But I couldn't see how any of this helped me with Wild Child.

Pali continued, "Just watch him test himself against his comrades in a herd of horses. They are practicing for the coming fight, for the right to breed. Watch his extraordinary play-fighting. He gallops, turns, stands up, and then kneels down, only to leap up again. There is a serious side to this play, just as there is to our training. They are testing to find their rank. Most stallions and geldings keep this ability to be playful and show off, if they are not afraid and they feel healthy. We should be able to play with our horses, but not fight with them; it is still serious business. They are bigger and stronger, and it is not a fight we would win."

I finally spoke up, "I don't want to fight with Wild Child."

"Yes. But to make that happen between ourselves and our horses, we have to change our human status in their eyes from predator into that of protector. A predator, you must flee or fight. A protector keeps you safe and stands guard against all dangers so you can relax. So you can rest. But a protector has also a higher status, that of a leader not a follower. This is the sacred bargain we make with our horses. You are above or below a horse in status. But you are never his equal."

I had to clear my throat to speak, and when I did it came out like a whisper.

"But what if the stallion in question is already aggressive toward humans?"

"I understand you. Aggression between a horse and a person can easily become a dangerous situation. But if you have earned his trust, then between the stallion and the man can come an understanding that there is a line that cannot be crossed. But earning trust takes time. The path is not an easy one and it takes courage and consistency. If he is aggressive, he must go away from you. He is banished. He is still a herd animal. Solitude is death in the wild, so this banishment is punishment enough. He must ask to come back into your circle, and he must want to come back into your circle, because you represent safety and security. When he asks to come in, hold no grudges; do not celebrate either. Just accept it as the natural order of things."

Pali had given me a new way to think about my problems with Wild Child.

Why did Wild Child fight with me but did not even offer pinned ears in the presence of that creep Patrick? Why? I took care of him, but he was always fighting me. Or was he "playing" with me to establish rank? It looked pretty serious to me.

We went back to the tent stables to check on the horses. Pali and Marco had plenty of grooms, but they still did bed-check themselves every night. I walked next to Marco, and up ahead of us walked Deb and Pali. I was nervous for some reason, and although I usually talked too much when I was nervous, we walked without talking. I noticed all the horses coming to the front of their stalls, poking their heads out into the aisle. First they looked at Pali, and he stopped to stroke each one and say their name. As soon as he walked on, they turned to look at Marco, and he did the same. Pali and Marco were clearly the kings of this stable. There was no doubt about rank here. Marco stopped an especially long time to stroke the jaw line of a white stallion; his long mane and tail were braided. I realized it was the magnificent horse in the liberty act. My favorite.

"Bernardo, my friend, are you getting some good rest?"

The stallion lifted his chin and set it on Marco's shoulder, the better for Marco to scratch between his large cheekbones, a place not so easy for a horse to scratch himself.

"Lizzy, this fellow came to us as an unmanageable stallion, and he has turned out to be a wonderful, if cheeky, performer. But of course, I devoted a year of ground work, several times a day. I practically slept with him. People often feel entitled to things they have not earned."

I let that comment sink in a moment before answering.

"I noticed him tonight. I could see the connection between you two. That horse couldn't take his eyes off of you. No saddle or a bridle; it was amazing."

I stopped to take a breath. The words had tumbled out. I was painfully aware of my breathlessness. I sounded like some teenage groupie at a rock concert asking for an autograph.

Marco just smiled at me, and I watched as he gave his horse a kiss on its dark muzzle.

I knew the spot. The skin there was delicate, soft, and warm. I kissed Winsome there.

I would never be able to dare to kiss Wild Child on his muzzle. I would lose part of my face. I was ashamed of myself for how roughly I treated him. It shouldn't have to be like that.

"I wish I could feel a connection like that to Wild Child. Mostly I'm afraid of him. He looks at me like he's going to eat me or something. And even when he's tolerating me, it's only because I'm keeping a watchful eye on him. I know he'd love an opportunity to get revenge for all the times I've been tough on him."

"I would like to meet him. Tell me more about him."

"Well, Wild Child is a stunning dressage stallion. Margot didn't do the training on him; she recently got him when we were down in Florida for the winter. Somehow someone trained him all the way to Grand Prix. The horse hates me."

It hurt to hear myself say that. I wanted to be loved by Wild Child, the way Marco's stallions loved him.

I continued, "I have my own six-year-old mare. I like to think she loves me. She's not like Wild Child, so his aggression can't be all my fault. Still, I wish I rode her better."

"I'd love to see them both. If you want help with that stallion, or your mare for that matter, you just let me know. They've extended our engagement here since we are getting great ticket sales. We go home after this and give the horses three months back on the farm to rest. Living in these little tents is so unnatural for them. They need a break."

"Thanks, Marco. I'm not sure how the farm owner would feel about that. She's not very... um."

What to say? Deb had made it clear that Francesca shouldn't know we were here tonight. But I had to say something.

"I don't think she likes me very much, and she's actually the owner of the stallion."

"Ah yes, Francesca."

I had blown it. This absolute god of a man, and genius of a horse trainer, had made an overture toward me and I had blown it. I had shut the door. What, was I crazy? Think, Lizzy, think. So I said, "But I'd love to watch you train your horses. Francesca can't control what I do on my time off."

He looked at me with his incredibly large brown eyes.

"What time do you get off work?"

Yes, yes, yes. My inner child was doing a happy dance.

"We feed at four, and then bed check at ten."

"Monday and Tuesday I have plenty of time. Those are 'dark' days for us. No shows. It can be just us; Pali never lets me get a word in otherwise."

I could tell Deb was going to have to keep more secrets for me. But no way was I going to pass up this opportunity.

"That would be fantastic. I'd love that."

Maybe I had joined the circus after all!

CHAPTER 12

Sparks

THERE HE STOOD, IN FRONT OF an open stall door getting out the big white stallion from the previous night. I remembered the stallion's name was Bernardo. Marco was wearing jeans, paddock boots, and a polar fleece jacket, looking like any other horse person, just an extra beautiful one.

My heart had been racing as I pulled through the security gate. Marco was taking me out for lunch, and I was late. Being late always made me anxious, but dang it I was always late anyway. On top of that, my inner voice was saying that Francesca could never know about this, and I needed to be careful. But Deb said I should jump at the chance to learn from Marco, and here I was, taking that leap.

"Hey, Marco. Sorry I'm late. Mondays are my day off too, but I love to spend some time with my own horse, and you know how it is, there's real time and then there's barn time. Once I start playing with my horse, I forget about everything else."

"Ah, that's how it should be. A horse trainer should be a horse lover first and foremost."

I nodded in agreement. Marco smiled back and gave the big horse a rub on the neck.

"We both live on barn time, you and I. So then you will understand why I am not quite ready to leave. But come with me while I take Bernardo out for a bit of grass, and maybe you could take another one? I'll give you Caruso; he is always a good boy. Believe it or not, lush green grass is growing along the edge of the parking lot. Good grass is a balm for their souls, don't you agree?"

I was looking at his mouth and thinking how even and white his teeth were. I was looking at his eyes and thinking how big and brown and soulful they were. I realized I was looking a tiny bit too intently, and I purposely shifted my eyes to the horse. The horse was even more magnificent than the man, but my eyes shifted back to the man anyway.

I finally replied.

"Yeah. They all enjoy grazing and having a good roll."

He smiled again.

"Ah yes, then we'll make sure they both get a good roll too."

Bernardo had a snow-white coat. He was clearly one of the Spanish baroque type horses; maybe Andalusian or Lusitano. His mane, forelock, and tail were braided up to stay clean, showcasing the lines of his arched neck and sculpted face. No forelock covered his large dark eyes today. And in his relaxed state, there was something soft-looking about him. It made me want to reach out and touch him.

Marco handed me the lead rope and opened the next stall door. Caruso, another white stallion, whirled around to the front of his stall with a low whinny. The horse lowered his head into the halter.

"Yes, yes my friend. You can come too."

"I can't get over how kind your stallions are."

"Well, this fellow has always been like that. He never has bred, and I don't know that he even realizes he is a stallion. But his friend there, Bernardo, remember I told you about him; he was a mess. Here, let's switch. You take Caruso, and I'll take Bernardo."

I wasn't sure how to quite pull that off. I didn't want to let the stallions get too close to each other. I backed away from the horse I was holding, Bernardo, to the end of the lead rope and then stretched my hand out to Marco.

Marco smiled at me. "Lizzy. Don't forget these two are allowed to be loose together in the arena. They groom each other. Sometimes they squabble, but really they love one another."

I noticed that Bernardo was now looking at me warily. His ears were pricked. My tentative handling of him had made him back up half a step and examine me, with a tipped head.

Marco remarked, "Bernardo wonders why you are afraid, and if maybe you know something that he doesn't?"

Marco handed me Caruso's lead rope, and I handed him Bernardo's. Then Caruso came to me and calmly touched my shoulder.

"You see why I paired Bernardo with Caruso? Caruso is always the one to reassure the others, and now he is reassuring you. Things can go wrong in a performance, but Caruso never stops. He leads by example. We had a show during a terrible storm once. The tent canvas and poles looked and sounded like they would lift off the ground and fly away. Honestly I was worried maybe it was a tornado coming or something. Caruso stayed calm. Bernardo was close to panic; I could see it. His eyes were open wide and showing the white. So Bernardo attached himself like glue to Caruso. I just worked Caruso, and Bernardo followed. I was so proud of both of them that day."

I followed Marco out to the parking lot. Along a temporary chain link fence stood a stretch of grass and weeds. The horses knew where they were going. Caruso started to lick his lips and chew before we got there. We watched in silence for a few moments while the guys plunged their heads down and ripped up grass so fast that it was falling out of their mouths before they could chew it.

Later at lunch I tried to eat my taco. What a terrible choice for a first date. I spilled taco filling on my shirt and almost knocked over my tea grabbing a napkin to dab at the stain. I had noticed Marco's really long fingers that seemed to completely wrap around his taco. He also had the foresight to lean over his plate. His sunglasses were propped up on his curly black hair. He looked so very European and sophisticated. He was probably more Emma's type. He even had a way of walking that commanded attention, although he seemed unaware of his effect. When he spoke, his voice was soft and lilting, with a hint of an accent. Every bit of him was polished and measured and, at the same time, relaxed.

We sat outside the taqueria at small tables. The sun was shining, and the breeze kept the bugs away. We were probably about the same age, but I felt very young next to Marco.

"So Marco, you grew up performing I guess."

"Oh yes. I even had a pony act. My mother was also a great horse trainer. She did a dressage act. But she died when I was small; cancer."

"I'm so sorry."

We ate in silence for a while.

"So Lizzy, you are going to be a dressage trainer like Margot and Deb?"

My voice suddenly sounded raspy. I lacked Ryder's utter certainty. I couldn't imagine ever being as good as Margot or Deb.

"That's the idea, but I'm not sure I'll ever be good enough."

Marco shook his head gently. "No one is really good enough are they? I mean you are never finished. The horses suffer a lot while we try to become horse trainers."

"I feel guilty all the time. You should have seen my poor mare tangled up in knots while I tried to learn walk pirouettes."

Marco smiled, "They are incredibly forgiving. As long as you keep a good attitude and never become angry or frustrated, I doubt there is any harm done. But it's a good thing as a trainer to know when to call it a day. My father is good at that. I try not to compliment him. He already has an inflated opinion of himself. But he is good at what he does."

"I'm afraid I do get frustrated. But my mare seems to forgive me. And I never get angry at her, only at myself. But I do get angry at Wild Child. And I do take it out on him sometimes."

"The stallion?"

"Yes. But the weirdest thing has happened, Marco."

I proceeded to tell him all about Kiddo's adventures and Deb's brilliant save until we were both laughing hard and I was wiping away tears. I also swore him to secrecy. Marco was still smiling but his voice was serious.

"Your stallion clearly needs a friend. Have you ever tried to be that for him?"

I had to digest that.

"What do you mean?"

"Well, Kiddo has shown you something really important. You think of Wild Child as vicious. But he wasn't vicious with Kiddo was he?"

"No. That was weird."

Emotionality is a sign of instability. I'm guessing this fellow, Kiddo, is a smart fellow. He wanted a friend for his midnight turn-out, and he chose Wild Child. Probably so he would have a guardian. A lone horse is not a safe horse. Kiddo chose the biggest strongest horse in the barn to keep him safe while he stuffed himself on spring grass. Kiddo was self-serving, but also non-emotive. Wild Child didn't intimidate him or incite aggression in him, but Kiddo did impress him with his smarts and offer him freedom. I'm guessing Wild Child was able to graze happily by his side and not bother Kiddo, wasn't he?"

"Yes. You're right."

I was stunned. Marco's insight was at once bizarre and brilliant.

"You have to work with horses from a non-emotive place. When you get angry at Wild Child, is it because you are afraid?"

I didn't need to think long on that.

"Yes."

"Why would a horse accept as his leader someone who is afraid?"

"I guess I need to be like Kiddo."

"Yes. Make him feel safe, and then he will become your guardian too; like he did for Kiddo."

"Marco, thank you. I have never thought about horses that way before."

I sat back in my chair and admired Marco's intellect as much as his personal beauty. He didn't seem to notice and kept talking.

"Caruso is like your Kiddo. That is why Bernardo looks to him in moments of stress. And you must be like Kiddo too. But you have to repair the relationship first. Wild Child sees you as below him; as erratic and emotional and unpredictable. So building a new relationship will take time. Look at it from his point of view. Why should he be glad to see you coming?"

Marco had given me lots to think about, other than just how gorgeous and talented and smart he was. Thoughts were sparking and crackling in my head, and soon had started a fire. I couldn't wait to get home. I began to formulate a way to help Wild Child and help myself too.

Kiddo was going to help me. Although Wild Child did not like to see me coming, he would be glad to see his new friend Kiddo. And he was going to have to accept a package deal; Kiddo, Margot, and me. But that was just part of the plan. I knew what I needed to do. I just had to get Margot on board, and in my gut I knew she would go for it. I thought a happier Wild Child on the ground just might be a happier Wild Child under saddle too. He didn't need a "firm hand" from that creep Patrick.

He needed to learn to trust.

CHAPTER 13

The Ghandi Of The Horse World

"LIZZY, YOU ARE A SUCH CLEVER girl. I'm always impressed at how well you read the horses. I think this is going to do Wild Child a world of good."

Margot was pleased. I guiltily took all the credit for the idea. So here we were; riding together.

Wild Child and Kiddo were wearing crocheted ear bonnets to keep the bugs out of their ears, and I had double-sprayed them with fly spray. Still I was swatting away bugs with the end of my whip. Margot jokingly said the state bird of New Jersey was the horsefly.

My hopes were high. The weather was warm; the air was still; and even the birds seemed quiet this afternoon. It was a good day for our first hack.

At first we tested Wild Child and Kiddo around the outside of the paddocks since hacking Wild Child was venturing into unknown territory. But it didn't take long to realize this was going to work. Wild Child followed Kiddo around the field like a puppy. If he balked for a second, Kiddo would automatically stop and wait, sighing dramatically for effect. And then Wild Child would relax and follow again. Margot was clearly impressed.

We bravely headed out the farm's front gate. Wild Child snorted at the gates as they swung inward, but he quickly tip-toed after Kiddo, not wanting to get left behind as we went through and turned right, heading down the road for the big hill. We finally turned through the sagging wooden gate and headed up the grade.

I turned to look at Margot. She looked relaxed and happy. She called to me.

"Shall we have a trot, Lizzy?"

"Sure."

Kiddo was in the lead, but not for long. Margot passed us in spectacular trot, reins loose. She was up in jumping position hanging on to Wild Child's mane. Wild Child had his ears up and his tail held high. You could say he looked happy, even joyful, an unusual sight. Margot was grinning from ear to ear. I had a fleeting thought that she should really have a helmet on. I would feel naked without one, especially out on a hack. She got so far ahead of us that Kiddo finally had to break into a canter.

Margot called over her shoulder to me, "I'm going to let him canter to the top of the hill, OK?"

"Go for it!"

Wild Child lowered his haunches, and the two of them kicked into a gallop and were gone.

Little Kiddo was loping along without any feeling of nervousness. He really was a golden boy.

Margot suddenly pulled up. We hadn't crested the hill yet. When I caught up to her, I immediately saw the problem. Wild Child's joy had turned to panic; he was twirling around kicking like a madman. Margot was saying, "Whoa" and pulling on the reins.

I saw the problem.

"Wire, Margot!"

Wild Child was frantically kicking; a ball of baling wire wrapped around his hind hoof.

Without thinking, I jumped off Kiddo and rushed over to Margot, grabbing a rein. Wild Child dragged me a few feet. He had stopped twirling and was now running backward. For a brief moment, I thought he would get a front foot in the wire along with the hind foot. I hung on and felt myself become airborne for a moment, and then he froze. I let go. All was quiet, but I realized it could start right back up again.

Margot was using soothing tones and stroking Wild Child on the neck.

"Margot, I'll see if I can just pick up his hoof and pull the wire off."

"Lizzy no, that sounds too dangerous. If he panics again you could get hurt. Call Deb on your cell phone, and tell her to bring the wire cutters."

"Uh, Margot that would take too long. He could really hurt himself."

Then I felt a little shove on my back. It was Kiddo.

Kiddo, had not left us, but had walked right up behind me, to Wild Child, and they were now touching noses.

"Let me try, Margot. Kiddo will keep him distracted."

"OK. But darling please be careful."

And then an incredible thing happened. Just like the night of their escape, they sidled up to each other and began co-grooming; ignoring the fact that Margot was sitting on top. Wild Child was holding his hind leg up, the large loose wad of wire dangling from his shoe. One strand of the damn wire was wedged between his shoe and foot; otherwise he looked unharmed.

In a flash my mind played out my tragic demise, trampled to death by Wild Child as the two of us became joined in a tangle of baling wire. But I caught myself. I needed to be a leader. Just like Kiddo was showing me; I needed to be emotion-free, matter-of-fact. I shuddered for a second but then tucked Wild Child's hoof between my thighs like a farrier would do. Wild Child knew this pose well, and I felt his foot grow heavy as he relaxed. Then I wiggled the wire back and forth, back and forth.

Margot whispered. "Lizzy, is it coming?"

"Pop" came the wire out of the shoe.

"Margot, you are free."

"Oh thank God. Darling, you are amazing."

I had trouble getting back up on Kiddo. Now the emotions came flooding back into my body. I was trembling. If a rider had nine lives like a cat, I had just used up one of mine. Wild Child could have taken me out. But he didn't. What Kiddo had done was just not normal. Kiddo was innately a genius. Just like Cara had said. He was hardly a horse at all.

After we walked a while, Margot said, "Wild Child isn't a bad boy really. I think he's been terribly misunderstood."

"Margot, you've got to be kidding me. I'll bet the mothers of all those guys on death row say the same thing."

We both cracked up. I figured it was partly just out of immense relief. But after we grew quiet, Margot said, "Lizzy, I know you find him challenging; I do too. But Walter always said, 'you have to find a way to love every horse you have in training.' Otherwise, you will fail. They know the difference, you see. They will stop trying for you. It's the same with children. Every child who is failing a class believes the teacher hates him."

We were silent again. Then I said, "But what if it's true? What if the child is right?"

"Then the teacher has to change the way she feels. You can't expect it to come first from the child, or the horse. That's why the horses make us better people. Wild Child is going to teach us both important lessons. And in the process, we are going to make him a better horse."

There it was again; the same theme. Emotions. Marco told me to have none, and Margot said I would need to be able to change my emotions at will. They were both asking a lot from me. I rubbed Kiddo on his withers. Kiddo had just saved us all.

"Margot, it was Kiddo who just did the heavy lifting."

"That's because Kiddo already speaks his language. We just used him as our interpreter."

I looked over at Wild Child. He was clinging to Kiddo, making Margot's stirrups bump into mine. Wild Child's ears were pricked forward, and he had a new look in his eye, with worry wrinkles over his brow.

He had let down his guard.

He had allowed us to see that he too could be afraid, but he had not fled. He had trusted.

I thought of Patrick.

"And some people think that what Wild Child needs is a firm hand."

Margot laughed, "Now you sound just like Francesca!"

CHAPTER 14

Training Wheels

IT WAS TIME FOR MY LESSON, but I started my warm-up with Winsome without waiting for Margot.

It was not Patrick's firm hand that was needed; Kiddo had shown me that. I had been shown how I could not be an emotionally unstable leader for Wild Child. In the same way, I shouldn't be an unstable leader for Winsome, even if she tolerated me. Interesting how powerful new thoughts could be. Overnight I felt I had become a better rider.

And Winsome felt fantastic. She was moving with great energy and was reaching for the contact with a swinging back. Music was playing on the radio. When I cantered, *Isn't She Lovely* came on, and Winsome was cantering exactly with the beat of the music.

She was lovely, indeed.

I admired our reflection as I passed the mirror, imagining an American flag sewn onto my saddle pad. We looked great.

I was all warmed-up and walking around on a loose rein when Margot walked in.

"How's she feeling today?"

"She's great."

"I've been thinking about a plan for you and Winsome."

"Yeah."

"Pretty big show plans have been made for me and Ryder for the spring and summer. Frank and Francesca want both of us to try and qualify for the National Championships at Gladstone at the eleventh hour. I'm sorry, Lizzy, but it will be sucking up all our collective energies. I don't want you to think I'm forgetting about you. But Ryder and I are both going to depend on your help at the shows."

I was back to being a groom. I felt a little lump forming in my throat.

"I understand, Margot. I can put shows on the back burner a while. I can't really afford them anyway."

"Good. It means you can concentrate on training. Training to show and training to advance to the next level are quite different. It's hard to do both well at the same time. I want you and Winsome out later this year at Second level, and I want it to be solid. I put you through those walk pirouette exercises for a reason. You and Winsome will be making a big step to demonstrate honest collection. Second level is the downfall for most amateurs who are training their own horses because the amateurs trip up on that big step."

I was listening to Margot and understanding her, but my head and my heart were in conflict. Maybe I wanted to show off in front of Ryder. Maybe I just needed some kind of reassurance. Would I become a Margot or a Deb someday? Or was I always going to be a groom?

I realized I was reaching my hand around something new but did not yet have a grip. At the same time, I felt that what I wanted was slowly being drawn away from me. Was it? Unlike Ryder, I knew enough to know there was still much I did not know.

Margot was looking at me intently with concern on her face.

"And, Lizzy, just think. Some people get hung up at Third level when they can't teach their horse a clean flying change. You should breeze right through because Winsome already does beautiful changes. The problem now is to teach you and her both about taking more weight behind. She needs a more uphill balance. I have complete faith in both of you. But these things take time, darling. You know what real collection feels like from your time on dear Rave; now we must put more of that into Winsome."

"She's not uphill enough for Second level?"

"It's developmental darling. It's coming. You know how most children learn how to ride a bicycle by first riding on a tricycle? A trike is very stable but not very mobile. You won't win races on one or be able to do tricks right? As the child's balance improves, she moves onto a two-wheel bike with training wheels. It's much faster and more mobile. Once she gets the hang of that, the training wheels can come off. Kids with super balance even learn how to ride a unicycle. Then we're talking about a Grand Prix kind of balance! They can turn that thing around on a dime and bounce up a staircase. But it would be foolish to expect a child to start with the unicycle, wouldn't it? They'd spend more time falling down and hurting themselves than riding, and would most likely just give up. So it is entirely appropriate that Winsome began her journey as a dressage horse in a fairly level balance. You've done nothing wrong, Lizzy."

"I'm still not sure what you're trying to say, Margot."

"Darling, it's time to take her training wheels off."

"OK. What does that mean?"

"Well, just like that three-wheel trike, or those training wheels, we've allowed her to be a little wide in her base; her hind legs. We have to narrow the base. We have to ask her to carry her hind legs a little closer together and, at the same time, rock her mass back over that narrower base, lightening the load on her shoulders."

"But I thought you liked how she was going."

"You have done a super job of fulfilling the requirements of Training and now First level. Your horse is relaxed and happy. She goes freely forward with a swinging back, and she is reliably on the bit. She has developed the thrust required for lengthening her stride in trot and canter. She does lovely leg-yields. But it's a big jump up now to a good Second level. That's all."

I still couldn't help but feel that Margot was telling me I was not cutting it. All the wind was now completely knocked out of my sails. But I tried to suck it up.

We went to work, starting with trot-walk-trot transitions. We moved on the shoulder-fore and then shoulder-in. This was one of Margot's "essential exercises," and she explained it by asking the inside hind to move toward the outside fore. We had effectively "narrowed the base" behind, taking off Winsome's training wheels, but only if we kept the outside hind tracking straight.

We did the easy shallow loop of counter canter too. Our final exercise this day was to add the rein-back, and I thought my effort was pretty awful. I felt my frustration level rise.

"Lizzy, don't worry darling. When you get one step, or even the feeling that she shifts her weight a tiny bit back, then you release, reward, and ride forward."

We tried a few more times. Margot jumped out of her chair and came to Winsome's side, touching her on the chest lightly with a whip when I asked for the rein-back.

"Don't pull back on the reins; just gather both reins. When she meets the contact, hold steady and only let her pull against herself. Don't worry about where her head is; it's the feet that she has to understand to move. If she feels really blocked, lift one rein and ask for a step of turn- on-the-forehand. We never want her to feel trapped; she has to feel that moving her feet leads to an immediate release and step forward. This is an important concept for the horses. Then the horses never feel stressed by the rein-back, and it will become an amazing exercise to rebalance the horse to the hindquarters. Training never begins with a finished product, Lizzy. You must break it down to tiny building blocks, and reward approximations. So you see; this is enough for today. Be satisfied."

But I was a long way from satisfied. I felt my emotions bubbling away in my gut; suppressed. I wanted to be non-emotive. I wanted to be like Kiddo. I had a long way to go.

I finished as we always did in rising trot, allowing Winsome to relax and release any residual stress from the rein-back exercise.

As I left the arena, I found Deb leaning against the door frame. She reached up and patted my thigh, the same way that Margot had done countless times.

"Who died?"

"What?"

"It's horse training, Lizzy. Let it come as it comes. No one needed your score to win the Olympic gold medal today, OK?"

That made me smile, considering my earlier daydream about the American flag sewn on to my saddle pad.

"It's a good thing too. I'd hate to disappoint an entire nation."

"I watched your lesson, Lizzy; you rode just fine, and Winsome is beautiful."

I looked over my shoulder at Margot. She was talking on her cell phone and drawing a circle in the dirt with the toe of her boot.

"No, I was terrible. I'm imagining I'm on a unicycle, but clearly I haven't even taken off the training wheels."

Deb smiled and nodded her head. She was the one in a million who actually understood what I just blabbered.

"You were not terrible. You are a good rider, but you're riding with too much intention."

"What the heck does that mean?"

"You're too emotionally invested in the outcome."

"But I care. I care a lot. I can't help that."

"I care too, Lizzy. But I know to leave my ambition behind me once I swing up on the back of a horse. Your noisy inner voice is drowning out your ability to hear."

"Deb, you make riding and training horses sound like nothing but a head game."

Deb just smiled.

Margot strolled up and linked arms with her.

"Deb darling, I'm glad you got to see Lizzy ride. I think she could be the next "you."

Deb threw her head back and laughed.

"Oh God, Margot, for Lizzy's sake I certainly hope not!"

And the two of them strolled off arm-in-arm, heads bent toward each other; whispering like schoolgirls.

I had the idea then that there were no secrets between those two, and that was good.

I didn't feel like I could talk to Margot about Francesca, or about Patrick, or about Wild Child's nighttime adventures. But Deb could.

And then my mind changed tracts.

Could I really be the next Deb?

CHAPTER 15

Trap For A Tiger

RYDER AND I WERE TACKING UP in silence.

Every attempt I made at chit-chat had been met with either a grunt or silence, so what the heck. I gave up trying.

Ryder was getting ready for her lesson on Petey, and Francesca was supposed to have had her lesson already on Lovey. Francesca had been delayed by High Horse Couture business and had asked Ryder to jump ahead of her.

So I was babysitting Lovey who was conserving his energy by taking a nap in the cross-ties. The halter was on over his bridle, and it looked really uncomfortable. The cross-ties seemed to be holding the whole horse up as he leaned into them.

Ryder led Petey out of the cross-ties. Petey sure was a handsome guy. He was a true black, not a spot of brown on him, with a powerful neck and butt and a large and intelligent eye in a masculine face. There was a lot of engine there. I had yet to really watch him go, but I knew it must be going well because Ryder was already talking about showing him at Third level.

I sat with Lovey for another fifteen minutes. At that point we were both in a stupor. So I walked to Francesca's office and knocked on the door.

"Yes."

I opened it a crack. Francesca was sitting at her desk on the telephone. She raised an eyebrow and put her hand over the receiver.

"Is it OK if I walk Lovey around the arena until you're ready?"

She didn't exactly answer, but waved her hand at me like she was shooing a fly. I did discern the slightest nod of her chin, so I guessed that meant "yes."

Good enough. I was dying to see Petey go.

"Door!" I yelled as I got to the indoor. Margot answered.

"Lizzy, where's Francesca?"

"Still on the phone; I told her I'd walk Lovey around for her."

"OK darling, come on in."

I swung up on Lovey and then tried to stay out of Ryder's way.

Petey was impressive. He was uphill in his balance, so he had taken off the training wheels for sure. His shoulders were free, and his front legs expressive. But something about him said "man's horse." Maybe it was just because he was tall and heavily muscled, although Ryder with her long legs didn't look too small on him.

Ryder was being really harsh with him too. He got pulled up sharply in front of every corner. Then they went back to trot and made a step of medium trot out of the corner. From there they went on to extended trots, to halt, to rein-back, and back to extension. He got fancier and fancier, but he also got hot and tense.

Margot was saying, "Gently, gently now."

Ryder was pushing Petey, and I couldn't help but feel it was partly to impress me. And Petey was complying. But he had a certain look around his eyes, a bit of white showing in the front corners, as if he was rolling his eyes back into his head. Ryder had impressed him through her strong riding skills. But it looked to me like compliance gained through intimidation. I wondered how long it would last.

Finally Francesca came in, and I walked Lovey over to her. She still wasn't ready to get on. She wanted to watch too.

I stood next to her holding Lovey, and I could see Francesca assessing Ryder. Her jaw was set, and she had a weird look in her eyes, the lids lowered and her chin tipped up. I thought she was probably approving of Ryder's "firm hand."

I piped up, "Ryder is being awfully hard on him."

Francesca turned to look me straight in the eye. "The stuff of champions, Lizzy. Petey is going to make Ryder step up her skill level. Especially once she has to show him."

I wondered exactly what that meant.

"You know something about Petey that you're not telling?"

Francesca smiled. It wasn't a nice smile. She was sabotaging Ryder, and she was expecting me to enjoy that fact. She was unbelievable. Whatever it was that Petey did at the shows, Ryder was about to be blindsided. Francesca gazed out into the arena and continued whispering.

"There are certain horses that come into your life for a reason. Isn't that what Margot would say? Petey has come into Ryder's life for a reason, OK? Now let's let Ryder experience what Petey has to teach her, shall we?"

"Francesca, what if Ryder gets hurt? Does Margot know? I can't believe Margot knows."

"Listen up Lizzy, you are not going to interfere. Anyway, even if you did, I don't think Ryder would believe you. She likes that you envy her ability. And she wouldn't consider your opinion important."

"Well, you're probably right about that, but..."

"Welcome to my world, Lizzy." Francesca zapped me into silence with that comment. Yeah, I got it. We all did not show her enough respect. I knew she was right. What did I care anyway? I hurrumphed a bit.

"She's not even listening to Margot."

Francesca pointed at me and then pulled an imaginary zipper across her lips.

And I nodded up and down silently as a reply.

"Hold Lovey for me over here at the mounting block while I get on."

I watched Francesca ride away while Ryder finished her lesson with canter half passes to single flying changes. Petey was a little hot in the changes, so he got to do more transitions to walk, ride through the corner, and then pick the canter back up.

Margot was still using soothing tones and encouraging Ryder to be gentle, but when Ryder did follow her instructions, I could tell it was without conviction.

Petey still looked tense but powerful. I guessed he wasn't dangerous. Francesca was mean, but she wasn't reckless.

This meant I had another secret to carry around. But it wasn't too heavy a load. I had no feelings of duty toward Ryder.

Maybe Francesca was setting a trap for Ryder, but for once I found myself agreeing that the horse would, in time, be Ryder's best teacher.

CHAPTER 16

Beautiful Pariah

I COULD FEEL THAT MARGOT WOULD rather not be here at all. She was here because Francesca wanted it. I knew Margot did not feel ready to bring Wild Child out yet. But she had given in. I guessed she had to. I had always remembered Emma's words to me on my first day; without Francesca we could all be out on the street.

For this first show, Petey would stay home. This show was for Wild Child and Margot to get their first qualifying scores. It was not all about Ryder; though I was not sure Ryder realized that. But Ryder would be showing Papa for the first time here. Her scores counted too, and she let me know that she intended for them to be high.

The one saving grace about this first show was that it was in New Jersey. We got to sleep in our own beds, just like the shows we did in Florida. And if we forgot anything, we could always send someone running home to get it.

And we had Alfonso. He was fantastic help; he hauled everything over on Wednesday and helped set up the horses' stalls, the grooming stall, and tack room, doing much of the heavy lifting, and all with a smile on his face.

With Alfonso's help, setting up was a piece of cake for me since I had learned the drill down in Florida. I still had Emma's laminated list of things to pack, and I checked them off with the dry-erase pen as they went up the ramp and into the trailer for the trip over. Plus, I had Ryder to boss around. So I made sure she pulled her own weight. Even though Ryder was showing, she worked for Francesca and Margot too. I got to act as the foreman, and it felt good.

Francesca had purchased lovely big potted ferns and bags of dark wood chips. With Ryder's help I put up the tack room drapes and valance. Down went the tack room floor mat, and we installed all the racks and hooks for bridles and saddles and coats. The table and chairs were set out along with a CD player. The stalls were bedded deeply with fragrant pine shavings, the buckets and feeders hung. When we finished set-up, I carefully swept and raked. Our show barn was pristine.

On Thursday we unloaded the horses early in the day, and already the place was humming with activity. It was a big show, a qualifier for both Gladstone and for the North American Young Riders Championships in August.

Wild Child bugled his arrival, and as usual he turned heads wherever we went. But I hustled him into his stall before he could get a good look at any of the other horses. I turned him loose, and he immediately marked his new territory and then tried to peek over the boards at his neighbors. He was excited, yet not really nervous. He clearly knew about horse shows. This was a chance for him to see lots and lots of pretty horseflesh.

It would be my first experience with the "high performance" classes. These classes were run under the FEI (International) rules instead of the USEF (National) rules. Not just anyone could enter them. You had to send letters of intent, or declarations, to the national governing body along with a fee to even be allowed to enter. Francesca had even had to pay extra for Margot to declare so late in the selection process.

There would be a national show running concurrently alongside the qualifier, but the horses entered in the qualifier had a separate barn and warm-up arena and something called a "jog," an inspection of the horse's fitness to compete.

The jog occurred the day before the classes began. Our separate barn even had security, and we would be given little wristbands to get access to the stables. Lock-down, or security, didn't start until 24 hours before the first class. I had seen people

KAREN MCGOLDRICK | 119

at the Florida shows with special little bracelets that admitted them to the FEI barn, and I recognized them as status symbols. This time I would be sporting one!

I was excited and nervous, even though I was just the groom.

I wanted Margot to do well, and I didn't want to screw up either. If this show went badly for Margot and Wild Child, then they were done with the race to qualify for Gladstone. I had gone online and read the rules so I wouldn't do something to embarrass Margot.

We had to do the "jog" later that day. But first Margot wanted the horses to have training rides on the show grounds. They needed to get around the show arena to have a "look-see." Papa and Wild Child were not terribly spooky horses, but there were still lots to be nervous about. The pressure was on, and since Margot had not shown Wild Child, he was a bit of a question mark. He had been shown by his previous rider, Ben, but that was before he was even on Margot's radar.

Papa was an insecure horse who responded to nerves by becoming tense. These first rides on the show grounds were all about getting the two horses familiarized with the new environment and getting them "on" the aids. It was not a time to work out problems. You tried to stay away from problems and simply loosen, relax, and bring your horse's focus onto you. Margot also wanted the horses to be a little tired and relaxed for the "jog."

The FEI jog was a formal event. Horses were braided and presented in a bridle, usually a snaffle. The horses were always polished to a "T," and riders liked to dress well too, but they needed good running shoes! The "ground jury" (i.e. judges) and an FEI vet would either "accept" or "not accept" your horse as fit to compete. I was not sure what the history of the thing was, but it was highly formulated, and people lined up to watch it.

Each horse had an FEI passport that not only identified the horse but also had proof of his vaccinations. It was handed over to the show office on arrival. A jogging lane was set up with potted plants. When your number was called, the rider came forward and presented her horse to the panel. The panel had the horse's passport in hand and compared the description to the horse in front of them. After the panel walked around and inspected your horse, you did the "jog."

You walked away from the judges on a straight line about ten meters, until you got to a marker (usually a potted plant); then jogged alongside your horse to the next marker; then walked and made a right turn around the last potted plant; and then jogged back to the panel. At that point the announcer said "accepted" or, God forbid, your horse didn't look right, then you would be held in a box to be re-examined by another vet. If your horse was still "off," you would be "spun."

My job was not only to put in damn-fine-looking braids and have Wild Child polished until he shone, but to hand walk Wild Child away from all the other horses until Margot's number was called.

Then Margot would have to do the "jog" herself.

I had peeked at Ryder's braids before. I was clearly a much better braider than Ryder.

Yup. I did something better than Ryder. Wild Child had been so obnoxious while I braided him that it was a miracle they looked so good. Horses were arriving, and he felt the need to welcome each and every one with a full body-shaking whinny. It's hard to hang onto a tight little braid when the horse is vibrating.

I kept each new piece of yarn waiting in my clenched front teeth waiting to be incorporated into the braid, while keeping a lot of tension on the three strands of hair I was folding. At the same time I worked to summon a Zen state of mind. Every so often Wild Child would smack his tail against his own butt just to be sure I knew how pissed-off he was. Clearly Margot had not worn him out enough in her ride.

Ryder walked into the stall and lightly touched one of my braids.

"Nice braids."

"Thank you, Ryder."

"You better finish up though. The Grand Prix horses jog first."

I flipped my wrist around to check my watch.

"I've got plenty of time."

"OK. Well, Francesca bought us some nice threads for the jog, so I'm going to go change."

I was happy to see her walk away. I did need to hurry. I hit my rhythm, fingers flying on their own. It was cool how I could disconnect my mind from my fingers, and watch them go, almost like a disinterested observer. It was only between braids that I could feel how stiff my fingers were. Wild Child had stopped smacking his tail around and was now stomping and pawing with his right front foot.

"Quit that!"

I gave his neck a swat, and he stretched out both front legs and rocked back, doing a horse-version of downward-facing dog. His stretch was accompanied by a loud moan.

"I'm killing you with all this beauty parlor stuff, aren't I?"

He stood back up and assumed a sullen look, both ears back and nose wrinkled.

I had finished his mane and had to attempt to do his forelock without having him eviscerate my belly with his teeth. You have to stand smack dab in front of the horse to do the forelock. The temptation to bite me would be fierce.

I fetched an extra lead rope and tied his mouth closed; tightly. Funny thing; he seemed to like it. I figured I had tied his mouth shut so many times that I had trained him to like it. Or maybe it was releasing some kind of endorphins. His eye got a sleepy look. I dove into this forelock braid at top speed. It's best to use a French braid on the forelock so that it lies flat and doesn't stick up, but I always felt like I needed six fingers instead of five to French braid. With him kinda' out of it, I got the thing in.

Then I stepped back and admired my work. He looked beautiful. As usual, his copper-colored chestnut coat flashed different tones as he moved. He was otherworldly beautiful. I unsnapped him and led him back to his stall.

As I turned him loose he went for the wall and leaned over to mess up my handiwork by rubbing his braids.

"Wild Child, you brat. No!"

I swung the halter and rope at him and then jumped back. That diverted him. So he charged the stall front.

This time I laughed as I pulled the door shut.

"Toro, Toro you big red Bull…Just don't tear out my braids!"
Margot had walked up behind me.

"Oh, Lizzy, doesn't he look beautiful. Great braids."

"Well he already has tried to rub them."

"Better put him back in the cross-ties until we get this over with; then you can pull them out."

Wow. I realized all my handiwork was only going to be in for an hour or so, and then I'd have to do it all over again tomorrow. What a crying shame that was.

I waited until Wild Child had peed and taken a drink of water, and then bribed him back out with a sugar cube; no carrots for Wild Child until after the jog. I didn't want him slobbering orange bits. At least the sugar made a nice white foam.

Margot and Ryder looked sharp too. Francesca had come through with her fashion-sense again. They wore white pressed jeans and crisp white shirts, with a short tailored dark denim jacket. The Equine Paradiso farm logo was embroidered tastefully over the breast pocket. Margot had pulled her shirt collar up and was looking sporty. Ryder had a short haircut that was kind of tomboyish, and Margot had her signature shellacked blonde bun.

I was wearing jeans and my EPF polo shirt and baseball cap, looking like the groom that I was.

"OK Lizzy, let's put his bridle and number on. They're calling for our class to come to the indoor."

"The indoor?"

"Yeah. That's the collecting area. I'm going to have you lead him around in there until they call his number, and then I'll take him for the jog."

I felt myself deflate.

"I have to lead him around in there with all those other horses?"

"I'm afraid so, darling."

"I hope I can manage him OK."

"Just keep him away from the other horses, and keep him moving and busy. He's done this before. Maybe we'll be lucky and he'll get called early."

I put on his snaffle bridle. It was two tones of brown and soft and supple in my hands. I had oiled it and then rubbed it with beeswax. I slid the aluminum piece of his bridle number into the left side of his brow band and pinched it closed at the bottom. Then I folded the top down so it couldn't come off the bridle, and I pulled it away from the base of his ear so it wouldn't tickle him.

Then it was time to go. I pulled on my heavy deerskin gloves. Wild Child was eager; too eager. Margot walked behind us. Ryder needed to stay with Papa until her class was called. Wild Child had his neck arched and seemed to know where we were going. He was leaning into the bit, and I had my elbow pressed into his shoulder, walking on my heels.

I couldn't wait to have him at least enclosed in the indoor arena.

We got to the covered "tunnel" entrance.

"Lizzy, hold on; let me see if the coast is clear."

I dug my heels in, and we skidded to a stop. But stopping wasn't so good either. He raised his head and gave an earth-shaking whinny. He could see other horses pass by the door to the arena. He wanted to be in there.

Margot walked ahead of me, looked into the arena, and then waved us in.

And we were off.

We stepped into the arena. It seemed full of naked horses, at least to Wild Child, so there came the penis lowering down out of his sheath. I felt my cheeks get hot.

And there was Patrick, walking his well-mannered gelding around. He called out.

"Your horse just grew another leg."

Margot called out, "Keep him busy, Lizzy."

I growled at him.

"Wild Child put that back! These horses are not for you."

I had to get his attention on me. I tried to channel Pali and Marco and Deb. I tried to channel Kiddo. I knew a "firm hand" would cause him to simply yank these reins right out of my hands and go breed himself to one of these beautiful horses. And I would die a thousand deaths.

So I went toward the middle of the arena. Most of the horses were just marching around along the rail, and I walked him around on a teeny-tiny circle. Every now and then I would notice someone giving me a dirty look. I was the pariah. The good news is everyone stayed miles away from me.

I tried to scratch his neck, but he didn't even register it. So I made him do a turn on the forehand, and then I tried to practice the right-hand turns. Then I did walk-halt-walk. Every time he tried to pick up his head and whinny, I made him do something different. I tried a sugar cube, but he wouldn't take it. One time I shoved it into his mouth and he just let it fall right back out. He was into candy, but only eye-candy, not sugar. He wanted the flesh-and-blood kind. Every now and then he would turn and look at me, and his thoughts were easy to read. He was thinking, "How can I lose this pest?"

One by one, numbers were called, and the arena population began to thin. He could see his opportunities disappearing. As each horse left, he would stop and look wistfully at their retreating form.

I almost wept with joy when his number was finally called. I walked him over to Margot who did not look at all happy to take him from me. She barely made eye contact with me. Her eyes were firmly on Wild Child, and her jaw was set.

It was then that it occurred to me that Margot never handled him. She was about the ride, and man she could ride. But that was clearly different.

At first I thought all was going well. He stood for the panel like a rock. His head was up and arched, his tail held high. He was an impressive animal; stunning. Of course he had to let out one of his mighty bellows. He was saying, "I am lion, hear me roar!"

The entire panel stepped back. No one wanted too close to this lion. Margot turned to walk him away. And he pricked his ears and arched his neck, still looking for horses; so far so good. When Margot picked up a trot I held my breath.

Margot was so slender, and not a spring chicken anymore. His huge neck coiled downward, leveraging against the bit. Each step of trot got a little more airborne. He was getting too far ahead of her. She pulled him up earlier than she was supposed to. He stopped sharply and stood up on his hind legs. Margot was not about to let go, and was pulled off the ground entirely for a moment.

Someone behind me gasped. Then I clearly heard Francesca's voice.

"Yes, you're right, he needs more discipline."

When Wild Child returned to earth he started backing up.

Thank God Margot moved toward him, keeping the reins slack and cooing to him. She didn't overreact or scold him, or she would have lost him for sure.

Margot was able to lead him again at the walk around the last potted plant, and oh so cautiously jig-jogged the remaining trot steps.

Then they walked and halted.

And the announcer said.

"Accepted."

Thank God.

Margot looked the picture of calm as she smiled and walked toward me. But as she handed him over, I noticed her hands were shaking.

She whispered, "Well there's a project for you, Lizzy."

"Gee thanks, Margot."

"Get Deb to help you with it."

Wild Child actually walked nicely back to the stable. The excitement was over; time to take out the braids, feed and close-up the stable, go home, and get some rest.

And set my alarm for zero-dark hundred, so I could put the braids back in.

CHAPTER 17

Blue Ice

Try as I might, I couldn't ignore that today marked the beginning of Ryder's quest to stand on the top podium at the North American Young Riders Championships. She was dreaming gold medals before having taken a single step down centerline. What happened today would either give her a big wake-up call or stoke her ego some more.

Only the top four from each region would qualify and then become a team to go to the very prestigious Championships in August. Ryder was certain she would be one of those riders. But to qualify you had to have a minimum of three shows to average your score, and you had to do a musical freestyle at one of the shows, although the freestyle was not added to the average.

In addition to the North American Championships, Ryder (and Franesca) wanted to qualify for the National USEF Championships for Young Riders at Gladstone. Margot was only required to show twice to qualify for her Nationals, but Ryder would need three shows. I had looked, and there were only two shows left within driving distance on our calendar. I hadn't asked how she was going to get three.

The tests that Ryder and Papa would perform were equivalent in difficulty to the Prix St. Georges/Intermediare level, not the Grand Prix level. So while this test was a step up for Ryder, it was actually a step down in difficulty for Papa, who had been training all the Grand Prix movements with Margot though he had never been shown Grand Prix.

According to Margot, the horses in the Young Riders division had gotten fancier every year and the young riders more like mini-pros than teens. Many of the riders were now home-schooled or used tutoring services. Not all of them would become professional riders. For some this would be their last hurrah. Some would not stay in horses, and some would make horses their life.

Ryder's goals were no secret. The Brentina Cup would be her next step. It was a special Grand Prix for the Young Adults who had graduated from Young Riders, but then at age twenty-five they had to get out and compete against the pros. To follow her plan she'd have to keep getting breaks just like this one she had riding Papa.

Ryder was getting my superior braiding job for her first outing.

She had been nice enough when she asked.

I pulled up my braiding stool and stroked Papa's neck. He was a tender-hearted softie, with the kindest eye I'd ever seen. He was kind of like a giant Bambi. He only lacked the antlers.

I was already feeling trembly inside. Maybe it was partly the coffee, the early morning, and the lack of sleep, or maybe I just couldn't keep myself from caring, even about Ryder. I wanted her to make Margot proud and do justice to Papa.

When Ryder checked in to see how I was coming, I asked if she was getting nervous.

She looked me dead in the eye and answered, "I never get nervous."

Uh-huh I thought. It just couldn't be possible. Could it?

"Well, Ryder, I'd be wetting my pants, but that's just me."

Ryder gave me a thin-lipped smile, "And I'm so glad I'm not you."

Surely she was nervous. I squinted my eyes, examining her impassive face.

"Ryder, everybody gets nervous. You should see Margot. Even Margot gets nervous. It's nothing to be embarrassed about."

"Lizzy. I'm not embarrassed. It's just the truth. I'm not nervous. I'm prepared. I'm competitive. Papa is top-class and very comfortable at this level."

I guessed I would take her at her word. She was serious. And she did look calm. I absolutely did not get her.

"Do you want me to tack him up for you?"

"Sure."

She turned her back and strolled away.

Thank you would be appreciated, I thought while I stretched and flexed the stiffness out of my fingers. Braiding always made my fingers so achy. Twenty-three and getting arthritis, I thought.

Ryder might not be nervous, but Papa was. As soon as I brought out his tack, he got wiggly. He kept shifting from foot to foot, and nervously craning his neck to see who was coming. Finally Margot came down the aisle. Clearly that was who he was looking for. He gave a pathetic little whinny. Margot heard it and called back to him in a cheerful voice.

"How is my darling boy today?"

She walked into the grooming stall and found the tub of sugar cubes. Papa watched her every move, ears pricked and neck reaching toward her. Margot had that effect on every horse she trained. They always wanted to be near her. They adored her. Just as I did.

Papa was timid to his very core, and Margot was his security blanket. Pali was right. Margot had earned his trust. I watched her stroke him. Her hands were small, her fingers long. He almost gave her a hug with his neck. She pulled gently on his braided forelock, and he slowly lowered his head. Then she began stroking his ears with both hands, from base to tip. His head went lower and lower, and he rolled his eyes and yawned. Then he sighed.

Margot crooned to him.

"See, you are just fine. No worries, Papa."

Watching her settle her big weenie almost made me cry. And then I felt a little angry with her. Why would she agree to give the ride to Ryder? It seemed wrong. Here Margot had done years of hard work and then handed the ride away. He was Margot's horse. He deserved to have her in the irons. Plus, Ryder always rode like she was going into battle. How could Papa enjoy that?

Oh crap. Who was I kidding? I was jealous.

Margot had done it for the right reasons. She felt that the pressure of Grand Prix was too much for Papa. That instead, all his training could benefit an up and coming talented rider, while allowing Papa to compete at a level where he could shine. Ryder had been the lucky "chosen" one. I thought again of Ryder.

"He may be worried, Margot, but Ryder says she's not nervous at all. Imagine that."

Margot shook her head and smiled.

"It's a good thing, Lizzy. With that attitude of hers, she'll give my boy confidence. He always wants to please, but sometimes he's an overachiever, and it makes him tense and worried. He needs a rider who has inner calm. I have a feeling they'll do great, just watch."

"She just doesn't seem human is all."

I noticed Margot had a little smile. But she said nothing.

I finished with Papa, and here came Ryder, dressed for success. She looked great and had even put a tiny rosebud in her lapel.

It was time to get her to the warm-up arena.

Margot clipped on the coaching system, and I grabbed the bucket full of supplies. I had a towel, fly spray, sugar cubes, and bottled water.

Papa pranced all the way to the warm-up, and Ryder sat up on top looking downright regal. Her tailcoat was dark blue with silver piping on the lapels, and her helmet matched exactly.

As Margot put her through the warm-up, I could hear the chatter of the railbirds.

"Who is that?"

"I don't know, but that's Margot Fanning coaching."

"Is that Paparazzi?"

I could feel the energy working for Ryder. She was feeling it too. Every step of Papa's nervous energy was being channeled.

Ryder rode like she was preparing to ride into battle. She was firm and focused but without nerves, without emotion. She rode with purpose, and Papa had no time to think for himself.

They were an army of two; she was General and he was a buck private. His job was not to think, but to do.

When it was time to go in, a flock of bystanders peeled off the fence and followed us to the competition arena.

I handed her the water, and she took it without looking at me. Margot and Ryder had their final words while I wiped off her boots.

Papa trotted in like a Grand Prix horse. Even before the judges finished writing their final comments on the test sheets of the prior competitor, their pens stopped moving as they peered over their reading glasses watching Papa trot around the outside of the boards. They knew they were about to see something good.

The bell finally rang, and Ryder walked, turned Papa around, and picked up the canter to head down centerline.

I looked over at Margot, and I could tell she was nervous as hell. Her jaw was clenched. I figured she rode every single step of that test. And of course it was a good test. The pirouettes were a bit large, which maybe I took perverse pleasure over. The only real problem was the walk work. Papa lost focus. He began to think for himself too much. He could hardly keep from jigging, looking up, and seeming to notice the crowd for the very first time. Ryder managed it, but "just," as the steps stayed in walk but were too bouncy.

At her final salute, the crowd applauded heartily. Margot and I stood by the out-gate and waited to catch her eye. But she wasn't looking for us. Patrick stood at the far side, leaning on the rails with his young rider standing next to him, still wearing her tail coat. As soon as Ryder found him standing there, she looked away. And then she smiled at us, and Margot gave her the thumbs up.

I took care of Papa while Ryder and Margot watched the video Frank had taken. I could hear Ryder criticizing herself for the tiniest of mistakes without a shred of emotion in her voice. She had done incredibly well. But she wanted perfection. She would do even better tomorrow. I felt sure of it.

Her idol, Patrick, came strolling over to visit. This time she would catch some face time with the creep. I hated that.

"Well hello, Margot. Where'd you find your secret weapon here?"

"Oh, hi there, Patrick. I have two new working students this year. This is Lizzy, and this is Ryder, who you just saw ride my Paparazzi."

"Pleased to meet you, girls."

He shook my hand only briefly.

I suddenly realized this was my perfect opportunity. So, I said, "We've met before, at Francesca's farm."

I glanced at Margot, who was now looking at me with interest. Good.

Patrick nodded his head, but moved right along to Ryder, grabbing her hand with enthusiasm.

He held onto Ryder's hand too damn long, not letting go while he spoke to her. He was holding her hand and zapping her with his pale blue eyes. Those eyes were made of ice. I had chills run right down my spine. They weren't making Ryder cold though. Her cheeks were pink.

He said, "I enjoyed watching you, Ryder. My Advanced Young Rider placed right behind you. I'm sure relieved to think you'll be on our team this year."

He finally let go of Ryder's hand and turned to Margot, but Ryder was still looking at him. She hadn't said one word.

"Margot, I look forward to seeing you show Wild Child. I've always loved that horse. He's a tough bastard though. I thought you were going to lose him in the jog and give some one's mare a free breeding."

Margot laughed.

"You're too funny! He is a super horse, but it's my first time down centerline with him, so I have no idea what to expect. I'm sure we won't threaten your supremacy out there, at least not today."

Margot looked impish. She didn't seem to mind Patrick's ribbing too much.

He shook his head and tsk-tsked.

"I know by now not to underestimate you. But anyway, I came over to say that my barn is throwing a party at our stalls tonight with lots of food and drink, and I want to see you and

Frank and Francesca there. Claire doesn't spare any expense, and she'll be devastated if you miss it. And I want to see you girls there too. No excuses. Ryder needs to meet her future teammate Suzette."

After he walked away, Margot muttered to us.

"I guess we'll have to make an appearance, but I intend it to be brief; very brief."

CHAPTER 18

Crossing Over The Line

MARGOT WAS BEING TOO CONSERVATIVE IN the warm-up. I could tell she was hesitant to "unleash the beast." I had never been invited to "coach" Margot, and I wasn't going to start here. But Margot needed to get on with it. I knew Patrick's ride had gone well by the applause. Ryder was sitting with Frank and Francesca in the stands. That was good. I knew she wouldn't be a help to Margot.

This was the beginning of the payoff for Frank's huge investment. Frank and Francesca would be keeping track of all the scores in the class and mentally tracking each ride as a threat or non-threat to Wild Child. I knew that Francesca would be watching Patrick's ride closely too.

I found myself biting the inside of my cheek. This was killing me.

And then I felt a presence at my elbow.

Deb.

Deb gave me a pat on the back.

"She's a wreck isn't she?"

"It's too much pressure too soon, plus that creep Patrick is in her class and was teasing her."

"It's not Patrick; she's always like this. Wait until Gladstone. She'll be running to the bathroom every fifteen minutes."

Deb was grinning broadly, her dimples showing.

Margot and Wild Child were trotting toward us, and as soon as Margot saw Deb, she pulled up.

"Darling, you came. I'm so glad."

"OK, so now that I'm here, get the lead out of his pants. That boy needs to shake his tail feathers."

"He feels terrible."

"He won't feel that way after some extended trot and canter."

"Well, you better stand back, and be ready to pick up the pieces because he feels like he could blow."

"Oh, I've got 911 on speed dial. You've got twenty minutes. Go find the 'on' switch."

And off they went.

I whispered at Deb, "I'm as nervous as she is Deb."

"Well, Wild Child's still an unknown quantity. Some of them change the moment they head up centerline and cross that invisible line at A. We'll see, won't we? That's why it's called a test."

Deb hollered across the arena.

"Give him a kick and go. More. C'mon. More! Now mix it up. Keep him guessing."

Margot was working him with energy now. She had listened to Deb. She worked extended trots to passage, and then back to extended trot, and all the way back to piaffe. And he didn't blow up. He was taking it.

I could see Margot's jaw was clenched, and when Wild Child got too strong, she set him back on his hind legs with a halt and a rein-back. She did an extended canter too, and it was huge; his front legs and shoulders lifted high, and he rolled like a wave over a ground that seemed to shake under our feet when he passed.

God, he was breathtaking in a scary sort of way. I saw he began to anticipate her corrections of halt in a good way and began to stay back over his hind legs, becoming lighter in the reins. Margot felt it immediately too and didn't make the transition to halt again after all, but instead gave both reins, momentarily patting him on his neck and breathing "good-boy."

You rarely heard Margot say that to Wild Child.

Deb smiled again without taking her eyes off of the pair.

"She is so damn good. But she needs a coach. She doesn't really like being in charge. That was Walter's job. She was the good-looking blonde protégée that he could mold into his greatest achievement. If Walter were here, she'd be unbeatable."

"But she's such a good trainer and teacher too."

"Yeah. She is. Reluctantly. It wasn't the plan y'know."

Deb hollered across the arena.

"Now you're cooking! But, don't let him lose his focus!"

Then she spoke softly to me, "But, she'll keep putting one foot in front of the other. Just like the rest of us. She's made of the right stuff."

Deb went over to the ring steward to check if the show was running on time. The answer was clearly yes.

OK, Lizzy, we'd better get the polos off that guy and send her up to the gate."

Deb gave a loud whistle, which garnered some dirty looks from the other trainers and grooms.

I handed Margot a bottle of water and then a clean towel to wipe her sweaty face. I used the same towel to wipe off her boots. Deb was pulling polo wraps off at top speed. Wild Child was puffing, so it was good that when we got to the gate, the other horse was still in the arena, and he could catch his breath. Wild Child looked a little shell-shocked. His eyes got big as he stared into the arena.

As soon as the horse and rider finished, Margot gathered up her reins. Then Wild Child balked. He did not want to move.

Deb sighed. "Stage fright? Really? You are such a bag of hot air, Wild Child. Get your big orange ass in there."

Margot turned his head to her left knee and gave him a jab with her left spur. He caused a bit of a flurry at the gate as he spun around; then she gave him another jab, this time with both spurs, and he jumped forward. I could see Margot's jaw clenched again, and I thought to myself, buddy, don't screw with Margot, she IS tougher than she looks.

Margot had turned the key in the ignition, and what had been a stalled engine was now on full throttle. They went blasting around the outside of the show-arena boards in extended trot. On the short sides, they did passage and then back again to extended trot. She was not going to give him an opportunity to shut down. But of course the first thing in the test was a halt. I was literally quaking. My jaw was clenched too.

And then I noticed Patrick.

And...what the hell? Ryder was standing at his side. Suck up.

Patrick was still wearing his tailcoat.

I knew he wasn't there to wish her well.

The bell rang, and Margot did a halt and a rein-back and then picked up the canter and headed down the centerline.

Deb could not help her now.

A disaster now would leave a crack in the door for Patrick to weasel his way in. Margot could not fail. ...Please God, don't let Margot fail.

Now she would cross that invisible line at "A." I held my breath as they stepped into the arena and headed for the halt at X.

She made too abrupt a halt, but at least it landed nice and square. Margot saluted and moved off before the halt could properly settle. I understood her strategy. No stage fright allowed.

Once they made the turn at "C," I could once again draw breath. I realized I had been hanging on tightly to poor Deb's arm and quietly let go.

They somehow squeaked out every single movement. He two-footed his pirouettes which were a little sticky, and he sort of threw himself weirdly from side to side in the canter zigzags. But boy could he piaffe and passage, and his two-tempis and one-tempis were mistake-free. His canter stride was so dramatic that the changes were flamboyant. Margot had pulled it off.

As soon as she got out of the arena, she was sliding off of him.

"That was the most exhausting ride ever. Please take him for me, Lizzy."

I ran up his stirrups and loosened his girth. His veins were standing up, and he was puffing pretty hard. But I lingered for the score.

Within minutes the score was up.

68.75%

Margot was incredulous. She mumbled through tight lips. "Well, that was an early Christmas gift."

Deb and Margot and I began walking back to the stables. Margot looked wiped out. She unbuttoned her coat and pulled off her hat while we walked. Her shirt was soaked with sweat. Margot never sweat.

Deb took care of Margot while I took care of Wild Child, who was too pooped to snarl at me.

When I got back from the wash stalls, Margot was looking at her video and was restored.

Frank was pouring glasses of champagne. "Lizzy, baby. We beat 'em all today!"

"Even the famous Patrick?"

Frank grinned.

"Yeah, how about them apples?"

Frank and I exchanged high-fives.

We had a few hours to relax, and then it was dress-up time all over again; the awards ceremony.

I was excited about the awards ceremony. I had never even seen one, except on a video of the Olympic Games. But in the high-performance classes, they were required; if you didn't show up, you forfeited your prize.

Ryder and Margot were both winners, so when their class was pinned, they would be leading the traditional gallop. The Juniors were being pinned first; then Ryder's class would be pinned; then the small-tour horses; and then finally, Margot's class.

For the awards ceremony and victory gallop, all horses would be braided, and unlike in the actual competition, they would be wearing white polo bandages. Because of Emma I knew my polos would be professional-looking. I had learned how by practicing putting them on over and over again until they had met Emma's standard of perfection.

The riders too had to be dressed as if competing.

When I first pulled Wild Child out, he was looking pretty grumpy, pinning his ears and reaching to bite my thigh every time I walked around him for grooming and tacking.

When I tried to put on his polos, he started pawing. When I smacked his leg, the polo I was trying to put on, slipped out of my hand and unrolled on the dirty floor.

"Aw crap, Wild Child. Now I have a dirty bandage."

There went my plan for snowy-white perfect polos. I rubbed it on my jeans. I knew we had brought along only a few sets of bandages this white and new-looking. It was no good to go and buy a new set. Until they had been through the wash one time, they were too loose in the weave and just wouldn't unroll properly. Emma had taught me that. Maybe it wouldn't show. I unrolled it and rolled it back up, nice and tight so it would unroll smoothly around his cannon bone.

Ryder was already pulling Papa out of the stall, ready to ride down to the collecting area where they would pin on the ribbons.

Wild Child bowed himself up and whinnied. He wanted to go with Papa. He knew what was up.

"No, no Wild Child, not yet."

Then I really had a problem.

Wild Child was pawing bigger and bigger and leaning into his cross-ties, having a little fit over Papa leaving him. Moments like this reminded me that Wild Child wanted the company of other horses. He certainly didn't want MY company.

I stood back and waited for Ryder and Papa to clatter off. Papa never just walked to the arenas.

I leaned back against the wall and folded my arms. God, I was tired. I was always tired. It seemed like the day would never end. I dropped my head and closed my eyes. I would wait him out. I knew in his mind he was still following Papa down to the arena.

"Lizzy? Are you OK, darling?"

I lifted my head to see Margot looking concerned. She was dressed and ready to ride.

"Oh, yeah. I'm just letting him calm down. He was upset when Papa left."

"I know how he feels. I just dread awards ceremonies."

Well that surprised me.

"Margot they're awesome to watch. And you won."

Margot smiled.

"Well, I have to admit, they are a lot better, and even safer, when you win. I don't think I've ever been run off with when I'm at the head of the line!"

"Well, I can't wait to see you and Wild Child wearing that neck sash!"

"Thank you, Lizzy. Let me give him some sugar so you can get those polos on."

"Don't let him slobber all over your beautiful coat."

Margot pulled off her white gloves and picked up a towel to keep the sticky off her hands.

It worked.

He stood like a rock as I finished his bandages. And the dirt smudges barely showed at all. I slipped on his bridle and led him up to the mounting block.

Margot gathered up the reins, and I could see her hands were shaking. She looked down at me and gave Wild Child a pat on his neck.

"Lizzy, keep a hand on the rein for a minute."

"Sure."

And so I lightly took a hold of her curb rein and walked by her side. I heard her take a deep sigh and straighten up in the saddle.

"OK, Lizzy, you can drop the rein. Just stay close-by."

I dropped the rein, and as we walked people stopped to stare. Wild Child was magnificent, and Margot was elegant.

We could see Ryder's class walking into the arena, with music playing. Ryder was of course at the head of the line, a beautiful sash around Papa's neck. Patrick's student, Suzette, was in second place. So our farm had even beaten Patrick's prize student. I hoped Ryder had noticed. Margot was the better trainer, no matter how famous Patrick was.

The music stopped, and the announcer was reading off names and scores beginning with the sixth place and moving up the ranks. Judges were moving from rider to rider congratulating and shaking hands.

And then it was Ryder's turn.

Ryder's smile for once was not a smirk.

The announcer asked Ryder to lead off the gallop.

Meanwhile we had made it in one piece to the collecting area, and Wild Child had a beautiful neck sash put around his neck. I protected the nice volunteer from being bitten. Then Margot walked circles away from the other horses while I watched Ryder canter by with music blaring. All the horses filed out of the arena except Ryder who took the customary solo lap of honor all by herself. As she turned for home, she slowed him up and broke to a trot, allowing him to make his huge and wonderful extended trot right up to the out gate, where she pulled up to a walk.

It looked like fun. It was something I hoped someday to experience myself. I would be on Winsome, and she would be sailing, tail flying behind her. The music was grand, and for a moment I felt like crying or hugging someone. And then I woke up. This was Ryder's moment, not mine. I was the groom.

I could understand how this was what Ryder was living for; the applause, the music, the first place sash around the horse's neck.

The moment was a fleeting one, but one you would want to repeat, over and over again, if you could.

But with the last crescendo, her music came to a stop, and the next class filed in to subdued music to take their turn. And then they were off, and their winner had her solo lap of honor and was still trotting as she passed us.

Finally it was time for Margot's class to file in.

Wild Child had set his feet and wasn't moving. The quiet entry music was playing.

I walked over to him and grabbed a rein.

"C'mon, Wild Child. If Deb were here, you would be getting a major kick in the pants."

I gave him a pat on his neck. With his eyes bugged out and blowing puffs of hot air out of his nostrils, I led a tip-toeing hunk of a stallion toward the arena.

He stalled out once more, and Patrick walked around us and entered the arena.

"Here ya' go, Margot, I'll pony you in."

I hated how he smiled at her. It was condescending.

But it worked. Wild Child took a big sigh and followed.

And then when they lined up, I was glad to see Margot take her proper place: First place.

Each time a rider's name was announced and the crowd applauded, I saw Margot stroke Wild Child's neck. He didn't move around like the other horses that were nervous. He stood like a rock. But his eyes were too big.

The announcer asked Margot to lead off the gallop; again Wild Child wouldn't budge.

Patrick once again gave her a lead. And then once Patrick had moved ahead of him, Wild Child came alive. He reared up a little, and even that little rear caused a gasp from the crowd. And then he plunged forward, overtaking Patrick. With all the delay he was causing, the line behind them was backing up, horses fretting and twirling to stay in the proper order.

I growled to myself, "Get your ass in gear, Wild Child."

Margot gave him another kick and passed Patrick at a good clip of a trot, and then made a transition into a huge passage.

Now all the horses found their place in the line as the music pounded out the familiar "Blacksmith's song," a classical piece with the rhythmic backbeat of a blacksmith's hammer hitting the anvil.

The crowd was clapping in time to the music.

The placed horses slipped out behind Wild Child, and he didn't seem to realize it until he was turned to head back home. Then Margot allowed him to strike off into a canter. But soon he was taking over and headed for home. He accelerated until it was really a gallop.

Holy crap. It felt like we were having an earthquake.

They zipped right past the out gate, and it took Margot a full circle to bring him back. When she pulled him up, he tossed his head in a complete circle. It was a macho gesture. He was strutting, quite proud of himself.

Patrick and the rest of the class stood outside the gate.

Patrick said loudly, "He's a beast!"

Margot managed to walk toward me as I walked toward her.

She was smiling and thanking those who were congratulating her and gushing over her beautiful new ride.

She slipped off him, and handed me the reins.

"Lizzy, he's all yours now, darling. I need a drink."

I whispered, "Margot, did you mean to gallop like that?"

Margot put her finger to her lips, and said out of the side of her mouth, "I had zero control out there...zero. That just shaved years off my life."

And then she was laughing and joking with all the other members of her class as they filed past us.

Francesca and Frank had come down from the stands and took a moment to congratulate Patrick on his second place, but only briefly.

Frank hurried over to give a sweaty Margot a hug, and then he turned and enthusiastically hugged Francesca.

"What do you think now, Franny? I knew we got us a good one."

The Jacks were bouncing up and down in celebration, and I thought Francesca did look pleased.

Patrick was watching and smiling and had pulled off his top hat, waving it our way.

"Ah, Margot, that big boy just about pulled your arms out."

Margot smiled and winked at him.

"Oh, Patrick, it was a chiropractic adjustment is all. And thanks for the lead by the way. You really helped get us unstuck."

"Anytime, Margot, anytime; now, don't be late for our party."

"Of course, darling; wouldn't miss it."

But Margot had turned her back to Patrick and fiddled needlessly with a girth I had already loosened.

Chapter 19
The Making Of Omelets

Ryder said, "Let's pull braids, Lizzy, and get the barn done fast. I'm ready to party."

I heard Margot moan from the tack room. She walked out in the barn aisle.

"We do need to put in an appearance. But we've got to do this all again tomorrow you two. No late night, girls."

Ryder nodded, "No worries, Margot. I just want to meet Patick's Advanced Young Rider. She'll be in all my classes this year. We'll probably be teammates this summer."

When did Ryder become such a social creature?

Ryder and I still had a lot of work to do, so we were the last to arrive at the party and the thing was in full swing.

Patrick's barn aisle was packed with people eating and drinking. The place was really done up with potted plants and flowers and a little picket fence around the front of his tack stall with rubber chips set down like mulch. His stall curtains had piping and braid and his name in huge lettering. They were red, white, and blue. Each stall had a rubber stall guard and a custom bridle box and tack trunk in front of it, all in red, white, and blue. The whole farm looked decked out to go to the Olympic Games to represent the USA.

The thing that really blew me away were the large framed photos hung on the front of the tack room curtains. All were of Patrick, most of victory gallops, and on many different horses.

The barn aisle was so clean it looked like it had been vacuumed. It didn't even smell like horses, although his were right there. I made a point of checking out Patrick's Grand Prix horse. He stood pressed against the back wall of his stall with his head in the corner, so I left him in peace.

I saw Francesca giving air kisses to some woman I did not recognize. Frank was laughing loudly with a man I also did not recognize. True to his word, Patrick had a table loaded with incredible-looking food. There was even an ice sculpture of a horse in the middle. Geez.

I grabbed a plate and got in line. I was going to take full advantage of free food. I got to the table and was picking up my napkin and cutlery. I turned around to say something to Ryder, but she was gone. Another girl was grabbing a plate, and I noticed she was wearing plastic wrist braces; on both wrists. Something clicked in my brain. I should know this person.

She was a short girl with her hair in pigtails. She looked up at me, and her freckled face lit up.

"Well I'll be damned. It's Mary Sunshine."

Oh yeah, it was coming to me now; her name was Natalie, but clearly she had forgotten my name. Last time I saw her, she was agitating for a barn workers' rebellion and making lewd jokes at the show in Georgia.

"Actually my name's Lizzy. Remember, from the Conyers show in Georgia."

"I know who you are, Lizzy. Hey, I'm sorry about your old horse. Everyone was talking about it at the show; sucks big time."

Even now it made my throat burn to think of Rave. I had to swallow a few times before answering her.

"Thanks, Natalie. I miss him so much. But I can't believe you're still working. I mean, you said you had carpal-tunnel syndrome. I thought you were going to go have surgery on those wrists. "

"Not yet, but it won't be long before I'm flinging off my shackles, and I don't mean the braces either."

"Are you getting out of horses?"

"I'm getting out of that shit's barn if that's what you mean. Here, load up your plate, sister. You're starting to look like Olive Oyl, and anyway, it's all free."

"Hey, I am not Olive Oyl. That's more like Francesca, OK?"

Natalie stood back and eyed me up and down and then took the tongs from the bowl of sesame beef noodles and piled a heap of it on my plate.

"You like Thai, Lizzy?"

"Yeah. I love it."

"Then let's do damage, girlfriend."

Instead of balancing a plate and mingling, we headed off to sit on a curb, away from the crowd, but close enough to watch. It was impossible not to be in a good mood listening to Natalie rant. She was a real malcontent, but a funny malcontent. I found that I really liked her. Letting myself laugh was a great stress reliever from the tension-filled day.

"So, Lizzy. I watched both your trainer Margot and that Ryder girl show today."

"Yeah?"

She was shaking her head while shoveling in a mouthful.

"Shit, Lizzy, they're top class."

"Margot and Wild Child are top class aren't they? He's a tough horse, but Margot pulled it off."

"Yeah, the judges were practically doing the wave they were so impressed. With your trainer now in the hunt to qualify for Gladstone, Patrick's probably shitting bricks. He jumped in late with a new high-dollar horse Claire shelled out big bucks for, and he's no sure thing to qualify. There's only one more qualifier, so if Margot doesn't go, or can't go to it, his spot is safe. If she goes and her average from the two shows is good, she may edge him out. I'd keep my eyes on your horse at all times if I were you."

"Patrick gives me the creeps. He's gotten real friendly with my boss Francesca though, and he's always got that big smile on his face."

"Dogs show their teeth too, and they're not smiling, are they?"

"Natalie, Margot's no dummy. She stays above the fray. I'm not worried about her."

I sounded more confident than I felt.

Natalie was working away at her pile of food and nodding her head.

"You're probably right."

Natalie took a huge bite but just kept talking with a full mouth.

"I like you, Lizzy. I'm sorry you have to groom for Ryder Anderson. She's good, and the horse is better than good, but I can tell that nose of hers is stuck up big time. Arrogance and naiveté are a wicked combo. I'm just saying."

"You're observant. Ryder's all of that, but she's not stupid. No, stupid so far hasn't been her problem. Papparazzi is owned by Francesca and was trained by Margot, and Ryder's damn lucky to get the ride and knows it. But she's naive. She's just out of high school. She thinks she's going to win the individual medal at Young Riders. After that, it's straight to the Brentina Cup and then off to the Olympics."

Natalie guffawed and nodded. She seemed satisfied with the information I had given her and even relaxed. But then she got quiet for a moment and just looked sad.

"I was never quite that ambitious, but I sure could have used a horse like Papparazzi. But I've aged out now. I'm off the radar."

"Oh, you were in Young Riders?"

"Yeah. I had a damn good horse too. But, he's broken. Just like me by that shit-for-a-human."

Her attitude suddenly made sense. Could it be?

"Patrick?"

"Keep your friends close and your enemies closer, I say."

"What?"

"I work for his friend Tommy now. Tommy used to be his assistant trainer, but he has his own business now. They still sell horses together."

Natalie's chin stuck out, and her lips pressed together. I could see genuine anger. She wasn't just all jokes. She continued, "You know when you see these hot-shot trainers out showing and being so successful, you don't see the horses that didn't make it. I'm here to tell you, when they play for high stakes like some of these shit-for-humans, they break a lot of eggs to make their omelets. And they don't care. But my horse, he was my only egg."

"Oh, Natalie. I'm so sorry. Margot isn't like that."

"I've always had to learn stuff by getting my ass knocked around. I guess I'm not too smart. My horse paid for my stupidity. I didn't protect him when I should have."

We sat there quietly for a few moments, looking at a party that was getting louder and louder. I could see Frank laughing at his own jokes. He could barely spit out the punch line. Clearly the free alcohol was loosening things up all around. I realized I had never spotted Margot. She must have made a very brief appearance.

Ryder stood to the side with another girl; both of them were holding beers. She wasn't old enough to be drinking a beer. Patrick was leaning in toward them, waving his hands around and looking very animated, and both girls were clearly absorbed.

Natalie took a big swallow and was nodding her head. "You see that, Lizzy? He's got them hooked, and he's pulling them in. He's making magic. He can put you in a trance. I was like them. It's like joining a cult, but you can't see it at the time. You become a follower. Blind faith it's called. Yeah. Blind faith."

"Hmmmm." I watched a while longer. I was stuffed and getting sleepy.

"C'mon, Lizzy. Let's load up a plate with dessert."

"Oh no, I'll be sick if I eat more."

"Load up a plate for me then. I'll take it home."

I walked Natalie back to her "home." A pickup truck with a camper on the top, parked in a row of assorted campers and horse trailers with living quarters. We traded cell phone numbers. Natalie was a little toughie, but she surprised me by giving me a hug.

"You be careful out there, Lizzy. I'd hate to see you lose your rose-colored glasses. I hope you realize most wannabe working students never make that bump up into trainers. You gotta' realize you are expendable, my friend."

"Natalie. I've been trying to tell you that Margot isn't like that."

"You'll see. You won't get included in a lot of stuff; you won't get to ride the good horses. You either get the horses no one wants to sit on, or the dangerous ones."

"Thanks Natalie, but really, I'm treated well where I am. Right now I just need to go to bed."

"Sweet dreams, Lizzy. I'll see you guys tomorrow, and at the next qualifier. Tommy has clients showing at every dog and pony show in the region. Plus, we've got horses to sell, and to sell them he needs to show them. So I'll be around."

"I wish you weren't quitting, Natalie. I wish you would come work for Margot."

"No way. I saw that Francesca bitch in action. "

"Maybe I'll see you tomorrow."

"Yeah. You take care of yourself."

There was very little light out, and hoses and extension cords ran out of every trailer. I walked carefully away from Natalie's trailer, but it was really dark.

I stepped on something slick that rolled under my feet, and I slipped and fell on my butt.

"Oof."

I was suddenly sitting down, one leg bent and one straight.

I felt around and picked up a large zip-lock bag and held it up, squinting in the moonlight.

Syringes and needles and latex gloves.

Used.

Shit.

Chapter 20

Fearsome Creatures

The dawn was cold and the horizon just beginning to lighten when Ryder and I arrived at the showground.

Wild Child was nested down in his shavings. He looked tired and grumpy, wrinkling his nose and laying his ears halfway back when he saw me.

I understood how he felt. I was tired of horse shows too, and they were just starting.

The loudspeaker came on and crackled with static as it played the national anthem way too loudly. No one was there to hear it except the horses and the grooms and the early morning Training level riders with their unlucky coaches. The FEI divisions wouldn't start for hours.

So I was surprised to see Patrick; and wary.

"Good morning, girls."

His blue eyes passed right over me and fastened on Wild Child, who was now standing at the back of his stall, butt toward the door.

It made me break out in a sweat just to see him eyeing our horse.

He glanced back at me.

"Margot's not here yet?"

Ryder came out of the tack room and eagerly answered.

"Not yet. Would you like some coffee?"

Such a suck up.

"Thanks Ryder, but I came over to invite everyone over to our stalls. Claire has set out an incredible spread. So please come on over. Ryder, Suzette is there; you have plenty of time and I'm sure lots to talk about."

Ryder was nodding, "Sure."

Patrick nodded my way, "You come too, Lizzy."

"Sure, thanks."

Patrick turned, but then stopped and waved at us when we didn't follow. "Well, come on then."

Ryder started to follow and then looked back at me.

Me leaving would leave Wild Child unattended.

"You go on Ryder. I'll be there in a minute."

Patrick said, "Well, I won't guarantee that I can save you a chocolate croissant."

I smiled and nodded, "I'll have to take my chances."

And off they went.

Margot soon arrived. She was dressed to ride, her hair and makeup flawless as usual, but she looked tired.

"Hey, Margot, Ryder is over at Patrick's barn eating breakfast."

"Oh. She did her chores first?"

"Oh yeah. We finished ages ago."

"Good."

"Patrick came over and was looking for you and invited all of us over for breakfast."

Margot seemed unconcerned, "And did you get something to eat?"

"No, I didn't want to leave the horses."

"Darling, you can go get a bite. I'll be here. And look, here come Frank and Francesca."

Chopper and Snapper were pulling Frank down the barn aisle, panting with excitement and periodically choking and gagging.

Frank was bubbling over with excitement.

"Good morning, ladies. Are you ready to do it all again? How's that big red beast I paid too much money for?"

I didn't think Frank was expecting any answers, but it was good to see him enjoying himself, considering what it must cost to keep his operation afloat.

He slapped me on the back. "I just love winning don't you, Lizzy?"

I grinned back nodding in agreement.

Frank continued, "We are causing a buzz, I can tell you. I got interviewed yesterday about him. Can you believe that! Me, who only knows which end bites and which end kicks. On to the next qualifier I say; we're entered. Did you know that? We're going to give our neighbor Claire a run for the money."

Francesca put her arm on Frank's arm. "Don't make Margot nervous."

Margot finally joined in, "Yes, Frank, don't make me nervous."

Frank went to give Margot a hug, but she shrieked and jumped back as the terriers made happy lunges toward her legs. "White breeches, Frank, white breeches!"

"Oh, sorry."

And then we all laughed.

***

THE GRAND PRIX SPECIAL TEST WAS a test of strength, with lots of passage to extended trot back into passage. I knew Wild Child was tired, but once Margot got his blood pumping, he didn't show it. Margot, too, managed to summon the strength for the ride, with Deb kicking her ass in the warm-up arena, that is.

Once Margot's number was up, Wild Child walked into the show arena without a fight. He was a little distracted, and strong in Margot's hand, but because of his wonderful piaffe and passage, his score was almost the same as the day before. Margot was happy to have gotten her debut out of the way. But she was wiped out. The margin was slimmer than the day before. Still, Margot had come out on top, and Frank was crowing.

Ryder had Papa tuned up to perfection for her test, and she was clearly relishing every minute in the spotlight. She didn't seem a bit tired. Today Papa performed with less tension, so the walk was swinging along and covering ground. Her score was verging on the magical 70%. She sat up there with her nose in the air. I noticed Suzette and Patrick were ringside for Ryder's test. And when Suzette rode, Ryder returned the favor, leaning on the rail and clapping and whistling at the final salute. I figured Ryder had a new friend in Suzette, despite having beaten her two days in a row.

When it was time for the awards ceremony, Margot went in and took her sash, but excused herself for the gallop. I knew Frank would be disappointed, but Margot said she did not have it in her today. And I couldn't blame her.

And we were done.

Frank and Francesca disappeared, as did Margot.

Quiet descended on the barn, leaving me sitting slumped in front of the stalls, and Ryder fiddling intently with her phone.

Alfonso showed up to help with the tear-down and to drive the trailer.

Once Ryder and I got Papa and Wild Child off the trailer back at home, Alfonso waved goodbye. We could unpack and do laundry tomorrow on our day off.

It was mid-afternoon, but I went straight to bed.

I was dead asleep when my cell phone woke me up.

"Lizzy."

"What?" I pushed the stem on my watch which lit up the face. My God, it was only seven PM but it felt like midnight.

"It's Deb. Let's go meet the guys for dinner."

"Deb, I was already sleeping."

"Great. You should feel refreshed then."

"I am dead tired."

"I'll drive. You just come along."

I looked in the mirror. My hair was still wet from my shower, and my eyes were puffy.

"I look terrible."

"Marco won't think so."

It hurt like hell to put my contact lenses back in. Soon my puffy eyes were red and tearing.

Marco would need to be blind tonight.

I pulled on jeans and found a nice blouse, but it was wrinkled. I gave it a few shakes and put it on. I braided my wet hair and put on some earrings and lip gloss. Staring at my reflection, I seriously considered diving back under the covers. But that would be the coward's way out.

"Grab your bag and let's go Lizzy."

I turned around to find Deb standing in my doorway.

"Deb. Hey. You're here."

I had never seen her in the main barn and was surprised to see her in the apartment.

"Yeah. I said I'd come and get you. Where's Ryder?"

"Probably asleep like I was."

"Nope. Her car's not here."

"Really. Wow."

Since she had only one friend that I knew of, I knew where she had gone.

"Deb, I have so much to tell you."

I grabbed my bag and followed Deb through the barn. We stopped at Winsome's stall. Winsome poked her head out for a kiss, and I dug a peppermint out of my bag for her. I never went to a restaurant without pilfering a handful, she loved them so.

"She's a beautiful girl, Lizzy."

"She's my treasure."

"Someday you should breed her. It's always good to have one in the pipeline."

"I guess. But not for a long time yet."

Deb pointed to Winsome's brand.

"Hanoverian. Wild Child is the same "W" line, huh?"

"They aren't anything alike, they can't be related."

"Lizzy, look at their hip lines; they're exactly the same. Look at the neck and face. I mean, she is very feminine and he is well, really macho, but c'mon, distinctly "W" line horses."

We walked down to Wild Child's stall. He was standing at the back of the stall. He turned to look at us, pinned his ears, and shook his head. But I could tell it was half-hearted. That boy was pooped.

I examined his conformation with a new eye. Deb was right. He had the same sloping hip line. His tail was set low like Winsome's. She was a much darker chestnut. Wild Child was an amazing burnished copper that glowed like no other horse I'd ever seen. But, yeah, Deb was right.

"But Deb, how could my mare be so sweet, and Wild Child be so mean?"

"They all have mothers. What's your horse's dam line?"

"B."

Deb was smiling, and then she was laughing, "For real?"

"What?"

"So is Wild Child."

"No!"

"Well, temperament isn't all inherited. There's nature and then there's nurture. It all starts with the mare. She teaches her baby a lot about human interaction."

I stood there staring at "cousin" Wild Child.

And then something shifted internally. My Winsome was related, closely, to this incredibly talented bona-fide Grand Prix horse. My little "needle-in-a-haystack" mare that I got for peanuts in a distress sale was related to a horse that Frank Cavelli paid some ungodly amount of money for.

Wild Child's success was now tied, at least in my own mind, to the value of my little liver chestnut mare with the moth-eaten blaze—my Winsome, who meant the world to me.

And I allowed a tiny bit of love for Winsome, intense and deep, to shift to this fearsome creature.

CHAPTER 21

Sitting With The Cool Kids

WE MET PALI AND MARCO AT the restaurant. Seafood. No matter how tired I was, I was never too tired for shellfish, especially dunked in butter. Probably not more date-friendly than tacos. I made a mental note to keep the butter off my shirt.

Pali and Marco were waiting inside for us. Pali had a commanding presence. His voice was deep and musical. He was the kind of person who filled up a room. He embraced Deb enthusiastically, and she almost disappeared in his embrace, she was so tiny compared to him.

Marco and I nodded to each other.

As soon as our waiter came by, Pali was ordering. It sounded like he ordered everything on the menu, plus a couple different varieties of wine. I had to butt-in to ask for a coke.

Pali made eyes at Deb who explained, "Lizzy doesn't drink. Not even a beer."

"Ah, Lizzy. Deb hasn't corrupted you yet?"

"No. But not because she hasn't been trying."

Deb smiled, "I don't know how she does it, working for Francesca and without any chemical assistance. Clearly I couldn't do it."

"Deb, my princess you ARE working for Francesca again. Or haven't you noticed?"

"Ah, but I still drink."

Pali's eyebrows went up, and he started pouring.

Deb was nodding and smiling and saying "more, more, now don't be stingy. I'm drinking Lizzy's share. She can drive us home tonight. Right, Lizzy?"

"Sure. I was the designated driver all through college."

Pali and Marco both looked my way, but Pali spoke, "A college girl?"

"Yes."

Marco asked politely, "What did you study?"

"English Lit and Creative Writing."

Blank looks all around.

And then Pali cooed at me, "What a luxury. Four years provided so you could read novels and write stories."

"Uh, yeah, it was great actually."

Everyone looked thoughtful for a moment.

Deb said, "I started college but dropped out to ride full time."

Pali's eyebrows went up again, "And Lizzy, did you realize what a privileged existence you had?"

"Not at the time, no. I do now."

Marco finally joined the conversation, "What was the best thing you got from that time?"

I had to think about it for a moment, but only a moment, "Reading great books…when I read, I can go anywhere. I can be someone else or enter a different world and a different time, just by cracking open a book. It's magical."

Marco was leaning toward me now, listening, "But Lizzy, this is magic for one, right? It sounds lonely."

"Not at all, if I read a great book, and then share it with you, we can talk about it and re-live it a little bit together. Plus, what if I write a book, and then give it to you and you read it."

"You could do that?"

I felt my cheeks get hot, "I'd like to; someday."

"Then that is what you should do, Lizzy. I think writing for an audience is a kind of performing, too. You create something that comes to life on the page, and someone else enjoys it."

I laughed. "Not like what you do Marco. I mean, writers can hide. A romance writer can be fat and ugly, and you would never know. Her protagonist can be slender and beautiful. In a way, writers are cowards and fakes."

"But it is all a miracle, no? The little black squiggles on a page become flesh and blood in our minds, performing amazing things. That you can do this is something I admire."

"Well what I admire is the connection you have with your horses. That's what I really want. What you have is real; you can't fake it, and you can't hide. I've only glimpsed what it must be like, and those little moments of insight for me just make me hungry for more. I feel so frustrated most of the time that I'm not better than I am."

"Then we admire one another."

Oh God. He was staring at me with those soulful big brown eyes, smiling with those perfect small even white teeth. His horsemanship wasn't all that I admired.

We had a delicious dinner, and I kept the butter off my shirt and didn't spill my drink or do anything else embarrassing. In fact, it was one of those evenings that I never wanted to end. I loved being with them, and they seemed to enjoy me, too. Now that was magic.

I did notice Deb was drinking more than eating, and hanging on Pali's every word.

Pali was making jokes and making us laugh with stories of performances gone awry and special horses in his life, all who had passed on years ago.

I couldn't remember a better evening. I was sitting with the coolest people I thought I'd ever met.

It was like being in high school again, and being invited to sit with the cool kids, not because they felt sorry for you, but because they had decided that you were cool, too.

I excused myself to go to the ladies room, and when I came back, Pali announced that Marco would be giving me a lift home.

Deb smiled and winked at me, showing me her dimples. Suddenly the tag inside my shirt was tickling my neck, making me want to scratch. I resisted the urge.

Marco and I chatted amiably all the way to the farm. He pulled up to the well-lit farm gates, and I gave him the code for the keypad. I had left my clicker in my truck.

Marco was awestruck by the beauty of the farm.

"Pali was right about this place. He talks about it all the time, but I've never been here."

I turned in my seat and nodded at Marco. He continued, "I guess you know they used to be together, and he spent lots of time here. He even gave Francesca lessons. But then it went all to hell so to speak. It always does eventually. Poor Pali."

He parked and we both sat dumb in our seats for a moment. I guessed Marco wasn't going to talk anymore about Deb and Pali. And I guessed nothing else was going to happen either. So I thanked him for bringing me home and got out of the car with a smile and a wave, but before I could close the door he leaned across the seat.

"Lizzy? Can I come in, y'know, just to see the barn and the horses."

Wow. A flock of butterflies lifted off inside my stomach.

"Of course, Marco, I'm sorry. I'd love for you to meet Winsome and of course Kiddo and Wild Child."

His face lit up, "That would be great, really great."

I led Marco into the barn. Instead of flipping on the aisle lights, I flipped on the wash stall and grooming stall lights. But it didn't matter to the horses, and they started whinnying. Most came to the front of their stalls and pricked their ears. I gave Marco an introduction to each one. He spoke softly, and he knew how to caress each horse the way they liked it. Winsome got rubbed between her jawbones. Papa lowered his head just like he did for Margot and got his forelock and ears rubbed.

I thought I could swear that Kiddo looked deeply into Marco's eyes and then sighed, recognizing a benign spirit. He let Marco put his arms all the way around Kiddo's face and totally relaxed in his embrace. But each and every horse seemed to recognize Marco as a friend.

And then we came to Wild Child, who I had saved for last.

"Ah, here he is. Oh, you did not exaggerate, Lizzy."

Wild Child had been watching and waiting. He stood regally on high alert. He tossed his head in circles and charged the front of the stall, with ears pinned and lips curled back.

"See. He's a bastard."

"He really feels threatened."

"He hates me. It's me more than anyone else, I swear."

"And are you devoting extra time with him?"

"No. I do only what I have to."

"Well, I don't want you to get hurt. I mean, be smart, Lizzy. But you need him to understand that you are for him, and not against him. You understand? What can you do for him to ease his mind? What you need to do is work with him after he has been ridden and is tired, so he doesn't have excess energy. Then start doing nice things for him."

"Like what?"

"Start with massages. Since you like to read, I have just the book for you to show you how. Once he begins to enjoy your hands on his body, then you need to be able to ask him to do things. Since you have to handle him on the ground, you must be the master of him on the ground. I can show you some exercises, too."

I had a hard time imagining being the master of Wild Child. But if Marco would be my teacher, I would be a willing student. I wanted to start right away.

"Actually, Marco, I thought I would die getting him through the FEI jog this weekend. He practically pulled Margot off her feet. I think he embarrassed her. Margot told me to work on it before the next show."

"Lizzy, tomorrow is Monday again."

"Yes."

"Your day off?"

"Yes."

"Would you...?"

"Yes."

We both laughed.

"I didn't say what yet."

I smiled. I had sat with the cool kids, but I couldn't play it cool. "Just give me a chance in the morning to unpack the trailer and do some laundry first, OK?"

"OK."

"He leaned in and gave me a sweet little kiss, light as a feather."

And then he said good night and turned and walked away.

I turned off all the lights and stood blind for a moment. My knees were like jelly, but I was flooded with joy.

The only light now was the glowing window in our apartment. I looked up to get my bearings, and noticed Ryder turning away and disappearing.

CHAPTER 22

Fight, Flight, Or Follow The Music

I WOKE UP EARLY, GOT MY cup of coffee, and leaned my head against the apartment window, watching the guys down in the barn aisle. I saw Alfonso leading Wild Child out, done up in his armor. He wore his mega fly mask, the kind with ear covers and the piece that flops over the nose. He had on four bell boots and four sport boots, and his coat was gleaming as usual. He did look tucked up. Probably a little dehydrated from the stress of the weekend.

Wild Child needed to stay in one piece physically, so turnout was a risk; but mentally he needed paddock time. It was a balancing act to keep the body sound and the mind willing. Even the strongest, healthiest horse could self-destruct in the blink of an eye. The same flight instinct that made horses win races could also incite them to run through a fence or tear a tendon. Even a stone bruise could take him out of contention by making him miss the final qualifier.

Worrying about the what-ifs could drive anyone crazy. I was already having a little anxiety-by-proxy for Margot's benefit. It didn't matter to anyone if I looked like a nervous wreck, but Margot had a reputation to uphold; and she had to look like she had confidence in her horse. Still, I wondered if she spent time at home chewing her nails. I figured she did.

I turned around to see Ryder had padded into the kitchen in her pajamas. She was pouring a cup of coffee.

"Hey, Ryder."

She was sipping her coffee. She always took it black.

"Hi." She walked over to where I was standing and looked down into the aisle with me. I had seen her looking at me and Marco last night, but I didn't bring it up. In fact I steered her away from even thinking about mentioning it by talking about our day.

"We still have to unload and do laundry. I'm beat though, how about you?"

I knew instinctively she would deny being tired. But she had to be.

"I'm good, just give me thirty. I want to get it done quick, 'cause I'm blowing this scene."

She was a closed book as usual, but I was not surprised that she had made plans.

"Oh, where are you going?"

"Suzette and I are going to the mall and a movie."

"Nice."

"And you, Lizzy? Going to the circus again?"

Smart ass. I looked at her as she sipped at her coffee. How could she know about my trip to the circus? She wasn't letting on. The girl was cool as a cucumber. So I would be, too.

"Mondays are dark."

"Oh," she nodded. And then she turned away and took her coffee with her.

So she had seen Marco last night. So what? Last night had been magical. I could get used to it.

I stopped looking through the window and instead focused on my reflection. I might not have been a beauty, but I was not plain either. I had been told I had pretty eyes and a good smile; my nose wasn't too big or weird. OK, I had this frizzy mass of hair I hadn't yet captured into a scrunchy, and I had absolutely no curves; which actually was an asset for a rider because nothing bounced. And my arms were starting to look like a boy's. That's where all my curves were. Actually my arms were getting pretty ripped. I picked up my right arm and made like a body builder. I cracked up then, but I also impressed the hell out of myself.

So then I put my coffee down and tried a few more poses, looking at my reflection and amazed at my muscles. I was buff and hadn't realized it. I refocused my eyes down through the window and saw that Alfonso was now pointing up at me with one of the other guys, and laughing too.

Arghh. I waved and turned around to hide.

Of course Ryder was dressed and standing there, and even she was laughing and shaking her head.

"Lizzy, you are such a freak. Pull on your jeans and let's get this done, OK?"

I tried to laugh at myself as I headed to my room to change. But I was embarrassed.

Ryder and I schlepped all the stuff out of the trailer's tack room. We cleaned all the tack and washed out the buckets and feeders and reloaded them. I still had the laminated checklist Emma had made down in Florida so we wouldn't forget to repack or clean anything. We washed the show pads and polos and cleaned out the trailer for Alfonso so he could go park it. Even the stall drapes had to be unfolded and wiped down and then folded up and put back into the canvas bag. The vinyl woven tack room floor mat got the same treatment.

Finally we were done. I could call Marco now, but I waited until Ryder had showered and changed.

I thought she was looking pretty sharp as she swaggered out the door twirling her car keys. She grabbed them in her fist and waved me a silent salute good-bye.

I carried my cell phone down to Winsome's stall and called from there. The guys had gone off to lunch, so it felt private. I was going to call a guy. I had to chew on a fingernail first. I couldn't remember when I last made such a call. I mentally rehearsed the invitation, looking at my watch to allow enough time to get Winsome ridden first.

Marco picked up after the first ring. We were brief; professional. We had an appointment rather than a date.

Winsome had done nothing all weekend except chew grass and swat flies. Although she was the picture of glowing health, covered with dapples with a coat that felt like satin, I noticed she was getting a little too round. She needed a good calorie-burning gallop up my favorite hill.

The damn gate was still a source of anxiety for Winsome, but for some reason leaving the farm was no biggie. It was coming home and hitting the keypad that was still tricky. At least I had managed recently to keep the horse between me and the ground.

By contrast, Kiddo's steadiness had become something I valued more and more each time I swung a leg over his back. He never minded the gate, or anything else for that matter. He was solid gold in my book. The feeling of safety I had on Kiddo was what I knew I needed to bring to my rides on Winsome.

Winsome was still young and flighty and totally my responsibility. If she had a hole in her education, it would be my fault. And I was nothing if not tenacious. We were going to keep at it until that gate phobia was conquered. I would become her Kiddo every day, every ride. As Margot liked to say, "Repetition is the mother of all learning."

We scooted through the gate after it was fully open and turned right, staying to the side of the dirt road. Soon we came to the old wooden gate, open and sagging on its hinges. It was the entry to another world. I went through the gate and turned left, keeping to the edge of the field.

To our right I spotted a family of deer grazing in the middle of the field, flicking their long ears and swatting their tails at the flies. Winsome hadn't seen them yet.

I knew if they flipped up their long white tails and bounded away, Winsome would spook. So I pulled her up and turned her toward them. She froze and raised her head to study them. I tried to take a long easy breath and relax myself in the saddle. She was used to seeing them all over our farm. But still, she was nervous. I could feel her heart pounding, her body pulsing under me. After a minute of standing like a statue, Winsome unlocked and started back up the hill. I had averted a disaster.

The area had been overrun by deer. They had no fear of the horses and were brazen really. The area farmers hated the deer because they carried the tick that spread Lyme's disease. They also hated them because they chewed up gardens and flower beds. Still, I couldn't help but admire their beauty.

I picked up a trot to let Winsome warm up and then let her break to canter. Then I gave her a kick and let her take it up a notch, which she did.

Winsome hunkered down like she had ignited her booster rockets. I left the reins loose and leaned forward, standing in my irons, letting my ankles and knees take up the motion. I floated above her but could still feel her hind legs digging in as she stretched her neck forward, blowing loudly in rhythm with her stride. This took me back to riding side-by-side with Ryan along the canal paths in Florida. The experience never failed to fill me with joy.

As we got to the crest of the hill, Winsome slowed her pace, and I started to pull her up. Then I felt her rear end drop, as if she was about to crumple and drop to the ground. But the deer had simply caught up to us, bounding all around us like they were on pogo sticks. Winsome didn't stick around to watch.

Good riders know by feel when to be passive and when to act. I had made the novice's mistake of being passive in the one split moment at the top of the hill when maybe I could have turned her. But once we were galloping down the hill and gravity was taking over, all chance of control was lost. Winsome was like a boulder rolling down the hill, gathering speed as she went.

She got faster and faster, and it felt like one misstep would send us crashing to the ground. I was bracing in the irons and leaning back, pulling like mad on the reins, gritting my teeth, and thinking about the pain of impact at this speed.

Winsome was bolting for home and had forgotten all about me, the flyspeck on her back.

At least when we got to the road, I got her to come back to walk, or rather a prancing sort of walk.

We got to the gate the same time as Marco.

He rolled down his window.

"Lizzy, look at you, still on your horse."

"Marco! Let me tell you what a miracle that is!"

"She looks hot. Can I help you cool her down and put her up? I don't mind."

"Thanks, Marco. Please put in the code and I'll slip in. My mare hates that gate."

So he keyed in the numbers while I walked Winsome in nervous circles. She wanted to get to the other side. I waved at Marco, and Winsome and I slipped in front of his car and scooted through to the "safe" side. When she got to the front of the barn, she gave a big sigh and her muscles slackened. I jumped off and almost didn't remain standing. My knees were wobbly. I fished a sticky unwrapped peppermint out of my pocket and handed it to her. She happily took the mint and then tried to rub her sweaty head on me, while I gently pushed her away to keep from getting knocked over.

Marco walked up and gave her a pat.

"Two pretty girls."

Marco had his hand on Winsome but was looking at me. I turned away from him to run up my stirrups and loosen the girth.

"Well, this pretty red-head just bolted off with me. It was a near-death experience galloping down that long hill."

"So, this one has a strong flight instinct!"

"I'll say."

"Interesting. And the stallion is a fighter."

I was shaking my head in agreement.

Marco continued, "Horses have two reactions to perceived danger, fight and flight. Some horses are fighters; most just want to run away. Clearly you're going to have to become good dealing with both types."

"I guess then there are two ways to die with horses."

Marco started laughing, "In both cases, this book will come in handy."

He handed me a gift bag.

"Oh wow, thanks. This is the one you were telling me about?"

"I wanted to help you with that stallion, but I see you need help with the mare, too."

"She just panics sometimes, and I have to hang in there until her brain re-enters her body. I actually have a really good relationship with her though."

"You need to read the section on avoiding the panic zone."

"And you use her techniques?"

"I've met her, and she even worked on Bernardo. She helped me a lot. I promise, if you start changing your approach with the horses, everything will get better. But it starts here."

He pointed to his head, "And of course, here."

He put his hand over his heart.

I opened the bag and lifted the book out. The title was about solving behavioral problems in horses.

"I can't wait to start reading it."

"Take time; it's not the kind of book you read straight through, cover to cover. Play with her exercises, and see what the horses tell you. They tell you what they need if you listen."

Marco walked in with me, and I showered Winsome. Of course I stuffed her with carrots. I washed her face and then gave her face a good toweling off, including the ritual rubdown inside of her ears. Even as reactive and nervous as she could be, she loved her rituals. But I had learned that she could press the panic button in the blink of an eye.

I had come to understand that was the way she was hard-wired. Her ancestors had been able to survive, to breed, and to pass on their DNA because they had outrun the lions...or perhaps horse-eating deer.

Marco followed me to her stall as I put her away.

"So when are you going to get this stallion out of his stall and show him to me?"

"I don't know, Marco. Francesca is so weird. I'm always worried about getting into trouble."

"Ah, yes. But you know, Lizzy, having a bad boss only makes you agile and smart. You learn how to manipulate the manipulator, you know?"

"No, I guess I don't know, Marco."

Marco answered me in a firm tone, "Then it is the same problem that you have with the stallion."

"No. That's not it. The stallion could kill me. Francesca could just fire me."

Marco smiled and nodded but was matter-of-fact in his reply, "But they both are the master of you, when you should be the master of them."

"I don't know how that could ever be."

"But it must be, Lizzy. You just need the right instructor, and I know Margot is your riding teacher, but I think I could teach you, too.

He was saying it with conviction. I was momentarily speechless.

"I would like to teach you."

I looked up into his face. He wasn't all that tall, but he carried himself like he was.

If he had been the pied piper, I would have been following his music.

That I would take him up on his offer was, in his mind, a given. And he was right.

Before I could even think, I was getting a carrot out to halter Wild Child. I was already following Marco. Was this the same way he got the horses to do his bidding?

"OK, but just to the grooming stalls. I've never just taken it upon myself to do stuff with other people's horses outside of their specific instructions, especially our top horse that's trying to qualify for Gladstone."

"You are already in trouble with this one. You think it will get better by itself?"

Marco stood back while Wild Child and I did our usual game to get the halter on. He charged the front of his stall, and I stuffed a carrot in his mouth. Then I dodged his teeth while he stuffed his head in the halter and went for my thigh. Next I wrapped the lead rope around his mouth. He did look really dirty from his morning turnout, so I did have an excuse ready if someone came in while I was grooming him.

"So, if he was my horse, Lizzy, I would want him to want to come to me. I would always let him make the decision, and then let him find out it was a very good decision to make."

"And how would you do that?"

"I teach all my horses to come when I call their name. Like anything else, it takes repetition. With the really wild ones, I've even had to withhold food and water, but that's an extreme situation. Not like this one.

"Usually I'll teach it first at liberty in the round pen, but you can do it here. Why not just call him every time you go past the stall. Carry a pocket of peppermints. Don't catch him at first; just call him to the front, and give him a treat; then walk on. Pretty soon he'll be coming every time he sees you. Then you slip on the halter for the treat and take it right back off again. Try it for a week. It won't take too long before he is whinnying every time he hears you call his name."

"That sounds easy enough."

"It's really not brain surgery. Now hand me that lead rope and let me show you a few simple things."

Wild Child looked pissed off, but also wary. Between the stall and the wash stall, Marco had Wild Child do walk-halt-walk transitions along with turns on the forehand. Wild Child even turned to me once, tugging on the lead rope, as if he was asking who was this guy and why would I let this guy mess with him?

But within minutes, Wild Child was engaged in the game of it all. Marco trotted Wild Child up and down the aisle, stopping suddenly and turning quick. Wild Child was soon chasing after Marco with his ears pinned but totally engaged. Marco slammed on his own brakes, and Wild Child stopped on a dime without Marco touching the lead rope. After Wild Child stopped, he surprised me by pricking his ears forward to look at Marco, with a question on his face that almost said, "What now?"

"He's a smart boy, Lizzy. I think I would have a lot of fun with this guy."

"Marco, when he trots after you, he still has the look of murder on his face."

"Ah, well, for now it's part of who he is, Lizzy."

Marco walked him into the wash stall, turned him around, and clipped him to the cross-ties.

"OK. I'll show you some of those massage moves. He's gonna' love it."

Marco started moving his hands over Wild Child. He pressed the skin down and moved it in little circles. Wild Child still had his ears pinned and his lips pulled back. But in a few moments he was dropping his head. Then Marco did some weird stuff. He actually put his fingers in Wild Child's mouth. You couldn't have paid me to try that.

He even massaged the horse's gums and lips. When he was through, he moved to the ears. I usually had trouble brushing Wild Child's head, but now his eyes were half-closed, and his head hung down like he had been drugged.

"You see, Lizzy, aggression is a tiring job. A horse that feels relaxed and secure won't feel the need for it. But don't let this fool you either. If I didn't have the right internal attitude, he would feel it and would feel the need to defend himself, to defend his territory, or to re-establish his dominance. You could still easily trigger a reaction, and it can happen quick as a flash, so stay aware. But this is a great start. I always try to finish every session with a horse that has attained a state of internal calmness."

I was impressed. Marco really was the pied piper. Wild Child couldn't fight it; he had to follow the music.

Just as I had done.

CHAPTER 23
Manipulation 101

EVEN AFTER I MADE MYSELF TURN out the lights, I still tossed and turned, mentally writing my own Disney story. I woke up early, even though I had stayed up late reading. I was going to be the master of Wild Child.

My difficult boss and her difficult stallion were going to make me nimble and smart. Was that what Marco said? I was going to be their master. They would both be eating out of my hand, and they would believe it had been their decisions.

I hadn't yet figured out how this applied to Francesca. But as for Wild Child, I could hardly wait to get down to the barn and try out my magic touches. I had practiced them on my own leg the previous night, and although it sounded like voodoo, I had seen Marco and his horses. If Marco believed in this stuff, then so did I.

Plus, I had seen Wild Child melt under his touch.

Ryder was finishing a bowl of cereal when I grabbed a cup of coffee.

"Hey, Ryder. Did you have fun with Suzette?"

"Yup."

"Whadya do?"

"Hung out. I saw Patrick's farm and had an awesome talk with Patrick. He gave me some great training advice. He has Wild Child figured out, too."

"Yeah?"

Yeah, right, I thought.

"Yeah. And I met the farm owners. They sponsor Patrick and Suzette."

"Kind of like Francesca and Frank with Margot and you."

"Yeah, except they're even richer."

"How do you know that?"

"Suzette."

"Interesting."

"She said the Cavellis are rich, but the Winstons are RICH."

"Yeah, well, you still have a better horse and trainer than Suzette, so you ought to count yourself lucky."

"You know I don't rely on luck."

"Yeah, well, I'm going to start feeding."

"I'll be right there."

As soon as I stepped into the aisle, the whinnying began. I rolled the cart out of the feed room and started dumping out the small buckets of feed that we had prepared the night before. Each horse had a customized diet with special supplements mixed in.

Wild Child rushed to the front of the stall as usual, ears pinned as he raked the stall front with his teeth and then tossed his head in a circle. After his first bite of grain, he shot me a dirty look.

"I am filling my heart with love for you, Wild Child, just like Margot said I should. I will not let you stay this way. You will be a happier horse because of me. You just don't know it yet, but you will."

I took a deep breath and tried very hard to believe what I was saying. Margot said I must love Wild Child, and Marco had said I must be agile and smart and get myself straight in my heart and mind. I must make the horse want to come to me. I must manipulate the manipulator.

These were the wisest people I knew in the business. I had to trust them. I had to believe them, Margot and Marco. Their names even sounded alike. I would use the advice of both because really they were sending me down the same path.

The last horse to be fed was Kiddo, waiting patiently with ears pricked. God, I loved him. He made me want to go in and hug him.

So I did. I walked into his stall and put my arms around his neck.

And I watched him chew his grain.

Poor Kiddo! Grain was dribbling out of the side of his mouth. Surely he needed his teeth done.

Francesca's horses saw an equine DVM dentist twice yearly. Winsome had only ever been "floated" by my vet, which meant he had manually filed down the sharp edges. I was not sure what a vet dental specialist did that was different, but I knew they used power tools.

I also knew that horses' teeth never stopped growing, hence the saying that old horses are "long" in the tooth. Any malocclusion could cause sharp edges to form on the teeth since they didn't get ground down naturally. Those sharp edges actually could cut the inside of the cheeks.

My vet just reached in with a big old rasp and started filing. It was tough work and never failed to have him dripping with sweat. Of course Francesca would have a specialist.

As I wheeled the cart around, I saw a small car pass by, heading for the gate. The driver saw me, too, and waved.

It was Pali.

Leaving.

Good for Deb, I thought. She was master of her own destiny, right? And that was how it should be for all of us.

Ryder had come down and was busy with the hay cart; and I wondered if she had noticed Pali.

I went into the tack room, filled my pockets with peppermints, and put Pali and Deb out of my mind. I had bigger fish to fry.

Today would be the day Wild Child would learn to come when I called his name (with a peppermint).

The problem was all the others decided their name was Wild Child.

This was unanticipated.

Peppermints come wrapped in plastic; and any horses nearby pricked their ears and came to the front of the stall as soon as they heard the plastic crinkle. Soon they were banging on their doors and making cute faces. Especially Hotstuff, who turned his head sideways, stretched out his neck, and poked out his top lip. I couldn't deny a peppermint for a performance like that.

Meanwhile, Wild Child kept his nose pointed toward the back of his stall and his butt turned toward me.

I decided to go ahead and pull him out and begin grooming him for Margot, even if it was early. So I went for a carrot, and I got my lead rope with a chain and a short whip.

I opened his door and there he came, guns a'blazing, all teeth, and a long snake-like neck.

"I love you, Wild Child, you son-of-a-bitch."

OK. So that wasn't quite what Margot meant by finding a way to love him. I knew that.

I held up the whip, and he spun around and showed me his butt again.

I held up the carrot again.

"Come nice this time, asshole."

I put the whip down and held up the carrot.

Same old show.

I held up the whip. He respected the whip, thank God.

We repeated this crazy routine until I gave up, closed the door, and walked away.

Ryder saw me.

"What are you doing? You need me to get him for you?"

"No, Ryder. I'm just trying something, OK."

"Whatever."

She had such a superior sneer on her face. I felt myself getting angry at her. But then I thought of Marco. Manipulate the manipulator. I had to work from the right place in my head and in my heart. I couldn't let Ryder screw with that.

I set out Wild Child's tack and polos. And then I went back.

This time I snapped the carrot. At the sound he spun around. At first his ears were up, but then as soon as he focused on me, they went back again.

So I did something really weird, but intuitive. I went and got Kiddo. And I stood outside of Wild Child's stall and fed Kiddo about five carrots, one right after another.

And OK, Hotstuff and Petey got a couple, too.

Pretty soon Wild Child was leaning out into the aisle begging. Begging! Wild Child!

I put Kiddo away, and he seemed to understand my plan. It was either that or he was just hoping for more carrots, but Kiddo stretched his neck over his gate and intently watched me go back down the aisle to Wild Child's stall.

Wild Child crept to the front of the stall and got his carrot. I put the halter on while he chewed. He had a sulky look on his face, but he forgot to try and bite me, and I had to pull him to the wash stall. He wanted to turn around and look at Kiddo, who was looking at him.

I had put Wild Child off his game.

As I clipped him into the cross-ties, Ryder crossed her arms and smiled. "You are such a freak."

She touched a nerve. "Ryder, for God's sake please stop calling me that."

And she replied in a voice that had no genuine remorse or regret. "Oh, sorry, Lizzy. You know I'm just kidding around."

I said nothing out loud but in my head I said, "I love you too, Ryder, you asshole." The same line I had just used on Wild Child.

Chopper and Snapper came flying down the barn aisle, which of course meant that Francesca was coming.

She looked like she had put her makeup on in the dark this morning. Like a kid with a coloring book, Francesca's lipstick had smeared outside the lines of her lip pencil. I tried to look away quickly, so I wouldn't initiate a conversation, but too late.

"Lizzy."

Just hearing her voice made my heart squeeze in my chest, and a jolt of adrenaline hit the old bloodstream. Francesca ruled through fear and intimidation. And yet, here was a woman with ridiculous red lipstick, and just to go to the barn.

I was afraid to say anything.

So, who was the most ridiculous here?

It was time for the new Lizzy.

Even if it was a tiny little baby step.

"Good morning, Francesca. Uh, you might want to check your lipstick. It's smeared."

There. Good for me.

Francesca raised an eyebrow, and then turned on her heel and headed for the office without a word.

Wow. That was easy. I was a wizard in training.

"Begone, Francesca!" And poof it worked.

Unfortunately she was back out in a moment and headed my way. My heart started to pound. I put my back into currying Wild Child.

Francesca stood silently watching. Her little terrier minions were stationed on either side of her. I could feel all three sets of eyeballs on me. Finally she spoke.

"Well. As I was about to say, since you and Margot are hacking out in the afternoons together, Ryder will now help Deb in the afternoons with the young horses, at least this month while we are working on getting Wild Child fitter."

"Oh." I felt a surge of jealousy. Deb was my friend, and I didn't want to share. OK, so now I was being really childish. I offered, "I can still go up in the evenings afterwards."

Francesca made a wicked little smile that was more like a grimace. She was taking perverse pleasure in realizing this made me jealous. I realized I had just shifted the power back to her.

"No need, Lizzy. You can't do everything, and Ryder needs to pull her own weight."

"Sure. OK."

Francesca started to turn around to leave. But I needed to tell her about Kiddo. I needed to step in for his sake, "Francesca?"

"Yes."

"Kiddo needs the dentist."

"And how would you know that?"

"I noticed he's having trouble with his grain. I'm sure it's his teeth."

"Cara usually takes excellent care of her horses."

"I'm sure she does. But..."

She waved her hand dismissively, before I could describe how the grain was dribbling out of his mouth. I wanted to show her I did know what I was talking about.

"I'll call and make an appointment."

Francesca had just taken a direction from me.

I kept my smile to myself.

I had Wild Child all tacked up and ready for Margot far too early. So I massaged him slowly, trying to imitate Marco's magic circles.

I did slow pulls on his forelock, while keeping a sharp eye on his mouth, and then grabbed small sections of his mane and pulled slowly. He was not as compliant under my hands as under Marco's.

He was suspicious and periodically snapped half-heartedly.

I thought he was sure this was some kind of trick. Surely I was going to perform an unpleasant procedure. He was guarding himself.

And I was always on the watch, too, ready to guard myself from him.

Margot was, of course, right as usual. I was the only half of this duo that required this relationship to change. He had no intention of changing. He had only the drive for self.

Margot's words were still in my head. I had to find a way to love him first if I had any hope for a change from him.

Because Wild Child was more of a biter than a kicker, I tried some of the tail massages from the book. At first he snatched his tail back out of my hand and gave me a swat with it. So I backed off and instead massaged the very top of his butt, and then slowly moved back down the dock. He started to relax. He rested one foot on the toe, and his tail went slack in my hand. We were both breathing slower.

"Well, I'll be."

I hadn't even seen Margot.

"Oh hi, Margot."

"Darling, look at Wild Child. I've never seen him looking so...normal."

"I'm taking your advice, Margot. I'm going to find a way to love this guy. I'm going to make him a better boy, and then maybe he'll behave in the jog!"

Margot laughed, "Now if you can just make him lighter in the contact and easier on my body!"

"You never know, Margot, maybe it will help."

"Darling, I appreciate so much that you care."

"I want the world to see how great you two really are."

"You sound just like Emma. Let me get this ride over with so I can ride Hotstuff. Wild Child is work. Hotstuff is like a Labrador Retriever. All he wants is to please me."

That made me laugh, because it was true.

"Yes, I'll bet he would just keep bringing you a spit-covered tennis ball until you had to hide it."

Then we both laughed.

I pulled Wild Child out of the cross-ties. He still made a snarly face at me. Margot was talking on her phone.

"Yes. Come on. Deb, darling, I need your help. OK."

"Lizzy darling, bring the video camera in about fifteen minutes, OK? It's in the office."

"OK. Cool."

Ryder started grooming Hotstuff, and I went into the office for the camera. Of course Francesca was in there.

"Hi, Margot wants me to video her ride on Wild Child."

"Oh. Good idea. It's in the top drawer, Lizzy. I'll come too. I'd like to watch."

I'd never seen Francesca and Deb in the same vicinity. But I couldn't think of a tactful way to mention to Francesca that Deb was in the indoor.

So we all traipsed to the indoor, me with the video camera and Francesca with Chopper and Snapper in their usual places as the advance guards.

The dogs didn't know about the rule of yelling "door" before entering the arena. When we got there, Wild Child was snorting and arching his neck.

"Francesca, I was just trotting down the long side when your little devils popped into the ring. He almost spun me off."

Francesca froze in her tracks. She wasn't listening to Margot. She was looking at Deb with her eyes narrowed.

"Don't you have work you should be doing?"

Deb looked uncomfortable. It was unlike her.

"Margot asked me to be her eyes on the ground today."

Margot blew through her nostrils loudly, clearly still irritated with Francesca about the dogs.

"Oh for goodness' sake Francesca, I need Deb's help. She has so much more experience than either of the girls. She shouldn't be shut away up in the breeding barn."

Francesca lifted her chin. "Of course Margot, whatever you need."

"Thank you, Francesca."

Margot straightened up and shortened her reins. "OK. Let me do a few transitions, and then I'll canter down centerline and try these damn zigzags."

Francesca and I sat down on the viewing stand. Margot called over her shoulder to me.

"Lizzy, please video this. I want to study it later."

"Oh. OK"

I had totally forgotten why I was there.

So Margot rode through the zigzags. Down centerline and three canter half passes to the left; a flying change; then six strides of canter half pass to the right; a flying change, which counted as the first stride back to the left to the count of six; a flying change and six more strides to the right; then three strides back to centerline; another flying change; and a turn right at "C."

The whole thing was a highly technical test, exponentially more difficult than the dreaded walk pirouettes that almost did me in.

Wild Child got through it, but he flung himself side to side, just as he had done at the horse show. It must have gotten a low score.

Margot made a transition to walk and sighed. She was sweating and shaking her head.

"You see what I mean?"

Deb crossed her arms, "OK. Don't panic."

"Darling, if you could feel this! By the end of the line, he's so heavy he's like trying to steer a Mack truck. I've lost the power steering."

"Yeah, actually, it's pretty amazing that he makes it at all."

We all stood there.

Francesca cleared her throat, "Why don't you walk through it, Margot? You had me walk through the one from Fourth level."

Deb looked over at Francesca, and Francesca lifted her chin like a challenge. I thought I saw the wheels turning as Deb turned to Margot.

"Francesca is right. Slow everything down and see what you feel. That's what you'd tell me. You need to feel where it goes wrong."

And whether they believed it would help or not, a silent agreement was made between Deb and Margot right there on the spot to try it for Francesca.

It turned out to be useful. I could see Wild Child start the half pass without Margot. When Margot tried to prevent him from half-passing the new direction, he got his legs all tangled up and wobbled like a drunk.

If there hadn't been so much pressure for Wild Child to "get it right," we would have been laughing. But no one laughed. Margot walked back over.

"Well that WAS illuminating. He can't even do it at the walk. No wonder canter is so hard."

Deb replied, "Those Grand Prix half passes are steep, and his stride is huge. To get to Grand Prix, he's been pushed beyond his level of balance."

"Yes. I agree. But I have to do this again in another week. What now, Deb?"

They stood there and looked at each other. Deb put both hands over her mouth, pulling downward and then crossed her arms again.

"He's not going to change his technique overnight, but we can make it better by having him anticipate going straight forward instead of sideways. That, plus, you're going to have to make a smaller stride."

Margot nodded, and Deb continued, "No sliding sideways allowed. That's when he loses balance. Just do the three to the left, and then don't do the change until he remains straight and in-front of your driving aids. Take as many strides as you need. If it works out, start the next one, otherwise don't."

Margot nodded, and Deb continued, "And let's not do the pattern from the test before the next show. Let's keep him guessing, and maybe we can get him back on your aids."

Margot's face was serious, "OK. It's worth a try."

Deb nodded, "Yeah. And Margot, one other thing."

Margot was already walking away but turned and looked over her shoulder. "Yes?"

"Chill, baby. It's going to be fine."

Now that was the Deb I knew and was growing to love. She turned to me, winked, and smiled in the broad way that brought out her dimples.

Francesca was not amused, and she showed her irritation by barking at me.

"Lizzy, film it please."

"Oh, sorry, Francesca."

Margot repeated the exercise three or four times.

It wasn't the Grand Prix zigzag, but I saw how it got Wild Child guessing, which brought him onto Margot's aids instead of his own program. That was a good thing, and he stopped doing the crazy lean and slide. And I got it all on film.

I led a sweaty Wild Child back to the barn with his stirrups run up and his girth loosened.

Ryder was unclipping Hotstuff from the cross-ties.

"That was a long session."

"Yeah. Margot is trying to fix Wild Child's canter zig-zags. Remember how he was sliding at the show?"

"Oh that. Patrick and I were talking about that yesterday, and he told me how Margot could fix it."

All I could do was wince.

CHAPTER 24

Bonding

"LIZZY, IT'S NO BIG DEAL, REALLY. Why are you so upset?"

Deb was pushing magazines out of the way so I could sit and have a cup of tea with her.

"I'm not sure."

That was a total lie. I was jealous. I wanted Deb and all her lessons to be for me exclusively.

"It's Francesca, right? It's always Francesca."

"No. This time it's not Francesca. It's just that Ryder gets to ride the good horses. And she is going to New York next week with Francesca and modeling for High Horse Couture. She'll probably get to keep the breeches, too. She thinks she's going to the Olympics, for God's sake. And now she'll be with you every afternoon. Working with you up here was something I got to do that Ryder didn't."

Deb smiled and shook her head.

"Lizzy, it only makes sense. Anyway, those rides with Margot, those are golden. You get one-on-one time with Margot, and you are really helping her. You certainly don't want Ryder taking your place on Kiddo do you?"

"No! I love those rides with Margot."

Deb leaned toward me, eyebrows lifted, exasperated. "OK Lizzy, you sound like you're twelve years old."

"Yeah. Sorry. I emotionally regress sometimes."

This made Deb laugh a loud. "Hah. You really are a college girl after all. I haven't met any twelve-year-olds who talk about emotional regression."

I was chuckling right along with her, but self-conscious, too, at how desperately insecure I must appear.

I had given up everything to be in this place, to have what these women (the Debs, the Margots, and even the Ryders of the world) seemed to own by right. And some days I was hanging in there by the slenderest of threads. I rarely put my insecurity into words, but I was on a roll.

"It's just that Ryder already has an inflated opinion of herself. And she's hanging out with Patrick's Young Rider now. So I have to hear about the famous Patrick, and how great he is, and how rich his sponsor is."

Deb sighed again. "Hey, the horses will take care of that in time. They always do. In the meantime, don't let her get to you."

"You're right. I need to remember how young she is."

"Speaking of young, my little twelve-year-old, I'm on foal-watch, and any time you want to come up and sit with me, you're welcome. I've moved my chair right outside the foaling stall. Wink is showing all the signs, and I know her well by now; she'll wait until it's dark and quiet, and she'll foal quickly."

I had forced Deb to take pity on me. I should have been ashamed of myself, but that twelve-year-old inner-self was celebrating. I had gained myself more Deb time. I won.

"I've never seen a foal born. That would be amazing."

"It never ceases to be amazing. It's a privilege to be witness to a miracle."

Then I couldn't help myself. I said it. "And can we just not tell Ryder about it? She worked for a vet in high school and would probably deliver it herself "C" section, and then be written up in the newspapers. In fact, Francesca would alert the media, and she'd be on the evening news."

Deb joined in, laughing, "Wearing High Horse Couture breeches!"

Then we both cracked up.

"OK, Lizzy. This one's just for you and me, OK? But let's be casual about it. I'd hate to be accused of, what did you call it… emotional regression."

"OK."

I waited until after dark and then crept up the hill. The first night was really fun. It reminded me of all those wonderful sleep overs in high school when no one sleeps. Deb and I didn't braid each other's hair or put on makeup. But we did talk boys.

She asked me all about Cam, and then I volunteered about Ryan. But there my story ended. And I didn't want to jinx anything about me and Marco. Of course there wasn't anything to tell. Yet.

And I asked her about Pali.

She said she fell in love first with his riding and training, and then she fell in love with him. He was a good man. But when Pali and Francesca had their big falling out, Francesca had made Deb choose. And she chose Pali. Who wouldn't?

But in time, she realized she was not the woman Pali really loved. She could never replace Marco's mother, and once she understood that, the life of the circus became too hard a life for her. She wanted to come home. She wanted to come home to Margot and home to Regina. She wanted to come back to her little house at Equus Paradiso farm.

But Francesca was punishing her for choosing "the Gypsy" over her, didn't want her back, and told her so. Margot almost lost her job fighting over it with Francesca, but Margot and Frank had gotten Deb her job back.

The problem was she still loved Pali very much. But she would never leave the farm again. If she did, the door would shut behind her forever. She knew that.

Those nights with Deb, sitting up late talking, were precious to me. I really did have something that Ryder did not.

A real friend.

Ryder finally did ask one night where I was going. And I didn't lie. I told her I was sitting up with Deb on foal watch. But I didn't invite her to join me.

By night number five, I was totally exhausted. Deb greeted me and simply turned me around and pointed back down the hill.

"Forget it, Lizzy. I'll come get you; promise. You are a zombie, and zombies make terrible dressage riders."

To be honest, I was grateful, even though I argued first before agreeing. I was so tired when my head hit the pillow, I felt myself falling right through the mattress and pillow, like Alice in the rabbit hole, and I was instantly unconscious.

I saw Marco riding toward me. He was riding Bernardo bareback and bridle-less. He reached out his hand to pull me up behind him. We had to hurry; we had to get away. My arms felt like lead; I couldn't lift them; and I couldn't take his hand. He would have to leave me. There was no time. I felt his hand reach out and touch my shoulder, and I heard my whispered name.

"Lizzy."

Where was I?

"Lizzy, wake up. Hurry or we'll miss everything."

The whiteness of Bernardo's coat dissolved into a mist, leaving only the lightest of touches on my shoulder.

I rolled over and opened my eyes to find Deb sitting on the edge of my bed.

"Wink is about to foal. Don't change; just put on your shoes and grab a jacket."

Deb and I crouched next to the water buckets, our backs against the stall wall, trying to be invisible.

The chestnut mare was clearly uncomfortable, but Deb reassured me. Wink had done this many times before. Deb said those births had gone well. I felt squirmy with excitement and cold in the damp air.

Wink was sweating. She circled around and then lay down in the deep straw bedding. A horse down the aisle whinnied softly.

Wink settled in the straw and then turned to look at her tail. A placental sack bulged, and two little white tips of hooves poked at the sack.

The little guy, or girl, was coming, and I could see the front feet and nose. My heart was pounding when the water broke and nostrils broke through, opened, and drew in their first lungful of air. Thank God. He was breathing. Deb crawled over and pulled the sack away from the head and freed the shoulders. Then he just slipped out and lay in the bright-yellow straw. Wink turned her neck around and gave a low-pitched whinny. A chorus of whinnies erupted from the rest of the barn.

I crawled over to be next to Deb. Deb put her arm around my waist and gave me a hug as I grabbed Deb by the wrist.

The little guy had a large star on his forehead; he appeared to be bay. His coat was wet. Little brown tufts of hair poked out of his tiny dark ears. He shook his wobbly head and then looked around. Deb lifted one hind leg to have a peek. A colt. We crawled back to our spots against the wall.

I wiped tears from my face. I was so grateful that Deb had gotten me out of bed.

I said, "Welcome to the world little baby," and I practically choked on my words.

The mare licked her newborn. Her tongue did not lick like a cat's or a dog's, but poked the baby here or there, sometimes only hitting the baby with the underside of her tongue. Since horses have a blind spot directly in front and directly behind, I wondered if she could see where she was licking.

But her baby felt it. He lifted his head and bobbed it.

Deb stepped out of the stall and came back with a small jar.

"It's a sterilized jar with iodine. The navel cord has to be thoroughly saturated so it can't get infected. I mean, the stall is full of bacteria no matter how hard we try to clean it."

Deb put one hand under the baby, dunked his navel stump into it, and held it there for a few moments, kind of swishing it around.

"There you go little man." She backed away.

Soon the foal was trying to unfold his front legs. He was barely a skeleton covered in hide. How could such a feeble little creature survive?

Within an incredibly short period of time, maybe twenty minutes or so, one spidery front leg jerked forward, landing on its first joint. He heaved forward onto the folded joint and immediately flopped over into the deep straw.

I caught my breath. Tears stung my eyes. Would it be a terrible thing to help the helpless?

I turned to Deb, "Can't we help him?"

She said, "He is a creature made to rise and run. It's his first test of survival. He's safe from predators. Just watch. His mama is watching. She'll cheer him on."

My knees ached. I longed to get up. I longed to help. But I willed myself to stay immobile.

Another attempt by the foal landed the other front leg forward to join the first. The hind legs pushed against the straw floor, the hock joints trembling. Again he did not find his feet and flopped over.

The mare stood, and reached down again to lick her baby, leaving her head down low. Once again, he hoisted his butt up into the air, his front legs splayed out. He hung there half up and half down. Wink's nose touched his curly short bit of tail gently as if to lift him.

"Get up, little baby," I breathed softly. "Get up."

He wobbled again and flopped over.

I thought to myself that he was doing it all wrong. That's not how horses get up. Front legs first and then the hind legs. Shouldn't the mare be helping him in some way?

"Deb, I think something is wrong." I looked over at her, and she was solemnly watching the foal.

"Don't panic just yet, Lizzy. Give the guy a chance."

But I couldn't help myself, I started to panic. I found myself tearfully breathing out the words.

"Please, little thing, stand up. Someday you will be a big fancy dressage horse. Someday you will fly across the diagonal in extended trot. But it all starts here. Or God forbid, it all ends here. Stand up, God damn it."

Once again I felt Deb's reassuring arm around my waist.

"Lizzy, calm down and watch a little miracle."

The foal launched himself again. This time front legs first, and then the hind legs. Up. He was up! Oh my God, he was finally up.

The mare whinnied low and deep.

And a small high-pitched whinny answered. I felt like cheering. Then Deb and I heard steps coming down the aisle. A familiar voice whispered.

"Hello, my darlings. Everything go OK?"

"Margot!"

The stall door that had been open only a crack opened wider. Margot's hair was down. She looked sleepy, but beautiful and somehow younger. She exclaimed, "Oh Mama Wink, look at your beautiful baby!"

Margot walked right past us, right to Wink, and wrapped her arms around the mare's neck. I slowly rose, my knees stiff as all get-out.

Margot turned to Deb. "Thanks for calling. I got here as soon as I could."

Deb walked around to lift the mare's tail and carefully tied up the placenta that was hanging out, still to be passed.

"She's still got to pass the afterbirth."

Margot stepped back and took a long look at the colt before speaking.

"Another beautiful colt. I think Francesca will be happy to have another Bounce, and so will you, Lizzy."

"Deb, is he weak? I was so afraid, he kept falling down, and he was getting up all wrong."

Deb turned around to look at me, still reassuring.

"Everything's going to be fine, Lizzy. Stop worrying. He looks perfect to me. Let's step outside the stall; he needs to nurse and bond with his Mama. Wink will guide him; she's an experienced Mama. That first nursing is when he gets his colostrum. Meanwhile, I'll call Doc to come give him an exam. But you don't look so hot. Are you OK, Lizzy?"

"Actually, I feel a little lightheaded."

I noticed Margot and Deb exchange glances. Deb spoke again.

"Hey Margot, I've got some of that imported coffee you like, and I baked scones last night. I've got that good marmalade, too."

"Deb darling, I can always count on you. Lizzy and I will go start the coffee. You stay with Wink. I think once the foal starts nursing, she'll pass that placenta."

Deb nodded without taking her eyes off the mare.

"You guys bring me some coffee with cream when it's ready."

I followed Margot on shaky legs, and when I caught up with her, she too put her arm around my shoulders. "As soon as Wink's passed the placenta, Deb can show you how she imprints the foal. You see, the training starts already, we are teaching them trust."

"That little baby looks so fragile. Do you ever get over it; the fear."

"It's the loss of control. We pretend that we have control. And sometimes it really feels that way. After all, we chose the stallion, we caused the breeding. But at the critical moment, it always strikes me that control is an illusion. We are simply spectators of something large and grand. That, my darling, is awesome more than fearsome."

"Well, I don't know how any of them survive to become dressage horses."

"We just do our best."

Margot and I carried out a coffee for Deb. I watched the two of them, heads bent together, examining the new guy. Margot put her hand on Deb's shoulder. The sight reminded me that they had a long history.

Deb looked over her shoulder. "Margot has to christen the baby. But while she thinks about that, come over here and help me imprint this one."

I walked over and found myself smiling. The foal had amazing whiskers, long and curly. They kind of matched his hairy ears. Deb wrapped her arms around the baby and then ran her hand down his leg and picked up his little hoof, which didn't really look like a hoof yet. The foal wiggled at first but then relaxed. Wink was chewing hay and ignoring Deb. She'd seen this all before, and she was tired and hungry.

"Here, Lizzy, look at the underside of the hoof; feel them. They're called feathers. See, this will be the frog."

The underside of his hooves reminded me of those plastic plants in fish tanks. They were white and soft.

"Is this normal?"

Margot and Deb both chuckled.

Then Deb picked up all four hooves and patted them as if she was the farrier. She played gently with every part of his body, even putting her fingers in his mouth and rubbing his ears. She rubbed all over his body with a soft towel as I watched, transfixed.

Wink finally passed her placenta. Deb examined every inch of it to be sure she hadn't retained any. She stretched it out in the aisle and showed me.

"See, Lizzy, here's the tear where the foal came out. This is the amniotic sac; here's the umbilical cord; and these are the horns. You absolutely have to see both, the smooth pregnant horn and the wrinkled non-pregnant horn. If she retained any, she would soon be really ill. OK, and this weird brown spongy thing, well it's called the Hippomanes. It all appears to be here."

She was satisfied and wiping her hands on her jeans. Then she turned to Margot. "All right, Margot. Are you telling us now, or do we have to wait?"

Deb and I both looked at Margot, and she had a coy little smile. "Are you two ready?"

Deb said, "I'm bracing myself, since they seem to live up to their names around here."

"Well, he's a Weltmeyer/Brentano II, so he ought to be a big impressive boy. They tend to be elastic with a super walk. But I also expect quite a bit of power. I know it's hard to imagine looking at this little boy and imagining what will be, but I hereby christen this foal..."

We both leaned forward.

"Bazooka!"

Deb groaned. But I didn't.

"I love it, Margot!"

"Thank you, Lizzy. I think it has a nice touch of whimsy, at the same time a Bazooka is a kind of weapon. I used to ride a horse named Boomerang, which is kind of similar, and that one was a super horse. We can call this little guy Zooky for short."

Deb nodded, "And when he launches us, we'll have you to thank.

Margot grinned and then turned to me.

"Now Lizzy, go and wake Ryder up. I don't want her to feel left out, and I'll go call Francesca and Frank. They all deserve to share in the joy."

I headed down the hill, feeling guilty about how I had conspired with Deb to exclude Ryder. And I wasn't proud of myself.

But I had loved every scary wondrous moment of it.

CHAPTER 25

Fear Of Falling

FRANK PULLED HIS CAR UP TO the front of the barn in a way that no one could miss it. It was a tiny, sort of mossy-green convertible, with the black leather top down; buffed to a high shine. He strode down the barn aisle, his voice booming and waving a brown bag around.

"Lizzy, Ryder, come see my latest folly, girls."

I set down my brush and looked over at Ryder. She had a smirk on her face, but picked up a hand to wave at Frank and said, "Cool car."

I left Winsome in the cross-ties and started walking his way.

"Wow Frank, what kind of car is that?"

Frank stopped in his tracks and looked mock horrified.

Frank pointed back down the aisle at his car.

"Lizzy baby, that's a Jag, a classic XKE."

"It's pretty."

He back-tracked to the car, and I followed him.

It was clearly old, but lovingly restored. The interior was tan leather and polished wood. Even the knobs and dials were polished chrome and wood.

"Frank, it really is a work of art. I'm impressed."

"Thank you, Lizzy. This is my kind of ride. Now where's Francesca? It's time to fess up."

"She's having her lesson with Margot."

"This guy in the village, he restores old cars, and I've been keeping my eye on this one. He finally finished it and gave me a call. He knew he had a sale. I just couldn't play it cool."

"Kind of like us and horses."

"Except cheaper."

Frank looked down at his bag.

"Oh and of course the bakery is there, too. You guys probably know about the bakery right?"

"No."

"You're kidding me?"

"No Frank, I'm not. And I might add I've been missing your donuts."

"I guess I've been falling down on my job. But for cryin'-out-loud Lizzy, haven't you explored the area at all? These lemon squares are to die for. Here, make sure Deb gets one, OK. They're her favorites."

Frank handed me the bag. I walked back to Ryder, dipping my hand into the bag and fishing out a lemon square. I had to close my eyes after taking the first bite. It reminded me of the homemade pies my Mom used to make. None of that fake lemon gel stuff. No, it was real and tart and sweet all at the same time. The pastry was dusted with powdered sugar, and it melted on my tongue.

"Oh my God, Ryder, we have to go find this bakery."

"You can if you want, Lizzy. You're skinny as a stick."

"You are too, Ryder."

"Well, I don't like sweets."

I looked at her like she was from Mars.

"How can you not like sweets? That's not normal."

Ryder shrugged and continued brushing Petey.

"Ryder, I learned in college that all babies are born with a taste for sweet; that and a fear of falling."

"Well, Lizzy, I am not a baby anymore."

She looked straight at me, did a two-beat pause and then continued.

"I don't care for sweets, and I don't worry about falling off because basically I don't do it."

Smart-ass; everyone falls off, I thought. I had never seen her come off, but she of course had seen me prostrate in the pansy bed. And it hurt, but it was part of the deal if you rode horses.

I tried to smile. "Good for you then, that means more lemon squares for me and Deb. In fact since you go next, I'm putting Winsome back in her stall and taking some up to Deb. I'll be right back."

"Fine by me, but shouldn't you save some for Margot and Francesca?"

"I think these are for us. But I'll go ask to be sure."

I walked toward the indoor and stopped a few feet from the door. I really wanted to shove one more in my mouth, but I shouldn't be a pig. I opened the bag and started counting squares. One, two, three, four, five, six... God, Frank must have bought them out of lemon squares. Maybe I should go ahead and offer. Margot might like one. I checked my watch. I had plenty of time. After I offered I could go have a quick tea and lemon square break with Deb.

I knew Bazooka and Wink were getting turned out for the first time today. Maybe I could watch. I was ready to yell "door" but froze instead.

Raised voices. Actually one voice, Francesca's.

"God damn Gypsy."

Then Frank spoke.

"I shouldn't have even mentioned it. Francesca, what does it matter really?"

"Frank, you know he'll worm his way in here again. Time to lock up the silverware. Next thing you know, Lizzy will be under his spell. And you remember he has that good-looking son."

Then Margot chimed in.

"Really Francesca, don't get too involved, please."

"He's a liar and a thief and worse. You know that. We don't need his kind around here again. If we need a man to help with the horses around here, we can call Patrick. Margot, can't you tell Deb to keep her trysts off my property? I mean Ryder is still a minor."

Frank's voice was now pleading. "Baby, come take a ride with me in the Jag and just drop it, OK? The girls will put away Lovey."

Then I couldn't hear anymore. The voices were lower, and I was nervous about being seen. So I turned and headed up the hill, clenching my bag of lemon squares, one of them now curdling in my stomach.

I thought, Francesca was too late. I was already under Pali's spell, or rather the spell of his good-looking son.

I found Deb curled up in the stall, with baby Bazooka napping in her arms. Wink stood over them both, a hind leg resting and her head drooping. She picked up her head, and her ears swiveled as I approached.

It is almost impossible to sneak up on any horse, and even trickier to sneak up on a mare with a new baby. But Wink was not a nervous Mama.

The foal slept with his head in Deb's lap.

I waved at Deb and then held up the bakery bag. She held her finger up to her lips, but smiled. I stood and marveled at how tiny Bazooka was now and how big I knew he would become. His legs were long, his knees big and bony, his neck short, and his mane and tail nothing but little wispy curls.

Deb whispered to me, "Hey Lizzy. What ya' got there?"

"Frank brought us lemon squares. Ryder doesn't want any, so more for you and me."

"Lucky us. Hey stick around a few minutes? I'm going to turn Bazooka and Wink out for the first time."

"Oh, I'd love to see that."

"As soon as he wakes up, and then he'll want to nurse a few minutes. Wink likes to show off her baby, and the other horses are fun to watch, too. They know they have a new member of the herd. It's really important for Bazooka to get moving on hard ground. It will straighten out his legs and stretch his tendons. This deep straw doesn't help with that."

As if on cue, little Bazooka lifted his head. Then Deb got up, and Bazooka did, too. It was still a rather awkward effort, looking like Bambi with his long bony front legs splayed wide.

He went to the milk bar straight away. I leaned in to watch his little tongue cup the teat, pulling it up against his upper gums, and then he gave a little tug and went to town.

"Well Deb, he certainly seems like he's gotten the hang of nursing."

"Wink is a good, patient Mama. She stands like a rock."

"She is indeed."

"OK, I'm going to put his baby halter on, and then I'll lead Wink out. I walk her really slowly since new babies get confused by doors and gates, and we don't want Bazooka on the wrong side of either. Baby can get panicked."

"You mean they don't just follow."

"Well, mostly they do, but you can't believe how many things can go wrong, Lizzy."

"With horses? Really?"

I was grinning, and Deb was smiling and shaking her head.

"OK, here goes. Give us a hand only if we need it."

We opened the stall door wide and headed out of the barn. Whinnying commenced from paddocks near and far. Bazooka was bumping along into Wink's hocks as Deb kept her walking at a snail's pace. Zooky's little powder-blue halter slid behind his ears and part-way down his neck. We made it through the paddock gate.

This was a special small paddock right behind the barn, reserved for new babies and Mamas; a nursery paddock. The grass was cropped close, and the fencing was a diamond mesh so small that little feet couldn't get caught. There was a good sight line to the two big-bellied mares in their own field. They trotted up to their fence line, and Wink called loudly to them. They answered her, the whinnies heartfelt.

Then Wink took her baby for a run. He galloped after his Mama, and she slowed down to let him show off his springy trot. She circled the paddock once each way and then put her head down to graze, but little Bazooka was not done.

He had discovered his legs. And they were cool.

He tried a few interesting capers. His legs almost got tangled up a few times, and I was afraid that he would fall. But he didn't. Wink seemed uninterested now. She was digging the grass.

The other two mares stood at the fence and continued to watch the new baby.

"Look, Deb. Regina and Glitter are watching."

"They know their turn will be coming soon. I really believe that. All three of these girls are fast friends. They have raised their babies together in the past, and as soon as all three are foaled out, they'll go back out together. The foals will wean at the same time, too. And the youngsters stay together as a class until they go to Florida to sell. You couldn't ask for a better childhood if you ask me. And my mares, well, they are the real gems here. I love my mares."

"They're lucky to have you, too."

So we stood there for about twenty or thirty minutes before Deb went in and caught Wink who really didn't want to pick her head up out of the grass.

"Sorry Wink, but we have to build up to this gradually."

We carefully reversed the process, and sure to Deb's word, Bazooka lost his focus and missed the turn into the stall. Wink immediately called him as he wandered down the barn aisle. So we took Wink back out, and she called him again. He squealed like a piggy and wheeled around, running down the barn aisle and whamming himself into his Mama who grimaced, wrinkling her nose and flattening her ears.

But she forgave him, turning her head to check that this time he was following as we guided her back into the stall.

"Whew, Deb. That was interesting."

"See what I mean?"

With the mare and foal safely back into their big roomy foaling stall, we headed to the kitchen, and I pulled out our lemon squares while Deb made tea. I checked my watch nervously. Soon my presence would be required down below. But I wanted to let Deb know what I had heard.

"Uh, Deb?"

Deb was wrestling with a stuck silverware drawer. It finally sprang open but after Deb pulled out a spoon it wouldn't close. She turned around and bumped it half-way closed with a few good wallops with her butt. It was clearly jammed. Now she couldn't close it or open it. She grabbed the handle and tried working it right and left, back and forth. Nope; going nowhere. I started to speak again.

"Uh, Deb, I think I heard Frank say something to Francesca about Pali."

Deb held up her hand to stop me from saying anything else. "I can only imagine. But just forget it, OK. Frank saw Pali leaving here the other night. I knew he'd say something to Francesca. Francesca is wrong about Pali, and so is Frank. You met him; you see what a masterful trainer he is. Anyway, I'm not a kid like Ryder. It's none of Francesca's business."

"Francesca mentioned me, too. She doesn't want me spending time with them either; she even mentioned Marco's name."

"You gonna' let fear make your decisions for you, Lizzy?"

And with that, Deb turned and gave a karate kick to the drawer, along with some kind of karate shriek. The drawer slammed back into the woodwork.

I didn't think that drawer was ever going to be opened again.

CHAPTER 26

Thinking Outside The Sandbox

MARCO SAID, "C'MON, LIZZY. I WANT you to try something."

We had taken Bernardo and Caruso into one of the training rings and turned them loose. After they had good rolls, Marco put them through their routine. Then he called them into the middle and gave them each a treat and petting.

"You want to sit on Caruso?"

"I would love to."

"Hold on one sec."

Marco walked over to the edge of the arena and came back with short stiff ropes that he put around each horse's neck. And he carried a mid-sized whip. Sort of like a carriage whip without a lash.

"Let me give you a leg up. On the count of three, OK. Bounce a little each count to help."

I grabbed the first braid of Caruso's mane and Marco took my bent left leg by the shin.

"OK, one, two, three!"

Marco was so strong he almost sent me all the way over to the other side. I gave a little shriek.

He swung up on Bernardo from the ground, seeming to defy gravity.

"OK, this is where the two horses go side-by-side around the arena. Caruso goes on the inside because the outside horse has to have the longer stride. First we trot."

Marco guided the horses with his long whip and voice commands.

Caruso's back was cushy soft and really easy for me to sit on compared to the warmbloods I usually rode. I reached for my neck strap at first, but Marco reached over and took my hands away.

"Just trust him to do his job. Here, put your hands out to the side, like so, or grab a little mane if you need to."

I put my hands out and laughed. "This is amazing."

"You look like a natural, Lizzy. OK, now we canter."

And with a cluck, the two horses picked up the slow and steady canter.

Marco reached over and gave my thigh a pat. "How nice to see you riding, you sit really well."

"This is fun."

"Ah, the fun is just beginning."

And with that he put his hands down on Bernardo's neck and swung up into a kneeling position. Then from a kneeling position, he made a little hop and was standing up. Just seeing him do that made me reach again for the mane.

"OK, Lizzy. I'm coming over."

And with a hop he was behind me on Caruso.

"Oh, that makes me nervous, Marco."

He put his hands on my shoulders. "You have nothing to worry about."

He hopped back over to Bernardo, slid back down into a riding position, and said, "whoa." And the horses pulled up.

"Now you try. Just here standing. Go ahead. I see you have good balance."

He took the strap off Bernarndo's neck and tied one end around Caruso's neck-strap, which allowed it to run its full length.

"See, I have made you a standing-strap. We hold onto this to find our balance when learning to stand on the back of a horse. Once you find your balance, you must let go. But first just get up into a kneeling position."

Even doing that felt really awkward. But I did it.

Caruso, thankfully, stood like a statue.

"Yes, good Lizzy. Now stand up and hold onto your strap."

One foot, then another. I felt sorry for the back of Caruso as my tennis shoes made dents in his back.

"Just lean back a little against the strap. Stand on your heels more than your toes, then center yourself. You are doing great."

I was fine but my knees were shaking.

"Yes, good. Now, to get back down, move one hand at a time back to the neck strap, staying over your heels; now straighten and open your legs and slide down into riding seat."

I got myself back to the riding seat position with relief.

"And now we move!"

Holy crap.

The horses moved off with a flick of the whip, back onto the rail. They picked up a slow canter.

"I'm coming over."

Marco stood up and once again was standing behind me with a hop.

"Now scoot back, I'm going to climb over you and sit where you are sitting."

That meant I had to let go of the strap. But OK. I trusted him. I put my hands on Caruso's shoulders and pushed myself back.

Pretty soon I was ducking my head, and Marco was standing in front of me, then sliding down back into a riding seat.

"OK now you just hold onto my shoulders and try standing up. You can do it!"

My legs were shaking hard, and my fingers were digging into Marco's shoulders.

"Oh my God. I'm standing up on a cantering horse. Oh my God."

I transferred my hands from Marco's shoulders to his head. I realized for a moment I was really pulling on his hair.

"Ow, Lizzy, leave me some hair, OK?"

"Oh, sorry Marco."

And then I took my hands off his head. I was fine. I was balancing myself. And of course the moment I realized I was doing it, I lost my balance.

"Crap!"

Marco grabbed at me behind his neck, but in that instant I reached for him too, grabbing his shoulders and then his waist as I pulled myself into him and onto Caruso's back.

"You OK back there?"

"Yes, thanks, I'm fine. But I'm glad you were there."

"Whoa, boys"

The horses pulled up, and they got pats and praise from Marco.

I still had my arm tightly around Marco's waist. I could feel the muscles through his tee shirt, flat and taut, with the sound of his low voice vibrating right into my fingertips. I was unable to move. I was babbling.

"It's just I really hate falling off, and it seems like I do it a lot more than I should. I knew if I didn't grab your shoulders and get myself back down, then I would be a goner."

"Oh maybe I can help you there. I fall off all the time. In a show it has to look like you meant to do it. And sometimes I do."

We sat there on the horse for a few more moments until Marco spoke. "You're going to have to let go of me eventually."

"Um. Sorry."

"It's OK. I was enjoying it, too."

And with that he twisted around and kissed me. But then, of course, I had to slide down to the ground where I found it hard to stand on legs made of rubber.

***

WILD CHILD HAD A MONSTER-HUGE WALK stride. Kiddo and I fell so far behind we kept having to trot a few strides to catch up. Then step-by-step poor Kiddo would fall behind again.

Half of what Margot said got swallowed up by the wind as Kiddo and I lost ground, but as soon as Kiddo and I would catch up, I'd ask her to repeat herself.

"Sorry, Margot, what was that?"

"Half-halts are effective when the joints in the hind leg are relaxed and springy, and the horse has energy. Creating energy, without creating negative tension that stiffens the joints, is the great problem of dressage."

"OK."

"You need positive tension. The kind that is required for any athletic endeavor. But if you go over-the-limit, due to over-riding, or fatigue, or things beyond your control like a flying plastic bag, then positive tension becomes negative tension, and that pretty much ruins everything. You hope to showcase your horse's brilliance by taking him to the limit, to peak-performance so to speak, without going over the limit, which often means disaster."

"And…"

"And Wild Child is still full of that negative tension. I don't have the ease and control I want. Then, Francesca likes to point out, the horse is never going to be any other way, and besides the horse could colic and die tomorrow; and damn it, she wants to go to Gladstone with him before something like that happens… an interesting point of view."

I pondered living life under such pressures, and I was glad it wasn't me having to show under those conditions. But Margot really didn't have a choice. She soldiered on doing what she could do to make things better on a tight schedule.

I knew I could help. I was helping.

These afternoon hacks were all about making Wild Child stronger so fatigue would not be a cause of negative tension. But the hacks were helping his mind, too.

Margot had shortened her reins and gotten into jumping position.

"Ready, Lizzy?"

"Yeah. Ready."

I got up in my jumping position and let Kiddo lope up the hill next to a trotting Wild Child. Wild Child soon broke into canter; and then out of his smaller canter into a bigger one; and with a slap of his tail, he galloped off.

It felt good to see him out of the "sandbox," breathing clean spring air, and kicking up clods of turf.

I caught up with Margot at the top of the hill. Wild Child was a sight, still alert, head up, panting, and surveying the landscape looking like an equestrian statue you would find in the middle of some European city.

I thought Wild Child figured he won every race up the hill against Kiddo.

Kiddo and I stood next to them.

I said, "A tired horse is a happy horse."

Margot smiled and gave Wild Child a pat. We started back down the hill on loose reins, and I even kicked my feet out of the stirrups.

The horses knew the drill by now and swung along relaxed and happy. Wild Child occasionally would stop, all by himself, to let Kiddo catch up.

What Margot didn't know was that Wild Child was going out of his stall each night with me. I was performing Marco's magic spells on the boy.

I took him out and massaged him and then made him follow me around like a dog on a leash. We practiced, "come," "follow," "whoa," "turn," "back-up." I'd also introduced "bow." I used a carrot to tease him down, until his nose was on the floor between his front legs, and then I picked up his left front hoof and let him touch down on his knee. Then he got his carrot.

It was all due to Marco.

Wild Child occasionally still charged me at the stall or paddock. When he did, I would first shoo him away. He would then look away, as if I had become totally boring to him and something else far, far away had caught his attention.

Then I would call his name again, and he would prick his ears and come to me, a different animal.

It was like breaking an evil spell. Once when I called him in the paddock, he had even whinnied to me. It caught both of us by surprise.

Of course he immediately reverted back to his snarly self. I thought he was embarrassed to have let his guard down.

I had discovered that inside this aggressive stallion was another horse. One that I thought needed me. After all, there had been a day when he had been like Bazooka, a spindly little thing bumping alongside his dam.

CHAPTER 27

Secrets

FRANCESCA HAD TAKEN RYDER TO NEW York for the day. It was the big photo-shoot for High Horse Couture. It meant extra work for me, but I didn't care. Well, maybe I cared a little bit, but not about the extra work.

They left so early it was still dark out.

I was up anyway, so I went ahead and fed. And after the horses ate their grain, I walked as stealthily as possible down the barn aisle. When I got to Wild Child's stall, I whispered his name.

"Wiiiiild Child."

Followed by pulling out a wrapped peppermint from my pocket.

He wheeled around and whinnied, and I laughed out loud.

"You're officially an addict now, Wild Child."

I gave him the peppermint and walked away, smiling to myself. He had become Pavlov's dog, or I should say Pavlov's horse, and was totally hooked on peppermints. It didn't mean that he loved me or trusted me. Yet. But I had won myself a little goodwill. I tried to ignore the other horses. Geez, it made me feel guilty. They had sweet and hopeful expressions. But I promised them each treats later.

Then I got myself a cup of coffee and headed to Winsome's stall. I slid open her door and plopped down with my back to the wall. I always found peace in just looking at her. I hadn't treated myself to this ritual in a long time; I had been so focused on Wild Child. She left her hay to come blow into my hair and ear, giving me chills. I put my hand over my coffee to try to keep things from falling into my mug.

"Go on sweetie, go eat your hay."

She soon got bored after mussing up my hair and snorting bits of hay onto my shirt, and she went back to eating.

Then I heard footsteps, and Deb popped her head into the partially-open stall door.

"Hey, you. What ya' doing in there?"

"Deb! Just chillin' with Winsome. What are you doing down here?"

"Well, Ryder said yesterday that she and Francesca would be in the city today, so I thought I would come spend some time here this morning. And I brought cinnamon rolls, homemade."

"Oh, man."

Deb peeled open a plastic container, and the smell of cinnamon and sugar walloped my senses. I reached in for a roll. It was soft and sticky and still a little warm. I shoved a good portion of it in my mouth, followed with a swig of coffee. Divine. Winsome smelled it, too, barged right over, and started pushing around with her nose.

"Lizzy, your mare thinks I brought these for her."

"Hey mare-mare, we are not sharing."

I shoved the rest in my mouth and then licked my fingers. Probably not the most hygienic move, I thought too late.

I gave Winsome a little push, and Deb and I left the stall. Winsome stuck her head out and watched us walk away, tapping her door lightly with her hoof.

I guessed I had spoiled an entire barn full of horses. I looked back down the aisle, and every head was sticking out, watching us.

I led Deb up to the apartment and poured her a cup, and we sat down.

"Deb, I've missed working with you in the afternoons. How is my "Boingo" getting along?"

"He's longeing now."

Deb looked at me like she had a secret to share, but hadn't decided whether or not to tell.

"That's great."

Deb tipped her head and appeared to be studying me, then got to the point.

"So, I had a nice talk with Marco. The guy is crazy for you. I get the feeling that it's mutual."

I felt my cheeks get hot. "He's... Well, I've learned a lot from him."

"Yeah?"

"He's helped me with Wild Child. I'm starting to get inside that horse's head, y'know? Plus, he let me up on Caruso. And Deb, I stood up on the back of a cantering horse. It was a total rush. I am doing new things and feeling new things with the horses. It's like my mind is opening up. Do you know what I mean?"

"Lizzy. I'm not going to rain on your parade. Not a bit. Just don't lose sight of your goals, OK? You still want to be a competitive dressage rider?"

"I do."

"Then believe me when I say, Margot is one of the best. And she is what many are not, which is ethical. And you are lucky to be here. The grass may look greener on the other side of the fence, but that's usually because it's Astroturf."

It took me a second to fully register the joke because her tone was so serious. But then her dimples appeared as she cracked herself up, and I joined in laughing.

"But Lizzy, I don't want to get you into trouble. I'm already in too deep myself, but I didn't mean when I took you to see the show for you to repeat history."

"Deb. Stop with the mystery. I mean I know you and Pali fell in love and that you left here and then you came back. But I need details."

"Yeah. I guess that's fair. But Francesca would kill me if she knew I told you this."

"Deb, since when does Francesca even talk to me?"

Deb grimaced and shook her head.

"OK. Well, things kinda' went south over a horse deal."

"A horse deal?"

"It wasn't just me that got involved with Pali. It was all of us. We all went to see the show that year. And we all were floored. Francesca was impressed more than any of us. It is magical; you've seen it. Even when you know a lot, it's impressive, but imagine if you know next to nothing. Pali's show works on the audience's emotions. He taps into every fantasy about horses. Francesca was especially taken with one of Pali's dressage horses. Babu. He was a fully-trained Andalusian. I mean circus dressage, but really quite beautiful. He did all the Grand Prix movements and also was super-good at some of the other stuff. Like Spanish walk and some cute Liberty moves. Pali used to put the prettiest girls up on him in fantastic costumes for the show.

"And Babu was brave. He would canter through smoke and work in a dark arena under a spotlight. Pali doesn't like to actually be in the show, but he can train almost any horse to do anything. Like Babu. But Pali also needs money just like everyone else. And Babu was getting older."

"And Frank and Francesca have a lot of money," I added.

"Yeah, but it was Frank and Francesca insisting on Pali coming out to our farm on the show's dark day. Of course we all hit it off, and Pali started spending a lot of time with all of us. He got along well with Frank. They loved talking food and wine."

"Pali was hanging out here?"

"Yup. That's when I learned how to train Regina with the neck rope. She was easy to teach, too. It was a fun time. Pali took Francesca back to his training ring and let her take lessons on Babu. He knew exactly what he was doing. He knew Frank would offer to buy Babu for Francesca."

"And did he?"

"Well, Pali played with him first and said no. Babu was a valuable part of the show. It would leave a hole in the performance, you see."

"So Francesca didn't get her horse?"

"Oh, she got him all right. Frank told Pali to name his price."

"Oh."

"And he did, and it was a big number."

"Oh."

"And Frank cut the check, just like that. Which was really kinda' stupid."

"Uh, Deb, I notice that we don't have any Andalusians here."

"Not even Pali could idiot-proof a horse for Francesca."

"Lovey's pretty close to idiot-proof."

"He is a rare jewel isn't he? But Babu would have been just fine for her, too. He was small, and she could sit his trot; and his canter didn't scare her either. It could have worked out if she'd stuck with it. But it takes some feeling to ride FEI."

"Francesca has no feel."

"Francesca has so little feel that when she rode Babu for those lessons, she didn't realize Pali managed every step of her ride. She still doesn't get how hard it is to ride well. She wanted a mechanical horse. Her reach way exceeds her grasp."

"What happened?"

"I think Babu was the most intelligent horse I have ever been around. He was kind of like one of Francesca's Jack Russell terriers, smart but full of mischief. And when he hit the show arena, he put on a show. Just not the show Francesca intended."

"And?"

"It was the funniest thing I've ever seen. Francesca was going to ride her first Prix St. Georges, which was already above her skill level, but she insisted. So there she was in her top hat and tail coat, cantering down centerline. She made a halt, and when she went to salute, she had the whip in her saluting hand, which meant she touched Babu on the shoulder with it. Babu started to go down on one knee to bow."

I literally felt my jaw drop and my mouth hang open.

"And that wasn't the worst of it."

"I bet Francesca was not laughing."

"Nope. As soon as he started to drop she freaked and she tried to pull his head up with her other rein, which pulled his head toward her left knee, which of course is the cue for "lie-down.""

"Holy crap!"

"Yup. He lay down, and Francesca had to step off of him. You should have seen the judge, even she was laughing. Francesca was eliminated; she had to tap him with the whip to get him to stand up and then lead him out of the arena. We all thought it was funny, our little circus horse putting on an impromptu show. Francesca couldn't let it go. She never sat on him again."

"Margot let her get away with that?"

"Francesca was sure she had been set up. It was irrational talk. Like Pali had trained Babu to humiliate her. She felt that Pali had fleeced her like a con man. To this day she will tell you that he is a lying cheating Gypsy who laughed all the way to the bank; that he ate her food and drank her wine, and screwed her young help, and then filled his pockets with her money and laughed all the way on his way out of town. She sent Babu to a trainer who sells a lot of Andalusians, and he sold quickly, but only for a fraction of what they paid for him."

"Wow."

"Yeah. When Pali heard about it he was livid. You see he thought his little Babu was set for life. Who knows what kind of a home he has now. Pali got drunk and called Francesca, and who knows what that conversation was like. Francesca took it out on me, like it was my fault."

"But why would Francesca be mad at you?"

"She told me that I was never to see Pali again. Can you imagine? I was in love. Of course I defended Pali, and I said a lot of things I shouldn't have said. And the things I said can never be unsaid. And I packed my bags and left in a huff."

"But she took you back."

"Only because Margot convinced her I had been under Svengali's spell just as we all had been."

"And was she right?"

Deb only shrugged. "I came back didn't I?"

I longed for Deb to tell me more. But Deb was done, and I had a work day in front of me. And I walked around feeling burdened by what I knew.

Surely Marco was no Svengali.

But he had me under his spell for sure.

And Deb had said he was crazy for me, too. That part of it made me feel great.

***

Wᴵˡᴰ Cʜⁱˡᴰ ᵂᵉⁿᵗ ꜰⁱʳˢᵗ ⁱⁿ ᵗʰᵉ line-up as usual, and Deb was
there to help Margot from the ground.

When I walked into the arena with Margot's next ride,
Hotstuff, I was surprised to see Margot standing by the gate
while Deb was riding Wild Child.

I had never seen anyone else sit on Wild Child since the
day Ben handed the reins over to Margot. Deb and Wild Child
looked beautiful.

"Oh Margot. Look at Deb."

Margot smiled. "It's fun for me to see what Wild Child looks
like from the ground. It gives me perspective. And frankly it
encourages me. It looks better than it feels."

I couldn't take my eyes off of Deb and Wild Child. I shook
my head.

"Man, Deb can really ride."

Margot crossed her arms and leaned against the kickboards.

"She should be the one competing, darling. My best days are
behind me. But Deb's could still be in front of her."

Deb rode Wild Child alongside the arena mirrors and
transitioned into piaffe. That was Wild Child's specialty. She
watched herself in the mirror and then carefully transitioned
out into passage. Then she walked and stroked him on the
neck, cooing to him. He was blowing but looked soft in his eye,
his ears relaxed. Deb was grinning. She called over to Margot,
"Geez Margot. You've never had one that piaffed like this one.
His technique is just about perfect. He really lowers behind, and
he is so active."

"He is working brilliantly for you, darling. He's being so
agreeable. I expected him to challenge you like he did me when
I first sat on him."

Deb pulled up in front of Margot. "Margot, you are making
the same mistake that we all make. I can hear your voice in my
head."

Then Deb did a pretty good imitation of Margot, "Forget
about that <u>old</u> horse, darling, you've already made him a
different boy."

I looked at Margot, and she was shaking her head, but smiling.

"Very cute, Deb darling, but don't you feel any resentment from the horse when you sit on him? Any at all?"

"Honestly Margot, I don't. Of course it might change if I brought in a mare in heat; but otherwise, nope."

Deb hopped off and gave Wild Child a pat. Then she turned to me. "Lizzy, you spend more time with him than anyone. What do you think? Do you think his attitude is improving?"

"I do. Sometimes he lets down his guard, and he's actually sweet. Of course when he realizes what he's done, he has to snarl at me. You know he has an image to maintain."

Margot turned to look at me and lifted one eyebrow. "You've had a change of heart about him, Lizzy?"

"We have a truce, although I always stay focused when I'm with him."

"Yes, do. He's a stallion, and we can't forget that."

"Well, I don't ever forget that. I do think he's beautiful and talented, and I've told him that every day. Haven't I Wild Child?"

Wild Child had left the conversation. He was staring past us toward the out gate, listening for horses. We stopped talking and just looked at his handsome profile.

So then I whispered, "Wiiild Chiiild."

And of course, on cue, he impressed Margot and Deb with his new trick.

His head whipped around, his ears pricked, and he whinnied a soft low nostril-quivering whinny.

Margot and Deb laughed.

I dug into my pocket and found an unwrapped sticky half-melted peppermint. But I still was holding Hotstuff. Hotstuff wasn't going to let that peppermint go to Wild Child. He practically knocked me down to steal the peppermint right out of my hand.

Well, we almost had a riot. Wild Child bowed himself up, arching his neck, and took a step toward Hotstuff. He would have whupped up on Hotstuff if Deb hadn't pulled him back. Margot came to the rescue.

"Wait, oh, gosh, I've got a sugar cube in my pocket."

She stuffed it into Wild Child's mouth, and for a moment we just stood as both horses deflated, the duel averted. Deb was laughing her easy laugh.

"Y'know, Margot, his life here is good. He gets to go out in a paddock and go with Kiddo on hacks, and he gets to work for an empathetic rider; plus he has the same sweet Lizzy grooming him every day. I think all these small pieces are coming together. You and Wild Child are going to rock by Gladstone."

Margot was listening. "You really think this crazy plan of Francesca's can work?"

"Not because it's Francesca's plan. It will work despite her. But you have to tread a fine line. You've got to get him in front of the driving aids where his motor is purring along and he moves with the scope he has by nature. But if you go too far, with that throttle wide-open, he'll take over. If that happens, he's going to drag your skinny little butt right out of the tack."

Margot was nodding her head in agreement. "Deb, how'd you get to be so smart?"

"Trained by the best in the business is all."

Margot took Hotstuff, and I ran up the stirrups on Wild Child and loosened his girth.

After Hotstuff, Margot was going to ride Papa and Petey and then tune up Lovey. Then I would have my lesson on Winsome.

Margot was treating Deb and me to lunch. After lunch Margot and I would hack Kiddo and Wild Child. I only wished this was the way it could be every day.

No Ryder, no Francesca.

No secrets.

Except, I did have secrets.

Deb and I were going out with Pali and Marco tonight. We would not be saying anything about it in front of Margot.

I never heard Margot ask Deb any questions about Pali either.

It would have felt good to unburden my soul and tell Margot about Marco. But I knew to keep my mouth shut. I was not to involve Margot.

Except that I never could keep a secret. And it was eating me up.

CHAPTER 28

Sophomoric

MARCO AND I TOOK WILD CHILD into the indoor after getting back from dinner, and I proudly showed off our in-hand work. Afterward, we leaned against Wild Child's stall door and kissed.

Wild Child wanted to be in the middle of it, too. He put his nose on Marco's shoulder and blew in his ear. I was a little nervous that Wild Child would escalate from blowing to biting, but he didn't.

Marco gently pushed the horse's muzzle away and then rolled me away from the stall front. Marco had turned serious and intense, and I closed my eyes and melted into him, but not without hearing Deb's voice in my mind. Would history somehow repeat itself?

I finally opened my eyes and looked up toward the apartment window. Ryder's shadowy form was back lit. She was back. She was standing very still, and did not seem to notice that I was staring right at her. I gently pushed Marco away.

He took the waistband of my jeans with his finger and pulled me into him again.

"Can we go upstairs?"

"Marco, I can't. Can't you see what I see in the window?"

Marco looked up too quickly.

"No. Don't look like that! Not so obvious."

"What do I have to be ashamed of?"

"Marco, it's Ryder. She could make trouble for me."

"The teenager?"

"Uh, yes, the teenager."

I watched her recede back into the shadows. What was she up to? I understood she could be my undoing.

"Marco, I don't think we can be together here. I'm scared she's up to something. I love my job here. I don't want to be fired."

Poor Marco looked confused. "Lizzy, just a moment ago you were kissing me like, like, you really meant it."

"Oh I meant it, Marco."

Then he whispered my name in a low musical way, not so differently from the way I called Wild Child for a peppermint.

"Lizzzzy."

And he pulled at my jean's waistband, reeling me in like I'd been lassoed, pressing us together again. Then he reached around, his palm now pressing the small of my back. My heart pounded against his pounding heart. And yet, even though the lights were out and I could no longer see Ryder's shape, I knew she was still watching. I pushed gently away again, and I could see the hurt in Marco's eyes.

"Marco, not here."

"Don't think of her, Lizzy."

"Marco, we can't be like Deb and Pali."

"What? We are not Deb and Pali, Lizzy. Why are you so afraid anyway? You aren't a little girl anymore. You are an adult. You have a right to have love in your life. No one has the right to demand that you live without love."

"Please, Marco. I hate that I am ending this wonderful day feeling miserable and sorry for myself."

Marco did look hurt. "Well, now I don't feel so great about myself either."

"I don't want that, Marco, really."

And he was turning on his heel, sighing, resigned. "OK, Lizzy. I need to go check on horses anyway. You have a good night."

"Marco. Wait."

He turned back around. "I had a wonderful time. And I'm learning so much from you, too. Thank you."

"You are welcome, Lizzy. Glad to be able to help."

At least he did sound sincere.

I watched his elegant form walk away, sighing to myself. Wild Child watched, too.

"There he goes Wild Child. I blew it big time. What a screw up I am."

I sidled back over to his stall-front and mindlessly began stroking his face, more to soothe myself than to soothe him. I was sniffling a little and wiping away a few tears.

Then it dawned on me; this was a first without his at least making a surly face. I was feeling like shit, but gradually I stopped feeling bad because I was transfixed by his tolerance of my hand on his face. My heart rate began to slow down. This was a breakthrough. Wild Child's eyes began to close, and I was able to stroke the soft, soft, skin around his nostrils, right next to his mouth. Right next to his teeth. He was leaning on the yoke front of his stall, and his lower lip was drooping. He barely roused himself as I backed away.

God, I was suddenly very tired. My legs felt like lead as I climbed the stairs. As I opened the apartment door, I heard Ryder close hers. But her light was on. I could see a strip of light under her door, so I tapped lightly, and then went ahead and opened it a little.

"Ryder?"

"Hey, Lizzy."

There she stood in her PJs, a slew of new High Horse Couture breeches spread across her bed.

I thought about busting her chops, calling her a spy and a Peeping Tom and whatever other names popped into my head. But I reined myself in. I was the one in trouble, not Ryder. I took a deep breath and moved toward the bed to admire her loot.

"These are from the photo shoot?"

"Yeah. Since they were all custom made for me, I get to keep them. Sort of like payment for the work."

They were, of course, beautiful. One thing about Francesca, she had exquisite taste. I stepped forward and touched each pair. The fabric was lightweight and stretchy. Each pair would retail for about three hundred dollars. I counted six pair. My cheeks got hot. Life was not fair. I had only the pair I was given when I rode Rave in the quadrille. I sure as hell would never be able to buy a pair, and the idea of owning six pair was unthinkable.

I swallowed hard, "So did the shoot go well?"

"Yeah. Francesca's pretty decent once you get to know her."

That thought sent a shiver down my spine. Ryder and Francesca buddies...like the kind that tell each other secrets, just as Deb and I had. Or maybe, like a flying monkey from the Wizard of Oz...ready to do Francesca's bidding? I got a grip. Since when had I become so cynical?

"Really? Well we had a great day here, too."

"How so?"

And then I nervously babbled like an idiot. "Um, well Margot took us all out to lunch. Oh, and Deb came down, and she rode Wild Child."

Ryder immediately narrowed her eyes. "Deb? I don't think Francesca would like hearing that."

I matched her narrowed gaze. Yeah, she was a flying monkey after all.

"Well, you're not going to say a word, OK? Deb rode him really well. She's an amazing rider. Besides, Margot knows what's good for Wild Child, and Francesca knows better than to second guess her."

"Whatever, Lizzy."

I sure wanted to believe what I'd just said.

Ryder had assumed a bored disinterested look. She started folding up her new breeches, and with her back to me said, "So Lizzy, you had a late night, too."

I startled like a scared rabbit. Instead of me confronting her, she was going to confront me. I was backing out of the room. "Yeah. I'm pooped. I'm rolling in."

Ryder turned and lifted one corner of her mouth. I noticed for the first time that she had a new haircut and color, and her nails were polished. She dismissed me with a little wave not unlike the one that Marco had made. "See you in the AM."

"Goodnight, Ryder."

I couldn't wait to get in bed and grab my journal. My eyes burned as I tried to get it all down. I still had a long way to go if I wanted to manipulate my manipulators. I had a long way to go to be able to manage my emotional state.

***

But in the morning light, my drama of the night before seemed ridiculous. Ryder and I had jobs to do, and we went about our routines peaceably enough. Francesca had the equine dentist coming in the afternoon for Kiddo. I was relieved because he was losing weight. He was getting fitter from our afternoon hacks, but he wasn't eating very much of his hay and was slow and sloppy eating his grain.

The morning had been a busy one. I had videotaped Margot practicing her freestyle. We were leaving next Wednesday for North Carolina, and Margot was feeling the pressure. She was going to be "winging-it" with her freestyle in North Carolina, but she didn't have a choice.

One of her qualifying tests had to be a freestyle. Frank had purchased Wild Child's freestyle music from Ben down in Florida. Margot had played with it a little in Florida but never had put it all together. It was crunch time. I didn't think she really had believed she would be going to North Carolina. She said it was her punishment for doing so well at her first show. Of course if things didn't go great in North Carolina, and she didn't make the cut, then life could go back to a more relaxed schedule.

Ryder had done so well at her first show at the New Jersey qualifier that she was practically panting to make the last-minute attempt at qualifying to ride in June at Gladstone in the National Championships for Advanced Young Riders. Her National Championships would be held the first weekend of the two-weekend competition at Gladstone.

Ryder's ultimate goal was the North American Championships in August in Lexington. But if she could squeak into these National Championships at Gladstone, it would be a feather in her cap.

Ryder felt the judges needed to see her in top company before August so the judges would be comfortable giving her the high scores she deserved. She wanted to ride into the North American Championships already the "favorite."

Francesca was all for it, but it meant Ryder had to do really well in North Carolina, and then they had to find one more competition. Ryder's qualifying rules required three shows, not two like Margot's. Additionally, Ryder was required to show a freestyle as one of her rides.

Ryder had made good use of her Francesca face-time, pulling Francesca into her plan. So if Ryder knocked it out of the park in North Carolina, there would be a hunt for finding another qualifier. It would mean heading to Canada.

Crazy.

I knew Papa would try his heart out for Ryder. I couldn't help but feel that Ryder didn't fully understand the generosity of Papa or Margot or even Francesca. She felt entitled because she was talented. It would all be a moot point if Ryder didn't score well in North Carolina. But to Ryder that outcome wasn't possible.

Ryder was also sure that Petey was going to make a splashy debut in North Carolina. I was called upon to videotape as she ran through the Third level test for Margot, and I agreed that such a debut was possible. Ryder had Petey powered-up and flying. She had him on the edge, but he put in a perfect test. I knew as I watched her that I could not have managed him. She was good, and she oozed confidence (or arrogance). Although her face was unreadable, her body language was not.

I had just piled feed buckets into the feed cart to feed lunch when the bright red vet truck pulled up to the barn. Poor Kiddo would have to miss lunch, and he so looked forward to his meals, even though he struggled to eat them. He wouldn't be able to have any food as he would need to be sedated for his procedure. But the rest of the barn wouldn't wait. I resolved to just give him a handful to pacify him while the vet got out and set up. All heads were hanging out of the stalls as I rolled the cart from stall to stall and dumped grain. Ryder had loaded up the hay cart and handed out hay, and she was putting it away when I passed her.

"Lizzy, did you forget to bring Kiddo in?"

"No, I brought him in."

"Well, he's not in his stall."

"Crap. The vet just rolled in. Finish for me will you."

"Sure."

Kiddo…not again, and in broad daylight.

I got to his stall and saw the clip, spring broken, on the ground.

"Aw, Kiddo."

I waved at the vet. She was still sitting in the truck talking on her cell phone.

I stepped out into the beautiful spring sunlight. All seemed peaceful and quiet. I scanned the paddocks and then slowly eyeballed the path up the hill to Deb's. Nothing.

The vet stepped out of her truck. She was a tiny woman with brown curly hair and a big belt buckle on her jeans. She stuck out her hand.

"Hi, you must be Lizzy."

"Dr. Turner. I'm sorry but I have to go find your patient."

"Oh, you can go get him in while I set up. This stall OK? I need a plug is all."

"Yeah that's his stall. But…"

I grabbed his halter off his hook and thought I should shut up and just go find him. I marched up the hill and walked behind Deb's barn to check out the back fields. No luck.

I walked back down the hill wearing his halter and lead rope across my chest like some kind of Bandito. I stopped outside the barn and hesitated. Kiddo was not a cat who could crawl under the foundations of a house or under a car. He should have been easy to spot.

No. I thought it unlikely, but I had to check.

And there he was. Standing in the indoor arena, looking at himself in the mirror. I walked in quietly, pulling the heavy wooden kickboard-doors closed behind me.

"Kiddo, how the heck did you get the memo? Come on, you bad boy."

He was watching me in the mirror, and he knew the gig was up. He stood quietly while I put his halter on, nosing me gently for treats.

"C'mon, Kiddo. The vet is probably tapping her toes wondering where the hell we are."

I dragged him toward the barn. He walked slowly, like a man condemned. But as we got to the vet truck, he slammed on the brakes. Dr. Turner walked out of the barn and quietly walked around behind him.

"I was about to send out a search party. I guess he's wise to us, huh?"

"Dr. Turner, you don't know the half of it."

I laughed, but Kiddo was dug in and leaning back, eyes glued to the vet truck.

"C'mon, Kiddo. You have to get your teeth done."

Dr. Turner made kissing sounds and then clapped her hands together, and Kiddo came unstuck and walked hesitantly into the barn. I tried to make a right turn into his stall, which had been transformed into his procedure room. Ropes hung down with a kind of harness covered in plastic tubing, but it had been pulled to the side. A stainless steel bucket sat outside his stall filled with some kind of mouthwash and a tube that looked like a caulking gun for squirting his mouth. Then there was the extension cord and all sorts of power tools, just like a human dentist would have, only in horsey size.

Kiddo was having none of it. He made a quick dart to the left, tucked his chin to his chest, and headed down the barn aisle, dragging me along behind him. The rope burned through my grip, but I was hanging onto the knot tied at the end.

"Kiddo, damn it you're getting your teeth done!" I was yelling.

Ryder heard me and made a dash for the other end of the aisle to close off his escape route. And Kiddo saw her. He slammed on the brakes again and wheeled toward me, his eyes rimmed in white with terror. He snorted at me like an accusation of betrayal.

Dr. Turner was right behind me. She glided right up to him needle and syringe in hand, pulling off the cap of the needle with her teeth. Then she smoothly and swiftly pressed down on his jugular and slipped in the needle, pulling back a ribbon of blood into the syringe and then slowly pushing in the tranquilizer. I had been holding my breath. But once the tranquilizer was in, I exhaled.

Dr. Turner pulled the plastic cap from her lips and covered the needle.

"OK, girls. That should help."

We stood there waiting for Kiddo to relax.

"Lizzy, let's see if we can get him into his stall now."

Kiddo's mind was still resistant, but his body had no power. We pushed and we pulled, and step-by-step we got the old guy into his stall. I did feel sorry for him as we slipped his head into the harness, cranking on the ropes and lifting his chin with the rubber tubing. Dr. Turner inserted a hinged speculum that held his mouth open. After she flushed his mouth out with the wash, she put on her head lamp like a regular dentist. It was equipped with a magnifying lens, too. And then her exam began in earnest.

I had never seen an equine veterinary dentist at work. I was fascinated, and Dr. Turner was friendly and easy about helping me understand what she was doing.

"Kiddo's really having trouble eating and losing weight. I'm so glad you're here."

"Well, I'm not a bit surprised. Want to see why?"

Dr. Turner stepped back, pulling Kiddo's cheek away from his molars. It would have been impossible to get such a good view if he hadn't been trussed up. But even I could see the gashes inside his cheeks.

"Oh, poor Kiddo!"

"Yeah, those are some deep oral ulcers due to sharp points and excessive ridges."

"Why would that happen like that?"

Dr. Turner pointed to the outside edges of his molars.

"These points are razor sharp."

Dr. Turner started working with her electric drill, one molar at a time. Kiddo leaned into his harness, his eyes closed. Between the short drilling sessions, she explained things to me while she stuck her gloved fingers into Kiddo's mouth to test the feeling of the edges.

"Horses' teeth emerge from the gum line almost their entire lives. Their upper jaw is wider than the lower jaw, so these outside unworn edges turn into something we call points. See the outside washboard exterior surface of the tooth? His are really excessive, and see how they've also abraded his cheeks? Wow. We'll have to put him on a round of antibiotics, too. We're going to make this boy feel so much better."

Dr. Turner worked up a sweat in short order. She had to squat and twist her body to really see into Kiddo's mouth. Just like a human dentist, she also used mirrors to check out the deep nooks and crannies. She explained that a horse has to be able to freely move his teeth forward and back, as well as from side to side, to chew properly. A horse's jaw can become limited in its range of movement by uneven wear patterns. Not only was there a problem called "points" like Kiddo's, but also "hooks" and "ramps." So not only can the teeth actually cut the cheeks and even the tongue, but when the jaw gets trapped, it can even cause TMJ joint pain and headaches.

I got the best look at the inside of a horse's mouth that I had ever had in my life.

Ryder stopped by to have a look and then a discussion with Dr. Turner about something called "bit-seating" which was a term I had never heard before. It involved a mild rounding-off of the edge of the first molar so it couldn't cause a pinch of soft tissue between the bit and the molar. Miss smarty-pants clearly knew all about it and discussed it like one pro to another before wandering away.

By the time Dr. Turner had cleaned up and driven away, Kiddo was waking up. I went to find an extra clip for his door and then went in to give him a lecture.

"Listen buddy, you are going to be able to eat again just fine. OK, maybe not tonight. Tonight I'm feeding you a slurry. I know it will look gross, and it will have yucky antibiotic powder in it too; but soon you can eat your grain and your hay and even carrots. Life will be looking up."

He leaned his grey-flecked head into my chest, looking pitiful. I proceeded to stroke his ears. I felt my lower lip wobble and tears sting my eyes. There was no way I could explain that all this torture we just put him through was a kindness. And yet, clearly he was not holding a grudge. I lifted his head by his chin and looked into his heavy-lidded eyes, shaking my head.

"How in the world did you know that the vet was coming, Kiddo? What did we do that tipped you off, huh?"

Whatever it was, Kiddo wasn't telling.

I realized that Kiddo, and all the other horses too, would always read me far better than I could ever hope to read them.

In the college of horsemanship, I was still a sophomore.

And Kiddo was a PhD.

CHAPTER 29

Crossing T's And Dotting I's

FRANCESCA SAT AT HER DESK STARING at her computer screen, and Ryder was leaning over her shoulder.

I was standing in the doorway. "Francesca, Lovey's tacked up, and Margot is ready for you."

She looked up from the computer at me as if she didn't recognize me. "Oh. Sure. One minute."

She pushed back her chair and turned to Ryder. "I'll see what I can do."

Ryder looked pleased. "Fantastic. I know you can make it happen."

"Well, I'm glad that someone around here has a little drive. Just be sure you're worthy of all the trouble you're putting me through."

"I won't disappoint you, Francesca."

Francesca almost smiled. Or maybe it was a grimace.

When Francesca headed out the door, Ryder did a little fist-pump behind her back.

I held my hands palm-up with a shrug. "So, what is that all about?"

"You ever been to Canada, Lizzy?"

"Nope."

"I think Francesca is going to let me show in Canada, so I can get three qualifiers in before Gladstone. I'm sure if I go,

I can qualify; and it falls right on the qualifying deadline for Gladstone."

"Won't that be a big drive?"

"Not any further than what we're doing Wednesday to go to North Carolina."

"But, I think I saw that show listing, and it's the very next weekend."

"Yeah."

"So we go trucking South one week and North the next? That sounds tiring for the horses. Does Margot want to do that?"

"Actually, I haven't said anything to Margot. She only needs the two shows, so she wouldn't have to go. But Suzette and Patrick are going."

Going without Margot? That was unthinkable to me. "Oh, Margot is so not going to let you go without her. Papa is her responsibility."

"Well, she could just come up to coach then. But Papa could ship up with Patrick's horses and stable with them, too."

"He offered to do that, did he?"

"Yeah. What of it?"

"I just think he's been awfully friendly is all."

"Lizzy, he's really involved with the Young Riders Program in this region. He's done free clinics for the Young Riders, and he will be the Chef d'equipe for our team at the North American Championships. Besides, he's got room on the trailer. The closing date was yesterday, so we'll see if Francesca can still arrange everything."

"Hmmm." I nodded my head and walked down the barn aisle to get Winsome.

I kept thinking about what Marco said to me. "Manipulate the manipulator." Ryder was working it, and I was interested in how she would pull it off. It took nerve.

I might also be a sophomore when it came to manipulation, but I was beginning to feel like I was surrounded by upperclassmen. Ryder's plan made me queasy.

Something else had been making me feel queasy. I had put off calling Marco. And he hadn't tried to call me. Not once.

I thought he had washed his hands of me. I was more trouble than I was worth. Plus, I thought he was used to girls swooning over him and falling into his bed.

He was swoon-worthy after all.

But I had decided I needed to chill if I wanted to keep my job. There was just too much brewing right now, what with this push to qualify. Margot and Wild Child had to be my first priority.

Not that I didn't love the thrill of his kisses, and I was flattered that anyone that good-looking was attracted to me.

I did want to see him again. But most of all, I owed him an apology and more of an explanation. I wanted to slow things down. I did not mean to chase him away.

So I did it again. I called Marco. And I was glad I did. I got an invite to the evening's performance. Gratis. I would get to watch from backstage.

I was not sure that Ryder noticed me slipping out. But I didn't have to ask her permission.

There was a special ticket waiting for me at Will Call.

And an usher came and escorted me to my spot.

I was just as excited as that first night with Deb.

I stood behind the curtain, stage right, which afforded me a good view not only of the stage, but of course, the backstage direction, too.

Pali had on a headset and lined up his acts, signaling when they were to enter from stage left. When the act or scene finished, the horses galloped off the stage to a line of standing stalls, kind of like parking spots. Once they found their spot, they shoved their heads into a waiting bucket with some grain in it. Horses flew into spots that clearly belonged to them, and they cut nasty faces at any horse who tried to crowd into their space.

Marco first did a six-horse Liberty act, and when that was done sent four horses of the six offstage at a gallop where they went to their parking spots. Then he had only Bernardo and Caruso together. For a moment as he jumped from horse to horse, I imagined myself out there with him. I could see it. I would be on Caruso, and he would be on Bernardo. For a moment the image charmed me. Yes, and I would be a circus wife, and our children would be circus children. Maybe trick riders or dressage riders; or maybe our son would do a Liberty act with his father, as Marco had done with his father.

And we would live on the road from one engagement to another, with performances every night and matinees on Sunday.

The fantasy bubble popped. I would hate that life. This was hopeless.

When Marco came off stage, he was dripping sweat and breathless. I could see he was happy and satisfied. He could only wave at me as he passed, shepherding his two loose stallions all the way back to their proper stalls. The audience roared their approval, but not for long because the trick riders were entering from stage left, galloping at speed across the stage, whooping and hollering and hanging upside down.

It was exciting to watch.

Then came the clown and his trick horse. The clown was dressed as a cowboy; and after yawning and stretching, he got off and built a campfire with a big pot of beans hanging over it. The horse and clown both sat down at the fire and proceeded to eat their beans. The feedbag on the horse, and the clown's bowl, had large print on them reading "beans." Then the clown and the horse lay down and shared a blanket that the horse kept hogging, pulling it off of the clown. When they finally got settled, the horse got gas. Somehow Pali had that blanket rigged so it rose up with the sound effects. The clown jumped up and ran off holding his nose. The horse picked up his head, looking around as if to say, "What?" One time they had the clown fart and point at the horse to blame him. At this, the horse jumped up and ran off with the blanket. Then it turned into a tug-of-war. It was hilarious, and the children were screaming with laughter.

Marco had come up behind me, and he was laughing, too.

"I still love the comedy acts."

"Oh, there you are. You were wonderful, as usual." I turned my head, expecting a kiss. But Marco backed up a step.

It was right that he did, I supposed. I tried not to show my embarrassment.

"Thanks Lizzy. No two shows are ever the same. Caruso was so lazy tonight, I was afraid it would be boring to watch, but I'm glad you're enjoying the show."

"It's an amazing show, Marco. Who could be bored with so much beauty? Hey, can I treat you to dinner after? I actually have money in my wallet tonight."

Marco seemed to study me a moment.

"Sure, Lizzy. You know we have to wait until after our meeting with Pali. Nobody leaves ever until after the meeting."

"I understand, Marco. Totally. Work before pleasure."

He continued to look intently at me.

"Yes, Lizzy. It's the way it always must be. Work before pleasure, and animals before people."

"It is just the way it is, Marco. You of all people know that."

"Yes. I'll see you after our meeting. Well, I must go see to my boys."

"Of course."

My chest felt tight as I turned back to the performance. The horse now was flat on his back, all four feet in the air with the sound effects of snoring. The clown was pretending to try to sleep, but putting his hands over his ears and looking at an alarm clock while the music from Jeopardy was playing. The crowd just kept laughing.

I figured Marco and I were good. We were friends. It was just how I wanted it to be.

I brushed a tear from my cheek.

***

I WOKE UP THE NEXT DAY feeling stressed. We had our own show to get on the road and a lot of preparation to do. This time there would be no Alfonso to do our advance set-up. We had to cram all our stuff, and Wild Child, Papa, Petey, and Hotstuff, in the trailer for an eight-hour road trip to North Carolina. I wasn't sure how it would all fit, especially the hay.

Hay is the clunkiest, heaviest, and bulkiest thing to ship, and it's messy, too. We had started feeding compressed bales of Timothy which were smaller. But they were heavy as all-get-out and hard to pick up because the plastic strapping was too tight to get your fingers under.

I couldn't believe Margot was going to allow Ryder to take Papa the very next week all the way to Canada. But she had agreed. Francesca had convinced her. Francesca wanted both her riders and horses to be at Gladstone. It was Francesca's dollar after all.

I had come to the arena to run the CD player while Deb watched Margot run through the freestyle. Margot was falling apart.

"Deb, I hardly know the music; the horse is too strong in my hand. I'm behind the music one time and then ahead of it the next time. Each beat is too exacting, and I don't like where the pirouettes are. I'm too close to the rail. I wish Francesca would let go of this idea. It's just crazy."

Deb's voice was low and slow. "Margot, calm down. If you panic and chase the music, it's no good. No one wants you saluting at the end and the music running on; so slow down. Fill the music with dressage, OK? Let's take it from the top, and I want you one or two beats behind where you think you should be. Don't let the music push you. You know what I mean?"

Deb looked over to me. "OK, Lizzy. You play announcer."

Then Margot gathered Wild Child again. I could see her draw into herself and take a deep breath. She had taken Deb's words to heart.

Margot did a few canter-halt-rein-backs and then raised her hand for the music.

I did my best imitation of an announcer. "Margot, your music is rolling."

Margot picked up passage as her swing music began, and in she came. And of course it was fine. She may have started her pirouettes ahead of the music, but she placed them in a better spot; and the good news was she finished her salute right with the final beat. I applauded like crazy, and Deb gave one of her wolf-whistles.

But most important, Margot had pulled it off. "Oh Deb, I wish you could come!"

"No can do. Glitter and Regina are about to pop. Lizzy here will take good care of you and Wild Child. And of course you have Ryder."

Margot cut Deb a look. It was fleeting, and she cut her eyes back to Wild Child's neck in a flash, giving him a heartfelt petting. But that look said volumes to me. They had been discussing Ryder. I knew it. I could imagine the conversation well enough. Ryder better watch herself. Ambition was OK, as long as it didn't run over someone else, be it human or horse.

I took a sweaty Wild Child back to the barn where Francesca was meeting with the vet. He was filling out our health certificates. Even though we wouldn't be stopping at an agricultural inspection station like we had to do leaving Florida, we were still required to carry our original negative Coggins tests and health certificates. If you got pulled over, you'd better have the right papers.

The vet needed to take temperatures and listen to lungs. Then he would look at the trailer so he could verify that it was clean and sanitary. I put Wild Child in the wash stall and started stripping off his tack as the vet approached.

"So how is this big guy doing?"

"Well, he's usually too tired these days to try and take me out."

I pulled off his saddle. The saddle pad was saturated with sweat.

"He's an impressive animal."

The vet lifted one hand to shake down a thermometer, lifting another hand to pet him. Wild Child pinned his ears, barging forward in his usual threatening manner, snapping his teeth in the air.

"Wild Child!" My arms were full of tack so all I could do was yell at him.

He whipped his head around and looked at me; startled. I was embarrassed at his bad manners.

"I'm sorry. He always believes the best defense is a good offense."

The vet just stepped back, looking at him and shaking his head. "Well, he looks healthy to me."

He turned and walked away without having touched Wild Child.

It was the same game Wild Child had used so effectively on me, except I never had the option of turning and walking like the vet just did.

"Well Wild Child, I guess you impressed that one."

He was looking at me with wide-eyed innocence. I hung up the dirty tack to be cleaned and threw the soaked pad in the laundry hamper. Then I opened the fridge to grab some carrots, triggering a whinny from the wash stall.

"Got your hearing-aid turned all the way up, don't ya'?"

I stepped out into the aisle with a handful of big long fresh-looking carrots, and he was pinning his ears and shaking his head up and down.

I scolded him. "Make a pretty face or you get nothing."

And "boing" the ears came forward. I actually laughed. "Wild Child, am I getting through your thick skull?"

As he munched I stroked his face; a soft look came into his eye; and I just let him take one carrot after another as I pulled gently on his forelock. I thought about how much you can tell from a horse's eye. When Wild Child relaxed, his eyes reminded me of Bazooka, young and innocent.

Then there were his ears, so relaxed they almost seemed loose in their sockets.

You had to be around horses awhile before you could fully appreciate how expressive horses' faces are. I had read somewhere that each ear had thirteen pairs of muscles, and the nostrils, mouth, and lips each had ten. Non-horse people typically would ask me what the horse was smelling; as if a horse was a dog; and it was true that stallions especially liked to sniff manure. But horses were mostly masters of body language. It was a language I was getting more and more fluent in, but I would never be better at it than they were. I would always be the foreigner. Kiddo had taught me that.

I was not sure how many muscles surround the eye, but a nervous, scared horse has a wide-open eye, often showing white around it. The ears are either pointed toward the source of anxiety, or quickly swiveling one direction after another.

A calm, contented eye is like that of a nursing foal, drawn inward; safe. Horses that develop trust in their riders get this expression during their work-outs. They feel surrounded by the rider; protected from predators. They often seem to me to blink more often. Their ears bounce or hang a little lop-eared; or just turn halfway toward the rider. They are still taking it all in, aware but not focused on anything external; even their breathing changes, becoming rhythmic with their stride. Tails too, get loose, bounce, and swing.

Then, there was the eye of the horse that was abused, distressed, or exhausted. Sometimes this eye seemed to roll part-way back into the horse's head so he appeared to be blind; a horse who had literally "checked-out."

Neck positions speak volumes because horses have to change their visual focus by moving their necks. A high neck helps them focus on distance, and a low neck allows them to focus on items that are close up. When a horse suddenly lifts its head, bugs its eyes, points its ear, and freezes, the rider must be ready to take flight. This is the posture of a prey animal that thinks it has spotted a predator. If you are sitting on a horse that strikes this pose, you can often feel the strong, fast beat of their heart under your legs. It's enough to charge your own bloodstream with adrenaline.

Mouths were also very expressive. Foals made an interesting gesture with their mouth when they approached an older horse. They pulled back their lips and smacked their gums (or teeth if they had them). It reminded me of a nursing gesture, but it was clearly a submissive gesture. A plea: "I'm a baby, so don't hurt me."

And then there was aggression. Wild Child was making me an expert on aggression. I had a lot of opportunities to study Wild Child's threatening displays, his ears, his mouth, his lips, his nose, his tail, his muscle tension, and really his entire demeanor.

One moment he could be fine, and then the next be ready to swing the first blow in a fight. When he spotted a target, for example, a dog in his paddock or even a butterfly that flitted into his path, he would lower his arched neck to focus on his target. His ears would pin back flat; his nose and lips would pull back; his mouth would open; and then he would charge, sometimes only one step or two. The dogs knew to run until they were safely outside his fence. Even the butterfly knew to find somewhere else to flit.

But he was beginning to understand that he couldn't chase me away. I was not going away. I was on his team. He was learning to look for me. There was security in the familiar, and we had forged an odd, grudging sort of friendship. It wasn't that I totally trusted him, or that he totally trusted me. But we were spending a lot of time together.

Meanwhile, my true love was getting the short end of the stick again. I seemed always to be apologizing to Winsome. And here I was getting ready to leave her again.

Margot was happy with my lessons, but I knew the facts; she had bigger fish than me to fry.

I was going on faith because I knew Margot had the big picture in mind. She knew the destination, and she knew the path to get there. I did not. I was taking Winsome with me on a path I had never traveled.

Down in Florida Margot had taken over the ride on Winsome while I had learned on Rave, and Winsome had benefitted from it. When I first started riding Winsome again, I had felt the difference. But the "trainer-effect" didn't hold for long once Margot had stopped riding her.

When I rode her, she was a beautiful First level horse. Her back was relaxed and swinging, and she was nice and steady in the contact and during transitions. But she was too much on the forehand.

How was I to make this leap while I was busy traveling to horse shows as a groom?

The world of dressage was passing me by. Natalie's words haunted me. Grooms don't necessarily graduate to become trainers.

I did not want to be a career groom. I wanted to ride. I wanted to be the star of the show someday and not forever a member of the chorus.

And I was saying goodbye. No rides on Winsome for the next five days. She would just chew grass and get fatter and fatter on that program.

I had to do something. And the answer was right in front of me.

Deb.

Margot thought it was a great idea. Deb would work Winsome for me while I was on the road. I begged pretty please and took her a case of her favorite beer.

I found her trying to pull the mane of a squirming two-year-old. The wash stall floor was covered in clumps of black mane, but there remained plenty of mane on the horse. In fact, it was still a bushy mess. Deb had more work up there than she could ever get to, and her two "girls" with pendulous bellies would soon be adding to her herd of charges. I felt guilty asking, cringing as I got the words out.

Good old Deb tipped her head, studied me for a moment, and then nodded.

"OK, Lizzy. Bring her up this afternoon with the longeing surcingle, her bridle, and side reins."

So I dutifully brought Winsome to Deb, and we headed to the round pen.

"I'll start the half-steps with her while you're gone. I'll show you one way to do it."

Deb longed Winsome first in the round pen with two longe lines. One went to the outside bit ring and through a standing ring on the top of the longing surcingle, crossing over her back and into Deb's hand; the other went like a normal longe line to the inside bit ring. Since we were longeing in the round pen, the outside line pretty much hung loose, and Winsome longed normally. Then Deb snapped a lead rope to the inside bit ring and handed me a baggie full of sugar cubes and a washcloth that she jammed into my belt. She walked a bit behind and to the inside of Winsome's left hip, holding the two longe lines, and I walked next to her head, holding the lead rope. We practiced walk halts, and every halt got Winsome a sugar cube. I used the washcloth to wipe the sugar slobber off my hands.

We went from walk-halt-walk to trot-halt-trot. Again, every halt got a sugar cube. Once we got that down, Deb made the transition to trot sharper, snapping the whip in the air so that the next few transitions to trot made Winsome jump out of her skin. We followed each of those with an abrupt halt and more sugar.

Soon Winsome was jumping forward into trot, then slamming on the brakes and whipping her head around for her sugar cube, which we gave with a ton of praise.

She was anticipating the whip and voice to spring forward into trot, and then stopping sharply to get her sugar. Finally all Deb did was lift the whip and cluck, and Winsome did three clear diagonal steps of trot almost on the place. Deb immediately halted her and had me "sugar-her-up." We undid the side-reins, took off the lines, and praised my little red mare to the skies.

Winsome had just had her first lesson in piaffe. It made my heart soar.

Deb would repeat the lesson each day with Alfonso helping while I was gone. I would owe Alfonso a case of beer, too.

I still had one more thing to reaffirm before I could comfortably hit the road for North Carolina. I had been doing my homework, but I wanted to make sure I had crossed all my "T's" and dotted my "I's." And I invited Deb to come watch and give her seal of approval.

CHAPTER 30

Social Antennae

"**WILD CHILD, THIS IS YOUR DRESS** rehearsal, buddy. You will behave for the FEI jog, even if I die trying."

I had him in the wash stall. It was past bed-check; late. I had put his snaffle bridle on, and I had called Deb and asked her to hike down in the dark so I could do an FEI jog rehearsal in the indoor.

But I didn't expect to see Pali and Marco, too.

And no matter how much I believed a romance with Marco had to be on the back burner, just seeing him caused my heart to pound.

I had to turn back to Wild Child and fuss over every keeper on his bridle to collect myself for a moment. Then I put on a carefree tone. "Hey, Deb. Hi Pali…Marco. Sorry I'm interrupting your evening. I didn't know you guys were here."

Pali spoke first, "We were just getting ready to leave when you called Deb. I haven't seen this handsome devil, but Deb thinks he is world-class. So I am treading across enemy lines to have a look-see."

Deb tugged at his arm, "Don't be silly Pali; the enemy is never here this late. Isn't he lovely?"

Everyone stepped a little closer, and I could feel Wild Child tense.

I was proud at how beautiful Wild Child was, and once I had collected myself, I realized I was happy to see Marco, too. I had a chance here to show off. I hoped I could.

"I've been working hard and using everything I've learned. I don't want Margot embarrassed again at the jog."

Marco nodded at me and said, "It's time to test it and see if it holds."

I pulled Wild Child out of the wash stall, and we headed into the indoor. Deb walked ahead of me so she could turn on the lights.

Ever since I had noticed Ryder spying on my late-night barn time, I had carefully waited until she was safely in her room with the door closed, and only then tip-toed out. Although I hated that I even cared, I felt I could only do my work in privacy.

Wild Child snorted as we walked into the arena. Francesca's lights were excellent in that they were bright and even, not a shadow cast across the arena footing. But Wild Child definitely was on edge. In a way, this was all good. I needed to test his submission. He slammed on the brakes and fixated on something. It was his image in the mirror, and he bellowed a body-shaking whinny at his own reflection, ratcheting up his tension and mine. I had to break his fixation and slow down my own heart rate.

I jiggled the reins a bit. "Hey, Wild Child, man I'm here. That's not another horse."

I put my hand on his ribs and moved him sideways. It broke the spell. Then I heard Marco. "Good, Lizzy. Bring him back to you."

Then I went through his routine, trying to keep it the same as we had been doing in the barn aisle every night. I looked up to see Pali and Deb laughing together, Deb elbowing Pali.

But Marco wasn't joining in. He was intent on watching and nodding his head in approval.

I really kept Wild Child busy until he was following my every body movement, staying close and attentive. Then Deb called to me, "OK, Lizzy. See if you can do the jog pattern now."

I started very cautiously, almost not letting him out of the walk. Then I repeated it a little more bravely, adding a rein-back for good measure, after the halt, to make sure he didn't barge ahead of me.

Deb called out again, "Wait here, Lizzy. Keep him busy. I'm going to add another little test, but don't worry, I'm just bringing Kiddo in as another distraction."

As soon as Deb entered with Kiddo, Wild Child let out another blasting whinny that could probably be heard in the next county. It was hard not to let that rattle me, and I heard Marco's reassuring voice. "You're OK, Lizzy, just keep drawing him quietly back to you."

And I did.

I moved again to the middle of the arena and engaged Wild Child in his exercises, sweet-talking him as we worked.

"Go ahead and do the jog again, Lizzy."

This time Wild Child was more relaxed. I figured he enjoyed having his friend nearby, and he seemed to understand the purpose of our session was no different from when we were practicing in the stable. I felt he was connecting the dots. It was as if he had finally said, "Oh, is this all we're doing?"

So I trotted away from my "ground jury," and this time I let him move out, running right by his shoulder, the bridle reins slack, bounding along but keeping my eyes on him.

And Pali and Deb and Marco were dead quiet now. I knew he looked stunning. Wild Child was going to rock the jog in North Carolina, and it was because of ME and my hard work. I pulled him up and made the right-handed turn back toward my ground jury.

And then of course, I saw them.

Margot and Ryder were standing with Pali, Marco, and Deb, who was holding Kiddo.

My heart sank, and my mouth went dry.

I finished my pattern. Then I told Wild Child what a good boy he was, because he had been. And I was proud of him.

Margot looked me straight in the eye and applauded slowly, the claps seeming to echo in the brightly lit arena. "Bravo, Lizzy darling, bravo!"

My voice sounded a bit shaky. "It's because of Marco. I've been working every night on it Margot, but I needed his help."

I looked over to Deb. And she came to my defense. "You know why we didn't say anything about Marco to you, Margot. We wanted you to be able to honestly claim ignorance if Francesca found out."

Margot crossed her arms and nodded her head. "I see; but now I <u>do</u> know."

Deb raised her eyebrows before answering. "No sweat. We've accomplished our goal, I think. Anyway, Francesca doesn't need to know, and who here would tell anyway?"

Then Deb smiled and even winked at Margot, who turned away as if she didn't see the wink. But she saw it.

Margot turned to Marco. "Well, Marco, I'm sure you are just as accomplished as your father. I'm certain Lizzy has benefitted from your help."

Then she reached over and gave Pali a hug, which he returned. "Pali darling, how have you been?"

I cut my eyes to Ryder, whose face was expressionless. Did she know they had all been good friends once?

Margot stepped back, but not before Pali gave her cheek a gentle pat. "Margot, you are looking as beautiful as ever."

"Ah Pali, you can't really mean that, but thank you, it still feels nice to hear flattery."

Her hair was down, and I always thought it made her look younger and more approachable.

Margot gave a sigh. "And now I really must go to bed or I'll be worthless in the morning. I don't know how you girls can keep these hours!"

Ryder had been silent and standing a few strides back while all the pleasantries were exchanged, but finally Margot turned and drew her forward to join the circle. She linked her arm through Ryder's. "Ah, there you are darling. Pali, Marco, this is Ryder, our newest addition and a real-up-and-coming talent."

Marco and Pali reached forward, shook her hand, and exchanged pleasantries.

Then Margot pulled gently on Ryder's arm. "Darling, come walk me to my car. Goodnight all."

And we answered with a chorus of goodnights.

I walked into the apartment after taking way too long to put Wild Child away so I wouldn't be likely to see Ryder.

And I was relieved to see her door was closed with no strip of light under it.

Hah. The flying monkey was a coward as well as a sneak. But if she really wanted me fired, she would have gone to Francesca. If she had, the scene in the indoor tonight would have played out differently.

That thought was so horrible that it made me physically shudder. And it also dampened the fire of my anger.

Why hadn't she called Francesca? Was this all about Margot? For sure Ryder had meant to knock me down a peg in Margot's book. I could only think that Ryder was jealous of my closeness to Margot. Even though hers and Margot's show success was the focus of the entire farm these days, and the rest of us were just support staff, it started to make sense.

Truthfully, she did have more than one reason to be jealous. One reason could have been those afternoon hacks with Margot that I counted as priceless. Ryder had never been invited to join us. Or it could have been foal-watch with Deb and Wink's foaling. By the time Ryder was called, it was me and Deb and Margot side-by-side. And I had purposely asked for Ryder to be excluded.

Or maybe it was that Deb had taken only me to the circus, where I had met the incredibly good-looking and talented Marco. I had closeness to Deb, and I was close to Margot; and then I had a gorgeous boyfriend that she watched me kissing. That was something to be jealous about.

She couldn't even-up that score by going to New York with Francesca for a day. No matter how confident, or even arrogant, she seemed, this little move showed that she really was insecure. She had tattled on me like I was a big sister who had stayed out after curfew. She had simply run to Margot like running to Mommy. I shook myself.

I had played a part in creating this monster, and Deb did, too.

How could I have been so dense?

The next morning I went about my business, but I felt jittery, slightly sick to my stomach, and full of regrets.

Margot came in and took Wild Child from the cross-ties. "Lizzy, Ryder, walk with me to the indoor please."

I braced myself, looking over my shoulder at Ryder. She stopped brushing Hotstuff and cast her eyes down, but spoke through tight lips. "Let me put Hotstuff back in his stall."

"No need, Ryder. I'll be brief."

And so we trailed after Margot, heads bent. I figured we both deserved a dressing down.

As soon as Margot got into the indoor, she turned to face us. And she was angry. I'd never seen Margot angry. She lowered her voice, and we both had to lean in a little as she whispered. "We are a team here. Do I make myself clear?"

I heard myself say, "Yes."

But I did not hear Ryder answer.

Margot continued. "This farm is a big endeavor, and there is plenty of work to go around. It's not a competition, girls. Sometimes one of you will be up, and the other down. It's the way it goes; but I need both of you, and I need Deb. I can't afford losing any of you right now. I put in a lot of my time to train you girls, and I don't want to keep starting over. Emma was here for eight years. That's about what it takes to make a Grand Prix horse, and that's what it takes to make a Grand Prix rider too, but only if you are committed. I don't want to spend my time on people who are not committed and waste my energies on petty jealousies. So, are you two committed?"

This time we both answered. "Yes."

"Good then."

Margot looked satisfied as if all were now set right. And then she added, "One other thing, I want my barn to be a place where I can find a sense of calm, support, and peace. A tall order I grant you. If you have some problem between you, just work it out between you and don't make it my problem."

Margot's eye contact was intense. I felt it physically. I had to clear my throat to answer.

"Yes, Margot."

"In fact, you two should have plenty of time to talk things out. Francesca and I are going to fly to the show. You girls can drive the trailer. That's eight hours of togetherness down and eight hours back."

I turned and looked at Ryder. Her face was expressionless.

But Ryder replied, "No problem, Margot."

"Great. Now I don't want to say another word about it, and neither will either of you. Got it?"

This time we both answered in unison. "Yes, Margot."

***

I WOULD NEVER GET USED TO driving a four-horse trailer. Getting gas was nerve-wracking, but the hardest part was maneuvering tight turns, especially on a two-lane road. Once I was up on the interstate, it wasn't so bad. But I could never forget that I had some ungodly dollar-amount of horseflesh behind me, and some of those animals had also become my dear friends. They depended on me to get them safely to the show.

I was flattered that Margot and Francesca trusted me enough to put me behind the wheel, but the responsibility was a heavy burden. I couldn't keep my mind off my "cargo."

Behind me was Wild Child, the horse Deb called "world-class." And then there was young Hotstuff, Margot's "wunderkind."

And Papa, the sweetest horse ever and Ryder's ticket to the big leagues.

And Petey. I wasn't sure Cara even knew that Petey was leaving the farm.

I spent eight hours driving, drinking coffee, and feeling stressed. I needed to stay on high alert and watch out for the other guy. I always kept my eye on the tail lights of the traffic ahead. I wanted no sudden braking for the horses. I tried to give them as smooth a ride as possible, and I took my curves with my foot gently on the brake.

We had hit the road armed with credit cards, cash, and also a special road-safety policy for horse trailers with an emergency number on the card. Kind of one of those things that you hope you never need to use. But it was there just in case.

Ryder was allowed to drive only if I was feeling fatigued, and only on the highway and not in the city. I was not sure I would be any more relaxed when she was behind the wheel. I was a terrible back-seat driver.

Margot and Francesca would be at the show hours before we would roll in, and they promised to have the shavings down in the stalls so the horses would be able to unload immediately.

Ryder popped in her ear buds pretty early on in the trip. But she couldn't ignore me for eight hours.

"Ryder."

She gave them a yank with a sullen look on her face.

"Ryder. Do we need to talk?"

All of a sudden, I felt a lot older than Ryder. The fact that I was driving this huge rig, and she was sitting there trying to tune me out, made me feel like I was a soccer mom saddled with a typical sullen teen.

"No, Lizzy. It's cool."

"That's it?"

"Yeah."

"So we're not going to talk to each other for this entire trip?"

"What do you want to talk about, Lizzy?"

"I don't know, Ryder. What are you listening to?"

"Papa's freestyle music. I'm visualizing our freestyle. I know every footfall, and I'm disaster-proofing myself."

"Disaster-proofing?"

"Yeah. Did you know that mental rehearsal is as powerful as real rehearsal?"

I did know some sports psychology stuff, but I wanted to encourage her. "No, tell me about it."

The sullen look faded from her face as she became engaged in her subject. "Yeah. They did an experiment where one group practiced throwing a basketball from the free-throw line, and the other group only visualized throwing the ball. But the group visualizing was told to see every throw go in the basket perfectly. And, of course, the other group couldn't help but make mistakes. Then they tested them."

"The visualizers did better."

"Yup."

"OK. So what's disaster-proofing?"

"So I've done my repetitions of visualizing the perfect freestyle ride on Papa. It's not as easy as you'd think. First off, you have to visualize it as you actually see it, not the judge's view, but the view from the saddle. I had to capture the <u>feeling</u> of a great performance too, not just the visuals. It's hard to do. And then the next step is imagining things going wrong and handling it brilliantly. You can't freeze when you have a disaster, and now I've watched myself handle it. I've practiced turning disaster into victory. I don't let anything distract me. I stay relaxed, and my heart rate and breathing actually slow down. It's like slowing time down so you can regain control. It's about discipline."

"Really? You can really slow down your heart rate?"

And so I let Ryder teach me more about mental rehearsal and sports psychology.

Ryder was smart and disciplined. I grudgingly had to admire that about her. I glanced at her face while she lectured me. Her face shone with animation and intelligence, absorbed in what she was telling me, and she was really very articulate.

"Ryder, y'know, sometimes you rub me the wrong way, and I'm sorry if I'm short with you, but I want you to know that I do think you are very talented."

It cost me a bit to say it. But I meant what I said. It was my peace offering.

"Thanks, Lizzy."

I put my eyes intently on the road.

And then the cab was silent, and the ear buds went back in. When I glanced back over at her, her eyes were closed. She was riding Papa in her mind, handling disasters with grace.

She would.

But Ryder, oh Ryder, had missed my cue. I expected some show of reciprocal feelings. I had made an opening gesture like the reaching of my hand toward hers. And she had kept hers in her lap.

I had said something honest, something nice, and expected something returned to me in kind. I did not feel angry. I felt a little sad for her. She was lacking something, some social antennae. But then again, I wasn't feeling superior in that department lately either.

CHAPTER 31

Ready, Aim, Fire

I ARRIVED AT THE SHOW GROUNDS and made my way to the stalls, nervously steering that behemoth of a truck and trailer around other trailers to our barn.

As usual, my butt was numb, my lower back stiff as all-get out, and the bottom of my right foot hot.

If I ever had pots of money, I swore to myself I would pay someone else to ship my horses—someone like me. That made me smile.

Margot and Francesca had been true to their word. Our stalls were bedded and ready for the horses. Francesca took all our paperwork and passports and headed to the office to check us in.

Margot stayed with us to orchestrate the unloading.

Wild Child came off first and, of course, stopped as soon as he hit the parking lot to lift his head and trumpet his arrival. The God of horses had arrived and expected all the other horses to stop and pay homage. He cracked me up.

I let him have his moment... just. "All right, Wild Child, you're blocking the exit, man, giddy-up."

We got all four horses off the trailer and into their stalls, and then I had to run to the bathroom.

When I got back, I was not thrilled to see who was stabled right next to us; Patrick.

On the bright side, I figured he'd have great food set out all weekend and invite us to partake.

Margot's job was telling us where to put stuff, and then she did "house-work." She set up her table and chairs, racks and hooks and such, and then got out the broom.

While Ryder and I were still running the drill and hanging drapes, Francesca returned with our packets and wristbands and numbers and, of course, the program. She and Margot sat down to look it over.

I noticed Margot nibbling on her fingernails. She looked up. "Girls, I want these horses to log some time in that coliseum. I have no idea what Wild Child or Hotstuff will be like in there. I know Hotstuff has never seen anything like it before.

"We'll ride Wild Child and Papa early tomorrow and then bathe and braid for the jog. The other two will have to wait."

I could see that this weekend was going to be an exhausting one. I was suddenly grateful that Winsome was at home. I knew who my first priority was.

"OK, Margot, I'm taking Wild Child into that coliseum right now."

"Good girl, Lizzy."

I hopped down off my chair that I had sat in maybe two minutes.

After a quick lick with the brush, I put on my deerskin gloves, ran the chain over his nose, and grabbed a short whip. "Now listen, you, we are going to have a look-see, but we are all business, buddy." Leading Wild Child around was never going to be a casual affair.

I called out hellos as I sighted Natalie, but I couldn't take my attention off my charge. He was swinging his head left and right and marching double-time. I felt like I was following more than leading. But funny thing, he seemed to know where we were going. He was headed for the entrance to the floor of the coliseum. I wondered if he had competed here before.

I made a circle to wait until there were no horses in the ramp-way into the arena. Once we had a clear shot, I headed in and took the inside track. Horses were already working in the arena, and a crew was busy setting up the little white dressage boards.

Potted ferns were sitting in a flatbed trailer behind a pickup, along with the dressage letters. It was a minefield of potential spooky items.

The audience would sit in tiers above the floor.

Wild Child and I did speed-walking laps. Every so often he called out or pranced at my side. But I was extremely pleased at how manageable he was. I found a small space to practice some of our drills, and even though I had to regain his attention a few times, he was OK. When I dug a few peppermints from my pocket, he was focused on me enough to eat them.

I finished our session by making him bow for the last peppermint and then headed for the exit. I was so proud of my new level of control. The hard work was beginning to pay off.

I looked up to the stands to see Patrick sitting by himself. His elbows were on his knees, his chin in his hands. And I saw the ugliest expression on his face. It was an angry face. He had been watching us.

I smiled up at him and waved.

It felt good.

***

BY THE END OF THE DAY, I was numb. Ryder and I were ready to go check in to our hotel, and I was ready to pass out. Margot had generously offered to do bed-check. As we stood at the hotel desk, I could see through glass doors into an indoor pool. Ryder followed my stare and soon was waving.

In the pool was her friend Suzette, with Patrick, and several other people that I did not recognize. They were splashing around and laughing. Plastic cups sat on the edge of the pool. It would never occur to me to bring a swimsuit to a horse show.

But not surprisingly, Ryder had brought hers. As soon as we pulled our rolley-bags into the room, Ryder was talking. "Lizzy, do you mind if I shower first?"

"No, that's fine."

"I want to go for a swim."

"Oh. Yeah. Sure. You go on and join the party."

"Thanks. Are you coming down?"

"No. But thanks for asking, Ryder. I'm going to find out who will deliver to the room and just order something and watch TV and then crash."

"Patrick's barn is going out for steaks and asked me to come, too."

At that I did feel annoyed.

"Ryder, we just put in a really long day, and the weekend hasn't even begun. You need a good night's sleep."

Here I was again, sounding like her mother. But no way was she listening. I could look at her and see she wasn't hearing me, and her mind was already pool-side. "No worries, Lizzy."

Soon I was sitting in my PJs waiting for the Chinese delivery guy to knock on my door.

***

I NEVER HEARD RYDER COME IN, but she was a lump under her sheets in the other bed when my cell phone started its wake-up music. The phone alarm started soft and then got louder and louder until I wanted to pick it up and fling it across the room. Ryder was rolled over on her stomach with the pillow over her head.

When we got to the barn, Natalie was raking up her section of barn aisle. She had already done her stalls. Her freckled face lit up as soon as she spotted me. "Lizzy, you are really slipping. I can't believe I beat you to it this morning."

Then she looked over at Ryder. "Not you; I'm surprised you're even standing this morning."

She turned to me. "Lizzy, this kid has a hollow leg or something. We were partying in Patrick's room last night, and she was putting them away!"

I turned and stared at Ryder. She pushed past me to the feed room, avoiding eye contact.

Our horses whinnied and banged at their doors. While Ryder fetched buckets, I went and gave Natalie a hug, and while Ryder wasn't looking, pointed towards her and mimed strangling myself.

I wasn't sure what to do about Ryder. I sure knew I wasn't going to go tattle to "Mommy" Margot the way Ryder had done, and besides, Margot had been clear about not bringing her into our petty squabbles.

Ryder may have found her little group to get drunk with, but I was going to enjoy every minute of time I could get with my friend Natalie. She was fun. I turned my back toward Ryder as she came out carrying buckets and began dumping feed. I whispered to Natalie, "Natalie, what in the hell were you doing hanging with that crowd?"

She winked at me and whispered back, "Purely for research purposes, Lizzy."

That made me giggle. "Does that mean Patrick was buying?"

Natalie smiled a devilish smile. "He bought everyone's steak dinner, and man, the booze was flowing in his room."

That only reminded me that Ryder was drinking, and she wasn't of age. Why was Patrick plying young girls with alcohol? What a creep. But I was still puzzled how Natalie had found herself in Patrick's room. "Natalie, how'd you get invited?"

"I invited myself. I needed a free meal, and I'm always busted."

I understood completely, since it was my usual state of affairs. But Frank had handed me some "road money," so I was feeling generous.

"Well, Natalie, tonight I want to buy your dinner. Yeah, but it's not free. I want a complete de-briefing."

Natalie's fist went into the air and she did a little shimmy, shaking the rake in her other hand. "Score! Two free dinners in a row!"

One of her pigtails had hay sticking out of it, and her jeans were filthy and wet from dragging the hose around. She was a sight. As she dragged the rake behind her to put it away, she was singing. She turned around to wave one of her plastic braces at me. She ad-libbed lyrics as she belted out some faintly recognizable tune at top volume. "When the sun goes down, Lizzy...it'll be you and me and a Margarita or three!"

Even though it was a non-competition day, I was almost sick with nerves, and I knew for Wild Child's sake I had to get control of my state of mind if I was going to help him.

Wild Child was an emotional mess while I tacked him up. He whinnied repeatedly and leaned against the cross-ties, trying to see down the aisle.

When he wasn't calling and leaning, he was pawing. I didn't try to stop him either. I knew reprimanding him for being nervous and pawing would be like yelling at me for having a big old knot in my stomach. It would only make it worse.

So I tried to be very quiet around him. I tried to breathe slowly and settle my own heart rate. I knew the real answer for his nerves would be provided by Margot. For a flight animal, freedom to move was the best reassurance, and Margot would allow movement in the controlled way that would truly settle him body, mind, and soul.

New national show rules meant that Margot had to wear a helmet while mounted on the show grounds. She could still wear the top hat for her actual qualifier classes that were still under FEI rules, but otherwise helmets must be worn.

I believed the wearing of top hats would die a natural death. They served no function and were uncomfortable as hell. But Margot would be one of the last to give hers up. The only time I'd seen her wear a helmet was in Florida when we first started riding the babies. I never saw her wear one in New Jersey. It never stopped me from wearing mine every time I climbed aboard though.

I ignored her fussing over her brand new custom-designed black velvet helmet. It was top of the line, costing over five hundred dollars. I thought it was beautiful, but Margot was as twitchy as a two-year-old trying to get it on. For one thing, her little blonde bun needed a big shift downward for the helmet to go on. I helped by giving it a yank, and she yelped and shot me a dirty look.

I could barely keep Wild Child still enough for Margot to mount. He jigged away from the stable while Margot was still adjusting her reins and patting the top of her helmet like she thought it would fly off her head. I had snugly adjusted her chin strap. It was going nowhere. But if she didn't watch herself, Wild Child would be the one taking flight.

I took a deep breath. Ryder got Papa out and started grooming.

"Ryder, you OK on your own?"

"Yeah. I don't need you, Lizzy."

"Good. I'm going to watch Margot."

I knew Ryder would never admit it, but I had a feeling she was hurting from her big night.

Maybe her second night she would actually go to bed and be rested for her first day of competition the next day.

I jogged toward the FEI warm-up arena. I knew Margot would already be in the ring.

There were only two other horses in the arena. Margot was trotting around, but Wild Child looked tight-as-a-tick. The only way I knew he was still breathing was that every few strides he would whinny.

I slowed to a walk, wishing like hell that Deb was around to talk Margot through her ride. Then as I watched, disaster unfolded, and I was powerless to help.

The pistol-style watering jets that were set at regular intervals onto the fence posts were slowly raising their barrel-shaped nozzles. You couldn't miss it for the sinister noise. Air was hissing through the jets as the oncoming water pressure pushed it through the pipes.

Wild Child had just trotted past the out gate, but the other two horses were on the other side of the arena. The noise stopped him in his tracks.

It seemed to be ready-aim-fire, as the pistol-like shower heads began spewing high-powered arcs of water.

"Chuck-chuck-chuck."

And all hell broke loose.

Wild Child ducked and spun on his heels, bolting back through the out gate and toward the barns. The other two horses scampered sideways in a mad dash to follow his lead, gaining a lot of speed as they hit the gravel driveways. The riders were no more in control than little rag dolls on their backs. The three were running on instinct alone, fleeing danger.

Meanwhile, Wild Child had a head start on the other two horses, but seemed to have slowed down to allow them to catch up.

Once he had his two friends, the three went blasting by me side-by-side, the women saying, "Whoa, whoa, whoa," pulling on reins to no avail, and spewing gravel. A couple pieces stung my legs.

Someone came out of the end of our barn with their arms spread wide and walking straight toward the bolting horses. Brave soul. All three horses came to a screeching halt in front of her. The two made a quick duck around the person, who made a grab at Wild Child's reins, catching the left curb rein and hanging on.

Yeah, it was Ryder.

One lady flipped off over her horse's right shoulder as it ducked to the left around Ryder, but amazingly she landed on her feet, still holding onto her reins before just slowly crumpling into a sitting position on the ground.

The other horse just stopped, and his rider jumped off on her own power. I looked back toward the arena, to see all the water pistols hanging down, barrels pointing at the ground, harmlessly dribbling water. Someone had shut them back off.

I finally caught up and took Wild Child from Ryder, looking up at Margot. She was white as a sheet.

CHAPTER 32

Not My Revolution

WILD CHILD GOT A BUBBLE BATH, and then it was time for me to put in his braids. This time he was almost motionless in the cross-ties. After his "near-death" experience fleeing from the horse-eating water-gun sprinklers, followed by Margot riding him for an hour, he was spent.

Unfortunately, Margot was wiped out, too. She had given Ryder a lesson on Papa and then gone to the hotel for a rest.

Peace settled on our little section of stable. I noticed that Wild Child even chewed his carrots slowly, letting pieces fall out of his mouth. I left him alone as long as I could, and I was glad to see him take a short nap.

But soon I had to bother him again to braid. He stayed snoozy until I braided his forelock. He woke up then. I kept my braiding stool as far away from his mouth as I could. He tried to lip the yarn off my apron, but he wasn't really trying to bite.

My goal for the afternoon was for Wild Child to get through the jog with Margot in an orderly way. I would find out if my training "stuck" under the excitement of an arena full of naked horses. Margot had endured enough stress for one day, and she still had to ride Hotstuff this afternoon.

Of course I also wanted to be proud of my work. Marco had sent me a text asking to report back how it went. And I only wanted to send back a good report.

When I brought out the snaffle bridle, Wild Child wouldn't open his mouth. My arms felt like lead holding it up, up, up, as he fussed like a baby in a high chair who didn't want to eat his strained peas.

"C'mon Wild Child, c'mon boy, open up. Open up, Wild Child."

Nope. Jaws clamped shut.

I slid my finger in the side of his mouth, pressing gently on the bars of his mouth. It was the space where the bit sat and where horses have no teeth.

Nope. His nostrils wrinkled. Bridles meant riding to Wild Child, and he had had enough for one day. He was on strike.

I sighed and put his halter back on and went for sugar.

First I just handed him a cube with his halter on, and of course he gobbled it up. His ears came up hopefully, as if he thought he had won this round and was off the hook.

Sorry, but no way.

As soon as I lifted the bridle up to him again, he turned his head completely to the rear, as if something at the back of the grooming stall was suddenly terribly interesting.

"Wild Child, I'm sorry but the show hasn't even begun yet; you and I have to put this bridle on NOW!"

I pushed his head around to the front, and he made a little threatening lunge and snap at me.

I took a deep breath. Patience.

Next when I slipped the halter off, I quickly wrapped the lead rope around his face. As I lifted the bridle, he clamped his jaw again, lifted his chin, and wrinkled his nose. I used the rope to gently pull his head back down.

Then I offered the sugar cube. He tried his best to part his teeth just enough for the cube and no more, but I pushed my thumb on his bars, this time getting a tiny bit more of an opening. I allowed the lead rope to loosen and slipped in the bit. Even though I felt like I needed another hand or two, I managed to wrestle the bridle over his ears.

"Gotcha'."

The whole bridle was askew, the brow band crooked and his braid twisted sideways. The lead rope was still twined around his face. Clearly we had done battle to get the thing on. I was glad there were no witnesses. I soon sorted it all out and got the lead rope off.

He shone like a copper penny, handsome as ever. But he was pouting, nose wrinkled and ears halfway back. I had won, and he was not happy about it at all.

When I put the number on his bridle, he threw his head up and down and then shook it violently, having another tantrum.

I had to twist it and bend the little metal stem until it didn't touch any part of him. He sighed heavily, retreating back into his pout. We were finally ready.

Then I waited for Margot to appear.

And waited.

They were calling for the Grand Prix horses to gather in the holding area, the covered arena next to the coliseum.

And Margot was nowhere to be seen.

Finally Francesca appeared. "Lizzy, I just got permission for you to present Wild Child for the jog. Get on down there."

"What?"

"Margot's pulled a muscle in her back."

"Oh my God. Is she OK?"

"She's at the Doc-In-The-Box getting some pain killers. She'll be fine but she simply cannot run alongside Wild Child."

"But I thought Margot had to do the jog to compete."

"Lizzy, stop dithering and listen to me. I just jumped through a lot of hoops for you to do it, so go."

"But Margot always dresses up for the jog. I'm all wet and dirty."

"Put on a ball cap and get down there."

Francesca ducked into the tack room and came out brushing off a cap. She crammed it on my head and then shooed me out of the barn.

I had to smack him with the end of the reins to get Wild Child to budge.

Then Francesca walked behind me, clapping her hands every time that he balked.

He perked up a bit once he saw all the beautiful naked horses parading around in the covered arena.

He gave one half-hearted whinny.

I went to the middle of the arena and put him through his exercises, which he did perfunctorily with a grumpy face. And then I practiced jogging a few times. He was reluctant to move but began to brighten up as he swung his head around to check out horses.

When his number was called, I knew what to do, and so did Wild Child. I could swear he knew he was on display.

He puffed himself up and stood perfectly still, posing, as the ground jury walked around him.

Then when they instructed, I marched him away and broke into a lovely trot, then back to walk, and then turning right around the marker, amazed that the reins were slack in my hands as I picked up my second trot.

The announcer's voice seemed to boom in my ears.

"Number 84, Wild Child, has been accepted."

I gave him a hearty pat, which was more for me than him.

As I walked into the barn, Patrick was handing off his horse to his groom. "Sorry to hear about Margot."

"She'll be OK. Margot's tough."

He nodded thoughtfully. "She got lucky. That stallion could really hurt someone."

I felt my cheeks get hot. I walked Wild Child right into his stall and kept my back to Patrick as I gave Wild Child a pat and pulled off his bridle and slid on his halter. I still had to pull his braids, but I wanted him to have a break first. He got a sip of water and then put his head in the back corner of his stall, turning his head once to pin his ears at me. He wanted me to go away, and I felt he had earned some private time. I hooked the door and walked away to clean his bridle.

But Patrick was hanging around. He plopped down in one of our chairs. What an ass, I thought to myself. I went into our tack room and cleaned Wild Child's bridle, and even though I was hiding behind the stall drapes, I still turned my back to Patrick, hoping he would just go away. I had taken a page from Wild Child's book on body language.

But there he sat, and when I glanced sideways at his form, I could see his foot jiggling away like a nervous tic.

Then here came Francesca alongside Ryder who was leading Papa back from his jog. Papa was champing on his bit, still a little keyed up.

Clearly Francesca was who Patrick was waiting for. He finally popped up out of our chair. "Ah, Francesca. How is Margot?"

His saccharin voice was full of concern.

"Hi Patrick, well I told her to go get a good massage and a bottle of pain killers. She's a real trooper. She'll be fine tomorrow."

Tomorrow? I thought about poor Hotstuff who had been circling in his stall trampling his poop into mush and calling every time a horse came or went out of our barn. I tried to interrupt.

"Uh, Francesca?"

Francesca turned and glared at me. I shut up and waited for her to finish her conversation with Patrick. He leaned in and said something to her that I couldn't hear, and then they strolled off together, whispering earnestly.

Ryder had put Papa in the cross-ties and was busily pulling out braids. Maybe she knew.

"Ryder, is Margot not coming to ride Hotstuff?"

"Doesn't look like it, Lizzy."

"Poor Hotstuff. He's anxious and needs to get out."

"Lizzy, chill. I'm going to go ahead and tack up Petey and give him his workout and then let him see the sights."

"Oh. OK. Glad you know what you're doing."

Great. I looked across the aisle at Natalie, giving her a weak wave. She was filling a hay bag. She mouthed the words, "Sorry about Margot."

I figured everyone had been talking about Wild Child's morning bolt. There hadn't been many people around to witness it. But tongues were clearly wagging. I figured that was to be expected, but Patrick's comment really bugged me. As if it were somehow Wild Child's fault. Any horse would have bolted. The other two horses in the arena had bolted, too. And no one could have done better than Margot in riding that bolt.

Francesca finally returned. "Lizzy, Margot has asked that you give Hotstuff a good longeing and then hand-walk him all over the show grounds. His classes are not in the coliseum, but he does have a class in the covered arena. See that he gets a good look at the judge's boxes and the flowers. Margot doesn't need any more spooking to tweak her sore back. It's up to you to see that doesn't happen."

"OK. I'll give him a good longeing session."

"No spooking tomorrow. Do whatever that requires."

"Sure, Francesca."

There went any chance I had at an early evening and early bedtime. I looked across the aisle again at Natalie, but had to cut my eyes away quickly so Francesca wouldn't see. Nat flashed both hands in the air for a split second of a double-handed rude gesture. Then while Francesca conferred with Ryder, Nat stuck the hose between her legs and opened the nozzle a bit, shooting some water in Francesca's direction. But she quickly twisted it closed and started singing a song while she dragged the hose down the aisle to fill her buckets.

I suspected Francesca may have sensed something.

Ryder had a smirk on her face; she had obviously seen Nat. I was working hard to keep my expression impassive.

Francesca rolled her eyes and let out a dramatic sigh to let us know that her burden in dealing with us was a heavy one; she started up again. "I'm leaving now girls. Be sure and be thorough in your preparation tonight. Margot has a big day tomorrow. Patrick will keep an eye on things for me until tomorrow, so if you take any shortcuts, I'll hear about it. Oh, and Lizzy, tonight you can do bed-check duty by yourself. Ryder has a very early ride tomorrow on Petey. I want her well-rested."

I narrowed my eyes as I looked at Ryder, hoping to convey my agreement with Francesca on that point. The last thing Ryder needed was another hangover.

I wondered if Francesca had heard about the previous night. Ryder dropped her eyes away from my glare. Maybe she was feeling a shred of guilt. Good.

My job this weekend was to work my butt off for Margot, and when required, for Ryder. I figured I could sleep again in New Jersey. Shit always rolled down hill, and that was where I was currently standing.

I noticed Patrick followed Ryder out when she got on Petey. He would be her ground-person in place of Margot. Patrick had used Margot's sore back to stick his big toe in the door; I knew Ryder was thrilled, and Francesca was on board. Slick move.

I longed Hotstuff in a special area set aside for longeing, and then I walked my legs off around and around with him, making sure every flower and judge's box became a total bore.

He was swinging his head left and right, accidentally bumping into me as he took it all in, whinnying only when he heard another horse whinny.

He was overwhelmed with all the strange sounds and sights, but Hotstuff was clingy rather than rude. I had loaded up my pockets with sugar cubes, but by the time we wearily dragged ourselves back to our barn, my pockets were empty. Hotstuff was wiped out more from the emotional drain of his day than any physical effort.

We had walked miles, and I was stumbling with fatigue as I hosed him off and toweled his face and legs. If he could have climbed into my lap, he would have; he wanted me to stay close. After I toweled off his face, he lowered it into my arms. His giant ears flopped left and right. If he had a thumb, he would have been sucking it. Poor guy. Growing up was stressful.

By the time I had finished with him and pulled Wild Child's braids, Natalie was slumped in our chair polishing off a beer.

"Nat, maybe I need a rain check. I can hardly keep my eyes open."

She shook her head. "Nope. You are feeding me tonight, remember?"

Ryder came out of the tack room, ears pricked. "You're going out, Lizzy?"

"Just going to dinner with Natalie. I can drop you off at the hotel first."

"Don't worry about me. Patrick can take me back. We're all at the same hotel, remember?"

Patrick again. What did he have planned for her tonight? I put on my Mommy voice before I could stop myself. "Ryder, I hope you won't stay out late."

Ryder rolled her eyes, looking like the bratty teen. And there we were again, acting out our parts. "Lizzy, you fuss like an old lady. Since you're doing bed-check tonight, I'm going to bed early."

"Got it. I'll try not to wake you up when I come in."

Natalie was sitting silently, but watching the exchange over the lip of her beer bottle. She caught my eye and blew a little oompa-oompa with her bottle. I was ready for a mental-health break from Ryder. Thank God I had Natalie to escape with.

"C'mon, Natalie. Let's find a big juicy steak somewhere. I might as well eat myself silly until bed-check. Let's go dirty."

"Now we're talking!"

Natalie's face was positively glowing at the idea of steaks.

It wasn't fine dining by any means, just one of those chain restaurants that line the busy roads along major interstates, right alongside the big-box home improvement stores. It was a good thing, since we were grimy from head to foot.

I went ahead and ordered the most expensive and biggest steaks on the menu and more beer for Natalie.

I was almost too tired to eat. A combination of shaky and sleepy, plus the soles of my feet felt bruised. I made a mental note to buy better shoes. Natalie was slathering butter and sour cream on her potato.

"So Natalie, what's up?"

"Lizzy, I've got a wheelbarrow full of shit to unload on you."

I took a bite of steak and chewed. It seemed like work to eat, but I kept at it, leaning back in my booth between bites and waiting. Nat was polishing off her potato, skin and all, before attacking her steak. I didn't know how she had so much energy.

"OK, Lizzy, because I really do like you, I gotta' tell you Margot needs to get her ass back here tomorrow and get in the ring."

"Yeah. I kind of get that feeling, too."

"Patrick wants the ride on Wild Child. Every time he sees that horse, he gets all antsy. He's been real cozy with Francesca all day, too."

"Why? He's got a fabulous horse. And money to buy whatever he wants, according to Ryder anyway. Ryder says his sponsors are richer than rich."

Natalie turned to her steak. She was eating fast and talking at the same time.

"Lizzy, the Winstons had another trainer before Patrick, y'know? Their former trainer was no match for Patrick. In fact he was a sweet young guy, wet behind the ears. But he got Claire started, and all excited about dressage, and the two of them got the husband on board to go flitting off to Europe to purchase kick-ass horseflesh at the elite auctions."

Natalie was waving her knife in the air to make her point.

"But they were all young horses. This young trainer, he seeks out Patrick to be his mentor, 'cause he's got to deliver now and he's not equipped. So, Patrick starts to come periodically to the farm to coach him."

Natalie had to pause, catch her breath, and cut her meat again. She sat back a moment to take a swig of beer and burp. Then she grinned at me.

"So, here comes Patrick to 'help' him, and of course he sees the Winstons' farm with a brand new state-of-the-art stable. All of it screams money; and then when he gets a load of the quality of horseflesh, well, I'm sure he played it cool while he was wetting himself."

"And..."

"Claire Winston traded up."

"So, the kid was out and Patrick was in?"

"The next thing you know, Patrick is the new trainer for the Winstons, and this kid's working in some small barn in west Bumble-fart."

"Poor guy."

"Yeah. That's one young trainer who learned the hard way who not to trust."

"How do you know all this, Nat?"

"Lizzy, I've been close to the players for a while now."

"And what's that got to do with Margot? She's no wet-behind-the-ears kid."

"Patrick's got his eye out for his next victim. Claire is just finding out how much he's cheated her. He got greedy. I mean, if you buy a horse for a hundred thousand and turn around in three days and sell it to Claire for three hundred, you would think you would keep real quiet about it."

"So you heard him admit that?"

Natalie shrugged.

"He likes to party. Let's just say Patrick, and my boss Tommy, they think people like us don't count, like we don't have ears. But when they knock back a few, they forget themselves and can't help but brag. They think I despise Claire the way they do. But I know they despise me, too. I'm still tolerated at the party though. I'm pretty good at telling jokes and getting the party rolling. But hell, I'm just a groom. Just like you."

Natalie lifted her knife and pointed it at me.

"But Lizzy, in time the 'fit will the hit the shan.' I'm about to prove to the Winstons that Tommy and Patrick have been screwing them over big-time."

I saw her face get very serious. And I got worried, too.

"What do you mean, Natalie?"

"I've got more than hearsay now. Y'know what I mean? I've got proof. I don't think anyone but me knows exactly what's coming down the pike, but still, I can see Patrick sniffs something in the air. Claire's not too good at keeping a poker face. I think she's been cool toward him. His job's safe for now; or at least until after the qualifying list comes out for Gladstone. Claire won't cut him loose yet."

"So, you think Patrick knows something's coming, and that's why he's courting the Cavellis?"

The knife got lifted and pointed again. "You can't be fired if you quit first, right?"

"Well, I think that Margot's position is secure, but I still don't like it that Francesca hangs out so much with Patrick. And then there's Ryder; she seems to think he's hung the moon."

"Yeah. Well, Suzette was green with jealousy the other night. She considers herself Patrick's girl."

That thought was shocking. "Are you telling me that he's sexually involved with his young rider? I don't know about Suzette, but Ryder's only eighteen. She's not old enough to buy beer."

"I can't say for sure, but my best guess is…duh? He tells the girls they're going to the Olympics. That he can provide them with world-class horses and sponsorships. And then they are swooning when he chooses them. They don't want to believe he's serving up piles of hot steaming horse crap."

"Does he ever deliver?"

"Sure, when he can. He drives his horses like the devil. They win their share for sure until they can't because they're lame. He promotes himself, and he promotes his students. But his real talent is that he's a dream-weaver. They call these types of guys con-men because they instill confidence."

Natalie drained her beer. Her nose was sunburned and covered with freckles. I noticed she was wearing soft wrist braces tonight instead of the hard plastic ones. They were spotted with stains, just like her clothes. She waved at the waitress and asked to see a dessert menu, and then turned back to me.

"Lizzy, once I settle my personal score, I want you to watch out for yourself. I like you too much. You remind me of me, before I was so angry."

We both sat in silence for a moment, all lightness gone. I had gone from tired to tired and despondent. None of this had anything to do with me, and yet I was somehow stuck in the middle of it. And as nutty as all of this sounded, I believed every word of what Natalie was saying. I thought of her as the lone wolf; the whistle-blower; the catalyst for the fury that was surely coming. I couldn't be part of any of it. But I admired her bravery.

"I admire your courage, Natalie; I could never be that brave."

"Lizzy, revolution begins with the proletariat."

I gave her a tired smile, and she continued.

"And that would be us, Lizzy."

I sighed again. "Natalie, this is your revolution. But I am grateful that you've told me what you have. It will help me protect Margot."

Natalie shook her head and leaned back in her chair studying me.

"I hope Margot deserves you. But, please, let Ryder make her own choices. You never know about loyalty until it's been tested. I get the feeling that she's about to be tested."

Chapter 33

Hammers And Nails

"**Shit, Margot, get your ass here**." I was muttering to myself.

It was time for Margot to be here. Wild Child was braided and resting in his stall. Hotstuff had been longed, bathed, and braided. Ryder was ready to take Petey to the warm-up arena. And Margot was MIA.

All I could do was pace back and forth, back and forth. I had raked and tidied and picked the stalls out for the umpteenth time. Natalie and I had exchanged concerned glances across the aisle.

And then finally, Francesca and Margot were there, Margot calling down the aisle. "Ryder, darling I'm so sorry to be late. These damn pain pills knocked me flat. You go ahead to the warm-up with Petey. I'll be right down."

She went into the tack room and started fussing. "Where are the headsets for the coaching system?"

I walked in and handed them to her. They were in the basket where they always sat, right in front of her.

"Margot, are you OK?"

"Yes, dear. I'll be fine. Let me get started with Ryder, and if you don't mind, bring a coffee to the ring for me."

"No problem."

Margot looked tired, but she was dressed to ride, her blonde bun low on her neck in its new helmet-friendly position.

Ryder was still standing on Petey outside our barn. He looked absolutely regal. He was solid black with a beautiful crest on his neck. His face was noble rather than beautiful, with a large round eye, his ears pricked forward. His tail was full all the way to the squared-off end. He could have been one of those military statues in some European park. In fact he was unusually motionless.

Ryder spoke up. "He won't move. I'm stuck."

Margot started clucking as she walked toward him.

I was thinking to myself that he was acting just like Wild Child. "Hey, Ryder," I yelled, "he's got stage fright. Just like Wild Child."

I could see Ryder clench her jaw, and then she growled like a grizzly bear, kicking him hard with both spurs.

"Errrrr! You will not do this to me!"

Petey threw his head down and pinned his ears. Then he started backing up really fast, disappearing around the corner of the barn, out of my eyesight.

Margot and I trotted together to the end of the barn, looking to the left.

No Ryder.

We quickened our pace, turning left alongside the length of the stable.

No Ryder.

But we could hear a scuffle, and then we saw her.

Petey was cantering a few feet, and then stopping and backing up again. And then jumping forward, as Ryder began to growl again and nail him repeatedly with both spurs.

Then he slammed on the brakes and flew backward, down the length of the barn and around the far corner, again out of our sight.

Margot and I exchanged looks, and for a moment she looked totally defeated. She moaned. "I do not need this, I do not need this."

"Margot, what should we do?"

"Lizzy, go get the longe whip please. I'll wait for you here, OK?"

I ran as fast as I could, my heart pounding.

When I got back, we had to go on a hunt for Ryder and Petey. Margot and I found them, still backing and twirling around near the barns, no closer to the warm-up arenas.

"Ryder darling, Lizzy and I are here to help. You just wait for us, OK? Lizzy, please take a rein and lead Petey, and I'll walk behind him. Ryder, you just sit relaxed as possible dear. We need to get the adrenaline levels down if we can."

And so we made a slow progression to the arenas. It was weird because the previous day he had gone to the arenas and worked fine. This day, the day that mattered, he was totally resistant to leaving the barn.

We walked and stopped and petted, and then asked him to walk again. If he backed up, Margot gave him pop on his behind, and he would nervously jump forward; and now and then he would shake his head, as if he were saying, "no, no, no!"

Once we got to the warm-up arena and inside the gate, we had to let go. No one is allowed on foot inside the warm-up arena.

But we weren't needed.

It was as if he could suddenly breathe again; he was once again just Petey, cruising around in the middle of a crowded warm-up arena.

Ryder put him right to work.

Margot hadn't put on the coaching system, so she had to yell her instructions to Ryder. There was no way she would have Ryder come out to put them on and risk him not going back in.

I was amazed at Ryder. She was tough. She showed no signs of stress now.

Her warm-up was brief. She had blown too much time twirling around the gravel driveways by the stables.

Ryder came out of the warm-up to head to the competition arena. I still had to get the polos off, but Margot kept her moving all the way to the competition arena.

I could tell Margot was nervous. As soon as Ryder pulled up, Margot was whispering to me. "Hurry, Lizzy, hurry. I'll get this side, you get that side."

"Ryder darling, try and keep him on your aids."

I did my best to hurry, but Petey was going stock still again, his neck lifting, his gaze fixated toward the show arena.

I heard Ryder growl. "Don't you dare, you son-of-a-bitch."

Margot handed me her wad of unwrapped polos, and the longe whip, and grabbed a rein from Ryder, putting one hand on Petey's ribs, right behind Ryder's leg, and pushing his hind legs sideways in a turn-on-the-forehand. Petey unlocked, and as the horse and rider in the arena had finished their test. Ryder was able to give him a kick and send him in.

Margot sighed loudly. "Oh thank God. They're moving forward again."

"So, this is Petey's problem." It came out of my mouth too fast to stop myself.

"What?"

"Well, Cara said that he was only for a really advanced rider. This must be why."

"Cara told you that?"

What to say now? I sure as hell wasn't going to mention Francesca's name. "She mentioned it, casually. And Ryder jumped at the chance to take him on as her project."

Margot turned away without answering.

Petey and Ryder looked great. They were warming up outside the little white boards, waiting for the whistle to signal that the judges were ready.

Ryder was being smart, testing his reaction to the forward driving aids. She even did a few canter-to-halt-to-canter strides, immediately lengthening his stride.

Margot was quiet, but I could feel her tension.

The whistle blew.

Ryder turned around and made a good approach down centerline. She was the picture of competence, her position in the saddle textbook perfect. She landed a perfect halt at X. It was straight; it was square; and it was immobile.

It was too immobile. They were stuck.

Margot couldn't bear it. She turned her back. "Tell me what's happening, Lizzy."

"Well, Ryder is kicking, and Petey is standing there taking it."

"He's not backing up?"

"Uh, yeah, now he's backing up."

Margot turned around now, and we both stared in horror as Petey backed all the way out of the arena, just as perfectly straight as the line he travelled in to get to X.

Ryder was not a blonde, nor was she particularly fair-skinned, but her face was beyond red.

It was more like a mottled sort of purple.

The whistle blew again. They were eliminated. The judge was standing in her booth yelling. "Bring him back in here."

And then, she yelled at Margot. "Margot, get him back in here."

And Margot stepped forward and grabbed a rein, and led Ryder back in as I walked behind clucking, my arms full of polo wraps and a longe whip stuck under my armpit.

Thankfully, although this was a big show, this was not an important class, and there was hardly a soul watching.

I knew how Ryder was feeling.

Ryder did not know what abject failure felt like. I did. And I was reliving it. My heart was pounding, and my mouth was dry.

We walked Petey back into the arena, and Margot had a few words with the judge. I heard words like "new horse in training" and "blindsided."

Ryder managed to canter around a few laps before they walked back out.

I couldn't bring myself to like Ryder. But I felt like crying for her. For Margot's sake, I told myself.

As Ryder passed, Margot reached for Ryder's leg, trying to give her a reassuring pat.

But Ryder quickened her pace, and Margot's hand only brushed the air.

Francesca and Margot were huddled in the tack room as I pulled Petey's braids. I was straining to listen.

Ryder had gone to the restrooms to change and was staying there an awfully long time. Probably pulling herself together, although she would never admit such a thing. She didn't have Papa's class until late in the afternoon, so there was no rush now.

I couldn't hear a word that Margot said, but Francesca didn't try to lower her voice. I could hear her clearly. "Too much success too soon is just terrible for a person. Petey was a perfect opportunity, Margot. Failure is what that girl needed."

I couldn't hear what Margot said.

"Cara was just going to throw Petey out in the field for the summer. What a shame that would have been. He is a handsome thing. If Ryder can turn him around, it will be an honest source of pride for her. She's only successful now because you trained Papa, and I pay for him. No one gets it free of charge, especially an eighteen-year-old."

Margot mumbled something.

Then Francesca again. "Let's see if she rises to the challenge shall we? Now she has something to prove."

And then she was off.

Ryder trailed back in. I didn't know what to say. But I saw Natalie, across the aisle holding the reins for someone to mount. She was smiling broadly, but turned her back as Ryder passed by. My guess was that everyone had heard about it, and that Natalie agreed with Francesca. All I could think was what a complete bitch Francesca was, and I wondered what additional failures she had planned for my future. Maybe I still fell off enough to keep her happy.

Ryder ducked into the tack room without even making eye contact with me. But I could hear her.

"Margot, I've been talking to Patrick about Petey. He thinks we should scratch the rest of the classes, and get permission to ride in the show arena at the end of the day; and if he pulls that stunt again, I should just beat the crap out of him. I mean, he has to go forward. That backing-up is just the worst."

There was a pause. I stopped working on pulling braids. Petey was now totally relaxed. Poor thing was emotionally spent. I was too, but at the mention of Patrick's name, I cringed. How stupid was Ryder to throw that at Margot. I was sure Margot was seething.

But Margot sounded composed. "Ryder, darling, I had no idea about this horse's problem. You know our preparation would have been much different if I had known. As it was, you and I were thrown to the wolves."

Ryder's voice was flat. "What do you mean?"

Margot was silent for a moment. Francesca deserved to be busted big time. But Margot let it go. "What I mean is, we don't know this horse. We don't know what he is capable of doing. You think backing up is bad? Let me tell you what is bad. Bad would be making this escalate to rearing. Bad would be him hitting the panic switch and flipping over backwards and turning you into a quadriplegic; that my dear, would be bad. And that isn't going to happen; not on my watch, darling."

As Margot talked, her tone became emphatic, her words carefully measured.

Ryder answered in a flat emotionless voice. "What do you suggest?"

"That we use our heads. It's the one thing we have that's more powerful than the horse's."

"Yeah?"

"Ryder, consider that yesterday he was fine. Today, he didn't even want to leave the stable. What do you think changed his mind?"

"Patrick said it's like a jumper that refuses his jumps. You have to go to the bat, or in our case the whip, and beat him over it."

"Typical male approach, but darling, a jumper that refuses his jumps feels over-faced. The thing you must do is lower the jump until he gets back his confidence. You lower it until he jumps again, even if you have to go back to a pole on the ground, and then work your way back up."

"I didn't do anything to over-face that horse."

"No, I don't think you did. I think someone else did. He knew it was show day. He wanted no part of it. Tomorrow we leave him unbraided and ride him early, before his class, at the break of day. See if it changes anything."

Ryder sounded incredulous. "Margot, are you saying that the braids made him turn into a total ass?"

"Ryder, I don't know this horse, and I can't promise you anything. When they wrote the book on training dressage, they didn't know about Petey, OK? But I can promise you one thing; if a small hammer and nail doesn't do the job, reaching for a bigger hammer and nail usually won't get the job done. It only splits the board."

I didn't think Ryder was ready to hear that. I thought she was so mad at the horse that only violence in some form was going to placate her.

Ryder came out of the stall, and Suzette was walking down the aisle toward her, jabbering like a teenager.

"Oh Ryder, I heard what happened. You poor thing! You should get Patrick to help you. He'd turn that jackass around in a New York minute!"

Well, I had been quiet as a mouse while eavesdropping, but I had been simmering with rage. I figured poor Suzette was a safe outlet for me to let off steam.

So I hollered. "Hey, Suzette, Petey is not a Jackass! This is a super horse who was scared shitless today. He's going to get an eighty percent one day. He just needs someone who can give him confidence, and then you'll be glad he's not in your class."

Oh man, that felt gooooood. But my blood was still up; it took all sorts of self-control to stop there.

I heard some weak laughter from Margot who was still in the tack room. And Ryder turned and scowled at me like I had no right to open my mouth.

Suzette put her arm through Ryder's and began pulling her down the aisle looking over her shoulder at me like I had three heads. They wandered off before I could say a word. But I felt like I should jump off the mounting block and go start a brawl.

Natalie did a little happy dance with her broom that included some rude gestures, including hip thrusts toward the departing girls. She was crowing with glee. "Get outa' here, Lizzy! I'm sure Petey there appreciates you defending his honor. I genuflect before you. You da' woman."

Margot stepped out of the tack room and stared at Natalie for a moment, and Nat froze like a deer in headlights. Margot's mouth was slightly open, her lips curling upward in a small smile. But mostly she looked bewildered. She said, "You look very familiar. Have we met?"

Natalie pulled her broom up tightly against her chest, and for a moment she looked embarrassed. And then she stuck out her hand and gave Margot's hand a hearty shake. "I'm Natalie."

CHAPTER 34

Folks Want Results

"Lizzy, is Hotstuff ready for me?"

"Longed, bathed, and braided."

"How is he feeling?"

"Better than the rest of us."

Margot smiled weakly. "We need to give Ryder a little space. Petey and I have just given her a lot to chew on. She's so incredibly adult-like most of the time that it's easy to forget that she's only eighteen and hasn't learned her own limitations."

I unclipped Petey and led him to his stall. As soon as I took the halter off, he shook vigorously and then threw himself down on the stall floor, rolling and rolling, pressing his mane into the shavings. He got up and shook again, his kinky unbraided mane full of shavings. As I hung up his halter, I realized Margot was standing behind me watching him.

"Look, Lizzy, that is one relieved animal. Those braids represent something terrible to him. He is going to be a puzzle we need to solve. Horses can become dangerous when they feel threatened. That's something to remember, Lizzy."

I thought, "No shit, Margot." The same could be said about people. I wanted to tell Margot everything I knew, but Natalie had made me promise. Nat had some kind of plan, and I promised not to blow her cover to anyone. But still.

"Margot, I heard what Francesca said."

Margot's mouth pressed into a line. "I'm sorry you had to hear that."

"Well, in a way, I get what Francesca was saying."

Margot's eyebrows lifted, and she shook her head. "No Lizzy, things are hard enough without intentionally trying to make them harder. Francesca was wrong. Just know that I would never do something like that to you."

"I know that, Margot."

"Good dear, now let's tack up my big black Lab puppy. I think we both need a long walk to relax, and I need to loosen my back muscles. Stress of any kind just makes it worse."

Margot turned away. This discussion was at an end. Plus, what Margot needed right then was to relax. She had to go and get her head in the game, too.

I had tacked up Margot's horse. I had cleaned Ryder's tack. I had taken care of Petey. I had picked up stalls.

Ryder walked into the tack room and saw that everything was finished. But she just couldn't seem to bring herself to say thanks. The cloud she was carrying over her head was too black and still rumbling with thunder. I could tell there was still another storm on the horizon.

Francesca, Ryder, and I stood by the warm-up arena and watched Margot warm up Hotstuff.

Hotstuff was a balm for Margot's soul. He was still an awkward-looking horse. We couldn't keep enough weight on him although he sucked down more grain and hay than any of the other horses; he was still all angles and bones. At least his black coat was shiny, a little sun-burned brown patch here and there. His way-too-large ears hung a little to the sides. They even bounced in rhythm with his stride. His front legs were long and spidery, and his front hooves looked too big for his slender legs.

But you forgot his awkward looks when he moved. He bounced off the ground like he was on a trampoline. That trot turned heads wherever he went, and people were buzzing about him on the rail.

It had been hard to find a saddle to sit still on him, but this one had been custom-made and fitted. He was growing so fast though that it needed constant tweaking. The only thing that seemed to connect Hotstuff to the ground was his incredibly thick tail, set low on a sloping croup, with hocks that stepped deeply under him like a stalking tiger. As Emma used to say, he was a total freak. But she meant it as the highest of compliments.

The fact that Francesca had bred him, and that he was out of Deb's Regina, was also a source of pride. He was a product of Equus Paradiso Farm and of Margot's training program.

It was clear that Margot loved him, and he felt the same about her.

Margot did a very short warm-up, and then we pulled off his polos and headed over to the covered arena for the USEF test for four-year-olds.

Even though this was only Hotstuff's second time to show, he looked like a cool customer. Of course I had hand-walked him around and around the arena, examining the flowers and the letters and the judge's box, until the bottoms of my feet were numb.

It had been worth it. He was relaxed and obedient. He even halted square both at the beginning and at the end of the test. Finally we had a reason to celebrate something.

At the end of the test, while Margot walked on a loose rein, the head judge stood in her box and addressed the audience, what few there were sitting in the bleachers.

"First of all, I want to congratulate you on owning such a horse." The judge had a distinctly German accent. "When we talk about the happy athlete, for me, this is what we mean, or should mean. I gave this horse a ten on submission."

A little gasp rose up from the stands. A ten on anything was almost unheard of.

She went on to rave about all of Hotstuff's fine qualities. His average score, between the two judges, was high enough that there would be no doubt, barring disaster, that he would be going to the National Young Horse Championships in August in Illinois.

Margot bubbled happily all the way back to the stalls. Francesca actually patted her big baby horse enthusiastically, and for a moment all was well for Equus Paradiso Farm.

But we still had two more rides and two more days to live through.

***

WHATEVER POISON PATRICK HAD BEEN FEEDING to Ryder, I would have thought Margot's amazing ride on Hotstuff would have been the antidote. But it was looking doubtful.

I thought to myself, "Wake up, Ryder. This is what dressage is supposed to be about."

But I still sensed an air of rebellion in Ryder. As she prepared to change again for her ride on Papa, she barely spoke one word to anyone. She was silently intense.

Petey had delivered the blow to her confidence that Francesca had so neatly planned.

I thought Ryder was boiling under her still surface, and I hoped she didn't take it out on sweet Papa.

I had once again put in Papa's braids for her. I did them slowly, rubbing his face and scratching his withers between braids. Papa was a big pussycat who always wanted you to touch him. Margot's touch was the one he wanted the most. But I would do in a pinch. I wasn't going to rush and rob him of what he needed to relax. But it put me behind schedule. He would miss his rest break between braiding and tacking up.

This class would be in the big indoor stadium and would kick off the evening classes which usually drew an audience.

Even empty, the stadium was a big scary echoing metal and concrete structure. You entered the arena on ground level through a narrow lane; some called it a tunnel, with all the seating above the head of the horse and rider. The seating was in tiers; and on an upper level, vendors set up shops and food booths. So there was plenty of distracting noise and movement. All that activity challenged the focus of both horse and rider. Plus, the horse was utterly alone; he couldn't see any other horse while performing. The next horse wasn't sent "up the tunnel" until the rider turned down centerline for the final salute. That aloneness created insecurity for some horses. They were herd animals by nature, after all. But they had to rely on their rider to replace the security of the herd.

Of course if you had any ambition, like Ryder, this is what you and your horse must be able to handle. All the big international contests were held in "electric" venues like this one and worse. You learned to go deeply internal in your focus and surround your horse with your aids.

Papa was a sensitive and reactive horse. But he was also a big-weenie who wanted his rider to take care of him. He would never challenge his rider's authority, but he could certainly freak out about something before checking in with his rider. Just like Wild Child's freak-out bolt with Margot.

But I knew better than to underestimate Ryder. Her impassive face and demeanor, her lack of nerves, added to the fact that she really could ride, made her one tough-as-hell competitor. But it didn't make her the Queen of dressage either. Petey had shown her that. She could fail, too. I had to agree with Francesca, that was an important lesson.

I stepped back to admire my braids. God, I was good.

Ryder was dressed and moving around quietly. She had set all his tack out for me.

I put extra care into his polos and set his saddle on carefully, sliding it from a little in front of where it would go toward the back, to his "saddle-spot," where it settled naturally. That way the hair was smoothed down, and his hair follicles wouldn't be irritated. I pulled the saddle pad lightly up into the gullet so it wouldn't bind at his withers. Then I put the girth on loosely.

Sweet Papa lowered his head into the full bridle, taking the bits in his mouth as I handed him some sugar cubes. I pulled gently on his forelock braid the way I had seen Margot do. He closed his eyes and tucked his head under my arm pit. I let him hide there for a moment.

I whispered to him, "OK, Papa. Come out to play buddy."

I smoothed the curb chain by twisting the links until they would lie perfectly flat and smooth in the groove of his chin. I tucked a cushioned pad over his jawbones before snugging up his noseband. I buckled all the buckles and checked all the keepers. Then it was time to snug up the girth and bring him out into the barn aisle.

One last spritz of fly spray and one last fluffing of his tail, and he was ready for Ryder.

He was beautiful. Unlike Hotstuff, Papa was a poster child of what a dressage horse should look like; he was massively muscled, a real powerhouse, but with a chiseled and elegant face with a large soulful eye.

I felt sad that he was not still Margot's Grand Prix horse, but his downfall had been the one-tempi changes. They made him crazy. And the piaffe also made him so nervous that he would break out of it by launching himself through the air, which Margot thought he might have worked through eventually by gaining strength and by tactful riding. But she wasn't so sure about the ones.

So Margot thought that he would be happier as a small-tour horse, meaning staying at the level that Ryder was showing him. Not all horses were made to be Grand Prix horses. It was better for everyone to let them be great small-tour horses and be happy, rather than push them to the place where they would be unhappy, or even break down mentally or physically.

Just another reason why I loved Margot.

As I watched Papa warming up, Natalie found her way to my elbow. "Well Lizzy, there's the proof that there is no connection between good and good riding."

"What?"

"She can obviously really ride."

I turned back to watch. Yes. Ryder was back in her zone. Papa was working with his ears trained back on his rider; maybe the only sign of his nerves was the extra sugar foam on his lips, as he played with the bit too much. But the reins were light, the curb hanging a bit loose, and the snaffle steady but without any backward tendencies.

In fact, Ryder had a beautiful way of hanging her long arms down and almost forward toward the bit. It was a soft and giving look.

I thought to myself that no matter how we all trained to sit exactly the same, to fit the classical prescription for a "good seat," we all were individuals, and our style was ours alone. It reflected not only our own body proportion, but also our temperaments.

Some riders even seemed to sit more with the downbeat of the trot, and some seemed to accent the upbeat or suspension of the stride. These were subtleties that most people never noticed because the overall impression of all good-sitting riders was that they simply became an extension of the horse; a Centaur.

My eye had become much more attuned to small things, both good and bad.

And as much as I hated to admit it, Ryder's position was not only classical, but also beautifully harmonic and simpatico, and uniquely hers.

Soon I was pulling the polos off, dusting off her boots, and handing her a bottle of water that she chugged and tossed back at me.

It was time.

Margot and I walked into the tunnel, and the ring steward held us back with a hand like a crosswalk guard.

Then we were waved in. Or I should say Ryder was waved in. Margot and Natalie and I walked through a gate and up to the first tier of seats.

Ryder was the picture of composure.

I looked around and was relieved that Patrick and Suzette were nowhere to be seen.

I elbowed Nat and whispered, "Wonder where Patrick and Suzette are?"

"Lizzy, Suzette rides right after Ryder."

"Oh."

Francesca walked casually down the tiers with a shopping bag in one hand and a coffee in the other. She sat directly behind me. So that meant no more conversation with Nat.

Margot turned in her seat and with pursed lips gave Francesca a few nods. Francesca nodded back, some silent communication passing between them.

The whistle blew, and Ryder walked, turned around, and lined up a perfect centerline, picking up a canter and nailing her entry and halt.

Then she proceeded to lay down a near-perfect test, with only one small mistake in her tempi changes. There was hardly anyone there to see it, but those of us who were there applauded like crazy, especially Francesca.

Francesca lightly touched Margot's shoulder, before getting up and walking away. Ryder had clearly just passed Francesca's sick adversity test.

Suzette came flying in just as Ryder walked out of the little white perimeter of the dressage arena on a loose rein.

Suzette's entry into the stadium scared Papa, who spun around and actually tried to go back into the dressage arena. Ryder gathered up his reins and steered him to the other side of the arena, away from Suzette and her fire-breather.

I could tell Suzette was nervous. She should be. She looked over-horsed. It was such a contrast to the controlled composure of Ryder and Papa.

Margot was heading down the stairs.

"Margot, I wonder if I can watch Suzette's ride?"

She stopped and looked surprised.

I could see that Ryder was turned around in the tunnel trying to watch Suzette too, but the ring steward was waving her out.

I added, "I think Ryder would want to know how Suzette's test goes."

"Oh, I guess so. OK, but hurry back."

I could tell within seconds of Suzette's entry that Ryder had beaten her. Yes, her horse was super-powerful, a flashy mover who did everything pretty cleanly, but no way could the judges place her first. The contact was so strong, and sometimes the horse's mouth was open against the pressure. The horse had an eye-popping front leg action but was missing the swinging relaxed back and tail.

Sometimes, too, Suzette looked like she was in a chair seat, her heels pressed down so hard that the foot was in front of her knee, and her upper body leaning behind the vertical. These were all signs that the rider was bracing against the horse, and/or the horse was bracing against the bit.

When the ride was over, I thought Suzette looked exhausted.

I saw the next rider trot in, but I had to run back and take care of Papa.

I knew one thing for sure. Papa would need to keep his braids in for the victory gallop.

I prayed that Margot and Wild Child would have an equally successful ride.

***

"NICE RIDING, LADIES!" PATRICK SANG OUT as he and Suzette walked back into our barn aisle.

Suzette hopped off. Patrick gave the horse a friendly sort of slap on its butt. He dwelled in front of our tack room.

"Ryder, if I could put those two rides in a blender and then divide by two, neither one of you girls would be beatable. You rode a perfect, but boring test, and Suzette here rode an exciting, but flawed test."

Margot was walking down the aisle toward our tack room, and Patrick's back had been toward her. He even startled a bit when Margot spoke.

"Ah, Patrick. But Ryder rode the exact test I asked her to ride."

Margot smiled at Patrick. And Patrick smiled back. They were technically smiles, but of the sort a Doberman makes when it sees an intruder. Natalie had pointed out that fine distinction to me.

Patrick regained his cool and answered her. "I'm sure Ryder is capable of doing whatever her trainer asked of her."

Margot was still smiling, "Yes, indeed she is."

Ryder was standing silently right there in her stocking feet. She had taken off her coat and hat and boots. Her hair and shirt were both wet with sweat.

Patrick laughed a short little humorless, "hah."

"Well Margot, I guess the children's hour is over. It's time for you and me to play the game now. I trust your back isn't too sore to ride?"

"My back will be fine, Patrick. Thanks for asking."

"See you in the warm-up."

"See you there."

After he left I wanted to say something along the lines of, gee, I really hate that guy. But I didn't have a chance. Anyway Margot wouldn't approve, and Ryder would only be pissed off.

Where was Natalie anyway? She would appreciate my comment. I guessed she was working; her boss Tommy had a rider in the division, too.

Margot sounded a little tense as she called out to me. "Lizzy, shouldn't you start braiding Wild Child?"

"Yeah. I'm right on it, Margot."

"And Ryder, don't you need to take care of Papa?"

"I'm on it, Margot."

Margot stood in one spot, aimless; she patted her tidy blonde bun and smoothed down her shellacked hairline. Every hair was in place, as usual. She felt each ear, touching her pearl earrings. Then she unlocked.

"Lizzy, Ryder, I'm going to go to the rental car and take a nap. If you don't see me in about an hour, call Francesca and tell her to come wake me up."

Ryder and I answered as a chorus. "Sure, no problem, Margot."

I pulled Wild Child out and started on his braids. He was quiet and snoozy, and just a little grumpy.

Ryder's score was announced. She had hit the magic number; seventy percent and change.

Suzette had a good score too, but not good enough.

Ryder had pulled Papa out of his stall and was heading to the showers.

I pulled braiding yarn out of my mouth. "Congratulations, Ryder."

"Thanks, Lizzy."

Suzette wandered down the aisle and met Ryder with Papa. She turned around and walked with her.

"Congratulations, Ryder. You beat me again. Sheesh."

"I wanted to watch your ride, but the ring steward wouldn't let me."

"That's OK. Patrick told me I was too hectic and sloppy."

"Were you?"

"I guess so."

After a moment of silence Ryder quietly added, "He told me I was boring."

Suzette giggled. "That guy is never happy."

"But Margot was happy with my ride."

"Must be nice."

"But Patrick's right. It was boring."

"He usually is."

"Yeah. If I want the really high scores, I'm going to have to take a little calculated risk here and there. But it's OK now to be a safe. I just can't be that safe at Gladstone or at the Championships in August."

"You're so smart about this stuff, Ryder. I just kind of' throw myself at each class; you're so... calculating."

I thought to myself that maybe Suzette wasn't as dumb as she looked.

They kept chatting as they walked, but I couldn't catch what they were saying anymore.

Natalie had come in, walking alongside her trainer's advanced Young Rider. The horse was dripping with sweat. Its teenage rider looked visibly upset, her face wadded up in anger.

She jumped off and turned to a woman trailing after her who was clearly her mother.

"Now do you see what we've all been telling you? If you want me to win, you buy me a decent ride just like you've been told. I don't know why I can't go on the trip to Germany to find something better. Now you've made me miss this whole qualifying season."

"Now darling, I think you aren't seeing the big picture."

"Mom, are you blind? You're wasting your money."

The kid flung her helmet in a chair, pulled off her jacket and threw it on top of her coat, and marched off in a huff. Natalie silently began pulling the tack off the horse.

The mother looked embarrassed. "Natalie, I'm sorry you had to hear that. I know Buster isn't the fanciest of horses. But this pressure to spend our way to Championships is just too much for me."

Natalie had her mouth twisted. She was holding back. She had to hold back every day. These were paying customers, and she was just the groom. She never forgot that.

I watched the woman dig into her purse and hand Natalie some bills.

It looked like a wad. Natalie nodded. "Thank you Mrs. Miller, I really appreciate this."

"Natalie you are a Saint, sweetheart. I for one don't know how you do this."

"I love the horses.

"Yes, I see that."

Mrs. Miller patted "Buster" a few times on his sweaty neck. "It's stupid isn't it, Natalie, but I'm more attached to this horse than she is."

She gave the horse another pat and then trailed away.

I got off my stool and went into our tack room and opened our cooler.

We had about fifteen pounds of carrots in there. I pulled five carrots out and walked across the aisle, stuffing one into Buster's mouth and handing the other four to Nat.

Nat let Buster suck one carrot down after another. Her face was grim. "That kid's a little shit-for-human in training. And her Mom's got a spine of jello. But she tips well."

"Does all that drama mean her test didn't go well?"

"Lizzy, here's the drill in my barn. Instead of teaching these brats how to train a horse, my boss churns horses. No one keeps their horse more than a few years, tops. Buy and sell, and pad the price, and take a fat commission off each transaction. That's the drill. If the kid can't ride, well, just keep buying and selling until you can find the robo-horse that can tolerate the kid."

"So she doesn't ride well?"

"She sucks. But no one will say that to the bank-account holder. It's always 'the horse.' And the kid believes it; and the parents believe it because they don't want to think otherwise. And ultimately, they will buy the horse that pulls it off despite the kid, not because of the kid. But they'll burn through a ton of cash first."

I gave Buster a pat. His eyes were soft and relaxed as he chewed the last of the carrots.

"Natalie, I feel sorry for Buster. What will happen to him?"

"He'll join the great horse lottery. Who knows? He may end up in a home where he's really loved."

"And what will happen to that little brat?"

"She'll get her way, even if they have to rip-off Grandpa and Grandma to do it."

"Wow."

Natalie nodded. "The lack of self-examination around here is stupefying, as is the amount of money these types shell out."

"I hate to think it's all about the money."

Natalie shook her head. "They get ripped off because they're too lazy to do the donkey-work it takes to become a real horseman. They need to listen to the horses. The horses never lie; they only go as they're ridden."

"I think I'll stick with the horses then."

Natalie laughed.

"That's all well and good, until you need to go to the feed store. We need the Cavellis and people like them, and those folks want results. Don't forget that."

CHAPTER 35

A Good Cook

WILD CHILD LOOKED AS BEAUTIFUL AS ever. But I could tell he was already tired, and he had yet to enter the show arena.

I was tired, too. Mostly of having to see and hear Patrick. I hoped next time that we could ask to be stabled far, far away from him. Was that possible to do without anyone knowing about it?

Patrick had the first ride in the class, and Margot was the last to go.

The day's first ride was always by draw, and Margot had just gotten lucky.

To ride later in the class was better.

The judges needed room to go up in the scores if a better ride came along, without having to give unreasonably high scores to anyone. So early in the go, they tended to score conservatively.

No rider liked drawing the first ride, but if Patrick was pissed about it, he didn't show it.

In my opinion, the unlucky part for us was that Patrick would be finished and no doubt would be sitting with Francesca, poisoning her mind while Margot rode her test on Wild Child.

I hated that.

Margot and Wild Child were almost too serene as they strolled down to the warm-up arena.

My stomach started churning.

The energy was all wrong. It was like they were both in some kind of trance. I gathered up my bucket of stuff. Ryder was silently walking along by my side. We parked ourselves at the warm-up gate and watched Margot stroll around and around. Finally I couldn't stand it anymore.

"Margot, they're on time. You have twenty-five minutes."

"Thanks, Lizzy."

I took a deep breath as she finally gathered up the reins and started trotting around.

They looked like they were warming up for a First level test. Oh man I needed Deb or someone. I turned to Ryder.

"Ryder, say something!"

Ryder snapped back at me. "What do you want me to do about it?"

"Margot's gone into some kind of trance or something. She doesn't ride him that way at home. He's asleep!"

"Since you know so much, you tell her."

I wished I had the nerve to strangle that kid.

"Margot!"

Margot trotted by and turned to look at me over her shoulder.

Well, I thought, here goes any feeling of job security. I tried my best to channel Deb, imitating her voice in an exaggerated way. "Get the lead out of his pants!"

As Margot circled around, I could see her lips had curled up in a smile.

She got it.

The clouds drifted above us, shifting the fading light from dim to bright and back to dim, casting shadows from the fence posts like a row of cavelletti on the ground. Wild Child took note, arching his neck as he lifted his feet carefully over the shadows. Then the wind picked up, blowing his tail out behind him and causing him to become even lighter and lighter on his feet.

One by one the other horses in the warm-up left to go into the coliseum. Soon it was just Margot and Wild Child by themselves. He stayed attentive to Margot, but I could tell he noted each horse's departure with the roll of his eye. He bellowed out a whinny, inflating himself. He may have been alone in the arena, but with his insecurity came the need to put on a display. This day that was not a bad thing.

He was now the big powerful stallion I recognized. Now the question became whether Margot could keep the energy just right; too much and he would be taking over; just enough and she could show off his impressive range of motion and elasticity. He had to be relaxed but not lazy, energized but not crazy. It was a fine line, and he could shift so easily from one to the other that it took amazing skill, concentration, and courage to manage him.

Once Margot was right in her head, she had the skill, had the concentration, had the courage, and had the most important talent of all; she had feel. She knew just what to do, how much to do, and when to do it. Like a good cook, she never had to measure her ingredients. She knew by feel how to shape and direct Wild Child without even thinking about it; just like Deb; just like Marco. Feel was something you didn't find in a book.

But both of them, Margot and Wild Child, still needed the confidence to go and show what they were capable of.

I nervously checked my watch and called her over. Regardless of the outcome, our day would soon be over.

Margot kept Wild Child on the bit and at attention while Ryder and I stripped off his polos, I wiped off her boots, and Ryder handed her water. We spoke not a word, but worked at top speed; an efficient pit crew.

Then we walked behind her toward the tunnel.

The ring steward was waving us forward.

Margot said anxiously, "I have a stallion. I don't want to be in that tunnel with another horse."

The steward nodded and held up his hand for us to stop. A horse soon appeared at the mouth of the tunnel.

The steward had on a plastic glove and quickly inspected the bit of the exiting horse; this was part of the protocol. The stewards had to check that the bits were legal, check behind the spurs for marks, check the nosebands, and in classes that allowed a whip, measure the whips. The FEI qualifiers did not allow whips to be carried at all.

The steward finished and waved for Margot to enter.

As the horse passed us headed back toward the barns, I saw Wild Child try to turn and watch, and he gave another mighty whinny, the kind that shook his entire body. Margot pulled his head around and gave him a nudge with her spurs. She only got him halfway up the tunnel. He froze and stared into the deserted show arena. Not a horse to be seen anywhere. They were all now back in the barns.

Once again, our big bully was having stage fright.

I channeled Deb again. "Wild Child, move it!"

I gave a series of clucks and waved my arms up and down.

But it didn't work. Instead he started to back up.

I heard Margot say, "Stand back, Lizzy."

And she gave him a hard jab with her spurs.

He backed up faster, threw his head down, and then stood straight up on his hind legs. It was the biggest rear I thought I'd ever seen. Margot leaned forward and grabbed him around the neck with both arms.

Margot managed to look cool as a cucumber, but I could see the fear in Wild Child's eyes. As soon as his front legs hit the ground, I jumped toward him, grabbing one of Margot's reins. "Wild Child, Wild Child, buddy, you're OK."

I looked up at Margot; she was patting her stupid little top hat back down on her head and straightening the brim. I wished like hell she'd had on her helmet. But her face was calm as she slowly reorganized her reins.

I held on to one rein, digging a sugar cube out of my pocket with my free hand. He had finally settled enough to take it from me. I thought that was a good sign. I knew the clock was ticking, and if Margot didn't present him by her formal ride time, she would be eliminated. All the trouble and expense, all the stress of making a last minute run to qualify for Gladstone, would be finished right here and now. I couldn't let that happen.

"He'll be fine, Margot. He'll follow me in. He just needs to take a deep breath, and then he'll be ready to go."

I looked up at Margot and couldn't believe what I had said. But I knew I was right. I had learned his every expression. I could tell by his eye. He was giving in.

Margot said nothing. We stood and waited a moment. And there it was; he took a deep breath. I gave him a hearty pat, and I stepped back to his side and did exactly what Margot had done for Petey; I unlocked his hind legs with a few steps sideways like a turn on the forehand.

It was one of the exercises that Marco had given us. We had done it every night. Wild Child put his ears on me, and his eyes brightened with interest. It was as if he said, "Oh, is that why I'm here? Well, then, no problem, Lizzy. I can do this."

Then I walked ahead and called him. "Wiiild Child, c'mon Wild Child, it's show time."

I turned and walked away, toward the arena, and he followed me in like a puppy. I walked about four or five steps into the arena, before Margot gave me a little nod.

Margot picked up the trot and off they went.

I turned around and headed up the steps where Ryder was waiting for me. We sat down in the nearest seats to watch.

By then my stomach had gone from churning to a dull ache. I wondered where the nearest bathrooms were, but I wasn't going to take my eyes off of Margot and Wild Child. I felt every stride as she rode around waiting for the whistle.

Margot did a few extended trots, then a transition to a stunning passage. The whistle blew, and they turned around and cantered down centerline.

And blew us all away.

I had goosebumps on my arms and, at the final salute, wiped tears from my eyes.

I finally felt like I could look around. I turned to scan the seats behind me for Francesca. I saw Patrick get up from his seat next to her.

Francesca never applauded her own horses and riders. But Ryder and I clapped and whooped. I did see another woman stop by Francesca's seat to chat. I knew she was gushing over Wild Child.

Who wouldn't? I couldn't wait to plant a kiss on his big old shark-face, whether he liked it or not.

CHAPTER 36

Not Waving—Drowning

MARGOT MET US IN THE PRE-DAWN hours so we could get Petey out before the show began.

Unfortunately, he wouldn't be allowed to practice in the show arenas, even before the show started. It was against the rules.

Margot looked tired, even as she made an effort to sound cheery. "Good morning, girls."

We answered in chorus, "Good morning Margot."

"Ryder, let's get this done fast; don't worry about how well he's groomed."

I helped Ryder get the tack on quickly, picking the shavings out of his tail and putting on a fresh set of polo wraps. We might be fast, but we wouldn't be sloppy.

Petey hesitated a moment to leave the stables, but only a moment. Ryder sat sloppy, kind of like a cowboy would. She left the reins loose and simply reached back with the flat of her hand and gave him a slap on his rump.

"C'mon, Petey."

The horse audibly sighed, then blew his nose and reached down to wipe it on his snowy-white polo wraps.

And then, surprisingly, off they strolled.

I thought, "Damn, maybe it was the braids."

The air was soft and cool, with a wisp here and there of ground fog that was quickly disappearing. Petey and Ryder made a handsome silhouette as they walked away. I turned back to the barn chores and was making quick work of it. Four horses were not a lot for me to take care of.

Natalie arrived, and I poured her a cup of fresh coffee from our pot.

"Thanks, Lizzy. Where's the rest of your gang?"

"Margot's coaching Ryder on Petey. He strolled out of here like a lamb today."

"The one that moon-walked right out of the arena yesterday?"

"Yeah. That's the one. Margot thinks maybe it's the braids."

Natalie practically choked on her granola bar. "Lizzy, that's funny. But you realize it's not the braids, right? He feels the tension. Some horses rise to the occasion, ready to go shoulder-to-shoulder with you into the fray, and some just snap under the pressure. Looks like Petey is one of the latter types."

"Yesterday with the braids in he was a maniac. So Margot said try him today without the braids. I couldn't believe the change."

"Lizzy, what do you think the braids signify to that horse?"

"I don't understand."

"Pressure. Probably rough riding. Or he may have had a rider who had show nerves. Someone who made him feel trapped and insecure, instead of giving him confidence."

"Well, that wouldn't be Ryder now would it? I've never seen her nervous or timid. No, he came with that problem. Francesca knew about it; she set Ryder up on purpose."

Natalie reached into my bag and took an apple I had snatched from the hotel breakfast bar. She took a bite before walking over to Buster and giving him the rest of it.

"Lizzy, you need to find a better hotel next time. These are tasteless."

Just then an elegant older lady came down the aisle. I admired her style, a brown printed silk scarf knotted around her neck, a wide leather belt with a horse head buckle on her slim hips, and carrying a butter-yellow briefcase. I'd never seen a briefcase that color before.

Natalie turned her back toward the woman and looked at me like a scared rabbit. "Holy shit. That's Claire Winston. She's way too early."

From a few stalls down, Nat's boss, Tommy, bellowed, "Natalie!"

Natalie snapped to attention. "Yeah. I'm coming."

Meanwhile Patrick had appeared and practically started groveling at the woman's feet. "Claire. I had no idea you were coming."

"Patrick, I was bored to tears at home. I thought I'd come watch you ride the freestyle one more time before Gladstone. Besides, I want to see Suzette's new competition. I keep hearing about this new girl with the name Ryder. I mean, whoever names their child Ryder must have been planning for this one a long time, right?'

Then she laughed a tense little laugh.

Patrick was nervous. I could tell. "Claire, sit down. We just started the coffee."

"Oh Patrick, I'm not interested in sitting just yet. I want to see all my horses. Hand me some carrots."

And then she proceeded to go stall to stall and feed her horses carrots and sweet talk them, rubbing and scratching them in all the right sort of places. She really did seem a decent sort.

But there was clearly strain between Patrick and Claire Winston.

I pulled out Hotstuff, put him in our grooming stall, and began to braid his mane.

He was wearing a fine layer of dust and shavings on his black coat. I thought it was a good sign. Our big baby boy had slept.

And he was still sleepy. He was one horse who seemed to enjoy having his mane braided. His top lip stuck out and wiggled; his ears hung to the side; and his eyes got heavy-lidded.

Straight across the aisle, Natalie had put a horse in her grooming stall and was ripping out braids and getting ready to re-braid.

"What happened, Nat?"

"Oh, I was hoping to get away with leaving these in from yesterday. He only has one class today, and then he's done for the show. But, alas; it's not to be. He rubbed them into a big frizzy mess. So, out they come and then in go a new set."

"Sorry. Margot makes us pull them out after each day."

Claire Winston had gotten her cup of coffee and was wandering down the aisle looking at horses.

And Patrick was dogging her every stride.

Margot walked in, Ryder and Petey right behind them.

I called out to them, "Hey guys, how'd it go?"

Of course Margot was the only one to answer me. "I for one am very encouraged. Ryder did a lovely job, too."

At the sound of Ryder's name, Claire Winston perked up. "Ryder Anderson?"

Ryder answered like she was in class. "Here!"

"Well, I've heard just wonderful things about you. I'm Claire Winston."

Ryder was such a suck-up. She hopped right off that horse and, with a smile plastered on her face, walked right over to Claire and Patrick, shaking Claire's hand.

Margot smoothed her hair back and patted her bun, tipping her head, looking slightly amused.

"Hello Claire. Patrick didn't tell us that you were coming. Francesca is here, too. I know she'll want to see you."

"Wonderful. I can't wait to see her. We have such a lot of catching up to do."

Natalie and I, the grooms, were indeed invisible.

While I braided Hotstuff, and across the hall Nat braided one of hers, we traded looks that no one noticed; some of them typical Natalie style, rude but funny.

Francesca walked in with her cup of coffee, looking sleek. She was wearing white slacks, crisply pressed.

Natalie mimed Francesca's walk while never getting off her braiding stool. She stuck her nose in the air and wiggled her butt, all the while keeping her fingers flying on her braid.

I thought, who but Francesca would wear white slacks to a horse show? I assumed it was a calculated move, planned so no one would dare hand her a horse to hold, or ask her to carry anything to the arena.

Francesca stopped a few feet inside the darkened aisle, pushed her Chanel sunglasses to the top of her head, and slightly squinted. "Why Claire, Patrick didn't tell us you were coming this weekend."

Claire was now sitting in a tall chair outside their tack room. Patrick was hovering over her shoulder as she examined the show program.

Claire looked up, looking surprised but pleased. "Hello Francesca. I didn't know you would be here either."

"Well, I'm not showing this time, just spectating. You know this run up to Gladstone is all about the pros. But I enjoy watching my horses go."

"I do, too. I hear from Patrick that you have some young talent this year."

"Hotstuff is an exciting prospect. We bred him ourselves, you know."

"Well, I don't know about Hotstuff. I'm sure he's special with a name like that. I meant the girl; the one with a similar sort of name as your horse. The one called Ryder. I just met her."

Francesca's lips turned up in a smug little smile.

Claire smiled and rose from her chair, waving Francesca closer, turning her back to Patrick, and walking away leaving Patrick standing alone, excluded.

Claire said over her shoulder at Patrick, "Ta-Ta Patrick, Francesca and I need to catch up. I am absolutely fascinated to hear all about her line of breeches!"

Across the aisle, Nat continued mincing around on her braiding stool; she wiggled her eyebrows up and down and made a tight little smile.

Patrick plopped down in his chair, his brow furrowed, his lips pursed together.

Then Natalie's boss, Tommy, started hollering again. "Natalie!"

"Down here, boss."

"Finish up those braids. I need you to make a run for ice."

"For icing down legs or making Margaritas?"

"How about you get enough so we keep our options open?"

Once his back was turned again, she stuck out her tongue like a spoiled brat.

It occurred to me then for the first time that Natalie and Tommy were maybe a bit too familiar with each other for a trainer and his groom. I mean, this was the guy that she never referred to except with profanity, and someone she said was in cahoots with Patrick.

But it would explain why she had been privy to all sorts of dirty inside information, and included in their partying.

I finished up Hotstuff, and Natalie went off for ice. Soon it was time for Margot to ride Hotstuff in another Young Horse qualifier.

Margot fussed over having to wear her helmet again, but as usual she looked great. She mounted up, and Hotstuff walked away from the barn eagerly. The boy was born to show. He was one horse with no stage fright as long as Margot was on top. To this point in his young life, he considered showing one big happy play date with his Momma Margot.

When they rode their test, Hotstuff was so chilled, his ears and tail bounced with every stride. He got a nine for submission and of course won his test.

And everyone from our barn aisle seemed to be there, Patrick, Claire and Francesca, Natalie and Suzette, and a few others that looked familiar, including Natalie's boss, Tommy.

Ryder was the next to go on our schedule. She would be riding the Advanced Young Riders Individual test, which really was the best test for Papa. It highlighted his extravagant medium and extended trot work at the same time that it made the canter work, where he could get tense, look easy.

Suzette and Ryder had changed places today in the order of go. Suzette was the ride before Ryder. Again everyone showed up ringside at the warm-up to watch. When Suzette went to the show ring, her gang peeled off from the rail and followed her. I noticed Francesca went with them.

Ryder as usual looked great, but this day she was even more relaxed, her intensity mellowed by the positive ride she had in the morning on Petey and yesterday's win.

I was not sure how Suzette's ride went, but a cheer went up from the stands when she finished. But no fear, Ryder was on. You could see it before she even turned down centerline to start her test.

She had her best score yet, 72%. I was happy for Margot's sake and for Papa who was one hell of a horse and deserved it.

I could see that Suzette was still sitting on her horse just outside the tunnel. She had been watching Ryder's test as best as she could from that distance, but most of her view was obstructed. Mostly she stayed to listen for the provisional score. In fact I noticed everyone had stayed for Ryder's ride.

Everyone that is except Patrick.

I guessed he had gone back to the barn.

The Young Riders had their awards at lunchtime, and we all gathered at the collecting area to watch them get ribboned-up and do their gallop.

Ryder had beaten Suzette by two percentage points. I could tell Suzette was disappointed. It had been her personal best score to date.

Patrick was nowhere to be seen, and I felt so sorry for Suzette that he didn't bother to come clap for her. But the rest of us there did a good job cheering for her; even Francesca clapped. Nat even whistled.

It was then time to pull Papa's braids and feed him carrots. I knew Ryder must have been exhausted, or would be as soon as the adrenaline wore off. I knew my legs felt like lead.

But I couldn't rest yet.

Soon the real drama would begin.

Both Patrick and Margot were riding the Grand Prix freestyle. And this time there would be a good-sized audience in the stands. I guessed Patrick would be anxious to improve his ranking and secure his spot for Gladstone. I had noticed his foot jiggling earlier when he was sitting down in front of his stalls. His spot was no sure thing now.

By then it was clear that Margot and Wild Child were a real threat.

I went for my braiding kit and a big carrot for Wild Child. But when I got to his stall, I was alarmed to find that he had dug a big hole in the corner of his stall. He had never pulled that one before. I froze a moment. The first thought in my mind was colic.

My voice came out squeaky when I yelled, "Margot!"

Wild Child spun around and whinnied. And it was his usual full-throttled whinny. The aisle full of horses whinnied back.

I drew a deep breath. Maybe he was OK.

"What is it Lizzy?" Margot had trotted to catch up and was at my elbow.

I cleared my throat and tried to sound calm. "Look at Wild Child. That is so not like him."

Margot was looking at him and frowning. "Pull him out of that stall and let's have a look at him."

He was puffed up and his neck arched when I handed him his carrot and put the halter on as Margot watched. He took it eagerly.

Again I heard myself sigh in relief. "Thank God, Margot, he passed the carrot test."

Francesca walked up, but seeing that her massive horse was highly agitated, as well as the chaos of his stall, she backed up a few paces. I laced the chain over his nose, which was a good thing; because when I opened his door he sprang out like something was after him, spun around to face me, and started backing down the aisle snorting. No matter what, I was going to hang on to that lead rope. I followed him down the aisle, calling his name. He slowed down finally and then stopped.

"Whoa, buddy. What the heck's gotten you upset?"

I caught up to him and stroked his neck. He was bug-eyed, and a fine network of veins stood up on his neck. I put him into the grooming stall and went to have a look at his stall. What a churned-up mess. The floor, which was clay, now had a big dip in the corner where he had clearly been working on an escape route.

"Geez Wild Child. Margot, come look at this."

Margot silently walked around the stall, pushing at the mix of red dirt and shavings with the toe of her shoe. Then she walked into the grooming stall and just looked at him. He looked right back at her, bobbed his head up and down, and then took a dump. That made me feel a little better. I heard myself once again exhale loudly.

"He doesn't seem to be colicking."

"No. You're right, Lizzy. He's just really agitated about something."

Patrick sauntered down to have a look. "Your stallion was having fits when we came in. I think someone walked through here with a mare. She was probably in season or something."

"Well that explains it then, Patrick. Thanks."

Patrick shook his head and smiled. "Stallions are a lot to manage, sure you girls are OK?"

"Thanks, Patrick, they are indeed. I'm afraid we're still learning this boy. We'll get him figured out."

As Ryder walked by, Margot gently touched her elbow.

"Darling, while Lizzy braids for me, please try your best to repair Wild Child's stall. Have Francesca order more shavings and bed him up thickly. I don't want him to hurt himself on those potholes he just created."

I started to put in Wild Child's braids, and he seemed to calm down. But when I climbed down off my stool, I realized he had an erection and was gently slapping himself against his belly.

"Oh Wild Child, she must have been in season!"

He had that half-lidded eye that didn't see me at all. He was in stallion fantasy-land. I would have been embarrassed except I was glad to be able to groom him and not have him biting or wiggling around. In fact I figured he might as well finish things up and have it done, rather than be embarrassing Margot in the warm-up arena. So I gave him some privacy and went and sat down with Natalie.

"Well Natalie, Wild Child is a complete sex-crazed idiot now. That must have been some mare."

For once Natalie had no snappy come-back, which really surprised me. A sex-crazed stallion was just the kind of subject that I thought she would love to riff on. Instead she just tipped back on her chair, leaning on the stall front, and looked grim faced.

But not for long.

"Natalie!"

"Here, boss."

"Sorry, Lizzy."

***

I WAS USED TO WILD CHILD being an aggressive son-of-a-bitch. But this was something different. His skin was still mapped with fine veins, and he was practically vibrating with nerves. Before Margot mounted she ran her gloved hand over his neck. "What do you suppose this is all about, Lizzy?"

I genuinely felt scared for both Margot and Wild Child. "He still isn't himself Margot. He's shaking all over."

Francesca stood behind us at a safe distance.

Margot looked at her, frowning. "Francesca, maybe we need to take his temp. This is just too weird."

"Patrick said it was a mare in season. He just needs to get his head back in the game."

"But Francesca darling, this feels like it could be more than that."

"Margot, you know you're not allowed to withdraw without a vet's excuse. Just see how he feels in the warm-up."

"OK. I'll give it a go, but if he feels low-energy, then I want you to get that vet to the ring ASAP."

Francesca's voice remained even in her tone as she answered, but her words made me clench my teeth. "Margot, remember that if you don't ride now, the run for Gladstone is over, so please be sure of yourself."

Margot was silent and swung up on Wild Child, gathering her reins quickly. She nodded to me to let go, and Wild Child whinnied again as he headed off to the FEI warm-up arena to join Patrick and others as they prepared to ride their freestyles.

We approached a warm-up arena where each rider was wearing ear buds and iPods, listening to their music as they practiced. They looked like a ring full of Secret Service agents on a security detail.

The sun was then low on the horizon. Inside the coliseum, spectators were sipping wine and nibbling cheese; the silent auction was getting ready to close. The items for bidding included business-class seats to Paris and of course, a pair of breeches from High Horse Couture.

I set my bucket of stuff down next to Nat, who was leaning against the railing of the warm-up arena. I was about to say something when she cut her eyes at me in an unmistakable signal to keep my lip zipped.

Patrick rode by.

I turned to watch Margot instead, feeling consumed with anxiety.

Wild Child did not look like a sick horse. But he was only one hair's breadth from exploding. I couldn't put my finger on what was wrong exactly. He clearly had tons of energy, but didn't look "fresh" either.

He wasn't pulling on Margot like he did when he was feeling too good and bossy.

No, he was wound-up and just a little too light in the contact, his neck a little too arched, his mouth a little open, and his lips covered in an unusual amount of white foam.

Margot pulled up abruptly in front of me. "Lizzy, can you check his mouth? I think he's gotten his tongue over the bit."

He didn't even try to bite me as I put my fingers in right at the bars of his mouth and felt for his tongue, and then pulled his lips back so I could see it, too. There it was in the proper place, so it hadn't come over. Yet.

But I understood why Margot was concerned. Sometimes a nervous horse would draw the tongue up so high in their mouth that it went over the bit. The pressure of the bit against the tender tissue under the tongue was extremely painful. The neck and the head would then curl up to avoid the pressure. You couldn't use the reins then at all, not without risking a violent reaction. From the saddle it felt like trying to ride a headless horse.

Of course Wild Child had never done anything like this before with us. Sometimes he was strong in the contact, but he never opened his mouth or played with his tongue.

On the other hand, as Margot picked the reins up and went through her practice, I noticed he was moving with incredible power. He always had a super piaffe and passage, but he was really pushing the edges today, lifting his knees and hocks higher than usual and breathing like a steam engine. I hoped like hell he wouldn't explode.

Francesca and Claire joined me at ringside, and they were whispering to each other. I couldn't help myself. I was straining to hear.

Claire tipped her head. "Francesca, I'm sure you're relieved, he doesn't look sick after all."

"We just don't have enough experience with stallions. And of course Margot is soft when it comes to the horses. He is world-class; look at him move."

Claire watched for a moment, and I thought perhaps she wasn't going to agree with Francesca. After a long pause she said, "Yes. I believe he is."

When the crew peeled off to go watch Patrick's ride, Francesca followed. She was so invested in Margot beating Patrick that she wouldn't dream of missing his ride and seeing his score. Also, she and Claire could sit and continue whispering to each other.

Ryder was the only other person to stay besides me, and I could see that she also understood that something was not right. But she was silent. I finally couldn't stand it.

"Ryder, what do you think is going on?"

I figured she understood I meant Wild Child.

"It's a tough business, Lizzy, and we all have our jobs to do."

I stood there and wondered what to say. "So just what is your job then, Ryder?" I turned and looked at her with narrowed eyes, really confused.

"To win, of course."

She looked down at her watch, and continued in a matter of fact tone. "You need to pay attention to your job too, Lizzy. It's time to get Margot to the ring."

Margot looked grim-faced as Ryder and I pulled off the polo wraps. She handed me her iPod and ear buds and turned down a bottle of water. I ran the towel over Wild Child. The foam from his overly busy mouth had flecked his chest. His coat was now wet with sweat and still just a bit "off" from its usual gleaming copper sheen.

Today he did not stall out going into the tunnel, although I had a hold of a rein as I led Margot into the arena. I gave his neck a pat before turning her loose. "You're OK, big stuff."

Margot put her leg on, and they bounded forward, focused; off to do battle.

Before long the judge at "C" had blown the whistle. Margot made her way toward the entrance at "A" and signaled for her music.

The announcer said, "Margot, your music is rolling."

And Wild Child's swing tunes filled the coliseum as Margot passaged her way into the arena.

Wild Child seemed to throw himself into every beat. But throughout, his mouth was too busy, froth once again being flung across his chest. I noticed Margot was riding on almost a slack rein, and when she did need to use the rein, it was brief, a small check and a big release.

The walk work was tense, and Wild Child never really uncurled and stretched his top line as required for the extended walk.

When Margot did her final centerline, matching her music beat by beat in a way that would have made Deb proud, disaster struck; Wild Child's tongue came out the right side, and not just a little bit. It was a long thing, waving around like someone who was drowning trying to summon help.

My heart sunk in my chest, and my eyes stung with tears. Wild Child was telling us all that something was very wrong. Whatever the cause, he was feeling distressed.

After Margot's salute, his tongue thankfully went back in his mouth, but not before I was sure all he judges had gotten a good look. If they had doubted the quality of the contact up to that point, seeing the tongue out made the problem undeniable. I wondered how many of Margot's scores were being knocked down a point or two at that moment.

For all the problems in the contact, Wild Child's score was still amazingly generous. His gaits had still dazzled the judges. I guessed because the music and choreography were great and well ridden, she scored a 69% and still placed second. But Wild Child was capable of so much more.

Patrick had won the class by a generous margin.

I knew Francesca would be devastated.

The weekend's events would have to be finished coast-to-coast before the final rankings would be posted on the internet.

And then invitations would have to be issued and accepted or not-accepted before we would know for certain whether Margot would be invited to participate in the National FEI Championships in Gladstone.

But at this point my best guess was that Margot had not made the cut, and that Patrick was in by the thinnest of margins.

Chapter 37
Thank You, Comrade

Margot looked exhausted, but she still had to live through the awards ceremony. I clipped the chain shank onto Wild Child's bridle and led him around down by the warm-up arena while Margot got off and drank some water and rested.

My legs felt heavy, and the bottoms of my feet were numb as I walked in endless circles. Wild Child had a weird flat look in his eye. He was no longer whinnying or looking for horses. He wasn't pulling on the lead or trying to bite me. In fact his head got lower and lower, and not because he was going to go for my knees with his teeth.

I put my right arm over his neck and stopped walking. We stood still, rooted to the ground. "Buddy boy, this just isn't you at all. You've gone from a nervous wreck to zonked-out."

Making Margot and Wild Child stay for the awards ceremony seemed like cruelty. But they had no choice. You had to show up for the ceremony or forfeit everything.

Finally the steward showed up with an arm full of ribbons. She called our number, and I took Wild Child over to her. She put a big ribbon on his bridle, wrapping the streamers around his throatlatch. I pushed the rosette down on his brow band to make sure it wouldn't tickle his ears, and then it was time for Margot to mount up.

Music played as the class paraded in. Scores were announced, and the judges shook each rider's hand as they walked from rider to rider and offered congratulations.

Wild Child looked comatose; he was even resting a hind leg, and Margot sat on him with her reins totally loose.

When the victory lap began, he took his place behind Patrick willingly and loped around like he was asleep at the wheel.

Then Patrick took his solo lap of honor, and the crowd hooted and hollered. Patrick slowed down so he had more time to put on a show; passaging, piaffing, and then leaving the coliseum in a huge extended trot to thunderous applause. He had put on a good show for the wine-sipping, cheese-eating, auction-bidding evening crowd.

Margot hopped right off Wild Child, ran up her stirrups, and loosened her girth.

"Lizzy, please set up his legs tonight, and come back in a couple hours to check on him, and make sure he's OK. Call me if anything seems amiss. I want you to take his temperature later. Right now it will be skewed since he's still warm from the exercise. Frankly I'm worried about him, even if Francesca's not."

I looked at Margot and knew she was on the edge of collapsing. "I'll take care of him Margot. You need to go take care of yourself."

"Thanks, Lizzy. My back hurts, and I have a splitting headache."

"Just go on back to your hotel, I've got Wild Child."

"I've got to find Francesca first; she's got the car."

When I got Wild Child back from his shower, I put him in the grooming stall and started pulling out his braids. Ryder was busy putting the barn up for the evening. Across the aisle Nat was doing the same. Suzette had plopped down in a chair. I guessed she was done already; she was texting at great speed. Finally she announced into the air, "Patrick's buying tonight. They're already in the pool, and we can meet them there."

Natalie announced, "Free meal. I'm in!"

Then Ryder, "Me, too!"

I couldn't believe these guys! "Ryder, are you sure? You still have to ride tomorrow early, and then we've got an eight- hour drive back home."

She just shook her head at me. "Lizzy, I'm good. I guess you're not coming with us?"

"No, I am not. I'm going to drive-through somewhere and eat in the room. Then I have a hot shower planned. After that, I'm coming back here for an early bed-check, and then I'm getting a good night's sleep."

Ryder just shrugged her shoulders. "Suit yourself. I gave Papa and Petey extra hay and topped off all the buckets, so don't worry about them at bed-check, OK? And don't be a Momma Bear and wait up for me. I can catch up on my sleep on the ride home."

I looked across the aisle at Natalie who was shaking her head. She said, "Gee Ryder, I'll bet you're great company on a road trip."

Ryder ignored her and turned to Suzette. "I'm ready. Let's roll."

Suzette was still glued to her phone even as she got up from her chair and started walking away. "Oh my God, Ryder, the scores are up from the Del Mar show in California. They've got some Young Riders that rock!"

"Suzette, it doesn't mean anything until we get a chance to go head-to-head."

"How can you be so sure?"

The two of them trailed off toward the parking lot, yakking as they walked.

Natalie didn't follow them.

I finished pulling braids and went for the bottle of rub for Wild Child's legs. I walked around and gave each leg a spritz and a brisk rub, then went and got four thick cotton wraps and four standing bandages to set his legs up for the night, and then started bandaging. I felt certain his legs were tired, although they couldn't be much more tired than mine. I admired my bandaging job. They were smooth and even, with just the right amount of wrap showing above and below the bandage, and the bandage finished off at the top with the Velcro closure on the outside.

Natalie walked over and leaned on the wall watching. "Great bandaging job."

"Hey, I thought you were going to grab that free meal."

"You notice how they cruised out of here without me?"

"Yeah."

"Little bitches. I've got my camper all hooked up."

"You need a ride?"

"Of course I do, they know that, too."

"If you wait a bit, I can take you. They'll still be splashing around in the pool for a while."

"It's OK, I have stuff to get done tonight anyway."

"You sure? You can come with me if you want. I'm just doing fast food."

"Nope. You enjoy. I'll see you at bed-check."

I finished Wild Child in a dark quiet barn, with only the sound of horses munching on hay. It was a good sound. Even with a fuzzy tired head, it was soothing to listen to. When all was settled, I locked our tack room and slung my bag over my shoulder. But I decided to take a moment to walk through the barn and have a look at all the other FEI horses.

The FEI barn was separate from the barns for the rest of the horse show. In fact there was security set up so that no one could come and go without a special little bracelet that was issued to all of us, including the owners. But I had only been asked to show mine once, and since then I had come and gone at will.

As exhausted as I was, I still wanted to see just how many mares actually were in our barn. I supposed any one of them could have walked by Wild Child's stall earlier and caused him distress. I would have blamed Patrick if I could have. I wanted to, but Patrick hadn't brought any mares.

And there were a few. But I knew, as a matter of fact, most mares competing in the FEI divisions were not allowed by their owners to "come into season" but were given hormones, either by injection or orally, so as not to play havoc with their athletic ability or focus. Most mares were famously moody and uncooperative while they were ovulating. So it was possible, but not likely, that one of these girls was in-season. But if it hadn't been a mare in season, what had it been? I didn't have an answer. But I thought I was getting to know Wild Child, and he had not been himself tonight.

I finally made it to the truck and then found a drive-through burger place that had old-fashioned grilled cheeseburgers and fries. You could tell from the smell in the parking lot that they were going to be good. They were the kind that come wrapped in paper and were sure to drip all over you.

When I got to my room, I sat on the end of my bed and watched corny episodes of the old Andy Griffith show. Here I was sitting in North Carolina (the site of TV's fictional Mayberry country), but in dressage, it was the same old sandbox anywhere you set it down. Some sandboxes just required longer drives than others to reach.

Then I took a long hot shower. With wet hair that I pulled into a scrunchy, I headed back out to check on the boys.

On the way I decided to swing back through that drive-through and pick up two chocolate milk shakes and some fried pies to share with Natalie.

By this time it was pitch black out. Once I got into the show ground's parking lot, I drove at a snail's pace along the RV section of parking. I couldn't find Natalie's small camper among all the long gooseneck trailers and big campers. Hers would be tucked between them along the row, so I had to gaze into the dark spaces between campers. I could see lights on inside of some of them, making the windows glow in the dark. I could even see a television. Someone else was watching re-runs of Mayberry; but no luck finding Natalie's camper.

I had gone down the whole line. I turned around and started crawling back down the line, aware that her milkshake was melting, and her fried pie was going cold.

I noticed a car parked between campers, and I instinctively slowed down a little more. It had blocked my view of Nat's camper. Just then, an interior dome light glowed and illuminated a skinny little ass clothed in white slacks getting into the car. The door closed and the dome light faded to dark.

Francesca.

The car started, its lights came on, and it backed out and drove away, while I just sat there, hopefully unnoticed.

I sat in my truck and stared at the space where the car had been parked.

Francesca had made a late night visit to my friend Natalie's camper. I couldn't get any kind of grip on that. It made no sense. I needed to march right in and demand some answers. But I didn't. Whatever Natalie was up to, and she had told me she was up to something big, I did not want to be part of it.

I had a painful muscle spasm in the arch of my right foot that made my toes curl. God, I was tired. I kicked off my clog and pulled on my toes. The spasm passed, and so did my anxiety. This stuff didn't concern me.

I drove to the barn.

A sleepy security guy sat in a plastic chair by the entrance. I walked past him with a little wave that he didn't even acknowledge. That had to be the dullest job ever.

I hated to do it, but I flipped on the lights for our section of the barn. I used a soft voice as I called out. "Wiiiild Chiiiild."

He whinnied way too loudly.

I unlocked our tack room and came out with a bucket full of carrots, visiting the big boy first.

He looked much better. His eyes were bright as he gobbled up carrot after carrot, lipping the entire length of carrot up into his mouth greedily, rolling it around, and finally crunching it. When I turned to feed carrots to the rest of our troop, he pinned his ears and lunged over the stall top in an effort to bite me.

For once, it made me smile. "Oh, so back to normal I see, you bastard."

He backed up and flung his head in a complete circle, tossing his kinky unbraided forelock around so it was tickling his ears, which just sent him into another round of head tossing and shaking, culminating in a small rear.

"Wild Child for heaven's sake. You've had as many moods this trip as any mare I've ever known."

I fed everyone their carrots and then pulled the muck tub around. Everyone still had plenty of hay and water. Before doing Wild Child's though, I pulled him out and stuck him in the grooming stall. I didn't trust him enough to go in there with him loose.

I texted Margot, "All is well. Hope you are resting."

She texted back, "Thank God. You get some rest, too."

I dropped the phone into my bag, and locked up the tack room. When I turned around, I almost screamed. Natalie was standing across the aisle, holding the butter-yellow briefcase; Claire's briefcase.

"Holy crap, Natalie. Are you trying to kill me?"

She cleared her throat before speaking, "Sorry Lizzy, I just tried to speak and nothing came out."

I had another one of those muscle spasms. This time it was in my throat. It made me grimace and bend over it was so painful.

Natalie reached over and touched my arm. "Lizzy, what's wrong?"

I put one hand on my throat and sat down in one of our director chairs. I finally whispered, "Muscle spasms."

"Lizzy, I watched you hand water bottles out all day long. Did it ever occur to you to drink any water yourself?"

I had to think about that for a moment.

"Actually, I don't remember drinking anything today, except tonight when I had dinner."

She shook her head, "You take care of everyone else, but who's taking care of you, Lizzy?"

"No one."

"Maybe you need to do something about that."

"But what about you, Nat? I don't see anyone taking care of you."

"But there's a big difference there, Lizzy. I learned the hard way to look after number one. They tried their best but they didn't break me. But you, you don't look like the sturdy type to me, I think you won't fare as well."

I looked at the briefcase. "Why did Francesca come to see you?"

"No one was supposed to see that."

"I was bringing you a pie and a milkshake, but Francesca was there."

"She brought me Claire's briefcase. Now I just gotta' copy some stuff and put it in here and leave it here for Claire to pick up tomorrow."

"Unbelievable."

"You were bringing me a pie and a milkshake? That's sweet of you, Lizzy. Still got them?"

"Melted."

"Pie would be still be good though."

"I can go get them…"

"Not so fast. Actually, I was looking for you. I did bed-check on our horses already."

"You were looking for me?"

"I saw your truck."

"What do you need, Nat?"

"Just a ride to the copy place."

"You've gotten Francesca involved and now me, too?"

"You don't have to take me. But, it's a pain in the ass unhooking and hooking back up in this pitch black darkness."

"What the heck do you need copies of?"

"I could tell you, but as they say, then I'd have to kill you."

"What am I saying? Don't tell me. But I'll drive you."

"Thanks, Lizzy, but not until I see you drink a full bottle of water."

And so I drank the water so fast it made me belch, and then I drove while she ate her pie. I pulled up to a brightly lit store on a major road. Nat turned in her seat, wiping crumbs off her mouth with the cuff of her sweatshirt. "You just sit here and eat your pie, which by the way was excellent even if it was cold."

When she came out, she was carrying the briefcase, and a manila envelope. She patted the envelope. "I have Tommy's password and pin numbers. I'm keeping my own set for security."

I wished she hadn't told me, but it was too late. I asked, "Financial records?"

"Yup. Some big deposits in there and some big withdrawals that went directly to Patrick. Shared booty, y'know?"

She had me drive her back to the barn. She picked up the briefcase, but left the envelope on my truck seat. We nodded to the security guard as we walked into the barn. There was really no need.

This time he was snoring.

"OK, now I'm going to climb over into Patrick's tack room, and if you would, toss me that briefcase."

"What? Shit, Natalie."

"I'm not going to be seen giving this back to either Claire or Francesca. I told Francesca I'd just leave it in Patrick's tack room."

Natalie pulled off her wrist supports before climbing on her braiding stool, and she had me hold back the stall curtains to look for a perch or something to climb on. It wasn't easy. She could start with the ledge, and then move to the conduit for the wiring. Then she put a foot on an outlet box and slung her leg over the top.

I was standing below her, clinging onto a very fashionable briefcase and feeling like I was involved in some sort of criminal activity, which in fact I surely was. "Natalie. Wait. Don't do it. What if you get in but can't get back out?"

"Not gonna' happen with you here to help me get out."

"Why are you doing this for Claire, I thought you hated all those rich women."

"Who says I don't"

"Well, you seem to be working for them."

"Nah, I'm doing this for me, although it's mutually beneficial."

Natalie lowered herself down into the tack room like Spiderman. She was clinging to the bars and walking her feet against the wall.

"Piece of cake. Now toss me that briefcase."

I looked down at the briefcase in my hand and stepped back.

It was kind of heavy. My first toss was just pathetic and the case came back and almost hit me in the head. I squeaked and jumped to the side as it hit the ground.

Natalie gasped, "Oh my God. That was the worst throw I've ever seen. You must have been the last kid they picked for the softball team. Not to mention you just scratched a Hermes briefcase."

"Really?"

I knew that meant the thing was worth a bundle. I picked it up and dusted it off, examining it for scratches.

"Hah, just kidding, Lizzy, but I'm sure it's some hoity-toity designer briefcase. It's Claire Winston's for God's sake. Try again, and this time put your back into it."

So I proceeded to sling the thing so hard it almost went into the stall behind the tack room. I startled some poor horse as the case thunked against the back wall.

"Lizzy, you are a trip. OK, at least I've got it. Claire said to put it under the tablecloth where no one can see it. Yeah. That works."

Then Natalie did her Spiderman crawl. She was grunting and swearing, and when she crested the top, she had to rest. It had been harder to get out than in, but she did it, while I nervously wrung my hands and kept a lookout. I pulled the curtain to the side, and she made it down safely. She was a dirty mess, but she dusted herself off, put her wrist braces back on, and put her braiding stool back. I drove her, and her manila envelope, back to her camper.

She got out of the truck and pumped her fist in the air, and then tapped it over her heart a couple times and said, "Thanks, comrade."

Maybe this wasn't my revolution, but I had just gotten pulled in... deep.

CHAPTER 38

Bolt

IT WAS TIME TO GET UP, and I had no pity on the kid. Who knew what time she had gotten in last night? She was flat on her back with an arm flung over her eyes. I had gone around and turned every light on in the room, as well as the TV. I pulled the heavy drapes back and looked out into the parking lot.

It was raining, and not just a spring shower. It was pouring and still pitch-black out. The security lights made circles of light on the blacktop, and inside each circle of light the rain was bouncing off the ground.

Ryder had her freestyle to do in the coliseum around ten, and then we were hitting the trail back home. But before then we had horses to care for, and we had to break camp and pack and load.

Then we had an eight-hour drive.

"Up, Ryder. It's time to pay the piper."

"Huh?"

"Up!"

"You've got to be kidding me?"

"Now. I can't leave you here, so get moving."

I zipped up my rolly-bag. Ryder was sitting on the edge of the bed.

"Yeah. OK. You go eat breakfast. I'll be there in a minute."

"Better be quick about it."

"Lizzy, there's no rush. I have oodles of time before I ride."

"Yeah, but as soon as Papa is cooled out, I want to get headed north. We have a long drive home, which means we do as much as we can ahead of your ride, which means you need to step on it so you can help me."

Ryder was staring at me like I'd gone berserk, and she needed to calm me down. "Lizzy, go get your coffee, I'll be right there, OK?"

As I was backing out through the door, I saw her grab her phone. Geez, she was probably already notifying her new best friend Suzette that Lizzy was in a mood.

I guessed Ryder wasn't the only one moving slowly. The breakfast area was totally deserted.

I sat by myself, looking through the windows at the rain pelting down. I hated driving in the rain. I especially hated driving a four-horse trailer filled with horses in the rain. I ate my scrambled eggs and bacon and hash browns, staring at my plate while resting my head in my left hand.

I heard the sound of another rolly-bag on the tile floor and turned around expecting Ryder. But it was Patrick. He was pulling a large masculine looking leather bag. It had an ID tag on it in the shape of the logo of the USET.

"Lizzy, good morning. Are we the first ones up?"

His cheeriness was another cross for me to bear this morning.

"We appear to be."

"Mind if I join you?"

This was almost too much, but I had no ready excuse. "Not at all, but as soon as Ryder shows up, I'm headed to the barn."

He parked his bag at my table and went to load his plate and pour his coffee. I went ahead and got a second cup; it looked like I was stuck. We both headed back to the table.

"So, Lizzy, I understand you ride, too."

He pulled out a chair and sat across from me. His tan face still had a pleasant smile plastered on it. We were going to chit-chat.

"Yeah. I have a really good mare. But she's only six years old."

"You should show her."

"Oh, I will. Margot wants me to wait until she's doing Second level."

"Well, I'm sure Margot will let you know when she's ready. In the meantime you're a fine groom, and that's something to take pride in."

I looked at Patrick's face. He was so relaxed that I started to relax, too.

"Thanks."

He was attacking his eggs with gusto. He drank his glass of orange juice practically in one gulp. Then he leaned in to say something in a confidential tone. "You know, I should warn you about something. I know the grooms like to hang together, but the fact is, Natalie there, she's a cute thing and so clever, but she has some serious problems. I just thought, y'know, forewarned and all that."

Oh yeah, I woke back up, Patrick was the enemy. I tried to look puzzled. "Should I be worried?"

Patrick leaned back and looked me straight in the eye. He took a leisurely sip of his coffee and paused a beat. "Lizzy, I'm sorry to worry you. She doesn't work for me. I wouldn't put up with her nonsense. But my buddy took pity on her. She and her horse were evicted from her last employer. I mean, they ordered her out of their barn one year in Florida, and she was literally sitting on the curb sobbing, holding her horse on a lead rope when he took her in. She's caused trouble wherever she's been. She's cracked. I always wonder if she's doing hard drugs or something. Anyway, just be careful. That's all I mean."

Patrick looked concerned and almost fatherly.

"Wow. Thank you, Patrick. Nice of you to be concerned about me."

"Well, any friend of Ryder's..."

"You guys talking about me."

What a relief to see Ryder. I pushed my chair back and stood up. "There she is, 'Sleeping Beauty.' Let's roll, Ryder."

"Don't I get to eat?"

"In the truck. Go grab something."

Patrick waved at the air. "Ladies, see you at the barn."

Ryder stuck her ear buds in as soon as we got in the truck. She remained hooked up and humming to her freestyle soundtrack while we fed and mucked.

Across the aisle, Natalie mucked. Next to me Suzette arrived and fed her starving herd. Then Suzette put out a CD player with little speakers and popped in some new age stuff that was actually nice music for first thing in the morning.

The rain didn't seem to be letting up. The black clouds were stalled out above us, dumping buckets on us before it began its projected northward crawl. It looked like it would be inching up the interstate with us later.

Margot and Francesca arrived. They had been shopping. Margot called out to us, "Darlings, we have presents!"

Margot sounded much cheerier today. I wondered how she really felt. The weekend had beaten her up, but you wouldn't know it from her tone this morning. She was made of tougher stuff than me, I thought.

She put a box of pastries down and started a pot of coffee. "I found some decent-looking pastries. Not exactly up to Peapack's standards, but it will do for now. You'll be happy to hear Francesca and I found cheap rain ponchos, too. We need to remember to leave them in the horse trailer."

"Thanks, Margot; brilliant!"

The show began at eight a.m. sharp. But standing at the end of the barn aisle looking out at the arenas, you couldn't tell. It was a desolate sight.

Judges sat in boxes staring at rain-drenched empty arenas. Dressage shows do not cancel due to rain. But riders can "scratch" and often Sunday class lists become one black line after another followed by the word "scratch." That was true even in good weather when people decide they and their horses have had enough fun for one weekend. With bad weather it often looked like an evacuation order had been handed down from FEMA.

But not for our barn, we still had the Advanced Young Riders Freestyle, which meant Suzette and Ryder had their rides.

The qualifiers were not treated as an ordinary open class. Scratches only happened with a vet's excuse.

And anyway, Ryder needed her freestyle score in order to be eligible for Gladstone. So she would ride unless the steward decided conditions were dangerous. Wet didn't count as dangerous.

I once again put in Papa's braids. Today he didn't even fidget. I figured he was as tired as the rest of us.

Ryder put her tailcoat and helmet on, and over it she put a clear riding raincoat. But it turned out not to be needed.

The rides in the covered arena had scratched, so the covered would serve as the warm-up arena for the coliseum. It even had a covered walkway from the covered to the coliseum. What a lucky turn for Ryder.

Papa's freestyle had been made for Margot at the Intermediare level. Ryder and Margot had changed the choreography so that Ryder could use it for the Advanced Young Riders division which was at the Prix St. Georges level. They had re-worked it in a short period of time, and it still wasn't totally smooth. But as usual, to Ryder it was no big deal. She had it all memorized and thought out in her mind step-for-step to the music, but she said, if anything went wrong, she could wing it and no one would be the wiser. She had it disaster-proofed.

Ryder had the lucky last-to-go spot, and even though she would never admit it, I thought she was nervous. Before she mounted up, she was pacing. I'd never seen Ryder pace before.

I held Papa while she got on. She pulled her ear buds off and handed them to Margot.

Margot looked surprised. "Are you sure, darling?"

"I'd rather have your feedback Margot. Hand me the coaching system."

Margot turned to me. "Lizzy."

"Sure."

I grabbed them out of the basket in the tack room and handed them to Ryder.

"Darling, turn the volume up. The rain on the metal roof will be loud."

The two of them got the volume adjusted, and then we were off.

We passed Suzette and Patrick walking back, deep in conversation. Patrick gave thumbs up to Ryder as we passed, but I didn't think Suzette looked very happy.

Ryder looked sharp even though I thought Papa looked tired. Poor boy didn't know he had to go to Canada and do it all over again next weekend. The thought made me sigh with weariness. The wind was picking up, blowing the rain sideways and making a racket on the metal roof. Papa went through his warm-up focused on Ryder as if he were deaf to the noise. Soon it was time to go in.

We had put on neoprene boots instead of polos for the warm-up. The boots didn't absorb water like the polos. It was good that we did since even in the covered arena they had become filthy, and my hands were covered with wet sand as I stuffed the sandy wet boots into my grooming bucket.

Ryder took her big swig of water and then gathered Papa up and walked under the cover all the way to the tunnel, picking up the trot and boldly entering into the arena.

Thunder rumbled in the distance, and then "BOOM" we were in complete darkness.

I couldn't see anything except the pale windows above us and literally "the light at the end of the tunnel."

The lights came back on in a moment, but only at half strength, glowing orange. Ryder was still trotting boldly around the arena. I didn't think she had flinched.

Around and around she went. And then the announcer said, "Ground jury, we appear to have power."

And the whistle blew.

Ryder made her way to the corner and signaled for her music. The announcer said, "Ryder, your music is rolling."

She picked up the canter and headed down centerline, the air around her a strange color in the hazy orange half-light.

The music was loud, but I could still hear thunder booming.

Ryder clicked along looking completely composed. Papa had become extra light on his toes, dancing to their music which had sort of a reggae beat that made Ryder and Papa seem carefree and happy as they bounced along to the beat.

But the thunder seemed to be getting louder.

I wondered how safe we were in this big metal building.

Ryder finished her freestyle with a bold extended trot down centerline that came to a halt right in front of the judge's booth.

As she dropped her hand in time to a cymbal, a bolt of lightning lit up the arena and then plunged us back into darkness. Quite impressive. It was like a curtain had dropped.

When the orange glow of the auxiliary power came on again, Ryder and Papa were strolling out of the arena like nothing had happened.

I turned to look at Margot who was applauding and turning to talk to Francesca at the same time. And then I noticed Francesca was smiling and clapping, too.

Ryder had held her stuff together through difficult conditions, and everyone was impressed, including me, but especially Francesca who wasn't so easily impressed.

Clearly it took an act of God to impress Francesca.

Before I made my way out of the tunnel, the announcer came on again. "Competitors, we are currently under a tornado warning. The show will be stopped at this point. Please, seek shelter now, and keep abreast of the situation."

Seek shelter? I figured I'd take my chances with the horses in the barn.

Everyone wanted to leave, but there we all sat at the barn, stuck, staring at each other waiting for the tornado warning to expire.

I noticed Claire Winston had retrieved her fancy briefcase and had placed it in front of her, tucked between her feet. I did not look at it long. I tried not to look at Natalie, or Patrick, or Francesca either. It wasn't easy trying to avoid eye contact with anyone but Margot. So I just kept moving.

At some point I needed to talk to Natalie. I needed to fill her in on what Patrick had said. But I couldn't risk anyone seeing me with her. Not now that Patrick had warned me off.

I walked through sideways-driving rain in my new rain poncho and hooked up the gooseneck, just to get out of the barn. I pulled it around the end of the barn and snugged it up against the aisle so the trailer's tack room door was facing in toward the stalls. That way I could load without going out in the weather. Not that it mattered. I was soaked even with the poncho on. Then I began the process of schlepping.

Ryder on the other hand was busy being euphoric over her ride, reliving every step of her freestyle and wandering around in her show whites talking to anyone. She hadn't even taken her boots off. The girl that never chatted was yackity-yacking with Patrick and Suzette and Claire and Francesca and Natalie's trainer, too.

Scores went up quickly, and the awards ceremony was cancelled. Once again Ryder had won, and Suzette was once again behind her. All was right in Ryder's little world.

My horse and my bed back in New Jersey were beckoning me. I wanted to talk to Deb, and with a pang I realized I really wanted to talk to Marco, too. I realized I hadn't even sent him the promised text message.

Finally we got the go-ahead.

Margot waited until Ryder and I got the horses loaded, and then she waved goodbye. She and Francesca headed to the airport, or at least the airport bar. They expected a long wait ahead of them too, with their flight delayed.

Patrick had his horses loaded, and Nat had hers loaded. It would be a mass exodus. Ryder hopped in, and I started the engine.

And then I saw Nat in my side mirror. "Ryder, I'm checking the hitch one last time."

"Suit yourself."

I hopped out. I no longer had on my poncho, but it was only a fine mist then.

"Natalie. Will you be OK?"

"I don't know."

She smiled weakly. That wasn't like her. I had the feeling that regrets about last night were too late, and she knew it.

"Patrick is on to you, I have no idea what he knows, but he knows something. He tried to warn me away from you at breakfast. He called you cracked."

"Yeah, well, I'm about to bolt. I think... I think... well, I think what I just did is a felony. But, hey, there's no turning back now."

"Oh my God, Natalie; a felony? That makes me an accessory!"

"Don't worry, Lizzy. My lips are sealed. I think maybe I'll head west. I'll send you a post card. But, of course, you have to promise to burn it."

Well, that made me laugh. "Natalie!"

But then when I looked at her, she wasn't smiling her cute Natalie smile. She was pressing her lips together and frowning like she might cry.

"Lizzy, I'm serious. These guys are capable of bad shit. I've seen it. I've photocopied it."

"What?"

"Take care, Lizzy. You're a good egg."

And as she turned and walked away, she put one fist up in the air, and pumped it several times.

The rain started up again, and I was getting soaked. I'd be sitting in these wet clothes for the next eight hours.

I walked into the tack room of the trailer and grabbed a towel. The trailer started rocking.

These boys wanted the wheels to start moving. NOW.

I slid in behind the wheel to find Ryder staring at me. "What were you doing out there?"

"I checked the hitch and then I said goodbye to Natalie."

I rubbed my arms and legs with the towel and then folded my ponytail into it and squeezed.

Then I put the behemoth of a trailer in motion. It always felt like I was pulling a train. I never forgot who was back there either. I was taking my boys home.

I leaned forward to concentrate on pulling around the barns, watching where the wheels of the trailer cut inside the turn. God forbid I pull down one of the gutters on the barns.

Ryder blurted out, "Patrick says Natalie's going to be fired."

At first I couldn't think of what to say. Anything I said would go right back to Patrick.

Ryder wasn't done. "You should hear how she talks to her boss. She's rude and crude."

"Ryder, why would Patrick care about Natalie? She doesn't work for him."

"Well he's business partners with Tommy. You know they import and sell horses together. Tommy has a great eye for a horse, but a terrible record with women. I guess Patrick finally did an 'intervention' with him over Natalie. She's been a source of embarrassment. She really is offensive, and he can't have that around top clients like Claire Winston. You know Francesca wouldn't put up with that crap for a moment. Anyway I just thought you should know. You don't want to be investing time and energy in a friendship with someone who is totally bad news."

"So what you're telling me is that Patrick asked for Natalie to be fired."

Ryder didn't answer. But I had one more thing to say. "Nice guy."

That silenced Ryder for about an hour.

But then she felt the need to bring up Patrick's name again and again. Patrick said this, and Patrick said that. And then she proceeded to tell me what Margot needed to do with Wild Child, according to whom? Patrick.

Barf.

CHAPTER 39

Green Hair

THE NIGHT BEFORE, WE HAD PULLED in off the road totally exhausted. Ryder helped as we settled in our four equally-tired horses. Winsome had hung her head out into the aisle begging for treats, but I had barely said hello.

With her in mind, I decided to get up.

I got my coffee, walked over to the window, and looked down into the barn aisle. Horses were already out in the paddocks, and stalls were being mucked.

I knew the filthy trailer would need to be cleaned. Loads of laundry would need to be started and tack cleaned. I shook my head and tried to put all that work out of my mind. Monday was supposedly our day off, and I really needed it.

I refilled my coffee mug and headed out to find my mare. On the way I popped into the tack room and grabbed an armful of carrots, then headed out to the paddocks, waving my coffee cup at the guys as I passed.

I spotted her in a far paddock; head down in grass that was getting too tall. Alfonso would need to bush-hog soon.

I stopped and called her name. "Winnnnnsome!"

Up popped her pretty face, and she whinnied. She had such an unusual blaze with moth-eaten patches of liver chestnut coat breaking through the white. And although every inch of her was familiar to me, I had an out-of-body moment where she looked foreign. I had only been gone five days, but it felt like I

336 | T<small>HE</small> D<small>RESSAGE</small> C<small>HRONICLES</small>: A M<small>ATTER</small> <small>OF</small> F<small>EEL</small>

had been gone a month. I had spent so much time recently with Wild Child, who was not only very tall, but imposing in every way. Looking at her I marveled at how my girl was as feminine as Wild Child was masculine, and now she seemed diminutive, almost delicate. I knew she couldn't have shrunk while I was gone. But that's how it seemed.

Before I made it to her paddock though, both Wild Child and Kiddo had spotted me and came to their gates begging. Since I had to walk right past them, I peeled off a fat carrot for each of them. I was happy to see Wild Child looking OK, if maybe a little tucked up, after his stressful weekend. He would need today to recover.

Winsome grew impatient, pawing at the gate, nostrils vibrating with her low, almost silent whinny, worried that I would give away all her carrots.

I slipped into her paddock clumsily; after all, I was balancing my coffee mug in one hand, and carrots in the other. Trying to unlatch and latch the gate was almost comical as I tucked the carrots between my chin and my lifted tee-shirt, rested my coffee on top of the fencepost, and simultaneously pushed my impatient mare back from the gate.

Then I found a seat on the ground with my back against a fence post and fed her what was left of my carrots. She stood with her head lowered, eyes half-closed. When the carrots were gone, she cleaned every little shard off the grass and then went back to grazing nearby.

The sun was warming, and my coffee growing cold. I tipped back the mug and finished it off. I closed my eyes and was drifting off when I knew for certain that someone was there. It had to be Deb. Without opening my eyes, I said, "I have so much to tell you."

But it was a masculine voice that answered me. "Really?"

I opened my eyes and looked up, the sun making it hurt to focus. It was Marco.

"Marco! I was sure it was Deb. What are you doing here? I mean, oh sorry, that sounded wrong. I just didn't expect you to be here."

"Good morning to you too, Lizzy. I went out with Deb and Pali for breakfast; Deb is exhausted from foal-watch and needed a break. We just got back, and I looked down the hill and saw you sitting here."

Marco climbed nimbly over the paddock fence and sat down next to me.

"So how was it?"

"A big fat drama. But the jog went well, except that I had to do it!"

"I thought Margot had to do the jog."

"She got hurt. Oh, Marco, I don't even know where to start."

And I proceeded to blather. I knew Marco had to be confused. Even I found myself hard to follow. But I could tell Marco was trying. His head was tipped, and he had a studious expression on his face. "And you're worried about Margot or Wild Child, or about Ryder?"

"All of them, but not nearly as much as I'm worried about Natalie!"

Marco's brow furrowed. "Who is Natalie again? I'm lost."

And I began all over again, taking the entire weekend from the top, but then back-tracking to give a full description of Natalie and how I first met her at the show in Georgia on our way back from Florida. I tried to make him understand that she was "the good guy." I was not sure he believed that when I told him about the butter-yellow briefcase, and the stolen financial records that I knew she had put in it for Claire Winston. It looked to me that she had exposed her boss, and in the process, exposed Patrick, who had been his partner in crime. And the scariest part was that I had helped.

I neurotically pulled up a handful of grass, placing the pile on my knee, and then split each blade one-by-one right down the middle while I rambled. When I finally looked up, I saw Marco's beautiful face staring intently at me. His lips were pressed together, and he was shaking his head. "Lizzy, this is what goes on at dressage shows?"

I stared back at him. It did sound ridiculous.

We probably sat there for an hour until I finally shut up. Then we sat companionably side-by-side in the grass. Finally he put his hand on my knee. It felt heavy and warm, solid and anchoring. My jittery insides settled again after the tumult of reliving the weekend and all the uncertainty and fear I felt about the future.

Marco stood up and stretched and looked up the hill. Pali's little car was backing out of the drive and headed our way. "Looks like I need to catch my ride back home."

I didn't want him to go, and an idea blurted out, "Marco, would you like to go on a trail ride?"

Marco looked surprised. "Who would I ride? I can promise you Francesca won't lend me one of hers."

"You can ride Winsome. She belongs to me, and I say you can ride her. I can ride Kiddo. I'll show you some stunning New Jersey countryside. I'll drive you back afterward."

Marco grinned. "I can't think of anything else I would like to do more."

Marco walked over to Pali's car and after a few words, patted the door. And Pali drove on.

This time when Marco and I rode side-by-side, it was my territory, and he was sitting on my precious horse. He probably didn't realize what an honor I had bestowed upon him. Even though he had put me on his horse at the circus, it was only because he was a brilliant rider that I had returned the favor.

I pushed the button for the farm gate from the safety of Kiddo's back, and we ventured out into the magical countryside of Peapack, New Jersey.

We headed down the dirt road, making our way to the familiar gate, sagging on its hinges. It always seemed to welcome me. Through the gate, and turning left, we headed to the well-trod path around the edge of the field. The path was wide, inviting us to ride side-by-side.

I turned to Marco, "This is where Margot and I let them gallop. Kiddo isn't very fast, but he can still have a little canter."

Marco smiled. "What a treat, Lizzy."

"Oh, and it's fine by me Marco if you let Winsome gallop ahead of us. Kiddo has trouble keeping up. She's fit, and I'm always safe on Kiddo."

We got up in jumping position and started out at a brisk trot. With our reins loose, we allowed the horses to set the pace. And after a few steps, Kiddo broke to canter. Winsome didn't try to outpace little Kiddo at first. Instead she lengthened her trot stride, doing a beautiful springy trot. I had an eyeful looking at my beautiful horse and Marco at the same time.

Winsome would usually pin her ears and make ugly faces at any horse that dared challenge her, or even ride this close to her, but not Kiddo. All the horses seemed to like Kiddo.

I looked over at Marco as he stood up in his irons and Winsome broke to canter. He stroked her neck in a relaxed way, not an ounce of tension anywhere in his body. He was a natural rider. No one had pressed him into any mold or ideal of a rider, but he was perfect as he was.

He winked at me and leaned a little forward, and Winsome kicked into another gear. In the blink of an eye, I was looking at her tail and round behind, while watching clods of turf fly up from her rear shoes.

Kiddo slowed into a trot, and then a walk. Huffing and puffing, he gave up the race. It made me laugh and pet him.

"It's OK Kiddo. They'll be waiting for both of us at the top."

And they were. They stood at the crest of the hill, making a stunning silhouette against a backdrop of green woods and blue sky. Marco called out to us, "Ah Lizzy, she's a delight."

"I'm glad you think so because she's the reason I am where I am. She's taken me down this road, and I know now that I'll never turn back."

"What do you mean?"

And then I found myself talking about finding Winsome and later leaving Cam. God, I hadn't even thought about Cam in a long time. But here I was blathering on about my college boyfriend; about the life he assumed we would have together.

But then came the purchase of Winsome, my incredible find, and then my mounting ambition as a rider. My "Black Beauty Syndrome" as Cam called it.

Marco listened respectfully, making small encouraging noises from time to time as we strolled along the edge of the field.

340 | The Dressage Chronicles: A Matter of Feel

I just kept talking. I had a lot of pent-up words, words that hadn't been spoken, but only scribbled down in my journal. But here was a willing set of ears, and all those words were unstoppable. And Marco didn't try to stop them either. When we had found our way back to the sagging gate, I was still talking. I pulled Kiddo up.

Marco halted Winsome, too. I felt that as soon as we passed through that gate, I would need to stop talking, and Marco must have sensed it. So we stood there until the horses began to paw the ground, confused. I couldn't blame them. It was time to move on.

I heard myself rush through my history, squeezing my story into our last few moments standing side-by-side at the field's gate as we restrained our horses. I brought Marco, and myself, back to the present, back to describing my life at Equus Paradiso Farm, and to Winsome, where this discussion had begun.

We stepped back through the gate, onto the dirt road that was hard packed enough that the clip-clop of hooves was audible, unlike the muffled sounds when we treaded on grass.

Marco was silent, and so was I, but in a comfortable way.

I warned Marco before I pushed the button on the farm gate, and Winsome spun around with Marco. Of course it didn't bother him in the least.

While she cautiously tip-toed through the gate, he reached back and stroked her on the butt.

I watched as he swung lightly down. She lowered her head and tucked it under his arm, while he scratched behind her ears and she poked out her top lip. Oh Winsome! She was flirting with him. Clearly she was not immune to his charm.

It was then that Chopper and Snapper came trotting out of the barn and broke the spell.

Francesca had to be right behind.

Marco reached down and patted and scratched the two terriers as they jumped all over his legs whining and panting.

He was smiling broadly. "Chopper, Snapper, hey boys. Long time, no see."

I shook my head and laughed nervously. I tried to stay calm, but my insides started to shake in anticipation of a confrontation with Francesca.

Marco cut his eyes my way and winked. "Lizzy, this is a test. Let's see how well you do."

But I gave myself a shake. This was the same Francesca who had acted as courier for Claire Winston. I realized Francesca Cavelli was one hell of a mystery woman, the ultimate double-agent. It confused me but also centered me. I wasn't nearly as afraid of her as I thought.

Francesca came strolling down the aisle, cell phone to her ear. Marco gave her a smile and a wave, and then the two of us walked the horses in and put them in the grooming stalls and began to untack.

Francesca hung up and caught up with us. Marco, having clipped Winsome into the cross-ties, walked up to her and shocked me and Francesca both by giving her a hug. "Francesca, it's been too long."

He let go before she could do or say anything. Her arms hung at her sides, her cell phone still gripped in one hand. She sounded a bit flustered when she said, "Marco, I'm surprised to see you here with Lizzy. Clearly you two have become friends."

He stepped back and looked her in the eyes, smiling. "You look fantastic. Life must be good."

"Yes, well, I stay busy."

Marco reached toward her with one hand, lightly tapping her on an elbow. "Hey, I was surprised to see Emma has moved on, but Lizzy here is your new Emma, and more than her equal. She's not only talented; she's really smart, too."

Francesca frowned and glanced at me quickly, as if to check and see if Marco was talking about the right person, but then turned back to Marco with a strained smile. "Now, don't go and give her ideas, Marco."

I decided to pipe up. "Marco is a hell of a horseman. He's teaching me a lot."

"No doubt."

Francesca's eyebrows went up in a suggestive way that made my face hot, but also made me just a little bit proud. He was a catch indeed.

Marco was so good-looking that just for a moment, a flash really, I thought I saw Francesca look at him in an open, sort of adoring, way. It would be unnatural not to notice his smooth tan face, and dark eyes, and then his head full of dark curls. Did Francesca have a real beating heart in that narrow chest of hers? Quickly of course, Francesca's guard went up, and she crossed her arms before continuing. "So I guess this means Pali is here too?"

"Ah, yes, I'm afraid so. But c'mon Francesca, it would be unnatural for us to be in town and for those two to be separate. He keeps hoping you see, but you shouldn't worry. Deb won't leave you. You won. Pali is too difficult on a daily basis, I know, I live with him."

Francesca raised an eyebrow, but didn't smile.

Then Marco said, "Lizzy showed me your stallion. Wow. What an animal. You must be really excited to own such a horse. I wouldn't be surprised to see that one make a team with Margot."

Francesca looked serious as she locked eyes with Marco. I could see she was considering the bullshit factor. Marco may have just piled it on a bit too thick.

"Well, Marco, I think the horse has what it takes. But you know it takes a tremendous amount of ambition to see that kind of thing all the way through."

Marco looked back with equal intensity. "Francesca, you and Frank have enough ambition for all of us. You couldn't be where you are today without it."

They continued a pleasant enough conversation. And I thought all had gone well when Francesca went back to her office. I shook my head and marveled. "Marco, how do you do that?"

"What?"

"Schmooze."

He laughed, "I actually like Francesca."

I found that idea shocking. "That is just not possible."

"Lizzy, she wants more than anything to ride at an advanced level. She can sort of fake it, but she has no feeling for a horse. She's too stiff and too old. I know; I used to watch Pali teach her on Babu. But look at the horse flesh she's producing, and buying, for others to ride and compete. Look at the facilities here. No matter how good she is at manipulating people, she cannot manipulate time. We all are living under the same curse. There is no breaking away from it. It's heartbreaking really."

Maybe Marco could find a warm spot in his heart for Francesca, but I couldn't go that far. "No, sorry Marco, she's nasty in little pin-pricking ways. She's gone out of her way to make me feel insecure and worthless."

Marco reached for my hand and gave it a squeeze. "Lizzy, if I told you your hair was green would you be hurt and offended?"

I was confused. "No, of course not, I know my hair is brown."

"So if I tell you you're worthless, you shouldn't be hurt or offended either. Because you know it's not true."

Well, that left me speechless. He continued, "Lizzy, you are a good rider and a reliable friend to all the horses in your care. Don't ever believe anyone who tells you otherwise."

He gave my hand another squeeze.

I stood frozen to the ground a moment, and then turned on my heel and headed slowly for the office, trying to gather my thoughts and take deep breaths.

My hair was not green. It was brown. No matter what she said, I was not worthless. In fact I was an important part of this operation. I was in fact important to her prized stallion and his success.

I figured Francesca could take the opportunity to chew me out, or I could take the opportunity to try and have a real conversation with her; like an adult. I stood for a moment outside the office door, and raised my fist to knock. But the door swung open.

"Come on in, Lizzy, and close the door behind you. You can't sneak up on me when I've got Chopper and Snapper with me."

I felt myself stiffen. And then I reached down and greeted the boys as they jumped all over my legs giving me kisses on my chin. At least I had two friends here, even though they were fickle in their support. I felt bolstered. "Francesca, I've got a few things I want to talk to you about."

She sat behind her big desk and motioned to a chair on the other side. Her desk had stacks of papers, and on the floor were books of fabric samples. Her desktop computer had a large screen with a photo of Wild Child and Margot as a screensaver. I had never seen the photo. I pointed to it. "Wow. That's stunning."

"Yes, just like Marco, outstanding physical specimens. You're enjoying Marco's attentions, I suppose?"

She was knocking me off balance before I had opened my mouth. I thought of Marco's words to "manipulate the manipulator." I took a deep breath. "Actually, yes I am, very much."

And then I grinned a big grin and tried to re-steer the conversation. I had real things to discuss. "I was wondering if the list for Gladstone is up yet."

"Yes. We are first alternates. I don't think all the West Coast horses will come. So I feel confident we'll go. Ryder still needs her scores from this coming weekend, but I feel confident she'll do it. She's very goal oriented. Why do you ask, Lizzy?"

"Did Patrick qualify, too?"

"Yes."

"I think he's one bad dude."

Francesca seemed to brighten. "And I should care what you think because..."

I thought I detected the faintest of curls at the edges of her lips. What I was saying was not funny. I was serious. I could feel my face heating up.

I was not going to run away. I was going to say what I needed to say. "You said that you valued loyalty."

Francesca pressed her lips together. Although her lipstick was perfect today, she had tiny lines that ran vertically into her lips showing her age. Marco was right. All the money in the world couldn't turn back the hands of time. But I couldn't feel sorry for her. No. She had too much power over me and over all of us, human and equine.

"Lizzy, Patrick is Claire's trainer. He's not your problem."

I got up from my chair, but damn it I had so much more to say. I had questions that I could tell she would never answer. She felt no need to share with me any more than she would share with Alfonso. Her attitude made my blood boil, but she still had power over me. I still did not want to lose my job. But I had information that she might like to know. That gave me some power. I tried to control my voice, to keep it steady and low, but it quavered as I spoke. "Patrick is way too old for Ryder."

Now she was looking interested. "What do you mean?"

"Francesca, you should be interested in what I see and what I hear, because I'm on the front line in a way that you can never be. I'm trying to tell you that Patrick got Ryder good and drunk for one thing, and I heard other stuff too that makes me suspicious. She seems mature, but she's only eighteen and susceptible to believe what someone tells her, especially if that someone promises to make her an Olympian."

Francesca stood quietly, and I saw her process what I had said. Her eyes opened back up and she nodded. "Yes. I see. Maybe I need to go to Canada and keep an eye on things."

She got it. Score one for me. My insides began to settle. I still hadn't mentioned anything about Wild Child because I really didn't have anything concrete to say. So I left it at Ryder. At least Francesca was listening to me. "I think that would be a good idea. No, that would be a great idea."

Francesca nodded again, but this time it was clearly a dismissal. "Close the door on your way out, Lizzy."

"Sure."

"Lizzy."

"Yes."

"Thanks."

"You're welcome."

Wow. I walked out, pulling the door shut in a gentle slow way, so that I could hear the latch click as the door knob released from my grip.

Oh my God, I really was the new Emma. I had broken through without getting my ass fired. I was manipulating the manipulator. I had passed the test.

But I had also unleashed Francesca on Ryder. I was sure Ryder would not be happy about that. But I still had lots of Monday left to enjoy with Marco, who was patiently waiting for me to drive him home.

Life was good.

It was late in the day before I got started on the trailer. There was still no sign of Ryder.

I rolled the muck cart around and scooped eight hours worth of poop from the trailer stalls. I pulled all the leftover hay out, too. I washed out the stalls with a sprayer attachment of disinfectant on the end of the hose. Then I swept it out with a stiff broom. The head divider and the inside of the escape doors also got hosed off and then wiped down with a rag. I left all the doors open and the ramp down to let it dry out. It finally smelled nice and clean. There was something satisfying about standing back and admiring my work while taking a deep breath.

I went into the tack room of the trailer and started pulling out everything to be washed and cleaned.

Ryder startled me. "Hey Lizzy, I can take it from here."

I twisted around, and there she stood in the doorway. I sounded more irritated that I meant to. "Ryder, where have you been?"

"I went over to Patrick's. I've got to get organized to leave on Wednesday, so we had a meeting over breakfast, and then I hung out with Suzette."

I noticed Ryder had dark circles under her eyes. In fact she looked so terrible that it made me tone down the irritation in my voice. "I can't believe you are back on the road again Wednesday."

"I'm fine. Hand me the laundry, and I'll get it started. You can leave the tack for me, too. I'll finish this up."

I couldn't do it. The kid looked too awful. "No, I'm going to help you finish unpacking and putting away, since you'll be packing right back up again for Wednesday. Plus, you won't have my help this time in Canada. You'll even have to braid your own horse."

"Suit yourself. But don't worry about me in Canada. I'll only have Papa. It will seem like a cake-walk after having the four horses last weekend. Plus, I'll hire a professional braider."

We were both trying to be decent.

Ryder started to put in her ear-buds. She was about to block me out again as usual. She had done it for eight hours on our trip home. I felt my face begin to burn. "Uh, Ryder, wait a sec."

Her eyebrows went up. "What?"

What was I going to say? I looked again at her face. She looked like hell, but she still thought she knew it all, that life had a clear step-by-step path that led to success and all that it promised. Those of us that had struggled to find that path must, in her eyes, be defective. She didn't want to waste her precious energies on defective people like me. Ryder was a fool, albeit a talented one. And Ryder was about to spend five days in the enemy camp. I could not be there to protect her, and I was surprised to find that I did want to protect her.

"Ryder, not everyone is who they pretend to be. Not everyone is worthy of your trust. Do you know what I'm saying?"

She stared blankly at me a moment. And then she smirked and shook her head. "Lizzy, I get that more than you do. You're the naive one who thinks every stray dog can be saved. I didn't want to say anything because I know you liked that nut-job Natalie, but Patrick told me some bad news about her, and I guess you should know."

I felt my stomach drop and my knees felt slightly weak. Something bad had happened to Nat. I instantly forgot the lecture I was about to give Ryder.

My voice came out in a breathy squeak. "What?"

I hated the look on Ryder's face. She was pitying me.

"She took off in the middle of the night, and she cleaned out Tommy's wallet on her way out. But it's good that she's gone since she'd been telling ridiculous stories to Tommy's clients."

"Oh."

I drew a deep breath of relief. She had gotten away unharmed. Thank God.

"So, y'know, maybe what you were saying about trusting the wrong people and all..."

I cut her off. "Ryder, don't be so sure of what you think you know."

"Lizzy, I know Natalie was a liar and a thief."

"Maybe, but in a den of really slick liars and thieves."

She clamped her lips tightly together, and then put her ear buds back in and snatched a plastic tub of dirty saddle pads and headed for the tack room to start laundry.

I watched her walk away, back straight and head held high, cocksure that she held the moral high ground.

That had not gone well. But what did I expect?

I stood there and thought the unthinkable, that it was too late for Ryder. Patrick had her hook, line, and sinker. The implications were racing through my mind.

Francesca had once fallen under Pali's spell and proven she was not beyond delusion. She bought his little Andalusian horse that she thought would change everything. Of course she had felt betrayed when reality slapped her back down, especially when her humiliation had been on public display. Then she had blamed Pali and by association, Deb, when it was Francesca's own damn overreaching ambition. I had believed that she could be that delusional again. I had believed Patrick's working on her could be successful. But I had been wrong.

Francesca clearly had enjoyed all of Patrick's attentions and didn't mind using him to try and fire up Margot's competitive drive. Now I understood it was Ryder alone who was heading for a hard landing.

CHAPTER 40
Home Sweet Home

I FOUND DEB ASLEEP IN HER barn aisle in that same old saggy-bottomed lawn chair that usually sat outside her front door. She had dirty horse coolers heaped next to it, and tipped over by her feet was a dented metal thermos. Two skinny black cats were curled up in her lap. When they saw me coming, they flattened their ears and hunkered down.

Her head was tipped back, and her glasses were just about to fall off the tip of her nose. She looked small and pale and I tried not to disturb her. I knew she was exhausted.

Inside the stall was Regina. Poor thing was huge, her belly pendulous. I could see milk dripping from her teats; the hair on the inside of her legs showed wet tracks.

I sat down on the floor. Regardless of how miserable Regina looked, she was still munching her hay with a calm eye.

I was glad that Pali and Marco had dragged Deb off to get something to eat this morning.

I sat there about twenty minutes, and then Deb began to stir. She gave a little moan, and put her hand up to her neck, grimacing.

I tried not to startle her. I whispered, "Deb, it's Lizzy."

She didn't open her eyes before speaking, "Ouch. Shit, I can't move my neck."

"Hold still."

I walked around behind her. No telling how long she'd been asleep in that awkward position. I rubbed my hands together until I was sure they were good and hot, and then gently placed them on her neck. "Ouch...careful."

"Just relax. Don't try to move yet. I know just how you feel."

I just let my warm hands rest on her neck, and then I slowly squeezed and released, squeezed and released. I supported the back of her head with my palm. After a few minutes, I asked her, "Can you move it yet?"

"Yeah, I think I can. Thanks, Lizzy."

I walked back around to face her. "Why don't you go to bed and let me sit here and read for a few hours. I have a novel sitting by my bed that I've been dying to get into."

One of the little cats hissed at me, and then the two leapt from her lap and vanished. Deb smiled. "Those two are totally feral."

Deb and her cats. I shook my head and marveled at her gift with wild creatures. "And yet, they feel safe in your lap, Deb."

Deb pushed her glasses back up her nose and got stiffly out of her chair. She did look rough.

"I really wouldn't mind taking a shift."

I expected her to protest, but she didn't. "Sure. OK. Thanks, Lizzy."

I helped Deb bring in all the rest of the horses and marveled at how great little Bazooka was doing. He totally ran amok up and down the barn aisle, doing all kinds of horsey gymnastic movements and getting all the other horses worked up and whinnying.

Then I went in with Deb to check on Glimmer. Glimmer was looking like she was about to pop, too. Deb was shaking her head.

"These girls are killing me. Regina is ready, and Glimmer is right behind her. But then again, Regina has always foaled in the dead of night, so I guess she's just waiting for dark and quiet. She'll probably foal tonight."

"Can they do that?"

"I think they can. But I don't know why she couldn't have chosen any one of the nights this long damn week. And when they foal it's fast. Fifteen minutes and it's done. If it takes much more than that, then you're in trouble deep. That's why I'm afraid to leave her side for a moment. She's sneaky. She's never had a problem; it's just she's getting old now, and I worry about her."

"Then why don't you go get some sleep now while it's light out? Not much chance you'll miss anything then."

"Ah, but now I'm awake and hungry, too. I'll go make us some sandwiches and tea. You sit there."

"OK."

So Deb made sandwiches, which she brought out wrapped in tea towels, and hot tea which was brought out in the dented thermos. She poured our tea into mugs that were only marginally clean-looking. The tea was hot and fragrant and had milk in it. The sandwiches were on her homemade bread with thick slices of ham and creamy white cheese. Afterward, Deb produced a margarine tub and peeled back the lid to reveal home-baked shortbread cookies.

I leaned against the stall wall, alternating a bite of cookie with a sip of tea, letting the cookie melt over my tongue. "Deb, you are good for my soul."

"Thanks, Lizzy. Hey, why don't you sit on one of the folded blankets here? The ground gets hard."

I grabbed a blanket and made myself a cushion. Deb was looking down at me though her granny glasses.

"So, now I want to hear all about the show. I've heard Margot's version. I want yours. The grooms always see and hear more than the trainers."

"Yeah. You know Emma used to say that stall walls have ears. I get that now. Margot and Francesca don't know the half of it. Or at least I don't think they do. I was the ears and the eyes for us all, even if I don't fully understand everything I took in."

I unloaded about everything. I didn't hold back. Deb was rapt. She nodded her head up and down and didn't interrupt once. I took a breath and rested, trying to think if I had left out any important details. Finally Deb spoke up, "I think I'd like this Natalie character. She's got guts."

"She was so brave. And Francesca blew me away, too. Francesca! She would never admit what she did, but she was the one who brought the briefcase to Natalie; I saw her myself or I would never have believed it. Then I ended up helping Nat pass on stolen records. I felt like a secret agent or something."

"Claire must have asked Francesca to do it. They are friends."

"But I can't believe Francesca said yes."

"And you said Nat had stolen these records from her boss?"

"Yeah. She had proof that Claire Winston was reamed on horse deals. I mean Patrick and that "Shit-for-Human" as Nat calls her boss, Tommy; they spent hundreds of thousands of Claire's dollars on horses that sometimes cost only a fraction of what she paid."

Deb didn't doubt me. I could see that. She was nodding. "I wonder if Claire will call the police, or at least her lawyers."

"And I helped. That thought scares the hell out of me. But then again, so did Francesca. But, Deb, what happens next to Natalie? Ryder told me that Nat has stolen money from her boss and hit the road. Poof! No one knows where she's gone."

"You sure that's the real story?"

"Yeah. I know it is, at least the part about Nat leaving. She told me she was going to bolt."

"She's made a run for it then."

"Yeah, after arranging the 'financing.'"

We laughed, but I was really worried.

After I had talked myself hoarse, I finally convinced Deb to go to bed.

I sat down in the lawn chair. It was a torture device. It was clear to me why she was practically crippled getting out of it.

So I stacked the dirty smelly horse blankets into the seat, and that helped. At least my novel was absorbing, but as the sun went down, the lighting got dim, and my eyes began to burn with strain. I hesitated to turn on the aisle lights. The horses needed to settle and rest, too.

After a while I closed my book and sat in the darkening barn listening to the music of horses munching hay. I got up to check on Glimmer one time when I heard her moaning. But she was just lowering herself down into her straw for a rest.

It started to get late. But I let Deb sleep on. I pulled out my phone and started working Sudoku puzzles.

Then headlights pulled right up to the barn and cut off. When the door opened, the dome light illuminated a familiar form.

It was Frank! He turned on one of those old-fashioned camping lanterns and started walking my way. As he got closer, I saw it was just a glorified flashlight.

I only had the light of my phone, and I aimed it at my face so I wouldn't startle him. But he still sounded startled. "Lizzy? What a good egg you are up here helping out Deb."

I felt myself relax. Frank always put me at ease. It had been ages since I last saw him.

"Oh my God, Frank. I've missed seeing you. Where have you been?"

"No one told you? I've been back in the old country."

"What?"

"Italy. I've been hired back to save a sinking ship. Those hip young guns who bought our company have run it into the ground. It's unbelievable."

"Well, you've missed a lot."

"Francesca's brought me up to speed. She sent me up here to give Deb a spell. She said everyone around here looks like the walking dead. Actually that's not what she said exactly, but you don't want to hear how she put it."

He was carrying a picnic basket and set it down next to the chair. Then he pointed at me.

"Is she still using this piece of crap for a chair?"

I laughed. Frank always said it like it was, but he meant it in the kindest way.

"Yes. And it appears to be the only one around."

I stood up and offered him the seat. But he was glancing up and down the aisle.

"Well, hell. I guess I need to come up here more often."

"It's not so bad now that I stacked blankets in the seat."

Frank looked back at me and at the chair.

"I guess if it's my only choice."

Frank sat down cautiously. He was much bigger and heavier than either Deb or me, and as soon as he got settled the seat gave way. Even the aluminum frame kind of imploded. Frank grunted as his butt hit the floor.

At first I shrieked, but when I saw he was OK, I started to giggle.

He looked up at me and deadpanned. "Lizzy, you're right, this is much better. Thanks so much."

Then I was out of control, laughing and snorting, which made Frank laugh, too.

Frank then stood up with the chair stuck to his butt. After a few shakes, the thing fell to the floor with a rattle, and Frank pulled the blankets out of it and folded it up while I was trying to wind down my attack of giggles. He walked to the end of the barn and hurled it out the door like some kind of Frisbee.

"I'll be OK, Lizzy. You go on to bed. If that mare so much as looks at her sides, or starts to sweat, I'll go wake up Deb. I know that much."

I wiped tears from my eyes. I hadn't laughed so hard in a long, long, time. I looked at Frank, and my heart swelled.

I wanted a Frank for myself. I spontaneously hugged him before I could even think about how Francesca would have fired my ass right then and there if she'd seen me do it. I made it brief, but still enjoyed feeling his mass and warmth before I jumped back.

Frank was smiling and holding up his hands. "Whoa. It's no big deal. I brought my e-reader that's back-lit and a bottle of really good wine. I just wish I had a chair. But I'll sit on these blankets and lean on the wall."

"Thanks, Frank. I'm glad you're back home."

He smiled again. "Good night, Lizzy."

I turned and headed back down the hill. The moon was almost full, so I had no trouble finding my footing. The next night it would be full. Suddenly I knew. That mare was not going to foal tonight. Tomorrow; it would be tomorrow. Tonight Deb would sleep.

We gathered around Francesca's desk first thing in the morning. Ryder, Margot, and I were clutching our cups of coffee. Francesca had made color copies of several layouts for her magazine ad for High Horse Couture.

The copy read, "My breeches fit like they were made for me…because they were."

There posing in the photos was Ryder, along with two beautiful Gordon Setter dogs wearing wide black rhinestone collars. Ryder's breeches were the same colors as the coats of the dogs; black with tan seats and tan piping on the waist. She was also wearing matching tan boots in the same color and style that the polo players wore.

Under the photo was the logo of High Horse Couture with contact information, and under that the line, "Ryder Anderson models the "Paparazzi," a full seat-breech in black and tan. Ask for our free catalogue and measuring kit."

Francesca was pushing the photos around with her finger, spreading the pages out so we could see the different poses and layouts.

In all of them, Ryder looked about thirty instead of eighteen. Her eyes were dark anyway, but with all that makeup, they looked huge and shiny-black and turned up at the corners along with her lips. Her hair wouldn't have lasted ten seconds in that do under a helmet. It was swept back in an arranged sort of disarrangement.

But the most striking part of every shot was how the camera focused on her butt. Yeah, it was a small butt, and I understood how a full-seat breech, especially with a contrasting-color seat, draws your eye that direction anyway, but it made me slightly uncomfortable.

Most of the shots were from behind too, with Ryder looking over her shoulder at the camera. In one she had one boot up on a chair seat with a spur in her hand. She had her signature smirk on her face in all of the shots. The expression was like a challenge. It was the kind of expression I personally would have liked to wipe off her face. She made herself so damned hard to like.

But Francesca looked pleased. "So I can't decide which to use. If you were shopping for breeches, which one would appeal to you? Margot, you go first."

Margot tipped her head and studied the pages, finally pointing to one.

"I like the dogs. They really make me stop and look at the ad, even if I wasn't looking for breeches. What luxurious colors their coats are! Plus, they give the ad a high-end look."

Francesca was nodding. "Yes, I agree. But which shot do you like the best?"

Margot pointed to the shot with Ryder putting on her spurs. "I think this one, although any one would do, Francesca."

"OK, Ryder, you next. Which one?"

Ryder pointed to the photo that made me squirm the most. In this pose she sat backward in the chair, her left arm along the top edge, her head turned to the right, her right hand stroking the top of one dog's head, while the other dog lay at her feet beside the chair.

But again, the camera was focused squarely on her butt, and the photo oozed with sensuality.

Francesca perked up. "Yes, I like that one, too."

I cut my eyes at Margot, and she quickly looked away, refocusing on the desk of photos. Francesca hadn't asked me which one I liked. But I was NOT going for the sexy one. "I like that other one better."

I pointed to the one Margot had chosen.

Francesca looked up and smiled at me in a pitying sort of way. "Duly noted, Lizzy."

We stood in silence for a moment, until Margot broke the spell. "Well, Lizzy, let's get you on Winsome first today. I hear Deb and Alfonso had a wonderful time with her. I want all the horses who went to the show to have a second day off today. They've earned it. That just leaves Lizzy and Francesca to have lessons with me. Ryder, would you please get Lovey ready for Francesca to ride after Lizzy?"

Ryder looked startled. "Sure, but don't you want me to work Papa?"

"No. He needs to rest. Tomorrow he has another long day in the trailer."

"What about Petey? I'll be gone for five days."

"No need to worry, Ryder, Lizzy will ride him while you're away."

I was as stunned as anyone. Petey...the horse meant for the talented rider?

I could see Ryder clench her jaw, while Margot continued. "Deb will have to ride Wild Child and Hotstuff for me, too, while I'm up in Canada coaching you; same with Lovey. The horses have to stay in work while we're traveling."

Then Ryder looked puzzled. "You're coming?"

"I just talked to Patrick yesterday to find out which hotel he's in. Francesca has kindly gotten a suite for the three of us and invited your friend Suzette to join us to make it four. We'll fly up on Friday."

I didn't think Ryder looked pleased.

"Wow, thanks, Margot. I really would have been just fine on my own. Patrick was willing to be my eyes on the ground."

"I'm sure you would have managed darling, but we wanted to come."

We headed out of the office, but not before I saw Francesca hand Ryder a stack of color copies of her poses. She went straight up to the apartment with them.

***

THIS DAY I WAS NOT JUST a groom. This day I was a rider. I might not be "fancy-pants" Ryder Anderson, but I was a rider, too. In fact, I had left Miss Fancy-pants back at the cross-ties grooming Lovey for her boss Francesca while I headed to the arena with Winsome.

It was a good day.

"Lizzy darling, go ahead and do your warm-up."

Winsome picked up her working trot with enthusiasm, and I felt a surge of joy. I belonged on the back of a horse, not just alongside one. For a moment I wondered what it would be like to sit on Wild Child. I thought it would be thrilling.

I reprimanded myself to focus on the task at hand. I pushed Winsome to trot her big trot, so big that a tiny bit of airtime came into each stride. I visualized her trotting like Wild Child, big and powerful, and she seemed to get it, responding with bigger and bigger strides.

I loved the feeling of surrounding her with my aids, my relaxed legs and arms swaddling her without disturbing her or impeding any of her movement, just being there.

Every bending line, no matter how easy, was an opportunity to supple her laterally, and I had to concentrate not to let the opportunity slip by. No motorcycle turns, she had to step away from the inside rein and leg, not fall against them, and I had to catch that step away from the inner aids with my outer aids.

The outside rein and leg and the inside rein and leg were both essential to shaping the horse in the same way the farrier shaped a shoe with a hammer and an anvil. The farrier couldn't shape a shoe without both his hammer and his anvil. In the same way, I had to ride with both reins and both legs, even if one was the active aid, and one was the passive aid.

Left and right, left and right, I constantly changed direction. It always reminded me of loosening a rusted hinge. Back and forth I went until Winsome felt smooth, and the shifts in direction felt effortless.

Then it was time for the canter departs. Again the first attempts were not smooth, and although Winsome was obedient, she lost power. So after each depart, I rode a few really forward strides in canter and then came back to trot and tried again. Before long the transitions smoothed out, back and forth, trot to canter, and canter to trot; yes, then I was satisfied. What else to do? Oh, yes, some long forward leg-yields.

At first Winsome drifted through the outside shoulder, avoiding the real work of the push of the hind leg. But I rode her straight and really forward for a few strides, like making stair-steps, and held the outside shoulder firmly with my outside rein and watched in the mirror as she stayed parallel to the track through the exercise. Yes. It was time to walk.

Margot had sat quietly in her director's chair, but I could see she was happy.

"You clearly didn't forget how to ride in five days' time."

"I'm so happy to be home."

"Shows are well and good, but there's no place like home, is there?"

It hit me then. I had just called this place my home. It caused a lump in my throat, and I had to pause before answering. "I love my job, Margot. But this is my favorite part. I think I'd almost forgotten just how much fun it is to ride. I've been consumed with worry."

Margot looked serious for a moment; then nodded her head, looked me in the eye, and answered reassuringly.

"Lizzy, things will sort themselves out. They always do. Regina will foal tonight I think, and Deb will relax. Pali and Marco will be moving on, which will be sad, but also a relief. Patrick will back off as soon as he realizes that Francesca is a dead-end. He'll refocus his schmoozing on a new victim. Ryder, too, will relax as soon as she has a little success under her belt. There is so much drama surrounding competitions. But it's just a side-show that matters little in the larger scheme of things. I know it doesn't feel that way right now. But, trust me, the world will continue to turn, and the sun will continue to rise in the East. You and Ryder are young. You don't have perspective yet."

Margot knew everything it seemed. I guessed my mouth was hanging open.

She laughed gently. "Darling, Francesca shares everything with me. Don't look so shocked."

"And you know about Natalie, too?"

I winced. I should have kept my mouth shut. I had just made it clear that I knew something about Natalie. Thankfully Margot didn't reply.

Instead she lowered her voice. "Let's get back to your ride shall we, before you run out of time. Francesca will be riding in on Lovey any minute. So let's have a little fun with Winsome."

Margot went to the wall and pulled down a long straight whip from a rack. It was an "in-hand" whip. "OK, now ride over here in collected walk."

I rode toward Margot, and Winsome saw the whip. Her ears sprang forward.

"Go ahead and walk along the kickboards. Yes, now halt."

Margot walked to Winsome's head and petted her. Then she dug into her pockets and fished out a sugar cube and fed it to her. "You're a fine girl, Winsome."

Margot put one hand on Winsome's neck and turned to face her hind legs. She quietly stroked Winsome with the whip, and then pointed the tip toward the ground and stopped moving.

"See, no worries red-head, no worries."

Winsome was on high alert.

"You just sit and do nothing, Lizzy. Just keep your nice steady contact and a relaxed seat and leg."

"OK."

Margot put her left hand on my inside rein, lifted the whip and began to cluck.

And Winsome piaffed a few steps. Margot stopped, and we stood still again.

"Ah, fine girl, very nice."

Margot lifted the whip again and clucked, and Winsome repeated her steps.

"OK. Walk on a loose rein through the short side. We'll do it again on the other side of the arena."

Just then Francesca walked in on Lovey. And for once I was glad to see her. I wanted her to see me. I was a rider today, practicing piaffe on my young horse.

Margot walked across the arena and up to Winsome, who was now turning to look at her. "Go ahead, Lizzy, pick her back up. Do another walk to halt to walk to halt. Yes, fine, now wait for me to catch up."

Margot petted Winsome and stroked her all over with the whip. Winsome started to shuffle. "No, now just halt and stand a minute. Let's be clear. Not yet, sweetie."

Margot again took my inside rein. "Whoa, stand, good girl. OK, here we go."

Up came the whip again, not even touching Winsome, but I could clearly see the steps in the mirror; step, step, step, step, good clear diagonal steps, even if they were modest in scope. Wow.

"Oh Lizzy, that was really good. Loose rein and pet her. Go take a lap around the farm on a loose rein. Deb taught her a lot while we were gone. Really and truly, Deb does a super job. You owe her a giant thank-you."

I threw my arms around Winsome's neck and hugged her. And while I was down there, I looked under her neck at Margot.

"I'm a lucky girl, Margot. Thank you, too."

Margot nodded. "Go get some rest. I think tonight Regina will keep us all up late."

CHAPTER 41

High Fidelity

I HAD FUN STROLLING THE STORE aisles and thinking up things to buy for the big night.

First off, I was buying a couple of good lawn chairs; the kind that reclined. I also wanted one of those lantern-type flashlights like Frank had. Then I wondered if Regina would like "birthing" music. OK, maybe that was a little overboard. So I restrained myself.

I did buy two balloons. One that said, "It's a boy" and another that said "It's a girl." That covered my bases.

Then I loaded up my cart with beer, cokes, chips and candy. I also bought one of those big containers of puff peppermints. Regina needed to keep up her strength, too.

I drove my goodies up to Deb's.

And as I staggered to Regina's stall with my load, I couldn't believe my eyes.

Frank had gone overboard.

He had dragged an old style leather recliner to Regina's stall. The thing was huge! He also had a large cooler placed next to it.

I set up my chairs and then fetched a feed bucket and put all my goodies in it next to the cooler. Then I opened up Frank's cooler and pushed the beers and a couple sodas down into the ice to chill. I could see a bottle of champagne and a stack of plastic cups in there.

I noticed Frank had added a clamp light to Regina's stall, too. We would have a bit more light tonight and would still be able to leave off the aisle lights.

Regina was standing in deep straw munching away at her hay. I guessed she didn't mind all the new stuff outside her stall. She had been a show horse after all. Usually horses don't like their home environment messed with. I opened up the puff peppermints, and as soon as she heard the plastic, she left her hay and came to investigate.

"Hey, big Mama."

I gave her long face a rub and then unwrapped a peppermint. The peppermint disappeared instantly, her soft lips sweeping it off my palm.

"Regina, you are a big coarse girl, but when you move you are a ballerina."

I gave her one more peppermint, and then she moved back to her hay. It was something to look at her and see Hotstuff. Regina stamped her foals with a bit of herself, jet black, full of power, with heavy thick tails and gigantic ears. She kept producing these exceptional movers, who were luckily more refined than herself, and all boys so far.

Francesca may have officially owned them, but I didn't think she would ever be able to sit any of them. It took an athletic rider to ride such athletic-moving horses. But the horses never knew who held their papers. Regina was and always would be Deb's and vice versa. And Hotstuff, I felt sure, was going nowhere. Margot would never let him be sold. No, he was hers.

"Hey, Lizzy."

I turned around, and there stood Deb. She looked a little puffy around the eyes, but otherwise much better.

"You rested!"

Deb pointed at the recliner. "What the hell?"

"It had to be Frank."

"How in the hell am I supposed to bring in horses past that monstrosity?"

"Now Deb, he was almost maimed last night trying to sit in your lawn chair. In fact, it met its end, although it put up a valiant battle. I found it out in the grass. It was totally mangled."

Deb's eyebrows shot up. "I loved my chair."

I couldn't believe it. "Just give it a proper burial and be grateful. This chair looks sooo comfy. Go on, sit in it."

She walked over to it and touched it like it was infected with cooties. I watched in total disbelief as she hesitated.

"C'mon Deb. It's just for foal watch. You can put in the apartment afterwards."

Out of the side of her mouth she muttered, "Over my dead body."

Well that surprised me. "Deb, these things are expensive."

"Lizzy, this thing would take up my entire bedroom. It's huge and it's ugly."

"Just sit in it, OK?"

"OK, OK, OK."

She slid in and I pulled the lever on the side. Out and up came the footrest. Ah, man. That thing looked cushy. Instead of propping her feet up though, she curled her knees into her chest.

Deb was so small that the thing did swallow her up. She looked like a baseball in a giant catcher's mitt.

After a big dramatic sigh, she popped up, the footrest snapping back into place.

"Now that you're here you can help me bring in and feed. Be sure not to get trampled as we lead our gang pass this genuine piece of Americana.

Deb had a sneer on her face. I couldn't let her get away with that. Not Deb. "Oh my God, listen to yourself; this from the woman who was sitting in a broken lawn chair?"

Then she was smiling so broadly her dimples showed. "Lizzy, I guess we all have that line that we just cannot cross."

Deb then rummaged through the feed bucket of treats, turning her nose up at every delectable salty, sugary, greasy treat I had stuffed in it. She was cranky. She didn't say so, but I knew it was just anxiety about Regina, and I cut her some slack.

Maybe I could have thought up some healthier goodies. I guessed I had gotten the stuff that appealed to me, and I hadn't thought enough about what Deb would like.

After I got only slightly stepped-on leading the snorting babies past the "chair-from-hell," I headed back down the hill to do the barn chores with Ryder.

The two of us hardly spoke as we went through our routine. Not that we ever exchanged words much anyway. But clearly Ryder's mind was not in the present. Mentally she was already in Canada. She was leaving in the morning.

Ryder had carefully stacked all of Papa's things at the end of the barn aisle. Papa's shipping boots sat outside his stall. Patrick and Suzette would be here early to pick up Papa and Ryder and head to the show in Canada.

I knew she did not want me intruding into her thoughts with talk about Regina or Deb or Frank or crazy big recliners.

I wasn't too interested in hearing about Canada or about any of her crowd either. I sure as heck was relieved that I wasn't getting back on the road to groom for her.

Up in the apartment, her garment bag and boot bag sat by the door. Coming in I practically tripped over them. I was sure I sounded annoyed. "Ryder, what time are they picking you up anyway?"

"Six a.m."

I thought how disturbing that would be to all the other horses.

"Well that will probably stir up the whole barn. Are you feeding Papa his breakfast first?"

"Yeah."

"I guess I'll need to get up with you and feed the rest of the horses."

"Lizzy, I won't turn on all the lights if you want to sleep in."

I nodded at her, but I still felt somehow put upon.

"No, I'll get up. I may be up already anyway. I'm going to foal watch with Deb tonight."

"Whatever."

She turned her back to me and grabbed her car keys, and then she was off to...I didn't know where. I guessed to get a bite to eat.

I picked up my truck keys, too, and twirled them around, trying to get Ryder out of my head.

What could I take to Deb for dinner that would pass muster? Considering that it had to be something already prepared, it posed a challenge. But I had seen one of those upper-end grocery stores out by the mall. I never had gone in, but tonight I would check it out. So I made the drive.

I wandered up and down the aisles and enjoyed tasting samples.

Finally I bought some fancy soft cheeses and cut fruit, along with some crazy-expensive pate' and crackers. I was pleased with myself. I knew Deb would like this stuff.

I grabbed my novel and then drove up to Deb's. Surprisingly, she was stretched out in the recliner, covered with a polar-fleece horse cooler, her eyes closed. Frank had won. She must have heard me though, since she opened her eyes with a start. I whispered, "Nothing is happening. I'll keep watch, OK?"

Deb made a little noise and then closed her eyes again.

I set up my lawn chairs and then made a makeshift table by turning over a muck bucket and using a towel for a tablecloth.

I started on a soda, made a stack of cheese and crackers, cracked open my novel, and settled in.

The sun went down, and it began to get chilly, so I went to look for another horse cooler. I found it and carried it back to my chair, but then I set down the blanket and walked to the end of the barn.

I stared out at the full moon. It was low on the horizon and was huge. I looked over my shoulder down the dark aisle, and all was quiet, except for that lovely sound of horses munching hay and moving quietly around in their stalls.

And I was overcome with loneliness.

There was no reason to well up with tears. But I did. I scolded myself. It had been a good day. I was home and riding my horse. I was being ridiculous.

Then I imagined Marco standing behind me, and I imagined leaning into him, the two of us admiring the enormity of that yellow moon; and I strongly sensed him there. I could almost feel the heat of his body.

I stared at the moon; and my phantom Marco put his chin over my shoulder and whispered into my ear. I almost leaned back, but I caught myself with a start.

The truth was that this state of loneliness might never change, and I felt a stab of panic. I looked back down the dark barn aisle.

There was Deb by herself.

And I knew that back in her condo sat Margot by herself.

I was not OK with that.

I thought that the idea, that the perfect love would come and mold himself around all my wants and desires and needs if I waited patiently, was just pure crap. Love was never going to be convenient or all about me.

But maybe I was being too pig-headed to see that this was my chance; maybe my last chance.

I had rejected Cam for horses, and I still felt it had been the right thing to do. I had no regrets there, even though it was tough at the time. The horses would have always been a source of conflict.

And then there was Ryan. He understood the horse passion, but Ryan would always be the center of his own world. No, I was right to let him go, too.

But I knew for certain at that moment that I did not always want to be admiring the moon by myself with nothing but my own shadow behind me.

I made my way back to the stall and curled up in the slightly stinky blanket. And I fell asleep.

Deb woke me up with a poke. My limbs felt paralyzed, and my mouth went dry. This was it. Deb went into the stall and squatted by the door. I was suddenly very cold and shivering. I pulled a fleece cooler around my shoulders and sat behind Deb on the barn aisle floor, gritting my teeth to keep them from chattering.

The clamp light flooded the stall with light that reflected off the deep bed of yellow straw and seemed unnatural. But down the aisle, out in the cool night air, the ground was also flooded with the yellow light of the moon that streamed in and illuminated the barn.

Regina started to sweat and paw. It was three a.m. Deb said this was right about the time Regina usually chose.

While I had slept, Deb had braided and wrapped Regina's long thick black tail.

The mare sank down into the straw, and there out behind her I could see the bulging placental sac, with tiny hooves and a nose positioned perfectly. Regina curled her neck around to have a look and then flattened herself out on the stall floor.

She picked her head up to look at Deb.

Deb crooned, "I'm right here Regina."

And Regina's head went back down. She was resting before the next contraction.

Another push, and a deep moan from Regina exposed more front legs and more of the foal's head.

Deb gently pulled the sac away from the head, folding it back along the shoulders.

"Ah, Regina, another black one. Not one white hair on its face."

The little foal was wiggling its head around.

"Look at that, Lizzy. This little one is a live wire. Once the shoulders clear it will come out fast."

Deb was squatting right behind Regina. True to Deb's words, Regina gave a loud moan, and the foal came shooting out with force, knocking Deb right over, sending her glasses off her nose and hanging over her chin. The foal let out a shrill whinny, and Regina answered in a long low rumble.

"Wow that was almost explosive. Deb, are you OK?"

"I'm great. Hand me that towel."

Deb saved her glasses and wiped them off with the towel before beginning to rub the foal. I marveled at how long-legged this foal was. I also noticed the ears.

"Deb, it's got Hotstuff's ears. Look at that. They hang to the side, and they're huge and wooly."

Deb was toweling off the baby and grinning. "He does look just like Hotstuff. He's like a clone."

After a short rest, Regina rose, came over to her foal, and sniffed it all over in short quick puff-puff-puff-puffs through her nostrils. Then, seemingly satisfied that this was indeed her foal, she commenced licking. Deb stopped toweling and stepped back. Then she walked behind Regina, grabbed up the slimy placenta hanging down behind her, and proceeded to tie it up.

"Oh, Deb, that's kind of gross."

"I know. But this way she won't step on it."

Deb wiped her hands on the towel and reached for her cell phone. It was time to call Margot.

I could only hear Deb's side of the conversation. "Yup. No not yet. What? Oh my God. I forgot to look."

Still talking on the phone, Deb walked in and lifted the foal's tail.

"I can't believe it! We have our first filly."

"OK. See you in a few."

Deb went and got her little jar of iodine and cauterized the navel. Then we waited for the foal to stand and nurse. And this little filly surprised us again.

There was not the prolonged drama of Wink's foal. The filly took a long time resting before trying to rise. But when she decided to get up, she just got up.

Deb and I looked at each other. Deb's eyebrows were raised. "Lizzy, I have never seen that before. That is one strong filly."

Once the filly was up, she didn't seem to know what to do with her long legs. She just stood in one place with legs stretched out in four directions.

She whinnied shrill and long, and Regina, after answering in her low rumble-rumble, actually sidled herself up against her baby and gave her a soft nudge on her butt, as if to direct her to the milk bar.

Well, that just did me in. I surprised myself by choking back a sob.

Deb turned and smiled. "Regina's the best damn mother ever, isn't she?"

I drew a deep breath to compose myself. "She's amazing, Deb."

Deb put her hands on her hips, staring at and assessing our newest herd member. "Just look at that filly. Every single one of Regina's foals is exceptional. But this filly is really special.

Look at those legs; look at how the neck is set on. It's another Hotstuff."

I took in some more long breaths and dried my eyes. I had finally stopped shivering when Margot appeared.

Regina was munching hay again while the foal nursed and bobbled around the teats for a few minutes. It looked like she wanted to lie back down and couldn't figure out how. The filly seemed thoughtful, standing there with all four legs quivering. And then very much like when she decided to stand up, she made the decision to go down, and she went in a heap all at once.

Margot went in and stroked her gently. "She does look just like her big brother."

Deb piped up. "You should have seen her stand up, Margot. She waited to gather her strength and then popped up right away. I've never seen anything like it. She's going to be awesome."

Margot sat down in the straw and stroked the filly's ears. The filly flattened out, putting her head in Margot's lap.

Margot looked up at us, and I said, "I think she just claimed you as her own."

"Oh yes, and I don't mind claiming her, too. This one's a keeper. Francesca would be a fool to let a filly of Regina's go. We need to keep this bloodline going."

Deb was shaking her head. "Aren't you getting ahead of yourself, Margot? Geez, she's only nursed one time, and you're already breeding her."

"Yes. I guess I am."

I saw Deb and Margot exchange a long happy look. This was a sweet moment when all things seemed possible. Who knew what this filly would do, but it could be great things.

Then it occurred to me that Margot hadn't christened the filly yet.

"So, Margot. What is this little girl's name?"

Margot had a gift to bestow, and she looked genuinely excited to give it.

"OK. I've got it, and seeing her makes me know it's the right name. I've decided that her official name is High-Fidelity because she absolutely is a true copy of her great and someday-to- be-famous older sibling Hotstuff. Her barn name will be Fiddle, and we shall see if I will be the one to play our Fiddle."

Deb smiled, "I like it."

I smiled, "Me too."

And then Margot laughed, "Thank you. Now I need to get Fiddle's head out of my lap. She's actually quite heavy."

**

I STAYED UP AT DEB'S UNTIL it was time to go help Ryder. Those first hours after foaling were critical. Regina needed to pass her afterbirth and have it examined to be sure she didn't retain any. Fiddle needed her colostrum.

I watched as Deb laid the placenta out on the barn aisle floor and examined it. Everything was OK, but the vet would be out later anyway to check mare and foal and do routine blood work.

When I left, little Fiddle was nursing vigorously, getting that essential colostrum that provided antibodies that new foals lack, while at the same time Regina enjoyed her breakfast.

Margot went home to get a couple more hours of sleep.

But foaling season wasn't over for us. Glimmer had yet to foal. Deb would not get any regular sleep until that happened. Even with just three broodmares, foaling season was almost too much stress and drama for me. I was floored by Deb's calm professionalism. I found the process an emotional roller coaster. On the other hand, welcoming this new little horse was a high. I had just witnessed another miracle, and looking at that leggy little creature and imagining what she would be one day was an intoxicating game.

I went ahead and flipped on the lights in the main barn. It was only five a.m., but I was fully awake and needed to burn off some of my edginess from the excitement of the night.

So I rolled out the grain and watched my charges rise, blink, pee, and yawn. Wild Child gave me a little whinny, as did Winsome and Kiddo.

All the horses had surely noticed the pile of equipment at the end of the barn. Horses noticed everything. It was hard-wired into their DNA. The inattentive horse had long since been extinguished from the gene pool by predators.

Papa had figured out that his number was up. He had seen the shipping boots outside his stall. He took a bite of grain and then poked his head out of the yoke opening on his door, spilling mouthfuls on the barn aisle as he glanced anxiously down the aisle.

I crooned to him. "It's OK, Papa. Eat your breakfast. The trailer's not here yet."

Ryder came down carrying her garment bag and suitcase. "Hey, Lizzy."

"Hey. Regina foaled. A solid black filly, strong and correct, with long legs and ears just like Hotstuff's."

Ryder's smile for once was warm. "That's great. I'll have to wait until I get back to see her."

"Margot named her High-Fidelity, and her barn name is Fiddle."

"Cute."

"You should have seen how she popped right up."

"Lizzy, you want me to get the hay cart?"

"No, Ryder, it's OK. You can go over your packing list. Make sure you don't forget all that paperwork to get through Border control."

"Lizzy, don't worry."

She was always so cocksure of herself. Still I noticed her going over Emma's laminated packing list.

The sun wasn't up yet, but it was still unnaturally light outside from the full moon when Patrick's diesel rig came rumbling up to the barn. I knew that Ryder would welcome my help then. The quicker we got her loaded, the quicker they could get on the road. Besides, I hated the idea of Patrick and Suzette loitering around.

Patrick jumped out and lowered the ramp. It was a trailer similar to ours; a four-horse head-to-head, nice and roomy. But when the ramp went down, I was shocked to only see one horse. It was Patrick's Grand Prix horse.

I felt the hair go up on the back of my neck. Where was Suzette's horse?

Ryder was still back at the cross-ties putting on Papa's shipping boots. I picked up an armload of her gear and turned to Patrick. "Can I put this in your trailer tack room?"

"Oh, hi, Lizzy. Sure. Thanks for the help."

I loaded Ryder's saddle and bridle and then squatted down to pick up the plastic tub of Papa's grain and supplements, bumping shoulders with Patrick as he went for the same tub.

"Let me take that, Lizzy. It looks heavy."

"Thanks."

In fact he was kind of attractive and pleasant, and he smelled nice, like some cool aftershave. This morning the cloak-and-dagger stuff all seemed silly and improbable. I felt OK about chatting him up. "So, what happened? I thought Suzette was showing."

"She was entered, but she had to go to urgent care last night. She has strep so bad she has ulcers on her tonsils. She's got a fever and all, too. She still wanted to come, but she doesn't need the scores, so I made her stay home. Ryder's the one who has to go. This trip's really for her."

He smiled, and the corners of his eyes crinkled. He was a man who had spent a lot of time in the sun, and his skin was rugged and the lines deep, but all sort of friendly and up-turned.

"Well it's nice of you to do this for her. She has her heart set on going to Gladstone."

Oh my God. Did I just say that? He was hard to resist when he turned it on.

"Will you be coming up with Francesca and Margot?"

"No, someone has to help Deb ride all these horses. Plus, it's still foaling season here. We had Regina foal last night, and Glimmer is due any day now."

"And who rides that stallion while Margot is travelling?"

"Deb. She does an amazing job on him. Just like Margot."

There, I had redeemed myself with that comment.

"I thought Deb didn't ride anymore."

OK. Now I remembered that I didn't like this guy. I looked him square in the eye. "I think that the best riders aren't always the ones in the show ring. Deb can ride rings around almost everyone."

Patrick laughed, "No doubt you're right. I remember Deb. She's one of those little terrier types, small but never to be underestimated."

Ryder led Papa as he clip-clopped down the aisle and up to the ramp. He was arching and lowering his neck, examining the ramp. But as always, he sweetly followed Ryder into the trailer. The other horse gave him a welcoming soft whinny as Ryder backed him into his slot in the trailer.

As soon as she got him settled and his hay net up, she jumped out and Patrick raised the ramp and turned to her. "You got all your paperwork?"

"Uh, yeah. Why don't you guys believe that I can pack?"

"Just saying. I don't want to turn around at the border."

Ryder started toward the cab and stopped in her tracks. "Where's Suzette?"

"Hop in and I'll tell you all about it."

I waved them goodbye, feeling suddenly queasy. Until Margot and Francesca got there on Friday, Patrick would be alone with Ryder.

That was not good.

After Patrick's trailer pulled out the gate, I realized that I was exhausted. The excitement of the night and the buzz of activity getting Ryder on her way had given way to a weird sort of dizziness. I wanted desperately to get horizontal in my very own bed.

I realized I had time. It was only 6:30 a.m. The sky was lightening and the birds chirping, while at the same time, the crickets were still making their night noise. I could see both the moon, then small and high in the sky, and the sun brightly creeping over the horizon.

My legs felt heavy as I climbed the stairs, pulling myself along with the handrail. God, I was moving like I was 100 years old.

I face-planted in my bed before I could even think of setting an alarm.

CHAPTER 42

Link Arms

I AWOKE CONFUSED TO THE SOUND of my cell phone. By the time I found it, I had missed the call. It had been Margot.

I stared at the phone's time display. That couldn't be right, could it? It said 3p.m. I called Margot right back and started talking as soon as I heard her voice. "Margot, I'm so sorry. I fell asleep, and your call just woke me up."

"Lizzy, darling."

I just kept yakking at her. "I'm so sorry, why didn't you come get me? I can't believe you didn't come get me."

"Lizzy, darling, listen. I'm up at Deb's but I'm coming down. Get up and meet me in the barn."

"Sure. Of course."

Her voice was weird. My heart squeezed tight in my chest, shooting adrenaline into my veins. I was up shit creek.

But as soon as I saw Margot, my knees went weak. This wasn't about me. Her lower lip trembled before she could speak, and she reached for my hand.

"Regina has died."

My legs betrayed me and crumpled. I sat down in the barn aisle. Then my throat constricted, and a stabbing pain flashed through my chest. I could hear myself making those horrible rasping sobs that sounded like they belonged to someone else, maybe not even a person, but a wounded animal. I had to get a grip. Margot just stood and held onto my hand.

"Go ahead, darling, get it done. We don't have the luxury of grieving long. Fiddle will need us."

I caught my breath and put a hand to my forehead. I thought of Deb. This would be too hard. And then I thought of Fiddle. Fiddle had just lost her Dam.

I looked up at Margot, "What happened? She looked fine in the morning. When I left everything was good. She was eating and Fiddle was nursing."

"And the vet came out and checked them right after you and I left. But then we all went for rest. And when Deb came out to check on them, Regina was gone. The vet said she ruptured an artery. She probably died in a matter of minutes. It's rare but it happens. And now we have an orphan foal that needs to be fed every hour or two, and that means all hands on deck until we find a nurse mare for Fiddle."

Margot still had my hand in hers, and helped pull me to my feet. I understood. I was needed.

I felt numb as Margot hooked her arm in mine, and we walked up the hill. I dreaded the scene that waited for me in that barn. That happy magic place where I had always found a friend now was the last place I wanted to be. But I could do it. I had to do it.

I had never seen so many cars there before. The vet's truck was there. Pali's car was there. Frank's car, too, was sitting right next to Margot's.

Margot and I walked past the foaling stall. I glimpsed in long enough to see Regina's huge form flat out on the floor. But Margot steered me along, past the large leather recliner, the cooler with champagne, the bucket of snacks, and the little pink balloon still taped to the side of the chair.

Further down, huddled outside a stall was the vet, talking quietly to the knot of people. Frank had his arm around Francesca, and Pali had his arm around Deb. And Marco was there too.

I stopped in my tracks a moment, and then Margot gave my arm a tug, and whispered in my ear. "We are going to get a little tutorial from the vet. We've never had an orphan foal before."

The vet addressed all of us. "I've put in a call for a nurse mare. Even if we have to be the ones to provide the real nourishment, a mare helps the foal develop a more normal personality and integrates the foal into the herd, if you can get them to bond. That's the trick. The quicker we can find a mare, the better. This foal is lucky in that she got her first nursing of colostrum. I've saved as much milk as I could from the mare, but we'll get the filly started on mare-milk replacer right away.

"It's great you have a crew here. I suggest you make up a schedule so the filly has round-the-clock care and feeding. We should keep a sharp eye out for any kind of infections and scours. We want the filly started on some solid pellets and hay as soon as possible, too. We can also teach her to drink from a bucket pretty quickly. But for now we'll need to bottle feed. Foals need milk for 16 to 20 weeks, and a newborn usually nurses up to six times an hour, requiring up to 25 percent of its body weight in milk every day. Right now that's about three gallons a day."

I kept my eyes on the vet. I just wasn't ready to look at Deb. I knew her grief had to be crushing her.

The vet produced a bottle and walked into the stall.

"Let's see how she does. You want to be careful about technique so the filly doesn't aspirate any milk into the lungs. Keep the head upright and the neck stretched to the bottle, just like she'd have to do to reach a teat."

Fiddle latched right on. She was hungry.

"You guys are lucky. This one is an eager eater with a good suck reflex."

We all stood quietly and watched Fiddle dispatch the last natural milk from Regina's udder. My eyes burned hot, but I steeled myself and did not cry.

Francesca spoke up first. "I'll make a chart, and we'll take shifts. We'll all pitch in, Deb. This foal will be OK."

Those were the kindest words I had ever heard from Francesca. Now tears stung my eyes. I braved a look at Deb, but she had folded herself into Pali, and he curled his arm around her protectively.

Pali was the first to speak up. "I'll take the first shift, Francesca. Marco, you run the show tonight."

Marco nodded, then reached over and gave my shoulder a squeeze, and then turned to Francesca. "You can give me a late night shift after the show tonight, Francesca. Lizzy, I'll check in with you later."

I whispered a raspy, "OK."

Little Fiddle looked so small as the vet pulled the bottle from her mouth. As he walked away, Fiddle tried to follow him out. He slid the door shut, handed Deb the bottle, and then went to his truck to get the tub of mare-milk replacer. We stood and looked at Fiddle through the bars. The vet came back and handed Deb the huge tub.

Marco grabbed my hand and squeezed it as he said goodbye. He had a show to put on.

The vet then pulled Frank aside, but I could hear as he whispered about the disposing of Regina's body. He said that perhaps he should be sure that the "girls" were not here when she was picked up. It was not a pleasant sight to see. The insurance company required that a necropsy be done, so she would be hauled to the vet school. What grim business that would be.

Our little knot began to disperse. Margot walked down the hill with Francesca and Frank. Pali and Deb walked with the vet out to the truck, and I walked over to Regina's stall and walked in quietly. The stall showed no signs of struggle. Looking at her huge form stretched out on the stall floor, I could feel no sign of her presence. I reached down to touch her, but she did not feel real. Still, I rubbed my hands and arms all over her, taking up as much of her scent as I could. I knew that Regina would have stayed to raise her foal if there had been any way for her to do it. Her body had betrayed her.

Then I walked down the aisle and went into Fiddle's stall. I held out my hands and let her tiny muzzle tickle my palms, taking in, I hoped, the scents of her mother. Then I wrapped my arms around her, rubbing her all over. And I let it rip, sobbing into her little ruffle of mane.

Soon I felt arms around me, and I straightened up. It was Deb. I should be comforting her instead of the other way around. "Oh, Deb."

Pali stood in the stall door.

"C'mon, Lizzy. You can sit with us for the first shift. You can help us move that recliner down here."

It was great to have Pali here. Deb was always so strong and confident, but looking at her now, her face pale and drawn and her hands shaky, I knew Pali's presence was essential. It gave her the gift of time; time to be weak, so that later she could be strong.

The three of us stood outside the stall and spoke in whispers.

I had so many questions to ask. "Deb, what's a nurse mare?"

"Oh Lizzy, it's a sad business."

Deb paused before continuing. "You either have to find a mare that has just lost a foal, or you have to rent one from a nurse mare business. We don't want to do that. It's a terrible business where they intentionally pull a new foal off a mare to make money renting the mare out. Horrible business."

Then Pali joined the conversation. "I have an idea, Deb, but it might not work."

We were still whispering when Deb answered, "I'm listening."

"Glimmer's an experienced brood mare, and an easygoing type, right?"

Deb nodded.

"Does she have a strong maternal instinct?"

"Yes."

"After she foals, we rub her placenta and milk all over Fiddle and try and convince Glimmer that she has twins."

"But Pali, Glimmer's foal will need the precious colostrum."

"Is Glimmer a good milker?"

"Always has been."

"She'll make enough for two, and we'll be sure the newborn gets its share. My Dad did it once with one of our mares. If it doesn't work, we can still try a nurse mare. Plus, we can supplement the foals with milk replacer by teaching them to drink from buckets and then eat foal-pellets to be sure they get enough nutrition."

"I guess that's what we'd do with a nurse mare anyway."

"Talk to the vet about it."

Francesca's voice startled us. "About what?"

Francesca had come up with a schedule to post next to the stall with four-hour shifts blocked out with a line next to the shift to write your name. She took a staple gun and posted it on the stall door. I noticed she had put herself with Frank in several slots, and Margot had put her name in, too. For once, we were all in this together. We were a team. Francesca and Frank didn't need to do that, but they had. I was floored.

Deb couldn't reply for a minute. She, too, was looking at the schedule. I thought for a moment one woman might make some sort of kind movement toward the other, but no. Instead, Deb just nodded her head and then turned to Francesca, "Francesca come into the kitchen with me while I make up Fiddle's bottle. Pali has an idea."

The two women walked away side-by-side and disappeared into the apartment.

It was a strange sight, one that if you had asked me the day before, I would have said was one that I would never see.

After Francesca left, Pali tipped the big recliner over and had Deb and me carry the backrest while he carried the heavier footrest.

We put it outside of Fiddle's stall, and I went and fetched the two lawn chairs, then the cooler, and then the snacks. We had broken camp outside Regina's stall, abandoning her. It seemed wrong to do so. It made me think of pioneers leaving their dead at the side of the trail and moving on.

But of course, Regina's body was a shell, an empty house where a thief had robbed the contents. And as the saying went, "life is for the living." And little Fiddle was very much alive.

When I went in to Fiddle's stall, she sidled up to me, and I thought maybe she could still smell her mother on my skin and clothes. I liked how friendly this filly was. She was smart too; she had caught on immediately about the bottle. I was gladly doing my turn with the bottle. It was fascinating to watch her little pink tongue wrap itself around the nipple, pressing it against her upper gum to suck.

Pali and Deb stood in the door and watched. Pali pointed at the filly. "She's good and strong, Deb. Just like her mother."

Pali kept his arm around Deb's shoulders and kept giving her little squeezes. Finally they went over to the recliner. Pali sat down, pulled Deb into his lap, and then pulled one of the horse blankets over Deb.

The filly emptied her bottle and then folded herself onto the straw floor. I sat down next to her and gently scratched her withers. Then she flopped flat out. This pattern would need to be repeated whenever Fiddle wanted to feed, until we had a nurse mare for her. I thought I'd better slip out quietly. I would go take care of the other barn and leave Pali and Deb alone together until Marco's shift started.

Francesca and Frank and Margot were standing in the aisle when I walked into our main barn. Frank was talking on the phone. He turned his back and wandered down the aisle away from me, still talking.

Margot spoke first, "Francesca and I already fed."

Another surprise. I had never seen that happen before. "Thanks. I was wondering..."

It seemed so unimportant, but I continued, "Did anyone call Ryder?"

Margot answered, "Yes, I told her. She knows Francesca and I won't make it this weekend. We are needed here. She'll be OK. Patrick will enjoy showing her off as his protégé. I really don't care."

"Did she mention what happened to Suzette?"

"No. What happened to Suzette?"

"Well, she didn't go. She has a bad case of strep, so Patrick and Ryder are by themselves."

Francesca and Margot exchanged a glance.

And then Margot sighed loudly, "Well, Lizzy, we have no control over that."

I narrowed my eyes and thought about Patrick, how he could make himself so attractive; and according to Nat, had no scruples. He would move on Ryder while he could, for no other reason except that he had the opportunity. I spat out my words with more emotion than I intended. "I think the man is a two-legged serpent. But Ryder is blind and deaf; she won't see or hear the truth about that creep."

To my surprise Francesca laughed, it was a sort of explosive, "Hah!"

Just then Frank walked back toward us. "Franny, go get Deb. The flatbed and forklift will be here any minute. She absolutely can't be here, baby."

Francesca nodded.

Frank turned to me. "You too, Lizzy, Margot. I don't want any of you girls here. Go down the street to the coffee shop. I'll call when you can come back."

Francesca headed out the door, and Frank called after her, "Don't take no for an answer. Tell her I said so."

Francesca held her hand up as she walked away. I knew instinctively that Deb would not put up a fight.

We four sat quietly around the table sipping our coffees and teas. If it was awkward for Deb and Francesca to be sitting side-by-side, they didn't show it.

At one point Margot remembered something and jumped up to call Frank. I knew what it was. She would tell Frank to save a bit of Regina's tail for Deb; to be woven into a keepsake bracelet.

I was constantly having "out of body" feelings. I was here, but I wasn't. Part of me was watching this really odd movie that featured people I knew in the major roles. Finally I folded my arms on the table and laid my head on my arms. Voices intruded quietly here and there, and once I felt Margot pet my hair, like I was one of the terriers. I heard someone say something about riding. And then I was being roused. It was Margot, "Lizzy, darling. We can go home now."

We stepped out into a starry-bright night, my limbs feeling leaden. I needed to gather my wits; I would have the next shift with Marco. What a relief to realize Marco would be there. I didn't feel competent to do much of anything, and I had an emotional surge of gratitude toward him. I looked at the three women around me and felt warm feelings toward all of them. Surprisingly, that included Francesca.

Francesca drove us home and dropped off Deb and me at the mare barn.

Margot leaned out the window to say good night. "Lizzy. Francesca and I will feed in the morning. You've got to look better than you do right now before I'll put you on a horse. When you finish your shift, I want you to get some rest."

"Thank you."

Deb and I walked in and stopped for a fraction of a moment before we passed the empty foaling stall. We said nothing. The door was open, and there was no sign that Regina had been there. The stall had been cleaned and banked with fresh bright straw. It was ready for Glimmer. Pali sat in the recliner outside of Fiddle's stall. He was sipping a beer, and next to the chair sat an open bag of chips.

Deb actually smiled, "You found some of Lizzy's health food I see."

Pali raised his beer. "Bless you, Lizzy."

Deb pointed to the stall, "How's the neonatal unit."

"Our unit is tip-top except that she wants to come out here and sit in the recliner with me. She'll be hell on wheels if we don't get her hooked to a mare ASAP."

"Yeah. I can tell she's an Alpha."

"Yeah, and it's only cute when they're newborns."

"Well, Francesca agreed that you should try to graft her onto Glimmer, so your plan has a green light. Remember, Glimmer is carrying a valuable foal, too. This one's from a hot young stallion from the "S" line, so we have to be careful not to endanger the new foal. I said we wouldn't let either foal be harmed. Please tell me we can make good on that promise."

Pali took her hands and pulled her into his lap and handed her a beer. "Glimmer and God both have to be willing."

I walked to the end of the barn aisle and looked out into a beautiful clear night. I could see the man-in-the-moon, but I was really looking for Marco's car and thinking of how comfortable it would be to look just like Deb and Pali in that big old ugly chair.

Finally Marco's lights climbed the hill. When he got out of his car and saw me standing there, he waved. As soon as he reached my side he pulled me to him.

He smelled like horses and wood shavings and something else wonderful that was beyond description. I pulled myself deeper into his embrace and felt the tension in my body release. I felt as though I had put down a heavy burden, and Marco had picked it up.

CHAPTER 43
Soul Sisters

PALI WAS SOON GRASPING MARCO BY the elbow and having him detail every minute of the night's performance, and then discussing this or that horse. They had investors that they had to answer to even though Pali and Marco owned their own horses. And then there were the many people who depended on the success of the box office for their living.

I began to realize that a lot rode on Pali's shoulders, and tonight that load had been shifted to Marco. I could tell by the earnestness of their tones that such a shift did not happen often, if ever, before this night.

Deb had gone and gotten Glimmer out of her stall and was leading her down to the foaling stall.

Glimmer's belly was pendulous and swinging from side to side. Deb stopped when she got to Pali and stood quietly, waiting while he finished his impromptu meeting with Marco. Pali finally turned to Deb and nodded.

He stroked Glimmer from her neck to her butt and then walked around and lifted her tail, nodding. Then he bent over and examined her udder.

He turned to Deb, "Get a good night's sleep, Deb. I don't think it will be tonight. But even if she surprises us, you've got eyes on her here all night. Just go sleep now."

She walked Glimmer to the stall and put her away, and Pali followed. I heard Deb say, "Please stay."

Pali ordered, "No. Sleep. Have a drink if you can't relax."

I couldn't see them, but I knew they were embracing. Then he walked out of the stall and headed for his car, waving silently to us before opening his car door.

Marco turned to me. "He'll go back to the show. He'll check every horse and walk through every tack room. He'll find something to raise hell over tomorrow. He always believes we are one show away from utter poverty, that if he relaxes for more than a moment, we will go hungry."

"And has it ever happened?"

"Not to me. But his parents had to flee Europe, and such a thing changes you forever. They had been part of a circus that luckily could plan a North American tour just before the rest of the family was rounded up and taken to a concentration camp. They lost everything that didn't go on tour with them. Of course that included the precious horses that were left back home. Pali said they were killed for their meat. And of course they lost every friend and family member that stayed behind, too. His father ground that fear into him every day of his life. He can never relax; not really. He only relaxes with a bottle. But he is a good man, Lizzy."

I sighed. It was a terrible story. But, yes, he was a good man. I nodded and added, "Yes, and an incredible horseman, too."

"Yes."

"Just like you, Marco."

He actually looked a little embarrassed. "Let's see if the filly wants her bottle, shall we?"

We took the empty bottle and tried to walk as quietly as possible into Deb's kitchen to mix a new one. We didn't speak as we walked back to Fiddle who whinnied her high-pitched little whinny when she saw us.

I held the bottle just as the vet had shown us, and once again I took pleasure in watching her suck, while Marco watched and smiled from the stall door.

"She's not depressed at all is she Marco? Does she understand that her Mommy died?"

"No Lizzy, I don't think so. She just has needs and a strong will to survive. We can feed her enough, but we cannot give her what she really needs. She can only get that from a mare. Let's hope Pali's plan works."

Fiddle finished nursing, and then she did some bucks and cavorts around the stall. I scooted out of her way, and Marco closed the door. We watched through the bars laughing. I reached over to Marco's hand and laced my fingers through his.

"That's the first time she's tried to play." I choked a bit. My emotions were still too close to the surface.

He replied, "She's nice and strong"

And then he gave my hand a squeeze.

My eyes welled up, and I pulled my hand from his to wipe my tears away. "Marco."

He turned to look at me, his brow furrowed, "What, Lizzy?"

"I live in this crazy world of women and horses. And when everything went wrong, and not even Margot or Deb could make it better, I was terrified. I realize it was a blessing to have men step in; to hand over this enormous burden to you guys, and then, to suddenly see all of us shoulder-to-shoulder working together. It was like something righted itself.

"I don't know if this will change anything around here in the long term, I'm so exhausted still I can't think straight, but I do know one thing..."

Marco leaned in, and I found myself whispering, "I'm not afraid of Francesca anymore." He squeezed my hand again. "And I'm not afraid of Ryder either. I'm afraid for her. But I'm not afraid of her."

"Lizzy, what are trying to tell me?"

"That you have been good for me."

Marco smiled and then nodded his head toward the recliner. "C'mon, I've always wanted one of those things."

I laughed. What a "guy" kind of response.

"Deb thinks it's hideous, but I've been dying to try it."

His arm curled around my waist, and he pulled me in for a kiss. Then he scooped me up behind my knees and carried me over to the recliner. Marco was incredibly strong for someone so slender. We slid in and pushed the lever so we were almost flat. We had four hours for each other, and of course, for Fiddle.

The next morning, I put on my breeches expecting that we would ride. But no one had the heart for it. Margot decided that the horses would get a mini-vacation.

Wild Child was confused and whinnied at me every time I walked past his stall. I felt guilty about it, too, and I made time each day to walk down the barn aisle and hand out carrots to every horse.

The weather cooperated, and Margot told the guys to leave the horses out a little longer in the paddocks if they seemed quiet. If they paced the fence or stood by the gate, they were to be brought in.

It was a precious time. Everyone was sad and sleep deprived, but I never heard a strained word exchanged.

Pali went back to work at the show, but he came and kept Deb company each night from midnight to four a.m. Marco and I did the four a.m. to eight a.m. shift, and then Frank and Francesca would arrive, bringing coffee and scones to share before they sat from eight until noon. Margot took the shift from noon until four, sitting with a novel and making phone calls. Then Deb would take the next one, and so on.

We never left Fiddle alone.

And somehow we took care of the other things like feeding horses, eating, and catching bits of sleep here and there.

We did call the vet out when Fiddle had scours, but we kept her little butt clean and thickly smeared with aloe vera cream, and the vet gave her some fluids to be on the safe side. The vet had impressed upon us that even though Fiddle was doing well, she was still considered a high-risk foal.

Ryder checked in each day with Margot, and evidently said very little except that all was well and she had won her class that day...every day.

And no one seemed to care. As Ryder herself would have said, "whatever."

We watched Glimmer like hawks as the days passed. Mares did not have reliable due dates. They could go anywhere from 320-370 days, which made it a long and uncertain wait. Meanwhile we worried that the window would close on Fiddle's ability to bond with another mare.

Finally, early Saturday morning, four days after Regina's death, Pali pronounced Glimmer "ready," but with the caveat that mares had made a liar out of him many times. He showed me how her belly had dropped to almost form a point. Her udder was so swollen that it no longer had the crease between the nipples which were exuding a wax that had turned opaque. Her muscles all around her tail-head had relaxed and softened; her tail felt almost limp in our hands. But the most important indicator, according to Pali, was her vulva. It had elongated. It was ready.

The foal was so crowded in Glimmer's womb that, as I sat and watched her munch her hay, I could literally see little bulges pushing her sides. I expected the birth to happen any moment. It looked like the foal was trying to paw its way out. Every now and then she would stop chewing and turn to look at her sides; but still, no foal.

The old-timers like Pali believed that a mare had the ability to choose the timing of giving birth, and that is why mares seemed to always foal deep into the night when it was the darkest and quietest. And so it turned out to be with Glimmer.

Marco picked me up at the end of our main barn aisle at four a.m. Sunday morning. He brought a thermos of coffee that I knew would be sweet and creamy. My head was still full of cobwebs when I slid in next to him.

Immediately when we walked into the barn, I knew. No one was in the big recliner.

We tried to be super quiet, and when we got to the stall, Deb was kneeling down behind Glimmer. The foal was in the straw, its wobbly head lifted, but hind legs still in the sack.

The foal whinnied, and Glimmer answered.

Pali's hands were hanging at his sides, wet. He looked over his shoulder at us. "Marco. Good to see you. Bring Fiddle in as quietly as you can. Lizzy, you help."

I felt my heart begin to race. This was it. This was the moment. I was terrified.

But Marco simply walked ahead of me down to Fiddle's stall.

She whinnied when she saw us and butted me when we went into the stall. Marco pressed his lips together and nodded, "Good, she's hungry."

Then he put one arm around her chest and with the other hand held her tail. He motioned to me to open the door. I pulled it open.

"Just walk behind us, Lizzy, and if I have trouble turning her, then come to the front and give a push."

"OK."

Marco sort of goosed her a bit and off they lurched; then they crabbed sideways to the stall. Little Fiddle grunted once and tried to rear, but Marco stuck with her and managed to make the turn into the stall.

Pali motioned to him to stop.

"OK, now hold her in the corner, Marco. Deb, let's get that placenta and wet Fiddle down."

I looked at the wet little creature in the straw. Its ears were up, it's eyes bright, taking in this new world. The sight still amazed me and stopped me in my tracks. I was smiling.

"What did Glimmer have, Deb?"

"Can you believe it, Lizzy, another filly? And she's the prettiest foal I think I've ever seen."

Without rising, the foal had scrambled free from the placenta and across the floor of the stall, and was being licked all over by Glimmer. She was dark bay and had a large star on her forehead. It was hard to tell, but I thought she had little socks on all four legs. There was a lot of light-colored foal coat on all four legs masking her true markings. Mother and foal were doing their bonding. Glimmer's eyes were soft as she explored the wet curls of the new filly's mane and then reached as far as she could to smell her tail.

Still Fiddle stood in the corner being restrained by Marco. Fiddle smacked her gums together in a gesture of submission. I thought she was afraid. I ran and got a rag. I came back into the stall and handed it to Deb, who saturated it with placental fluid, rubbing it all over Fiddle. Pali took it from Deb and wetted it again and handed it back to repeat the process. She got Fiddle's coat good and icky.

Pali waited until Glimmer rose and then went for her halter. He had Deb hold her while he expressed a little colostrum on the same rag and then he rubbed that all over Fiddle, too.

Then he held onto Glimmer's lead rope while she continued to lick her own foal who was still in the straw. We waited while the new filly found her legs. Each minute seemed like hours to me. I was sure Marco must have been getting tired restraining Fiddle, but none of us spoke unless we had to. And even then it was in hoarse whispers.

Finally, the new baby stood. Pali practically lifted her and placed her on one side of Glimmer to nurse.

And Glimmer turned her nose into the foal, licking and nibbling at her tail.

Then Pali motioned to Marco to bring Fiddle to the mare's other side.

Marco used his knee to give Fiddle a push. Bending over her back, he used his knee and both arms to walk Fiddle to Glimmer's other side, pushing her nose toward Glimmer's teats and her butt right up against Glimmer's side.

Pali pulled the mare's nose over to Fiddle's butt.

And Glimmer huff-huff-huffed in the smell of Fiddle and then began to lick.

Fiddle was the one who wasn't sure.

She gave a little squeal and moved away, and Marco kneed her right back into the mare.

Then Pali turned Glimmer's neck back to her own foal who had finally latched on and was nursing.

Glimmer licked and licked. Then Pali turned Glimmer's head back again to Fiddle. And Glimmer licked and licked. Again Fiddle squealed and this time kicked out. But Marco kneed her right back into the mare. Then Fiddle ducked her head under Glimmer's belly, and God bless Glimmer, she gave Fiddle's butt a little shove with her nose, as if to say, "There's the milk, dummy."

And once Fiddle had a drink, the light bulb went on. The miracle we all had prayed for happened. Both little foals were nursing at the same time. Sisters.

Glimmer tugged at her lead rope toward her hay bag. She was hungry, too.

Pali unclipped the lead and we all carefully stepped back to the doorway. We watched Glimmer carefully step forward to her hay, the little foals losing their teats, but bobbling after her, nudging their way back and latching on again.

Deb sat down in the doorway, put her head in her arms, and sobbed with relief. Pali rested his palm on her head, while Marco and I slipped away. We waited until the sun was on the horizon before calling everyone with the good news.

The vet came out first and did his exams. He was grinning the entire time, even while cautioning us that we might not be out of the woods yet and to keep an eye on the threesome. It was a rare event for a mare to accept another foal alongside her own, and he was impressed with what Pali had accomplished, especially with Glimmer. He kept stroking and cooing to her; calling her, "Mother-of-the-year."

The vet finally left, but reluctantly because as he said, for him, "moments like these are what it is all about."

Margot got there next. And even though she still looked exhausted, probably just like the rest of us, she was smiling broadly. We finally had something to be happy about.

She and Deb went into the stall while both babies were napping after another session of nursing. First she went and gave Glimmer carrots. "Darling, girl. You are a treasure."

She rubbed Glimmer on her rather large head, and Glimmer lowered her head for more rubs while taking a carrot. She pulled all but the stem end of the carrot into her mouth. The end she bit off and let drop to the floor.

The next thing I knew, the terriers had whisked past us all and ducked into the stall, making a beeline for the carrot butt. Margot gave Chopper a kick with her toe, backing him off long enough that Snapper nabbed the carrot. Then they both scampered away.

Margot hissed, "Damn dogs." Frank and Francesca had clearly arrived.

The foals had gotten sleepier and sleepier, and finally both of them splayed out flat on the floor. At least Glimmer and the foals seemed untroubled by the dogs.

Francesca and Frank looked in, and Frank was shaking his head. "God damn, you pulled it off, Pali. You did it."

Pali shrugged, "Only works if the mare says, 'yes'."

We were all quiet for a long moment, no one taking their eyes off the scene in front of us.

The foals looked precious and cozy, sleeping in the bright straw. Everything was clean because Deb and I had tidied up and taken out the soiled bedding and added new. Not even Francesca would be able to find fault here.

Frank grabbed Francesca's hand, "Franny, I'm never going to sell that mare. Never."

Deb finally broke the silence, "Margot, you haven't told us the filly's name."

"Ah. Everyone ready?"

We whispered our chorus. After all, the babies were sleeping. "Yes."

"Well, the reason I held back is that I had to see how this was going to play out, but happily, our new filly had to have an "S" name. I hereby christen her: Soul Sister."

I gave a little gasp, "Oh Margot, that's perfect."

It choked me up, but then everything choked me up these days.

Deb, and then everyone else, added their approval.

It was a good name, and she was going to become a good horse right alongside her big sister, Fiddle.

Frank had put his arm around Francesca, and she had ever so slightly leaned into him. And I swore Frank's eyes were shining extra bright.

I knew that all three of these girls had a home for life at Equus Paradiso Farm.

CHAPTER 44

Thorny

I COULD TELL ALL OF OUR riding horses were getting restless and needed to get back into work. Margot said we would take Monday off and begin training again on Tuesday.

We had only a week and a half until we shipped to Gladstone, which took place over two weekends. Ryder's championship took place on the first weekend, and then Papa could come home. But Wild Child and Margot had to compete both weekends.

The first weekend she would do the Grand Prix and the Grand Prix special. The second weekend she would do the Grand Prix and the Grand Prix freestyle. Each test was weighted, and the combined scores determined the national champion. It wasn't an Olympic year, but the top four riders would receive training grants to compete and show in Europe, and those who did well would find themselves on the short list for a coveted spot on a U.S. team.

It was a huge deal, but after the week we'd had, its significance had faded for all of us; all of us except Ryder that is.

She returned home Sunday evening. I helped Ryder get Papa settled and her gear put up. I tried to ask her how the show had gone, and she had answered with an economy of words. I tried to fill her in on our dramatic events, which she seemed to know all about. I guessed Margot had given her blow-by-blow descriptions. But I forged ahead.

"Ryder, I can't wait to show you Fiddle and Sister. I feel like you've been gone for a year!"

"Can I go tomorrow? I'm exhausted."

"Well, yeah I guess. I go up at four a.m. and stay until Frank and Francesca come at eight."

Ryder scowled, "I thought Fiddle was nursing on Glimmer now, and you wouldn't have to do that anymore."

I guessed she was right, but no one had told me not to come. I was dumbstruck at the thought. Of course it meant there would be no more cuddling in the predawn hours with Marco in that big old recliner.

I was lost for a moment in thought, relief mingled with regret. Ryder was shaking her head looking at me. "Lizzy, hello?" She almost looked angry at me.

"So you don't want to go up with me to see the babies?"

"I'll go tomorrow after we feed."

"And Deb lost Regina..."

"I'm sorry for Deb, and I know everyone is upset. But I don't have it in me to go tonight, OK? I'll go up tomorrow."

She was talking to me like I was a pesky child. "Yeah, OK."

I started a load of Papa's dirty saddle pads and polo wraps while Ryder silently put up his bridle and saddle. Then she pulled her ribbons and a prize cooler out of her trunk and walked out of the tack room to deliver them to Francesca's office where they would be displayed in a trophy case with countless others.

She poked her head back in. "I'm going up to shower and start my laundry."

"OK. I'll be up in a few. I haven't had dinner, have you?"

"I'm having a bowl of cereal and going to bed."

"Oh. OK."

I walked back up the hill. And sure enough, the recliner was empty. I poked my head into the stall. Fiddle pricked her ears, but she did not come to me to butt and beg for her bottle. She was feeding on demand now; bless Glimmer.

Sister had evidently just finished nursing and had the tip of her little pink tongue still curled and sticking out of her mouth. I noticed what long whiskers she had and how her large dark eyes examined me without fear. I backed away quietly.

Deb had taken Francesca's schedule off the stall, which answered my question. I did not want to knock on Deb's door. The crisis was over, but the grieving had hardly begun. She had lost the horse that had been her companion for a huge chunk of her life. Regina had been the horse that made Deb a trainer. The era of Regina and Deb was over.

I walked back down the hill and into our barn. But when I got to the stairs to the apartment, I hesitated. I just did not want to see Ryder. I had been honest when I told Marco I was no longer afraid of her. But, damn Ryder, she should want to be my friend.

So I did what I always did in moments like this one. I went into Winsome's stall, sat in the corner, and found the peace that always came just quietly looking at her. She came and tickled my knees with her nose, let me stroke her soft nose, and then went back to her hay, ignoring my presence.

The sound of Winsome's jaws munching hay was my lullaby, and I fought to keep my eyes open. The weariness of the past few days paralyzed my limbs and fogged my brain.

The barn darkened. I guessed we had cloud cover tonight.

Then I heard her.

"Shit."

Followed by some stumbling around.

I rose and realized my knees and hips had stiffened up. I flexed and straightened a few times, then made my way out of Winsome's stall, and called into the darkness, "Hey, who's there?"

A female voice ignored me and just kept muttering, "Where's the damn light switch?"

I hated to flip them on, but I made my way to the switches by the wash stalls and hit them. They were garishly bright. I squinted down the aisle and there stood Suzette, with a hand over her eyes.

"Shit. Those are bright."

I noticed she looked terrible, her hair loose, and wearing what looked like pajama bottoms, sneakers, and a quilted barn jacket.

"Suzette! What are you doing here?"

"I'm just coming to welcome my best friend back home is all. What are you doing skulking around in the dark, Lizzy? You just about scared me to death."

"Sorry, Suzette. Come on upstairs. Does Ryder know you're coming?"

Suzette shrugged her shoulders. "I don't know. I've been texting."

When I got closer I noticed she was glassy-eyed, like she had a fever or something. She did not look well. "Suzette, are you OK? I know you've been sick. I'm sorry you missed going to Canada."

Now she waved her hand at me in a gesture of "get-outta'-here."

"Antibiotics fixed me right up. I knew they would. I told Patrick I could still show, but you know Patrick, what he says is law." She sighed a long sad sigh.

"Well, even I can see you aren't recovered yet. It was probably the right call, Suzette. It's only a horse show after all."

At that she said, "Hah!"

And then she stepped in close to whisper.

Then I finally realized she was stinking drunk.

"He just wanted me out of the way; probably, probably..." Then she paused before finishing her sentence, "...infected me on purpose."

OK, she was drunk and paranoid too.

"Suzette, I'm not sure that's even possible."

She lifted her two hands and formed a circle, and her face grew serious, "The inner circle."

Her arms dropped to her sides and she squinted at me. "You probably don't know what it's like, do you?"

I was watching her sway a little, and her eyes were sort of unfocused. But she was on a roll. "No, you've never been there. Let me tell you, it's great; exciting. Anything seems possible. Yeah."

She leaned her stinky self a little closer and wagged her finger, "Horses you could only dream about riding. You are the envy of everyone who ever said you wouldn't make it. Negative soul..."

She paused again, and I thought maybe she was done, but no.

"Crushers... wanted you to become a ...secretary."

I watched her try to take a step back and wobble.

"Suzette, you're drunk."

"Well, what am I supposed to do now? Ryder is the center of his magic circle now. I think I should warn her, and I came over to warn her. But, you know what, Lizzy?"

"Suzette?"

"I'm not going to. No. You are right. I'm drunk, and she's a stuck up little prig who thinks she's better than everyone else. I was only her friend because Patrick told me to be her friend, so he can take credit for her success and worm his way in with Francesca. Ryder's probably never had a real friend in her life."

Suddenly I felt sorry for Suzette. And I felt sorry for Ryder, too.

"Suzette, do I need to drive you home?"

"I drove over, I can drive back."

I looked at her swaying and shook my head. "Nope. If you get killed on your way home, I'll be the one everyone blames."

"You can't. Patrick might see you drive in."

Suzette's face had gone waxy, and she had beads of sweat on her forehead. Then she belched. I grabbed her hand and pulled her into the bathroom in the tack room, just in the nick of time. I didn't even get the seat up. There is nothing more demeaning that having someone hold your hair out of the way while you vomit. Suzette didn't seem to notice, but I was pretty uncomfortable about it. And Suzette was a moaner, too. She did not suffer in silence.

I led Suzette up to our apartment and put her on the sofa. All I had for blankets were a stack of polar fleece horse coolers from the tack room. She really wanted to drive home, but I wouldn't let her do it.

The coolers smelled horsey, but they would do. I folded one and put it under her head. I took two others, opened them up, and tucked them around her feet. She scowled at me, "Man, the bed is floating off the floor and turning."

She kicked one leg out and put it on the floor. "That's better. I just gotta' hold it down."

She still looked pale and sweaty.

"Are you going to get sick again?"

She was dozing off, but she opened her eyes and looked earnestly at me. "Lizzy, stay out of this mess, OK? Patrick already doesn't like you. You were hanging out too much with Natalie."

"Good night, Suzette. We'll talk this out in the morning, OK?"

I only heard her blow through her nostrils. She sounded just like a horse.

And I turned out the lights. But when morning came, of course she was gone.

Ryder came out of her bedroom as I was folding up horse coolers. She walked over to the coffee pot smirking at me and pulled out coffee filters and the tin of coffee. "So what the heck, Lizzy? You miss sleeping in the barn aisle that much?"

She looked so pleased at her own cleverness. "No, we had a sleepover guest last night."

She ignored me for a moment as she scooped out coffee. Then she poured in the water, and finally turned around. She was still smirking. "Marco on the couch? You guys have a fight or something?"

I felt myself begin to rise to my own defense. But this was not about me or Marco, and I shouldn't let it become about me or Marco.

"No. It was Suzette. She was here to talk to you, except she was so drunk that she got sick, and I had to put her on the couch to sleep it off."

Ryder nodded her head and pursed her lips. "That sucks for Suzette. She's got a drinking problem. It's gotten pretty bad. Patrick's concerned about her."

I was gently shaking my head. How much should I play along with this insanity?

"Ryder, you seem so young to me sometimes."

Well that was clearly the wrong thing to have said. Her face went pink and she launched into what was meant to be a lecture to set me straight. "Oh, please Lizzy, stop. I'm fed up with you talking down to me. You're so holier-than-thou and a total kill-joy to boot. And you gossip like a little old lady. You and that nut-case Natalie are so bored with your own lives that you skulk around spreading nasty lies about Patrick and who knows what else. And then you go cozy up to Deb and try to poison her against me, too. Even Margot seems like she's been influenced by you. You've been nothing but a thorn in my side because you're jealous that I can ride circles around you. Thank God Francesca is so centered and balanced."

I was dumbstruck. I listened to the coffee as it dripped and hissed and steam rose from the top. I had to process that rant, especially the part about Francesca being "centered and balanced."

I tried to respond, but I only got a few words out before she was off and running again.

"Ryder, I'm sorry if I haven't been very understanding, but..."

"Lizzy, I don't get you, but I never got the girls and guys that are my age either. That's why I get along so well with Patrick and Francesca. These are people who are accomplished and have made their way in the world, and they "get" me and my goals. And I appreciate what they can do for me and what they want from me in return. That's only fair. But I'm old enough to run my own life. If I'm old enough to model breeches, then I'm old enough to have a drink or two if I want them. I don't need your permission."

"And what about Suzette?"

"What about her?"

"She's been where you are now, and things aren't looking too good for her."

"I can't help that Suzette drinks too much. She's screwed up."

"Ryder, who's been pouring her drinks?"

She narrowed her eyes at me and paused a beat before answering. "You blame everything on Patrick. You are on the outside looking in and misreading everything you see to fit your little fantasy. I know Patrick, and you don't know him at all. He's a fantastic coach, and he's twice the trainer that Margot is. Maybe that's what's killing you. As far as I'm concerned, this conversation is over."

That she would say such a thing about Margot physically hurt. I sighed, then walked over and poured myself a cup of coffee.

Ryder had turned the narrative around and clearly believed what she was saying. To Ryder, it was not Patrick who had a problem, but me. I was a vicious gossip who was undermining her relationships with Deb and Margot and running down Patrick because I was jealous.

And if Suzette had tried to warn Ryder, the story would be the same. Suzette had a drinking problem and was only jealous. And of course, Natalie had no standing; she was a nut-case with an axe to grind.

Patrick, on the other hand, had managed not only to keep his image clean, but at the same time, in Ryder's mind, burnish his reputation as a trainer and coach. I felt sure no one other than Patrick had been the one to shine that up, although I was sure Suzette had played her part.

I wished I could tell her that not only was Claire Winston planning on firing Patrick after Gladstone for his rip-off horse deals, but that Claire had shared the information with Francesca. Patrick had no chance now of getting the ride on Wild Child. But I had promised Nat. My lips were sealed.

Of course Ryder was right. I didn't know Patrick at all. I had made my mind up the first time he stepped into our barn aisle; the first time Wild Child moved away from his touch. My intuition might be flawed; but horses never lied, and I didn't think Natalie would lie to me either.

All this drama was giving me a serious headache. There was work to be done, and it was going to be a long day. We had to get ourselves and the horses back into the training routine with Gladstone looming.

We still had fragile young foals up the hill, and I worried about Deb sinking into depression over the loss of Regina. I felt the responsibility of making everything OK. But that was foolish. Pali would be checking on Deb.

Margot would work out her nerves by going through her test figures and by galloping up the hill in the afternoon side-by-side with me and Kiddo. I would help her shake the cobwebs out of Wild Child's ears, and I felt sure he would feel great after his break.

We all just needed to get through Gladstone, and then things would settle down. After Gladstone, Patrick would have to find a new sponsor and new clients, and Ryder would either have to settle down or pick up and follow him.

But I knew she would never give up the ride on Papa now that he was a sure thing for a spot for the North American Championships. No. She would stay focused like a laser beam on that. She wouldn't dare leave us until after the Championships in August.

After August, if Patrick had a new sugar-daddy or mommy, well then she'd probably be gone. That is if Patrick would still have her.

But until then, what we had finally said out loud to each other could not be taken back. Our positions were stubbornly set. And so we would continue to be thorns in each other's sides.

CHAPTER 45

Stand Off

WILD CHILD WAS A HANDFUL. HE was fidgeting and snarling at me as I tried to get him ready for Margot. I had to sort of sling the saddle up onto him as he danced to the side, and everything landed catty-wampus. His twitching skin had made the saddle pad slip back toward his tail, and the saddle had landed almost on his neck while the girth fell to the ground.

Ryder had Hotstuff next to me, and she sneered sarcastically over her shoulder, "Well, I see that's getting better."

I tried to ignore her, but her comment made me angry at Wild Child. He was making me look bad. I slapped him on his neck, and he pinned his ears and opened his mouth wide like he wanted to eat me; but I knew it was all show.

I managed to wriggle everything into its proper place while Wild Child pawed. Pawing was a no-no too, but I had to let it go if I was ever going to get the tack all strapped on.

Meanwhile Hotstuff, the teacher's pet, was craning his neck in the cross-ties next to us, horrified by the goings-on.

I knew I was being punished by Wild Child for all the days I had ignored him. I hoped he wasn't too horrible for Margot to ride. I handed him off without tattling on him.

After about forty minutes, Margot brought Wild Child back to us covered in sweat. Margot was pink in the face with dark rings under her armpits. I knew better than to ask if it had been a good ride. She stood quietly watching while Ryder unclipped Hotstuff from the cross-ties and tightened his girth.

As Margot handed me Wild Child and took Hotstuff, she gave Ryder and me our assignments. "Ryder you can ride Petey next, and then Lizzy will go on Winsome."

Ryder just nodded and then headed down the aisle for Petey while I started pulling tack off of a now quiet and compliant stallion. I brought him a carrot and watched as his eye softened and partly closed while he chewed. He was feeling much better now; Margot had worn down those sharp edges that always expressed themselves in downright nasty behavior.

Ryder and I had successfully avoided speaking to each other all morning. She might have tried to play it cool, but I could detect the large chip on her shoulder. She seemed to be taking special care tacking up Petey. I noticed her run her hands over all four of his legs and then feel each of his feet, placing the flat of her hand across the front of each foot like she was checking for heat.

I put Wild Child away and brought Winsome in to the grooming stall next to Petey. Just to be annoying, I felt carefully over all four of her legs, and then felt her hooves, too. Of course they were cool as a cucumber; they wouldn't be any other way after a week of rest.

After about thirty minutes, Margot brought me Hotstuff, who was barely out of breath. "That horse is better than a therapist. I had to slow him down and tell him to do less. And then all I did was sit there. He's not even sweaty; just brush him off, and then tell Alfonso to leave him out as long as he wants to stay out; and be sure and give him a carrot."

"Sure, Margot."

Then she turned to Ryder. "Ryder, go ahead and walk Petey around in the indoor, and I'll be right with you."

I watched the two of them leave and felt like I could finally take a deep breath. Then I had a nice uninterrupted time to polish Winsome as I would polish my boots. I grabbed the curry and rubbed, rubbed, rubbed. Winsome leaned into me, and I put my back into it, changing hands when I got tired. I used the stiff brush, then the soft brush, and then the towel. I sprayed her tail with de-tangler, carefully separating each hair. Then I oiled her lips and muzzle, and even oiled her hooves. Snowy-white polos and a clean white pad finished off the picture. I stepped back to admire my girl. I could see the dapples spread across her round rump, even though she was a dark liver-chestnut. Her tail had natural finger waves, in the shorter strands that hung along the sides, that I found fetching.

Although I was at a barn with horses far fancier than mine, and much more advanced in their training, the difference was this: Winsome was truly mine. No one could change that fact. Not even an annoying teenager.

Once I got Winsome tacked up, I headed to the arena. I figured I could walk around and start my work while Ryder finished her ride on Petey.

Before I could call "door!" and walk in, I heard Ryder talking to Margot. She sounded pissed, "I don't know what Lizzy did, but he feels like crap! He's back to his old screwed-up self, like someone's shoved something up his rectum."

I froze in my tracks. Then Margot's voice was raised, "Ryder, for God's sake, what are you talking about? We didn't have time to ride anything. The horses have been off for a week. Besides, if you're up on his back, it's your job to get Petey in front of the driving aids. Now get going."

I saw Ryder's back as she walked away gathering up Petey's reins.

My face went hot. I called out "door" and went in.

I looked at Margot. She looked at me with pursed lips and shook her head. Clearly she knew I had heard Ryder.

Ryder picked up the reins and started trotting. Petey was almost swimming the backstroke. He was trotting big and slow like passage, but without the power that passage needed; and his hind legs were trailing, pushing more behind himself than under himself.

Ryder was right. He felt like crap because he looked like crap; and he was blowing her off too.

Ryder said, "I shouldn't have given him that walk break. It's like starting him all over again."

And Margot answered, "So make your point, Ryder, and then leave him alone. He might have to feel the whip today, but be sure when he gives you the right answer he feels the reward. Then you must leave the front door open and allow him to go through it. You must get a good honest forward reaction, and then you must relax and do nothing. Stop fussing, Ryder, and ride."

And then Ryder and I locked eyes for just a moment. She was looking at me like she hated me. And I knew it was because I had seen her riding badly.

Then I heard the whip whistle through the air like an incoming missile. I flinched as if it had landed on my back instead of Petey's, and Winsome jumped, spun, and almost ducked back out the door. I climbed down quickly and took the reins over her head. But I looked back up in time to see Petey launch through the air like some kind of rodeo bronc. Ryder leaned back to lever herself deeper into the saddle, but I could still see a bit of daylight under her butt.

The whip whistled through the air once again. Ryder was making her point, and the message was delivered both to Petey and to me. Petey had his head down, his tail clamped, and all four feet off the ground, humping his way across the arena. But Ryder was still in the saddle, and Petey hadn't given her the right answer yet.

Whoosh came the whip again. This time Petey spun left and headed for the door.

Margot rose from her chair as Petey and Ryder ducked out and left the arena.

Winsome scooted, but I hung on, bouncing on my toes as I went with her. Luckily she stopped, and I could circle her back around.

I knew Petey would try and run to the stable, but Ryder had pulled his head to the side to stop him, and the whip landed again and again as he twirled a circle.

Margot and I walked to the door of the arena and stood side-by-side watching. Margot had one hand on my arm, and her fingernails were digging in. Both of us couldn't speak except to say, "Oh" and "Oh."

Once Petey stopped spinning, the whip came again and again, this time on his rump behind him. And this time he took off. Ryder aimed him up the hill, towards Deb's. And she just kept whipping.

He started off at a gallop, but the hill took the starch out of him pretty quickly. At the crest she pulled him up and then jigged him right back down the hill and straight back to the arena.

Margot and Winsome and I parted to let them in. Then Margot walked behind him and clapped her hands. He balked at the entrance, but another slice of the whip and he was in.

Margot and Winsome and I silently walked back in, and once we were in, Margot closed the heavy kickboard doors.

I could see Petey trembling all over, his veins a fine map on his black coat with welts already forming on his sides and butt.

Ryder picked up the trot, and they flew around the arena looking like a Grand Prix horse. The whipping was over. Petey had tested her with all he had, but Ryder had won. And now she sat on top like a princess. Then she tested him with stop and go transitions. And just from the lightest touch of her leg, he jumped forward. I knew that I could never have done what Ryder had just done. I would have fallen off in the first set of bucks. Neither did I have that hard core of resolve; that "do or die" tenacity.

Margot said nothing, but she had finally let go of my arm. Her arms were crossed, and she was tipping her head as she watched Ryder doing canter-trot-canter transitions.

After about five minutes she finally spoke up. "OK, darling. That's enough. I think you've made your point."

Ryder pulled up in front of Margot, and Petey stood there puffing away. But his eye still had a bit of a wacked-out look about it. Margot looked into Ryder's face, placing one hand on Petey's rein and the other on his neck. "Darling, are you OK?"

Ryder grinned, "I never felt better. But that bit about leaving the front door open for him to go through...I think maybe tomorrow we close the door. I never liked cross-country riding much."

Margot laughed weakly, and then Ryder laughed too.

"Oh, Ryder!" She patted her knee. "You are too funny."

Then Margot's tone turned serious, "Darling, you ARE made of the right stuff, I give you credit for that. But if this horse doesn't shape up soon, I think we just turn him out until Cara gets back. I just can't take much more drama these days. He's not worth you getting hurt over. There are many more fish in the sea."

Ryder was shaking her head, "Oh, I don't want to give up. I believe in the horse. He's going to turn around."

"Well, let's see how he comes out tomorrow. I don't want to see that performance again. Let's close the door and see if he learned anything from today."

Ryder nodded back, "Deal."

And then Ryder walked out, and as she passed me she grinned a shark-face grin right at me.

She was proud; she was strong; she was skilled; and in a way that I never would be. Yeah, I got the message. She was made of the right stuff, and I was not. And although Margot and I had been afraid, Ryder clearly had not been. In fact she looked radiant. She had loved the battle.

Even though I knew Ryder was out of earshot, I still whispered to Margot, "That scared me half to death."

Margot nodded back, "Me too, Lizzy. Thank God he didn't rear. Ryder might be right about that horse, and if she gets him reliably in front of the leg, and he stops shutting down, it will be a feather in her cap. She's right about him being a quality horse."

"And if she can't?"

Margot tipped her head and seemed to examine me. "Petey had been very good for her until we hit that show. He's been out of work a week, and he felt that he could test her today. Ryder wants to show me she's up to the challenge, that she can do more than ride a well-trained horse. And I need to let her do it, too. On that point Francesca has been perceptive. It's not all about the ribbons and award ceremonies."

I nodded back in agreement, then put my foot in the stirrup and mounted with legs that felt wobbly.

Watching Ryder and Petey had made me anxious and jittery, and now I had to ride Winsome in my first lesson in forever. I took a deep breath and looked at Margot as I gathered up my reins.

Winsome was cold in her back and excited by what we had all just witnessed. Who knew what she thought of all the drama. But it had affected her. It felt like someone had inserted an air bubble under the saddle, and I was perched on top of it. Not only that, but I could feel only my right leg making any contact with her side. Her tight back muscle was pushing me to the right. The right rein felt heavy, and she barely had any steering. Ugh. So this is what a week off felt like.

Winsome did her normal puff-puff-puff breathing, in time to her trot stride which felt too quick and short. Where was my usual horse? This felt terrible. Margot said nothing but sat back in her chair and watched, and I tried to stay patient and just work through it.

I chose to ride diagonals in a really forward working trot, and the bubble slowly began to deflate. I kept going on faith. My mare was trying.

After a few laps of strong canter each way, I tested her back muscles by sitting the trot. I knew if she was still tight in her muscles, she would try to stiffen and shorten her stride. I tried, and she did tighten momentarily. But within a few strides I could once again feel her back alive and swinging under me, and I could feel both of my legs hanging down around her sides. I was finally sitting "in" my saddle, instead of "on" my saddle, and I was down and around my horse. From this place I felt like I could influence the entire body of my horse. Or at least steer!

Winsome and I were both wet with sweat when I took my walk break.

Margot was nodding her head. "Today we are all being punished for ignoring our riding horses for a week. Wild Child was a 'bull in a china shop' today. They each express it differently, don't they? But, that's OK. They are not machines after all. You did a good job. She looks ready for work now. So, let me see you gather her. She needs that uphill outline and to put a bit of power in her work for Second level. Now that Deb and Alfonso have explained the idea of half-steps to her, we can use that idea to help us."

We started with trot-walk-trot transitions. Sometimes Margot had me make the transitions out of the walk, sharp and really forward, taking a few strides of lengthened trot, and then coming back to walk. Then we did the same with trot to halt and back to trot. In one of the transitions, Winsome anticipated the trot off and made one little half-step, at which point Margot had me trot out and praise her. Then she had me turn down centerline, and without halting at X, Margot sent me through a Second level test.

It was by no means perfect, and I lost my way and had to add some circles. Margot even had me add a few trot-halt-trots here and there, but I was doing it, and I thought Winsome was awesome. After a square halt and salute at X, we finished the lesson with Winsome doing the exercise of chewing the reins down in the working trot on a twenty-meter circle. This exercise proved that we had not lost the relaxation, and Winsome did it "by the book." All three of us were content.

***

MORNING QUICKLY BECAME NOON, AND RYDER and I got the riding horses in and fed them their lunch. The tack room was clean and the washer and dryer humming; time for our lunch.

It was a happy feeling; a feeling of normalcy.

Chopper and Snapper came bouncing into the tack room. Chopper had a torn up plush toy in his mouth. I thought it had been a rat with a squeaker, but they had torn the squeaker out. Stuffing was hanging out of it. He dropped it at my feet. When I reached for it, he snatched it back up and gave it a vigorous shake. Then Snapper dove for it, grabbed the other end, and started pulling and growling.

Of course it made me laugh; and I began cheering them on.

I joined the growling. "Grrrrrr! Go get 'em Chopper. Get 'em Snapper. You kill that ratty!"

Ryder used the edge of her boot to push them out of her way as she hung up the last cleaned bridle. Chopper cut his eyes at her but kept a firm hold of the toy. Chopper and Snapper were at a stand-off; each pulling hard but frozen in their tracks, and neither one with any intention of letting go of the prize.

"Look at how tenacious they are, Ryder! Aren't they something?"

Ryder smirked her smirk, "First dog to let go is the loser."

When Francesca walked through the door, both dogs dropped the toy at the same time. Francesca would always be the Alpha dog here. They wiggled their way over to her, and I scooped up the toy.

"Francesca they are too cute with the toy, but they've pretty much killed this one."

I handed her a flattened plushy toy with its innards hanging out.

"Here, Lizzy, this came in the mail for you."

Francesca's eyebrows went up. I wiped my hands on the back of my breeches, and Francesca handed me a postcard. I glanced at Ryder and realized she was watching, but she headed for the door.

"I'm going to lunch. I'll be up at Deb's all afternoon."

"OK. See you later."

Francesca stood there while I looked at my postcard.

On the front was a photograph of a cowboy riding a horse in a round-pen with a bunch of people sitting on the top rail watching. The caption read: "Colt-Starting Time at the Flying W Ranch"

I turned it over to find it blank; no note and no return address. Of course I knew immediately that Nat was telling me where she was, and that she was OK.

I looked up at Francesca. Although I said nothing, I realized she knew, too. But she simply nodded and walked away.

CHAPTER 46

Let The Games Begin

PACKING DAY FOR GLADSTONE CAME TOO quickly. We had one tack room and two stalls, one for Papa and one for Wild Child. We usually had a grooming stall too, but space was limited. Still, this was Gladstone. To be stabled in the historic old barn was an honor.

And here was Ryder, riding in that prestigious contest on her first effort to qualify. However the weekend unfolded, she had made it here. That was something.

We didn't need Alfonso today. Not with just two horses' worth of hay and grain, and no grooming stall to set up. Gladstone was only a few miles from the farm, so this trip, although ostensibly for set-up, also allowed Ryder and me to get our bearings.

But Deb came, which cheered me up; she knew her way around, unlike Ryder or me.

I had passed the driveway to Gladstone many times. I usually slowed way down to gawk, and when I was a passenger I had turned around in my seat. But there isn't anything to see from the road except a small sign with the USET logo in red, white, and blue, and a little building that looked like an old one-room school house. The tree-lined driveway disappeared over the rise of a hill, and the only thing else visible from the road was the golf course that once had been part of the farm.

Deb became our tour guide as we finally pulled up the driveway lined with leafy trees and wound our way alongside the golf course.

Ryder was quiet. But I babbled, "Oh Deb, I'm nervous just pulling in."

I gasped as the old stable came into view. There it was; the image I had seen only on printed materials; mostly fund-raising materials for the foundation.

This was Gladstone, or more properly, Hamilton Farm, located in Gladstone, New Jersey. It had once been a five thousand acre farm. It was a monument to the days before income tax, when people like the Vanderbilts and Carnegies were building their own monuments.

But after equestrian sport became a civilian endeavor and was no longer run by the Army, the farm had been the home of the United States Equestrian Team. Over the years it had housed many legends of equestrian sport, both horses and riders. It was hallowed ground. Now I was here, and I would be a part of it too, in my own small way.

A volunteer waved us over to an unloading spot, and Deb pulled in and cut the engine. She just sat there a moment before turning to us. "C'mon and have a look around before we get to work."

We jumped out, following Deb who made a point of leading us into the main rotunda first. She stopped and looked up at the vaulted ceiling and then opened her arms. "We are looking at history here."

We stopped in front of a guest book, and Deb pointed at it. "Go ahead both of you. My signature is in here from years ago. Who knows, someday maybe someone will look at your signature and say, 'Man that one went on to do great things.'"

I could tell Ryder liked that, and she was the first to grab the pen. And I didn't mind letting her go first; it gave me time to gawk.

This was a solid building, built to last. The entire thing was stone and tile and concrete with vaulted tile ceilings. Above us in the rotunda entrance was an oval of glass looking into the floor above. I pointed up at it.

Deb nodded back. "The trophy room. Maybe we'll do the full tour later, but just imagine the riders who have lived above the stables during training sessions; just like you guys do now at our farm, but in greater numbers. Can you imagine the great parties and rivalries and romances, and all the other drama that goes with horses and riding and making teams?"

I grinned as I nodded my head. Deb continued. "Some things don't change do they? There's a library, too. That side is all offices now." Deb pointed to the right side of the rotunda on the ground floor.

"But back in the day, that side was all carriages. If you notice, the weathervane on the top spire out there is a coach and four. Yeah. There is a lot of history here."

We turned left into the barn aisle under vaulted ceilings of tile and walked over herringbone terrazzo floors. The stalls on either side had nameplates of famous horses on them. They were fronted by wood, but each iron upright was topped with a brass finial.

I stopped and put my hand on the cool iron post. "Deb, this is almost spooky."

"You feel it too?"

"Yes."

"That feeling always hits me too, Lizzy. But once the horses are shipped in, it changes. It's like the living horses chase away the ghosts and turn it from a museum back to a living place full of excitement. Just watch the transformation."

All three of us stood in awe for a moment, but Ryder broke the spell. "So where will we be stabled?"

"It won't be up here. Follow me."

We walked behind her as she led us to the end of the barn aisle, and then we turned down a ramp. We were going down to a lower level. This was certainly something I had never seen before. We now looked at a daylight basement full of stalls.

I was almost speechless. "Wow. I've never seen anything like this before."

There was a stabling chart on the wall, and Deb found us pretty quickly.

"We are down this little turn all the way in the corner. I guess Wild Child, being the pain in the ass stallion he is, was put here so he won't bother anyone."

I looked at the dark stall, "He's like in solitary confinement down there."

"We can use the last stall for the tack room, Lizzy. That way he won't feel quite so lonely."

"OK."

And then we went and started to schlep and set up.

Before we left, we walked out the end of our basement to check out the indoor arena where Margot and Ryder would do their pre-test warm-up, and then up the back hill to look at the other two outdoor arenas. It was really a very small, compressed, and hilly show grounds, and soon it would be full of horses. We then turned around to hike down the hill past the indoor and then back uphill to the main show arena, to the spot where Margot and Ryder would enter the arena and have their chance to impress the five judges sitting in their nice little wooden huts; three along the short side behind "C" and one in the middle of each long side at "E" and "B".

Just standing there, beneath a huge electronic scoreboard that was dark, I felt slightly sick. This was it; the place where dreams were made, or broken.

We stood and watched a few minutes as the arena was being set up; a flatbed filled with ferns and flowers and stacked letters sat near us. Tents covered the bleacher seats that ran the length of the arena behind "B," and banners were being put up against the low stone wall that ringed the arena. I had seen it many times on videos and in photos, but here I was. It felt surreal.

I noticed a truck unloading porta-johns in a courtyard up another rise behind another old stable. It was an impressive building, too, and probably just as old as the iconic main barn. I smiled to myself that even at Gladstone we would still be using porta-johns.

***

THE NEXT DAY WE SHIPPED THE horses over.

Wild Child trumpeted his arrival as soon as his feet had left the trailer ramp. Ryder and I walked them right to their stalls and pulled off their shipping boots. Wild Child felt enormous as I crouched down next to him, his body quivering with excitement, his neck held high, his small pointed ears flicking forward and back looking for danger. I peeled the Velcro back with loud rips that made him flinch, and as each boot came free, I chucked it out the door. Then I stood and gave his neck a pat.

"Wild Child, no worries buddy. I promise no sprinklers will get turned on you here."

He paid no attention to me at all.

I said a silent prayer for Margot. At the same time, I thanked God that I was not riding. I could admit it; this was way too high-pressure for me now, and maybe forever.

Ryder only seemed to stand taller, to swagger a bit as she walked. She had made it here, and she intended to prove that she belonged here. Even if it was on someone else's trained horse.

For once Patrick was not stabled near us. What a relief. I knew he and Suzette were here somewhere, but I hadn't seen them or their horses. I focused on getting through the day ahead and pushed them out of my mind.

Ryder and Margot would get their rides done first, and then it would be time for me to braid and groom and get both horses ready for the FEI jog in the afternoon. This time Margot would be presenting Wild Child herself in the jog.

Margot wanted Wild Child to have a bit of time to settle in his stall, so I felt I had time to watch her coach Ryder on Papa.

Papa was nervous, and as soon as Ryder swung up, he was prancing away toward the arena with Margot at his heels. Ryder had put on the coaching system, and Margot was already cooing into her mike.

"Let him walk for ten minutes, Ryder, and see the sights."

And off they went.

I tidied up our area and then strolled toward the arenas, but I didn't get far before I spotted Suzette, and she spotted me. She was actually friendly. "Hi, Lizzy."

"Hi, Suzette. I'm so happy you made the cut. Are you excited?"

"Very. In fact my horse feels like a million bucks. I've tweaked my program a bit."

I felt a bit surprised at her chirpy tone. The last time I had seen her I'd been holding her hair while she was vomiting.

"That's great. What have you changed?"

She leaned in close and put her hand to my ear, "I've stopped riding with Patrick."

Well, that blew me away. "You've moved?"

She shrugged her shoulders, "I'm not going anywhere."

She grinned and then wiggled her fingers. "Got to' run. We'll talk more later."

"See ya."

I knew for sure then that Ryder and Suzette's friendship was finished. I sidled next to Margot and then focused on Papa and Ryder. They were regal. Papa was tense, but Ryder was completely in charge. As they progressed through the ride, Papa began to let go of his tension and actually made a good flat-footed walk when they took a break. I could tell Margot and Ryder were pleased.

Then they left the warm-up arena to go let Papa have a look at the show arena. No one was allowed to ride inside the little white boards, but today everyone was allowed to ride around the outside of the boards. Papa did spook and scamper sideways a couple times, but just as a compass returns to true north, Ryder quickly returned his attention back to her line of travel. Soon he was all business.

I didn't see the end of her ride; I needed to go get Wild Child tacked up for Margot. This time I had to tack him up in his stall. But he was surprisingly good for me. I had my secret weapon; a pocket full of peppermints. He was now a fool for peppermints.

When I pulled him out of the stall, he gave a full-body whinny, just so everyone would be sure to look at him. And he was an eyeful. I put the chain shank on the bridle and hung on to him.

***

AFTER SHE FUSSED OVER HER HELMET and tidied her blouse, Margot gave me a nod. "OK Lizzy darling, it's up to me now; turn him loose." I unclipped the lead, and they were off.

Deb appeared at my elbow, "How is she?"

"You better get down there and do your magic. I need to bathe and braid Papa for his jog."

Deb saluted me and walked off. I wished I could be there, but duty called.

I turned around and almost stopped in my tracks at the sight of Patrick, laughing and chatting up a pretty lady who I knew was our equestrian team manager. Patrick was working it. Yeah, I thought; he'd better.

I spent the next few hours doing my job. Bathe and braid, bathe and braid. The day wore on, and finally it was time for the jog.

Ryder changed for the jog into pressed slacks with a button-down shirt under a tailored blazer with a small scarf around her neck. She looked like a flight attendant. But Papa glowed and behaved beautifully, floating along her side for the jog, and standing like a statue while the judges walked around him for the inspection.

Margot presented Wild Child dressed with her usual sophisticated elegance, her collar stylishly turned up; her scarf knotted. Wild Child was puffed up. He bellowed loudly as he stood for inspection. One of the judges said something to Margot that cracked everyone up. I figured his reputation preceded him. Thankfully, Margot was able to keep her feet on the ground this time.

Deb stood at my elbow and whispered that he had been "on" today for his ride, skating the edge of control without ever going over it, and that's pretty much how he looked in the jog.

As I made my way back to the barn with him, we trailed behind an Olympian leading his horse back from the jog, and my fingers tightened around Wild Child's reins. Just the sight of someone that famous had my inner voice scolding, "don't let this horse misbehave in front of him, please God."

I put Wild Child up with relief and started pulling his braids. Ryder was sitting outside her stall repolishing her boots.

"Hey, Ryder."

"Lizzy."

"I haven't seen Patrick riding today, have you?"

"Yeah, his horse is going the best ever."

And then I couldn't help myself. "I saw Suzette."

Ryder stopped polishing and shook her head. "Did she tell you she's going to be Claire's trainer now? She's gone mental."

I couldn't believe what I had heard. I answered incredulously, "So Suzette is the new trainer for Claire Winston?"

I could see Ryder tighten her jaw. She thought I knew more than I did. "Patrick's tired of Claire Winston and her drama anyway. If Patrick is in the top four and wins a training grant to Europe, he's got the investors to buy her horse, and then it's adios to crazy Claire. Suzette can have her."

"Where will Patrick go?"

"He's got people watching him here, but it's all confidential right now, so I'd rather not say."

I couldn't stop myself. I said sarcastically, "I hear the Chinese are looking for trainers."

Ryder's tone matched mine, "Ha, ha, very funny."

I finished pulling the last braid out of Wild Child's mane and ran my fingers the length of his crest through the kinky hair. As soon as I turned him loose, he gave a good all-over shake. I felt it was his way of showing his appreciation.

"You rest well you red-headed land-shark. You have a big day tomorrow."

And as if he understood me, he pinned his ears, twisted his head toward me, and snapped his teeth once while I slid the bolt on his door.

I could only smile as I walked away. I was already tired, and I was looking forward to the fact that at this show I would be able to sleep in my own bed at night. Since Ryder had bed-check duty I couldn't hit that pillow fast enough.

I slept surprisingly well. But my nerves woke up when I did.

Ryder and I got to the showground before sunrise.

We had hours and hours before Papa's test, and even longer before Margot did the Grand Prix, so I could linger over every chore. The sun was peeking out from behind puffy white clouds.

It was going to be a beautiful day, and a warm afternoon, but I was cold and jittery and grateful again that I wasn't riding.

I felt grateful when the time finally came for Ryder to get on. The waiting was killing me. Regardless of my nerves, I thought Papa's braids were close to perfect, and his polos and pad so snow-white they almost glowed.

He champed the bit nervously while Ryder swung up and headed for the indoor for her warm-up. I grabbed my bucket, towel, fly spray, and Ryder's water bottle and headed down to the ring, planting myself next to Margot.

And then I saw him. He was no longer Suzette's coach; he was here to watch Ryder, and I wished he would go away. Margot saw him too, and Patrick raised his hand in greeting. Margot gave a curt little nod, and kept coaching Ryder.

Ryder for her part was totally focused. It was her gift.

When her warm-up was over, I stripped off Papa's polos and handed her some water while she and Margot had final words.

She rode into the competition arena like the champion she was destined to be. I wondered what it would feel like to have that confidence. Papa wasn't as sure. He uncharacteristically whinnied. Then he had a horrible loose BM.

And the judge at "C" rang her bell. It was showtime.

Ryder's entire demeanor bespoke an inner calmness. She sat tall, yet relaxed. Her legs seemed to drape around Papa loosely. Her shoulders and arms did not show a trace of stiffness; her curb rein hung a little slack. Papa rose up in front of her, brimming with contained power as he headed down the centerline. Already I was blown away.

The conservative ride of North Carolina was gone. Ryder was going for it, taking a chance in her extended trot and riding her tempi changes in almost a medium canter. In the extended canter, Margot actually grabbed my arm. It was, I thought, the ride of Ryder's life. When she headed down centerline for her final salute, I couldn't help myself; I had tears in my eyes.

I turned to Margot, "Holy crap."

And Margot just grinned back, her eyes sparkling, finally releasing my arm to greet Ryder who would be exiting as soon as the steward finished his bit and spur check. But first the score went up, and yes, it was the highest score ever for Ryder and Papa, 75%.

Ryder was going to be even harder to live with after this. Margot and Ryder finished their hugs, and I took Papa. Margot walked off chatting excitedly with someone, and then I watched as Ryder walked over to Patrick. I saw him give her a hug, and then a kiss.

Disgusting.

Suzette was correct when she said her horse was going well. I got back to the arena purposely to watch her test and marveled at how she and Ryder had actually followed Patrick's earlier advice in North Carolina and it had served them both well.

Ryder had added power, and Suzette had added relaxation and harmony. I hated to admit it, but Patrick's assessment of both riders had been correct. I despised the fact that such a crappy person could be right.

Suzette finished a point below Ryder. It had to kill her. But it was going to make for a very interesting weekend. Those two would be in a shoot-out for the Advanced Young Riders National Championships. Only one could be the winner. Today's Team Test counted for 50% of the final score, so tomorrow's Individual Test would be of equal weight. I wouldn't be sleeping a wink if I were Ryder.

They still had an awards ceremony for the class, and for the cameras at least, you would have thought Suzette and Ryder were the best of friends.

I could see Patrick on the far side of the arena, standing with the heavy hitters in the VIP tent. He was leaning in and listening to someone whisper in his ear. He still had to ride his Grand Prix test this afternoon, yet I marveled how he was relaxed and acting the social butterfly.

I left Ryder as she was having more pictures taken, and headed back to the "cave" to get Wild Child's mane braided.

The act of putting in each braid felt like a little prayer for Margot. There was something soothing about the repetitive action of my fingers. They moved without conscious thought, and Wild Child had come to like it, at least until I did his forelock.

As I pulled the yarn through and began to tie up each braid, I imagined I tied in a perfect half-pass or a straight flying change. Wild Child had gone half to sleep. When I snipped off the last hanging piece of yarn, I stepped off my stool and said out loud, "Amen."

Wild Child opened his eyes and turned to look at me. I fetched him a carrot, and then it was time to give him an hour to himself. This day he left his braids alone and attached himself to the back wall of his stall.

When it was finally time to put Margot up on him, I thought she was going to need more than prayers. Margot looked ashen. She was silent as I held on to Wild Child. She fussed an extraordinary amount of time over her hat and her coat.

Deb, Ryder, and I lined up along the open gate of the indoor arena. I watched as Margot's lips pressed themselves into a grim line. She looked almost angry. I whispered to Deb, "What's going on with Margot?"

"Well, right about now she's probably cursing Francesca for putting her in this situation. She'll be OK, just give her a few."

And Deb totally left her alone and let her putz and grumble around the indoor in rising trot which only messed up her tails on her tailcoat.

Meanwhile Patrick was doing his final preparations, flying around the arena and showing off his horse's extensions, creating a hot and lathered horse.

Finally Patrick left. I could tell Ryder was torn. She would want to watch Patrick's test. I shook my head and found myself crossing my arms, but then I said to her, "Go ahead Ryder. Come back and tell us how it went."

"You don't think Margot will mind?"

I gave a little snort, "I don't think Margot will notice."

And off she trotted.

Deb barely seemed to register. She called to Margot, "OK Margot, time to put the pedal to the metal."

I saw Margot grow an inch taller, sit down in the saddle, and arrange her damn tailcoat one last time. And then she turned our big boy on. I thought Wild Child was relieved to have Margot give him some real work to do, the kind of work that occupied his mind. There was no doubt that he had a world-class piaffe; but she had a lot of test to get through around those piaffes, and he was a clever boy about taking weight off his hind legs where it belonged and plunging it into the bridle. Deb and I both worried that she would ride him too conservatively, too defensively.

Which is exactly what happened. But it wasn't a bad test.

I still felt disappointed. Every time he piaffed, the running total on the scoreboard jumped up, but then flat-lined again. This was not the kind of test that would blow anyone's hair back in the judge's boxes.

Wild Child stayed soft in Margot's hands. His neck stayed relaxed, and he marched around like a good soldier. I realized he probably felt great to Margot because he stayed so rideable and there was a tremendous amount of harmony. He was beautiful to look at, his copper highlights gleaming, but he did not show the power he was capable of.

He finished with a score of 68% which was of course a better than respectable score. But not the kind of score that wins a National Championship, or even makes a coveted spot in the top four.

Patrick, on the other hand, had hit the magic 70% and change, enough to stand fourth after round one, still "in-the-money" for a training grant. I reassured myself that we had plenty of time to make up the difference. I couldn't bear the thought of Patrick beating Margot. Tomorrow would be round two, with the Grand Prix Special, a very good test for highlighting Wild Child's piaffe-passage tour, and then next weekend would be rounds three and four, finishing with the freestyle.

I was sure some naive wealthy patron in the stands was now seriously considering opening up their checkbook to Patrick. They would imagine owning that horse-of-a-lifetime with all the trappings; the farm, the trailer, the farm banner loaded down with blue ribbons. Didn't we all?

Ryder wanted to go be part of the night-time party scene, no doubt with Patrick. But Margot only wanted to go home and get a good night's sleep. She had watched her video, and had been disappointed. That video was worth a thousand words. The ride had felt better than it had looked. Tomorrow she had to force herself out of her comfort zone. This was not the time or place to play-it-safe.

It was my turn to do bed-check, and I didn't mind. The night air was pleasant, and I wanted to check on "my boys" anyway.

I was surprised to find our corner of the stables very dark and quiet. Wild Child greeted me like a long lost friend, and Papa walked anxious circles, turning his hay into the bedding and making it inedible. By just going into his stall, he began to calm himself. I gave him a good wither-scratching, then raked and swept out a corner of his stall, and put down a fresh flake of hay. He went directly to it and pawed it right back into the middle again where he proceeded to mix it into his bedding. Once he got it good and dirty, I knew he wouldn't touch it; so much for that.

I did every bit of tidying up I could think of, mucking and watering, then sweeping and coiling up the hose neatly. Then it was time to go home and get some rest myself. But first I thought I would walk the barn aisles and just have a look at the other horses. When I got to Suzette's horse, she startled me, her voice coming from her tack room.

"Hey, Lizzy. Watcha' doing?"

"Suzette, Hi."

I peered in her open door and saw she was stretched out in a lawn chair, not unlike the ones we had used to do foal watch. She had a notebook computer on her lap, and it looked like she was watching a movie.

I was a little confused. "You didn't go to any of the parties?"

Suzette smiled, "Nope. I'm not leaving my horse for a minute. Besides, I don't need to be around free booze."

"So you're giving up drinking?"

"Yeah. I promised Claire. I'm not going to mess up this great opportunity she's giving me."

"Suzette, I think that's great."

"Thanks, Lizzy."

"So you really feel the need to stay here all night?"

"It can't hurt. Patrick hates me. He can do all kinds of sneaky terrible things to make a horse tired or cranky."

"Like?"

"Like take away their water all night, or tie a leg up. All he'd have to do is come and dump my water buckets. Ryder and I are so close in the scores, just the tiniest edge, and I won't have a chance. He's angry enough at me he'd do it, too."

"Should I be worried about Wild Child?"

Suzette shook her head.

"Not if Margot keeps riding like she did today. He had been stressing about it, but she's no threat to him if she's not breaking 70%. I don't think he'll be out here tonight anyway. He's targeted a new sponsor and is working it hard."

"Well, I'm hoping Margot pulls it out tomorrow and gives Patrick something to worry about."

Suzette grinned, "Me too, Lizzy. Personally I think Wild Child is the best horse here, but it's too early still for him. Next year Margot will trust him more, and he'll be stronger, too. Patrick knows it. That's why he thought if he got the horse away from her he'd get him just in time to peak in the fall and make himself look like a miracle-worker."

Wow. Suzette had the real inside line. She glanced back at her notebook, and I thought I'd better go even though I had lots I wanted to ask her.

"Well, I guess I better go get some rest. Are you sure you're fine here?"

"Totally. Don't forget, I know where all the bodies are buried."

She grinned again, and I wasn't quite sure that she was kidding. She turned her movie back on and leaned back in her chair.

CHAPTER 47

Best Laid Plans

RYDER AND I WERE BOTH EDGY and bored when Frank arrived with terriers in tow, loaded down with breakfast pastries and fresh fruit for us. But after a few moments, he wandered off saying something about being expected in the sponsors' tent where there was a Mimosa reception.

Today there would be expert commentary all day by top professionals, one of them an "O" judge, the highest level of licensed judge. We only had three such persons in America.

Spectators could rent a headset and listen to the comments as they watched. The commentator was seated in the second story balcony of the stables while cameras recorded the ride from several different angles. It would be broadcast online live and on-demand. People all over the world would see Wild Child and Margot for the first time.

I thought Wild Child was a little too subdued while I groomed and braided. He forgot to try and bite me. He even interrupted our session by doing a "downward-facing dog," followed by stretching out each hind leg with a dramatic moan. I got the feeling that our quiet corner had been restful for him and that he had slept well.

Papa, on the other hand, was still fretful. I doubted that he had slept at all. He pressed his face against the stall bars and picked at his grain, dropping more on the floor than he chewed or swallowed. He was like a caged big cat, and his ride couldn't come too soon.

Ryder had shadows under her eyes. I was sure it had been a late night. But she was totally professional, and I knew she would do her job and do it well.

This day's rides went in reverse order of the prior day's placing. So Suzette went to the arena right before Ryder. Only Claire was there to send Suzette off to her test. Patrick was there to watch Ryder warm up, but turned his back to Suzette when she came out of the arena.

I could tell that Claire was nervous about pulling the polos off of Suzette's fidgety horse, so I turned around from watching Ryder and offered to do it. She looked relieved. In fact, she seemed afraid of the horses.

I also offered Suzette some water, which she refused. But I gave her boots a final swipe with my rag and wished her luck; with a nod of thanks, she was off.

Claire reached over and squeezed my hand, mouthed the words "thanks," and then turned to climb the hill to the arena. After about ten minutes, I heard applause from the show arena.

It was time. Ryder came out of the warm-up arena, and I pulled off the polo wraps. Ryder chugged her water like always while she and Margot had their last conference. Then the three of us climbed the hill.

Suzette was leaving the arena, looking thrilled. I saw her wipe a tear from her eye. She had scored 73%. As she passed Ryder, she turned and waved and smiled at someone, real or imaginary, in the other direction.

But it didn't matter; Ryder was already "in the zone." She knew what she had to do to beat Suzette.

She came in bold and nailed a square halt, saluted, and made her turn at "C." Papa was up and light, springing over the ground. Ryder rode her corners deep, like you would in a Grand Prix test. Papa stepped out just the tiniest bit with his outside hind leg in the turn, but whacked the plastic board right at the juncture with the plastic post. He whacked it just hard enough to make the board pop out of the post, shifting an entire section of white boards and leaving the short end of the arena mis-shapened. The crowd made an audible, "Awww."

But Ryder, to her credit, didn't seem to miss a beat, and the test flowed on. That should have been the end of the boo-boo.

Except that it wasn't, because when Papa had to come back through the messed-up corner, he didn't want to go anywhere near it.

He tried to stop. Ryder sat deep and closed those long legs around him, and he stuttered past his handiwork, tipping his head sideways and keeping an eye on it until it was well behind him. But even as he crossed the diagonal away from the offensive corner, he tightened his tail down and scooted.

Somehow Ryder finished her test, her scores dropping every time she had to pass the corner, and rising as she worked at the other end of the arena. But she had slipped well below 70%.

She finished with a 66%. She gracefully patted Papa, and I saw her search the rail. I followed her gaze to Patrick, and I watched as he turned his back to her and walked away.

But there stood Margot at my side, thoughtfully watching. Ryder stood while the steward did his bit and spur exam, and she simply kept her eyes down. And then Margot and I met her at the out gate.

I couldn't believe my eyes.

Ryder was crying.

Margot turned to me, "Lizzy. Please take Papa. Keep the tack on. The awards ceremony is soon."

"Sure, Margot."

Margot took Ryder gently by the elbow.

"Darling, you come with me. I want you to look happy in that awards ceremony."

And off they went together. I knew Margot would work her magic, just as she had with me when I had been eliminated at my first show on Rave. In fact losing was something Ryder needed to learn how to do with grace. It was part of the game. In the meantime, I needed to put fresh polos on Papa. He wasn't going to be at the head of the line today, but he still had to be in the ceremony.

Ryder had moved all the way down to fourth place. She put on a happy face and smiled while she shook hands with the judges and received her white ribbon. She restrained Papa as he took exception to staying in his place behind three other horses.

And then I stomped and hollered and clapped while Suzette took her solo lap of honor. I thought what a great start she had made as Claire's new young trainer. Claire had to be very pleased. When I searched the crowd, Patrick was nowhere to be seen.

But now it was Margot's turn, and once again Margot was a pale shaking wreck. Deb was there though, and I was counting on her.

All the hotshot west coast Olympians were warming up at the same time as Wild Child. Patrick was in there, too. It was a weird sensation looking at Margot in that exalted company and realizing she and Wild Child would be considered the weakest combination in there.

My face felt hot, and I pressed my teeth into my bottom lip. I wondered how Francesca and Frank managed, knowing they owned a horse that clearly had the makings of a world-class horse but had no chance at besting this field. Not this day. After the last few weeks though, I had developed a new level of trust in Francesca.

This day Francesca stood right next to Deb at the warm-up arena, but thankfully kept her mouth shut. Deb left Margot alone for the first ten minutes, but she wasn't going to stand back and be as quiet as the day before. She had made Margot put on the coaching system, and she was on Margot like a drill sergeant, pushing her to "get greedy."

"Margot, test him. You're already out of the money, so what have you got to lose?"

Then Margot stepped it up. Bit-by-bit she added firepower.

Deb was rocking back and forth in her paddock boots. "Now that's what I'm talking about. Hell, yeah."

Deb got so excited, she turned and slapped my shoulder.

When the time came to take off Wild Child's polos and wipe off Margot's boots, I was shaking so hard with nerves and excitement that I kept dropping the polos. Wild Child was on, and this was his test, the Grand Prix Special which really highlighted his piaffe-passage and extended trots.

Wild Child hit the arena without hesitation today. He was moving. Margot had watched her video and read her test, and Deb was right, she had nothing to lose. She pressed Wild Child to the limit of what he could do. She took her chances without allowing his throttle to go wide-open. She kept her skinny little butt in the saddle and stayed in control. Her passage and extensions were big and bold, and her piaffe, as usual, was sitting and really on-the-spot.

I wondered what that "O" judge sitting in the balcony was saying. Patrick was still warming up in the indoor, but he couldn't help but hear the crowd roar at Margot's final salute, or have someone pass along Margot's score of 71%.

Margot had proven that she did indeed have what it took to come to Gladstone and compete among our country's very best.

I was back in the barn when Patrick scored just over 69%.

Margot would take her place in the award ceremony today in front of Patrick.

I was tingling all over with pride in "our" boy and admiration for Margot.

Then it was time to pack the trailer and head back to the farm; to let Papa have a deserved vacation and to let Wild Child laze in his paddock for a day or two, before we shipped right back for the second weekend. Then the contest for Grand Prix National Champion would be settled after another Grand Prix test on Saturday, finishing with the Grand Prix Freestyle on Sunday.

***

MONDAY I WOKE UP FEELING THAT reality had made a monumental shift. Regardless of how the next weekend unfolded, Margot had proven something important about her abilities and the abilities of Wild Child. I knew Patrick would be moving on, and I hoped it would be far, far away from all of us. I felt I had a new friend in Suzette, and I hoped in time Ryder would reconnect with her, too. And maybe most important of all, Ryder had gotten to feel what it was like to be a mere mortal in the competition arena.

We had several days to rest and regroup before Wild Child would head back to Gladstone. It was a time to rest on laurels, ride my horse, and spend a little time with Marco. The thought sent a shock of a thrill that started in my stomach and ran right down my legs. Smiling to myself, I grabbed my coffee and headed down to the barn.

I found Ryder already hard at work. She was intently interested in laundry and tack- cleaning. I was gripping my hot coffee as I watched her unload a big wad of tangled polo bandages from the dryer.

"Ryder, throw me that wad and I'll untangle them for you."

"That's OK, Lizzy. I got it."

I sat down in one of the tall director's chairs that Ryder had unpacked from the trailer and gestured for her to toss me the wad, which she again ignored. Once I was seated, I realized the seat was wet from being washed. I jumped up and grabbed a towel and then sat on that. Ryder was clearly on a manic cleaning spree.

"Where'd you get all this energy?"

Ryder shrugged and started tugging at the polos. "I couldn't sleep, so I figured I'd get something accomplished."

From Ryder that was a huge admission. Something had shifted for her, too. She was letting me in. "Ryder, you rode beautifully yesterday. You've got nothing to feel badly about. Stuff like that happens to everyone. It just wasn't your day."

With that she finally chucked the ball of polos at me.

I continued, "Besides, Ryder, you should let Suzette enjoy her win. Be happy for her."

Ryder sighed, and her tone stayed soft, perhaps resigned. "Lizzy just stay out of it."

My new mood had emboldened me, and I just said what I was thinking, "Ryder, you guys are going to be on the same team in August. You'll need to get along somehow."

"Yeah, right. And Patrick is still our coach. It will be oh-so-cozy don't you think?"

Well, that was a thought. It shut me up and made me reflective. All I could do was sip my coffee and think to myself that a lot could change by August.

***

BY MID-DAY RYDER HAD SEQUESTERED HERSELF in her room, and I actually felt sorry for her. There would be no hob-nobbing today with Suzette at the mall, and as far as I could tell, Patrick wasn't calling either.

But Marco called to say he was coming over with lunch, and then I suggested we take Winsome and Kiddo back out on the hill, which he eagerly agreed to.

Marco came striding into the barn just as I was bringing Kiddo in from the field. He was drinking a plastic bottle of soda and carrying a sack from the Deli. When he walked up to us, he put his soda into his left hand with the sack, and he reached up to give Kiddo a rub on his neck with his right hand. Kiddo reached down and grabbed Marco's open soda bottle by its mouth and pulled it right out of Marco's hand.

We both stood there giggling while Kiddo proceeded to upend the soda into his mouth.

I was squealing, "Kiddo. Oh my God. Sorry, Marco."

Kiddo got a good bit of soda in his mouth, and the rest spilled all over the barn aisle and, of course, on his face and chest. I grabbed the end of the bottle and tried to pull it away from Kiddo, but he was hanging on.

"Lizzy let him have it. Look, he's so proud of himself."

I let go, and Kiddo nodded his head up and down as if he was agreeing with Marco. When every last drop of soda was gone, Kiddo dropped the bottle, and then out came his huge tongue to lick his lips. Marco and I just stood back and watched. When Kiddo finished licking his lips, he reached over to Marco with his top lip pointed and started pushing at Marco's sack.

I shrieked, "Oh no, not our sandwiches, too. Marco don't let him take our lunch."

Marco hid the sack behind his back.

"You want treats old man? OK, but you're going to have to work for them. Here Lizzy, put our lunch somewhere safe. Let's go play with him in the arena for a few minutes."

So I put our lunch in the tack room and grabbed a box of sugar cubes. We took Kiddo to the indoor, and he quickly picked up the cue to shake his head for "no" and nod it up and down for "yes." Then Marco climbed all over him, sitting backward and standing up on his back. He hopped down lightly and rubbed Kiddo's face.

"What a smart fellow you are! OK, one more trick and then we'll have our picnic. Lizzy, don't try this on just any horse."

He encouraged Kiddo to lower his neck. Then Marco laid over Kiddo's neck on his stomach, rubbing and cooing to him. Marco then put his right leg over Kiddo's neck and clucked. Kiddo lifted his neck and Marco slid down onto Kiddo's back.

"Ta-da! This is neck mounting. We use it all the time in the clown acts. Watch the different variations."

Then he lowered Kiddo's neck again, and this time he got on facing backwards and clucked. Kiddo lifted his neck again and Marco slid down his neck, this time sitting facing Kiddo's tail, where he gave him a good vigorous scrubbing with his nails. Kiddo lifted his lip and stretched his neck out, clearly enjoying himself. Marco did it one more time, this time getting on behind his ears but facing forward. Kiddo had picked up the drill and knew exactly what to do.

"OK, now you try, Lizzy."

"Me?"

"C'mon."

So he had Kiddo lower his neck, and I lay over his neck on my stomach, and as soon as Marco clucked Kiddo raised his neck. We did it again, and this time I slung my right leg over his mane, and slid right onto his bare back."

"Oh Kiddo, you are so smart."

I did have a little rush; I was proud of myself. I handed him a sugar cube from his back, and he reached around practically putting his head on my thigh. I gave his forehead a good rubbing. And then Marco had me get on Kiddo sitting backwards.

"You and Kiddo could be an act in the show."

I had to laugh, "Just what I've always dreamed of doing, Marco."

"I know. It's not exactly dressage is it? But it's a good use of a horse like this. He's a thinker."

"He's a natural comedian, that's what he is."

Marco's eyes were twinkling, and he was smiling. It was a look that made me feel warm all over.

The magic of the day continued right into the night. We had our lunch and then rode, and I still couldn't bear to part. So I went with Marco to tend to Bernardo and Caruso, and I swelled with pride as right in front of Pali and others at the circus, Marco wrapped his arm around my waist. I knew it was a public declaration to all that we were indeed an item.

Our small respite was over in a flash. It was time to take a deep breath and put my shoulder back into it. We were shipping back to Gladstone. Wild Child had been allowed two days to simply relax in his paddock.

Turning him out made Francesca and Frank nervous, especially since he had to buck and fart and run the perimeter of his paddock like a nutcase the first day we turned him out. He also made a point of getting as dirty as possible, rubbing the dirt deeply into his coat.

Francesca kept going on about his staying "sharp," whatever that meant. Margot had answered, that meant resting him as well as going out on the hill with me in the afternoon. We had a joyous gallop up our hill the afternoon before shipping over. Standing next to Margot at the top of our hill felt like standing on top of the world.

And although I knew Margot wanted to do well at Gladstone, I also knew Margot well enough by now that win or lose, she would still be the Margot I had come to love when this was all over.

This weekend Ryder would work alongside me as a groom, although I didn't really need her. When we arrived at Gladstone, I proudly took my big boy off the trailer and let him trumpet his arrival. He puffed himself up, dwarfing me at his shoulder. But I had the chain over his nose to remind him that his munchkin-sized minder was still there and that he was on a job assignment.

He wanted to linger as we passed horses being ridden and horses in their stalls. I had to smack him on with the end of the lead shank and practically drag him into his dark stall. I stayed with him, pulling off his wraps and letting Ryder do the schlepping. It was her turn to be a pack mule. I had earned this.

Today Ryder could clean up the stall and organize our tack room while I walked down and watched Margot have her schooling session with Deb.

This time, even with the west-coast rock stars back at work in the indoor, I knew the buzz was around Margot and Wild Child. People were talking. I could feel it.

I loved taking Wild Child from Margot after her ride and leading him back to the stable. This weekend he seemed to know why he was here; he was much more relaxed, and after his ride he seemed satisfied, as if he knew we were all happy with him.

Ryder held him while I pulled off his tack out in the barn aisle, and the biggest riding superstar of all, a multiple Olympian, found his way to our stalls and began to chit-chat with us, the lowly grooms. I was so incredibly proud of Wild Child, and I enjoyed showing him off. Here was a guy who could have the best horses in the world, admiring Wild Child. The guy ran his hand over Wild Child's neck, and I could see Ryder jiggle the chain on his nose. Wild Child still pinned his ears and wrinkled his nose, barely tolerating the guy's touch.

We got Wild Child bathed, and then I put in his braids for the jog. Margot arrived looking fresh and smelling of lavender. Her blonde hair was freshly coiffed into its stiff little bun; her make-up was flawless. Today for the jog she was wearing pressed white jeans with a wide blue belt and a fitted white, dress shirt open at the collar, showing off a plain silver chain. No one else would have been able to keep all that white clean, but then again, Margot didn't have to touch Wild Child until I handed him to her for the jog.

Once the announcer said "accepted," he was handed right back to me to return to the stables where I proceeded to pull out all those perfect little braids and then give the crest of his neck a good scratching.

When I finished his neck scratch and pulled off his halter, Wild Child turned his butt to me and put his head in the back corner of his stall. I had been dismissed from duty.

Ryder took bed-check duty, and I collapsed in my bed early and dreamed of victory gallops. In my dreams I was riding

Wild Child, and I was leading the gallop. I woke up smiling. I somehow knew this was going to be a good day.

I didn't feel the need to say any prayers while putting in his braids. And when Margot showed up for her ride, she did not look pale or shaky. She was smiling and laughing with Frank.

The previous weekend's tests had accounted for 55% of the total score toward the National Championships. Today was the Grand Prix test, which would count for 30% of her total score. Then tomorrow was the Grand Prix Freestyle, which only counted for 15% of the total, but was always a crowd favorite and would cap off the entire weekend on an emotionally high note.

Patrick was closely ranked with Margot, and we all knew the Grand Prix test was better for his horse than for Wild Child who would still lose points for his zigzags. It was also clear that the first three spots were taken. Neither Margot nor Patrick was a threat to those guys. The real battle was for that fourth spot and the training grant. For Patrick, the stakes were much higher. He had a potential sponsor to impress.

Our tests didn't begin until the afternoon. The morning rides were for the Brentina Cup, a Grand Prix test for those young adults who had graduated from the Advanced Young Riders program. It was the last step before a young person had to compete against the pros. I watched it with interest because it would be the next step up for Ryder, and for Suzette. But you had to have a Grand Prix horse to do it.

I managed to steal away and watch an hour or so of the competition, and as I sat there in the cheap seats, Suzette found her way to my side.

"Hey, Lizzy."

She leaned in toward me and patted my knee, "Look. I'm driving him crazy."

"What?"

"OK. Just sort of glance across the arena, up on the hill."

"What am I looking for?"

"Oh, Lizzy. Him of course. He's sure I'm giving away deep secrets."

So I cut my eyes across the arena, and at first I couldn't see Patrick anywhere. But when I did find him, Suzette was right. He wasn't schmoozing with anyone. He was pretending to watch the ride with interest. But he was looking right at us.

"Suzette, don't bait him."

She leaned in so much our heads were touching, and we hunched up and whispered so softly it was barely above breathing, "If Margot beats him by enough of a margin today, it's over for him. You see, Claire and Francesca had a little chit-chat with his would-be sponsor last night over nibbles and drinks. I don't think they said much, but it made Patrick sweat."

"I better get back to my post."

Suzette nodded, "Damn straight, Lizzy. Damn straight. You take good care of that horse."

I nodded.

And it was while I was walking back to the barn that I made a decision. I would stay with Wild Child tonight, just like Suzette had stayed with her horse last weekend. Margot had more than hit the magic 70%, and Wild Child and Margot were now a real threat to Patrick. I didn't want my water buckets removed in the night or any other of his sneaky tactics that Suzette had hinted at.

I decided to tell only Marco. I wanted Marco to come and stay with me. Honestly, I was thinking of romance as much as I was thinking of Wild Child. I could bring one of those lantern- style flashlights, and we could have a late-night picnic and cuddle. It would be like our nights doing foal watch. The nights had been mild. All I needed was a pillow and a blanket. I couldn't wait to call Marco and invite him to come after his show tonight. I would just need to connive to get an extra wristband so he could have access.

***

AFTER DAWDLING AROUND THE STABLE ALL morning, time suddenly sped up on me and soon it was time to kick into high gear again. I got Wild Child ready. Deb, Ryder, and I got Margot up. I turned her loose, and the three of us trailed behind her to the warm-up arena. Today Margot was more relaxed. She had said to me that she could see the finish line of this race and, no matter what, she would feel great getting over it.

Patrick was already riding his horse around the indoor with a quiet intensity that unnerved me. I watched him for a moment and then gave Deb a nudge and whispered to her, "Deb, watch Patrick's horse. He looks tired."

Deb had been watching Margot intently and looked annoyed at me at first. But then she focused on Patrick. After a moment she whispered back, "That horse looks washed out. Look at that piaffe. His horse isn't quite regular behind."

I watched closely as Deb turned back to Margot.

She was right. Patrick's horse was going through the motions, but without his usual energy.

Patrick had to feel what was going on. When it was his time to go, he headed for the competition arena alone. He no longer had a team fluttering around him. Ryder stood at my side.

Margot was oblivious, and in her zone.

This time Patrick's score was 69%.

The door had suddenly opened for Margot.

There was a chance now that she could actually make that coveted fourth spot. None of us spoke a word about it on our walk to the arena. Margot had to focus. But I knew that all of us had registered the news.

Deb reached for my hand as Margot cantered down centerline. Wild Child was relaxed, but still fresh enough from his rest. They nailed her first halt and salute.

Margot began cautiously, and Deb whispered under her breath, "Take a chance Margot, c'mon."

It was as if Margot heard her. The next extended trot was breathtaking, and of course then it was time for the piaffe, which was almost textbook perfect.

Wild Child lost a little power into the passage, but gained it back as he went, finding it in himself to practically bounce in and out of his next piaffe-passage transition. He exhaled into a monster extended walk...his holier than thou movement proving that his trot was not produced from tension.

Of course his canter tour had small problems. The dreaded zigzags were still his weakest moment, and his flying changes could still be straighter. But he bounced out his two-tempi and one-tempi changes without any mistakes. He got a little labored in his pirouettes. But he nailed his final centerline and salute. When the score went up, Deb and I screamed and bounced up and down and hugged one another.

Margot had her best Grand Prix score ever...72%.

Even Ryder looked pleased. And I knew Francesca and Frank were being congratulated by all sorts of bigwigs up there in the sponsors' tent.

Wild Child would be in front of Patrick in the day's award ceremony. And unless something changed, Patrick would still be staring at Wild Child's butt tomorrow.

CHAPTER 48

A World-Class Horse

SUZETTE HAD BROUGHT ME A WRIST bracelet for Marco. I hummed as I cleaned up the tack room and hung up Wild Child's tack, and I looked forward to my date.

But I got a phone call and apology instead.

Marco was held up after the evening performance. One of the circus horses was colicky. He would have to stay until he was sure the horse was comfortable and then check on it through the night. He promised to call and check in on me, too.

Of course I was here because of Wild Child. So I opened a bag of carrots and went to check on him. He would have to be my date tonight.

He had put his head in the back corner of his stall, hanging it low, and had a hind leg resting. He heard me; his ears swiveled back, but he didn't move until I called his name.

"Wiiiiild Chiiiild."

He turned his head to check me out. I crooned to him.

"Carrots."

He gave me a nice low whinny and brightened up, coming to the front. I slid the door open and handed him a big fat one. He allowed me to rub his forehead while he had his carrots. His eyes were sleepy, and even though I know he wouldn't be like this without the bribe of carrots, I enjoyed moving my hands all over his face and forelock and ears while he permitted it.

I let him linger over each carrot until my bag was empty. Then he poked and pushed at my empty bag and hands with his nose to check for small shards of leftover carrots. Satisfied he had cleaned me out, he pinned his ears, turned around, and went back to his private place in the back corner of his stall.

"Goodnight, Wild Child. Rest up buddy."

The night was cool, and I was stretched out on some plastic bags of shavings. They made a pretty good mattress, and I was comfy. I ripped open the bag of chocolates I had brought and dove in; then I pulled a show cooler over myself.

I was wishing Marco was there, but the next day was an important day, and I tried to focus on that. I closed my eyes and saw visions of Margot and Wild Child dancing in my head. I could practically hear their music. I wondered if Wild Child had similar thoughts. Did he dream of his music? He had heard it often enough.

Some small sound woke me. I checked my cell phone. It was 2 a.m., an hour when no one should be awake. It was then I clearly heard the whispered word.

"Asshole."

Someone was here.

I felt a rush of adrenaline through my veins; my face went hot, and my heart began thudding; my limbs froze in fear.

I found the contact list on my phone and hit "Marco" and texted one stupid word.

"Scared."

Then I crept to my feet.

I was here to keep an eye on Wild Child. Tomorrow was his day. Tomorrow he would show the world not only that he was truly a world-class horse, but that Margot was a world-class rider.

It was my job to check on him. I was scared, but I would find out who was swearing at 2 a.m.; probably just another one of the grooms. In which case I needed to let Marco know it was a false alarm.

With my phone clutched tightly in my hand, I ventured out and noticed immediately that Wild Child's door was half open. My heart sank in my chest and my mouth went dry.

At a glance, even in the dark, it registered; it was Patrick. At first I couldn't make a sound.

I saw then that Patrick had Wild Child's top lip twisted tightly in the chain loop of a long-handled twitch; the long wooden handle was tucked under his left armpit so his hands could be free. He had backed Wild Child into the corner of the stall, and Patrick's back was to me. But I could see what was in his right hand; a syringe. He pulled off the plastic cap on the needle and put it in his mouth, and then I watched as he grabbed a pinch of skin with his left hand, the syringe and needle ready in his right hand. He was drugging my horse.

Without thinking, I screamed, "Noooooooooooooooo!" It sounded like someone else's voice. It was high and unnatural.

And then I flew into the stall to stop what I could not stop.

He pushed the needle in.

I kept screaming "no." I was too late. He had drugged Wild Child.

He was yelling back, "You little bitch. Get off me, you little bitch."

The needle and syringe were still sticking out of Wild Child's neck, now bouncing as the horse rocked back on his haunches and reared.

And I started pummeling Patrick with my one free fist, still clinging to my phone.

But Patrick simply let the long-handled twitch fall from Wild Child's lip, and took a left handed backward swing that wrapped around my waist and struck my back.

The impact knocked me off balance and I fell forward under the horse.

I rolled on the floor and saw Patrick raise his arm up again; this time he was aiming.

I scrambled back to my hands and knees. I was directly under Wild Child's belly. I headed for the back corner of the stall to hide behind Wild Child. The second swing only landed on the back of my left leg, but it landed hard.

I still had my phone in my hand, and it began ringing, I quickly pushed the green button next to Marco's name.

But Patrick saw me and yelled, "Oh no, you don't."

Wild Child was practically cantering in place on top of me as Patrick just kept swinging, landing more hits to Wild Child than to me. Miraculously, Wild Child's hooves kept missing me. I put my arms up over my head to protect myself, but I clung to my phone and felt some blows land on my back, making me exhale and cry out in pain.

Wild Child ran backwards and that gave Patrick a better shot at me. I had no place to hide now, and felt more blows. Patrick was raging.

"Stupid little bitch. Damn it, I'm going to have to kill you now and they'll kill him too, when they see what he's done, and it's all your damn fault."

I was screaming at each blow that landed, screaming and kicking, scrambling to avoid the swings of the twitch, but between screams I was yelling right at him.

"You drugged our horse; you drugged him in North Carolina. You shit. You shit. You shit-for-human."

And then I saw Wild Child behind Patrick, freezing at the sight, so that Patrick landed a blow hard and painful against my shins. But I knew when I saw Wild Child what was coming, and Patrick did not. Wild Child's ears were pinned, and his mouth was open. He had coiled himself, rocking back on his haunches, to strike like a snake. I knew Wild Child; I knew that expression. He was serious.

He caught Patrick at the base of his neck. Patrick bellowed like a bull, and reached up and grabbed Wild Child's halter with both hands, trying I thought, to take the pressure off his neck. But Wild Child was not letting go.

Then Wild Child backed up one step and started spinning, and as he spun he accelerated. The force splayed Patrick's legs out and they kept hitting the stall walls with sickening thuds. I tried to get up on my shaking legs to run, but they kept buckling. I had to put my hands over my head and turn to the wall, flattening myself out to avoid getting smacked by Patrick's legs.

Patrick had finally stopped bellowing when Wild Child dropped him.

And then he was still.

I was still clinging to my phone and picked it up and held it to my ear. I could hear Marco's voice, "Lizzy? Lizzy? Lizzy?"

"Marco?"

"Are you OK?"

"No."

"I'm already in the car on my way. Can you call 911?"

"Marco, call Frank. Call..."

And then I had to vomit, but I was not going to drop that phone.

I could see Wild Child pawing the ground between me and Patrick, and I saw him bow himself up, preparing to finish Patrick off. It would have served him right, but I didn't want to witness it.

I somehow hurled myself from a kneeling position at Wild Child, and grabbed the dangling lead shank; yelling.

"No!"

He startled and then shook his head angrily, still pawing.

I still couldn't get to my feet, but I sat in the straw and pulled weakly on the lead shank, turning him away.

Patrick moaned and rolled over, reaching for his neck, and then seeing me, "Stupid little bitch."

My voice still sounded like someone else's. "What did you give him you shit-for-human?"

"Why should I tell you?"

Patrick managed to sit up and even though he was breathless, his voice was strong.

"Well, Lizzy, what now?"

I saw the twitch in the bedding. It was too damn close to Patrick and too damn far away from me.

"What?"

The man was broken to pieces. What the hell did he mean?

"I told Francesca this was a man's horse. Stupid to let a little slip of a girl handle him."

"What?"

I couldn't believe my ears. He was rambling on.

"I'll tell them I tried to save you; damn near killed myself trying. Ryder won't miss you though."

Then he actually smiled. And it was a relaxed and friendly smile. He was still playing the charmer.

Patrick tried to stand, but I figured his legs were broken because he couldn't do it. But he had seen the twitch. And I watched as he reached out and pulled it toward him, closing his fingers around it.

"Patrick, all I have to do it let loose this lead shank and Wild Child will finish what he started."

Patrick shook his head, "No chance, Lizzy. You calmed him right down. Look at him. You should have let him finish the job. Ryder was right about you; you're too soft. He's done; and anyway, if he tries now I'll break his legs with this thing."

I saw Patrick's grip tighten on the twitch handle. Wild Child arched his neck and blew a hard warning huff toward Patrick; and then he lowered his head and started gently touching my head.

I realized Patrick was going to kill me and then probably break Wild Child's legs. I only had one way out and I would have to scramble past Patrick to make it. I knew I couldn't do it on my legs and that I'd have to drop the phone…my lifeline. So I did.

I reached up and grabbed Wild Child's mane. It was short and wavy from his braids, but I gripped it tightly. My legs were killing me and useless, but I clung to his mane and managed to put one leg over his lowered neck. And then Wild Child lifted his head, and I slid down his neck right onto his back.

Patrick looked stunned, and his voice changed to a desperate scream, "I'll break his legs!"

He lunged at us, making wild swings.

Wild Child plunged toward the half-open door, and I clung onto his mane and his lead shank; and he hopped over Patrick's body, the twitch landing blows to Wild Child's legs as we scrambled past. I knew we wouldn't make it through the narrow gap of the stall door, so I let go and gave the door a desperate shove. I ducked low, grabbing his mane again and clinging to his neck as we squeezed through the narrow half-opened door. I could hear the door bang and bounce on its runner as Wild Child's hips knocked into it hard. But we were out.

And we just stood there in the aisle, me weakly cursing, trembling, and sobbing, and Patrick cursing and dragging himself toward the door of the stall. Wild Child stood like a statue, but trembled all over, his heart pounding between my knees. I knew we could get away. All I would need to do is tell Wild Child to run. But I didn't think I could hang on. And so I waited for help. I knew Marco would be there soon; and if Patrick ever made it out of that stall, he wouldn't get far crawling.

"Lizzy!"

"Marco!"

He had made it. I felt the tension drain out of my body. And my teeth began to chatter. I leaned over and hugged Wild Child around his neck to keep from sliding off. I realized it was the first time I had ever been on Wild Child's back, the first time I had ever hugged him around his neck. What a beautiful big round neck it was.

Patrick started babbling a story behind me, even while he still had the damn twitch in his hand.

Marco started to run to me, but Wild Child pinned his ears and made a small lunge while I clung onto his neck. Marco slowed down his movements, and Wild Child pricked his ears in recognition and let him approach. Patrick was still going on while Marco started to look me over. Then over his shoulder he snapped at Patrick.

"Shut up. Just shut up now! I heard it all on the phone. I picked up when Lizzy called and I heard it all. Shit, you're a psychopath."

I hoarsely whispered, "Marco, quick before he destroys it. There's a needle and syringe somewhere in the stall."

Patrick wasn't done; he wouldn't shut up.

"I saved her hide, and the damn thing nearly killed me. That's my story and I'm sticking to it. I saw her drug that horse in North Carolina, too. Ryder will back me up on this."

Marco's face went dark, "Would you like me to kick in a few ribs? No one would know but me, you, and Lizzy."

I shrieked, "Marco, no!"

I saw Patrick try to stand again, but it was no use. His face went white, and I was sure I heard a bone crack. He crumpled.

And then I saw Frank coming down the aisle with Security. And soon there were EMTs. Marco gently pulled me off of Wild Child, and someone wrapped me in heated blankets that could not warm me up. I was shaking all over, but I was talking and couldn't shut up. There were things Marco and Frank needed to know.

"Wild Child's been drugged. Wild Child's hurt. He hit his hips on the door. His legs were hit with the twitch. Please call the vet."

And Marco promised. And Frank promised. They would take care of Wild Child. They would take care of everything. My shift was over.

They would take it from here.

CHAPTER 49

Not Broken

"**GOOD NEWS, LIZZY. NOTHING IS BROKEN.** You're just really beat up."

I had been shuffled around to different rooms and X-rayed, but now I had been admitted for observation.

I was quietly enjoying looking at Marco.

I, on the other hand, had seen myself in the mirror when the nurse had helped me into the bathroom. I was hideous. I was swelling from the blows, and here and there bruises were already forming, including under my left eye and cheekbone. Even my scalp hurt and I couldn't bear to brush or comb my hair. Instead I had gingerly finger-combed it and put it into a scrunchie.

My legs had failed me when I needed them, but miraculously, now that the crisis was over, they were working again. I could walk just fine.

And sweet Marco had stayed nearby the entire time, while Frank had taken care of all the paperwork.

Then I began to get agitated.

"Marco, is Wild Child OK? Margot can't ride him in the freestyle like that. And if he gets drug-tested, she'll be ruined."

Marco blinked at me, "Lizzy this show is over for Wild Child. A vet is taking care of him, and he'll be just fine. Margot has just been granted permission to withdraw from the competition. Let everyone else take care of things now. The important thing is you're OK. You're safe."

I relaxed back into my pillow for a moment. My head was throbbing, but my mind was racing. "Patrick. What's going to happen to him?"

"Wild Child almost killed him. He was this close to severing Patrick's carotid artery."

Marco held his right thumb and index finger an inch apart. "Not to mention the two broken legs. He's somewhere in this hospital, but Frank made sure he's under guard, and the Winstons are here, too."

The details of the night were playing over in my head like a horror movie. The close call I had was sinking in. I looked at Marco, and my chin wobbled as I blurted out, "You and Wild Child saved my life!"

"I had very little to do with it. Patrick had no idea what he was up against." Marco was smiling at me.

"I only escaped because Wild Child defended me, and then because I remembered the neck mount you taught me."

Marco's eyebrows shot up, "You impressed the hell out of me. And I felt so helpless listening on the phone."

And then I started to cry in earnest. And Marco moved to the bed. I sat up and put my very tired and sore arms around his neck and let it rip until I was all out of tears. But they were grateful tears. And when I was done, I hunkered down under the terribly stiff and thin sheets and useless cotton blankets on the hospital bed and drifted off to a deep and dreamless sleep.

***

I WOKE UP TO FIND IT dark again outside. I had slept through an entire day. And there in the corner of the room was Frank, reading glasses perched on the end of his nose, a book open in his lap.

"Frank?"

His voice was soft, so unlike Frank. "Hey, sleeping beauty."

"Did Marco leave?"

"He had to go to work."

"Is their horse OK?"

"What?"

"The horse that colicked?"

"Oh yes, baby cakes, all the horses are just fine."

I tried moving my legs. Check. Then my arms. Check. I rolled my neck around.

I answered sarcastically, "Now they work. It was like a bad dream, Frank, where you can't run away, except it was all real."

"That crazy Patrick looks a lot worse than you do."

I smiled, "Wild Child did his best to kill him."

"He almost did. That horse scares the hell outta' me."

"He's a world-class horse, Frank. He saved my life."

"Mean as a rattlesnake though."

I smiled a big smile and felt warm all over. "Yeah. I love that about him."

Frank smiled back shaking his head, "You girls."

"Frank, what's happens now?"

"Lizzy, don't you worry about it baby. The Winstons and I will take it from here."

I was suddenly filled with anxiety. The level of crazy I had just lived through was stunning.

I kicked my covers off and started to get up, but I had a damn IV line attached to a pole with a drip bag.

"Ugh. Frank I want to go home now. Can I at least get this thing out?"

"Not until the doctor orders it. You want me to help you to the bathroom?"

"No. I want to go home. We have a herd of horses that depend on us. We have the babies on the hill. We have Wild Child. I have Winsome. I want to go home."

I was anxious, and my voice sounded panicky.

Frank came over to the bed and sat on the edge. He reached around the metal frame and pulled me into his arms.

He was a solid guy, but with a soft belly; a big guy who made me feel small, and I felt a measure of my anxiety begin to recede.

He crooned to me like I was a baby, "You and Deb are two peas in a pod. We'll manage somehow until you are healed up, but you need to stop worrying. You have a home with us as long as you want it."

Those were probably the sweetest words I had ever heard. Francesca would probably have a coronary if she heard what Frank had said. But I had a home; if I wanted it that is.

Margot took the next shift. I realized I was on a chart somewhere, just as Fiddle had been. It was now Lizzy-watch instead of foal-watch. The thought was embarrassing.

Margot looked beautiful but tired. The last few weeks had placed too great a strain on all of us, and it showed on our faces. Well, my face, I didn't even recognize.

Margot was full of apologies.

"Lizzy, I never dreamed it could come to this. I feel somehow responsible."

"Margot, I never thought I was in danger. I surprised Patrick is all."

We sat silently for a few moments. There was a lot I wanted to say to her. But I wasn't sure where to start.

So I changed the subject, "Are the babies OK?"

Margot almost startled, "Why yes, Deb has her hands full, but they are all going out together now. It's something to see; two mares and three foals."

"And Wild Child?"

"He's going to have time off; but he's being turned out, and all he suffered were bruises. He'll be fine. He'll just be terribly cranky to be out of his schedule. You know how he is."

"Can I call Natalie? I know where she is."

Then Margot grinned, "Francesca and Claire already did."

Then I was surprised, "It was supposed to be a secret."

"Francesca saw that postcard and figured out what it was all about. Francesca and Claire have taken care of your friend Natalie. By the way, in an entirely different way, Frank's taken care of Natalie's horrible boss, too."

I was shaking my head, "What an incredible mess."

"Ah, but this sort of thing is Frank's specialty. The Winstons are happy to let him take the lead here. It will all be taken care of, darling. You are safe and that's the important thing."

"And Gladstone?"

"There will always be another Gladstone."

"So Margot, what did you tell show management?"

"Well, the word going around is that Wild Child had been severely cast and Patrick and you were terribly injured trying to get him up."

I was shocked, "You totally lied to everyone?"

"Oh no, not me; we have other people to do that for us. For now, that's a good enough story for the press. We just say the typical "no comment" when asked and always add that we are only focused now on the swift recovery of the people who were injured by our quite wonderful horse."

***

I FELT RIDICULOUS BEING DISCHARGED FROM the hospital in a wheelchair. Marco insisted it was a hospital rule and I should enjoy the ride. Still, when I walked up the stairs to the apartment, I was shocked by the weakness in my legs.

He insisted on putting me in bed, and although I protested about that too, once I was tucked in, I was overwhelmed by fatigue. I kept protesting anyway.

"Marco, I'm not sick and nothing is broken."

He sat on the edge of my bed, and he looked at me in a way that made me melt down into the mattress and become totally compliant.

"Lizzy, I'm going to take care of you this week as much as I can, because after that I won't be around."

My stomach dropped. I always knew the circus would move on, but now was not the time to lose Marco. I needed him now. "Marco, not now."

"Lizzy, I've been meaning to tell you, but I knew you'd be upset. We've been winding it down for the last two weeks. The horses are tired, and that colic confirms our decision. The horses need fresh air and grass under their feet. They ship to the home farm in Canada Thursday. Pali and I will spend a couple days with the break-down crew, and then we follow them."

My chin wobbled, and words began to tumble out, "Maybe I should go with you."

"Lizzy."

Marco was shaking his head.

I hated how frantic my voice sounded. "Please Marco, I've had enough of this insanity. I'm so tired, Marco. I don't care about winning ribbons. I'm not made like Ryder with some kind of relentless drive. I want to rest and just enjoy the beauty of horses. I could be your groom. I could help you."

Marco smiled. He thought I was kidding. But at that moment, I was dead serious.

"You and Kiddo want to do a clown act?"

"We could."

Then he laughed, "You told me you wanted to be a competitive dressage rider. That you had walked away from your former life and embraced this life so you could study with Margot; that you were living your lifelong dream."

"I was so foolish."

"Lizzy, you're not thinking clearly. You just being a groom, or doing a clown act, would be a waste of a good horseman. You just went toe-to-toe with evil, and you won. Lizzy, you won. But if the experience makes you pack it up and run away to the circus, then you've given away your victory. I won't let you do that."

I searched his big brown eyes for sincerity, and the words I said did not match what I saw there, "You don't love me."

He did not get angry. He just shook his head and ignored my remark. "Lizzy, I know I have to leave you here where you belong."

"And you can't stay here with me?"

"No. I belong with my horses."

"Then it's no use is it?"

He leaned down and gave me a tender kiss. Then got up and turned off the light. "You're exhausted. You rest. I'll be checking on you later."

And Marco pulled the door shut as he backed out. The room seemed very empty and quiet.

At first I was angry at him, but slowly my fatigue pulled me into a semi-dream state. But just as I was drifting off, there was a light tap on the door and it opened.

It was Ryder.

She walked in, pulled a little straight-backed chair out of the corner, and sat next to my bed. Her voice was matter-of-fact, "I sat with you in the hospital, but you never woke up."

"Thanks, Ryder."

"I just wanted you to know that I did my shift."

So she was here for what? Credit? I watched her pick at her cuticles for a few moments. She had a terrible scowl on her face.

Then she whispered hoarsely, "People love you, Lizzy."

Ryder was struggling. Was that some weird form of an apology? I knew "I'm sorry" were words that would cost her too much to say, and I didn't want her to try. But I could say them easily enough for both of us.

"Ryder, I'm sorry for you."

She snapped back with passion.

"Lizzy, don't feel sorry for me, please. I can stand almost anything, but not that."

"OK, Ryder. But I'm not angry with you either."

Her face bunched up for a moment. My attempt at kindness had only increased her suffering. "Well, you should be, maybe more than you'll ever know. But, just know this, I'm still here, and I plan to do one amazing job by Margot and Papa and Petey and Francesca. I'm here as long as they'll have me. And I'm going to help you achieve your dreams, too. Winsome is a good enough horse. You're good enough, too. I'm going to help you."

I knew that was it; my apology. That was Ryder. She was indeed a force to be reckoned with. I was not sure how much I was going to appreciate all her help, but I accepted her apology.

"Thanks, Ryder, I'm going to hold you to that; OK? I do envy your talent."

"I have plenty I envy about you too, Lizzy."

Well that made me grin. And then I just couldn't help myself, "What about Patrick?"

Ryder flinched, but then looked me square in the eye, "He accepted a sweet deal."

"You mean he's not going to prison?"

She huffed, "Prison? No way! Frank has too much of a sense of humor. Patrick and that guy Tommy that Nat worked for have signed five-year contracts to go teach for a huge riding club in China."

I couldn't believe my ears. "China?"

Ryder actually smiled. "Yeah, China!"

And then we started laughing, and we couldn't stop until we were both wiping away tears.

I had gotten my wish.

CHAPTER 50

The Sweet Spot

SUDDENLY IT WAS SUMMER, AND THE bugs were terrible. I had bought Winsome crocheted ear bonnets; a plain one for everyday use, and the one I was putting on today for showing. It was brown with a pretty amber-colored ribbon, beads sewn in along the edge, and a short fringe that hung down in a point between her eyes. I thought it was quite fetching against her liver-chestnut coat.

Natalie had begged to put in Winsome's braids, but I wouldn't let her. Frankly my braids were much prettier. But Nat would be the one by the arena with a bucket and rag and a bottle of water. Nat would be there to pull off my polos while I handed the coaching system to Margot and got my final words of wisdom, just as Nat had been the one all weekend busting her butt for everyone. She would be sure and say something silly and clever and crude and make me laugh just before I went in the ring.

Nat now lived with Deb and had already proven to be a natural working with the babies and young horses. Although Francesca constantly looked down her nose and made disparaging comments, the truth was Nat had put laughter into our day-to-day routine at the farm.

I pulled Winsome out into the aisle, admiring our farm banner and row of blue and red ribbons. Deb had made her debut on Wild Child and had looked damn good. Francesca had finally ridden her first Prix St. Georges, and it had been acceptable enough. Margot had, as usual, impressed everyone with Hotstuff. And the biggest surprise of all was that Ryder and Petey were currently sporting the unbelievably high score of the entire show; 80% at Third level. They even had received an 8 for harmony, which had us all laughing as Ryder said the horse still hesitated to move off from his first halt and slowed down slightly every time he passed the gap at "A;" but you sure couldn't tell by watching.

It was now my time. I swung up on Winsome and made my way toward the warm-up arena. As usual, my legs were tight and my stirrups felt too long, but I took a few deep breaths, adjusted the coaching system clipped to my belt, and felt how eagerly my mare was walking toward the ring. I slipped in the in-gate, while giving my number to the steward. Then I heard Margot's voice in my ear.

"Darling, you look beautiful. Now take your time and warm her up just like you do at home."

The routine began to do its magic. Winsome was breathing in her rhythmic way, and she felt light on her toes and responsive. My legs began to let go; when I went to sit and work transitions, I found that sweet spot in the saddle where I could sit into the horse. I tested her forward and back. I tested her sideways. And finally, just for that magic feeling of sitting, I did a few half-steps. We were ready.

I entered the arena as soon as the rider before me dropped her hand in a salute. Winsome was a little nervous, but I sent her forward and let her work through her tension by using every part of her body. Movement with your horse was liberating even while it was a test of obedience. I knew now that I needed to risk losing control in order to gain control. Hold nothing back, but do it with a deep level of confidence. Movement was joy, and life was meant to be filled with joyful moments; but you had to believe you deserved them. I knew I deserved this joy.

The bell rang, and I made a transition to walk and turned around. In a flash I saw them all lined up and leaning on the arena railing—Frank and the terriers straining at their leashes, Francesca, Deb, Natalie, Ryder, and Margot, who gave me a curt nod.

I refocused and picked up a good strong collected trot, almost verging on a medium. I made a wide turn so I could line up a straight entry. The judge was standing, and I put the letter "C" right between Winsome's ears and entered, crossing that invisible line at A into the competition arena.

There was no more thinking to be done now. There was no need for worry; there was no need for nerves. Now was a time to be in the moment; to be swept up in the flow of energy coming from Winsome's hind feet and flowing up and over her back; to catch the wave and become part of it.

I guided Winsome with the right aids, at the right time, in the right intensity, without conscious thought. I directed without disturbing. I was cooking without a recipe.

It was simply a matter of feel.

ABOUT THE AUTHOR

KAREN MCGOLDRICK RIDES, TEACHES, AND TRAINS dressage at her own Prospect Hill Farm in Alpharetta, Georgia.

She is a United States Dressage Federation certified instructor/ trainer; earned her USDF Bronze, Silver, and Gold medal rider awards, all on horses she trained; and she graduated "With Distinction" from the USDF "L" program.

Karen got her first "working student" job by answering an ad in her community newspaper at the age of 12. Before, during, and after college, she worked on and off for a variety of trainers until she and her husband bought their first farm in 1992.

Karen is an award-winning contributor to *USDF Connection* magazine, and she is a regular columnist for the Georgia Dressage and Combined Training Association newsletter.

Karen feels that the best part of being a dressage instructor is sharing the insights, joys, and sorrows that riding, training, and loving horses have brought to her life. Writing a novel is one more way to do this.

The Dressage Chronicles comes straight from her heart.

You can contact Karen via her website:

www.thedressagechronicles.com

CPSIA information can be obtained at www.ICGtesting.com
Printed in the USA
BVOW02s0026040916

461011BV00001B/47/P